William Gordon Gordon-Cumming

Wild Men and Wild Beasts

William Gordon Gordon-Cumming

Wild Men and Wild Beasts

ISBN/EAN: 9783743383982

Manufactured in Europe, USA, Canada, Australia, Japa

Cover: Foto ©Andreas Hilbeck / pixelio.de

Manufactured and distributed by brebook publishing software (www.brebook.com)

William Gordon Gordon-Cumming

Wild Men and Wild Beasts

TO

COLONEL WALTER CAMPBELL.

My Dear Walter,

As the perusal of the writings of "The Old Forest Ranger," in the days of my early youth, first turned my thoughts to the hunting-grounds of **India**, to him the following pages are dedicated by

HIS AFFECTIONATE KINSMAN,

THE AUTHOR.

Auchintoul, *April* 1871.

PREFACE.

At the suggestion of friends, I have here given a short account of some of my doings during a long residence in India. The propriety of the suggestion may be doubted, but having been adopted, the book must stand for what it is worth.

Tiger stories have been told before, and as I generally find them received with incredulity in England, it seems only fair that I should aid in establishing the veracity of my brother-sportsmen.

But I should hardly have had the temerity to appear in public, had I not received the valuable assistance of Colonel R. Baigrie, late Assistant Quarter-Master-General on the Bombay Establishment, to whom I am indebted for the principal illustrations by which the book is enlivened.

Himself an ardent sportsman, and a keen observer of forest scenery and all its surroundings, he has well portrayed the incidents described.   His vivid sketches have been reproduced by Mr. Dallas of Edinburgh by a new and beautiful process.

The pen-and-ink sketches are copies from drawings by my friend the late Harrington Bulkley, with whom I was associated during several pleasant years in Guzerat.

W. GORDON CUMMING.

AUCHINTOUI, *April* 1871.

CONTENTS.

CHAPTER I.

CHAPTER II.

CHAPTER III.

CHAPTER IV.

CHAPTER V.

CHAPTER VI.

CHAPTER VII.

CHAPTER VIII.

CHAPTER IX.

CHAPTER X.

CHAPTER XI.

CHAPTER XII.

CHAPTER XIII.

CHAPTER XIV.

CHAPTER XV.

CHAPTER XVI.

CHAPTER XVII.

CHAPTER XVIII.

CHAPTER XIX.

CHAPTER XX.

CHAPTER XXI.

CHAPTER XXII.

CHAPTER XXIII.

CHAPTER XXIV.

LIST OF ILLUSTRATIONS.

CHAPTER I.

I HAVE often been surprised that the game of India, with its wild and varied character, does not more frequently attract sportsmen from England.

In many new and comparatively savage countries, uninfluenced by British or any other rule worthy of the name, there is no doubt grand and exciting sport to be got ; but then it is accompanied by an amount of hardship and discomfort, not to say personal danger, which scares any but the most determined hunters. Servants are with difficulty obtained, and much of what may be called the dirty work of the expedition has to be done by the master. Large supplies of all kinds have to be carried, and, owing to the difficulties of transport, many comforts have to be left behind. The time, moreover, to be taken up by the excursion is uncertain, owing to ignorance of the ground to be traversed and the difficulty of locomotion ; and, in the event of sickness or accident, medical aid is not to be had for love or money. Lastly—and to many not least—no approximate estimate can be formed of the probable expense.

In India there is none of this ; the country is either British, or under native chiefs, protected by or tributary to the Queen; locomotion is easy, and not expensive, carts being almost everywhere procurable, or, failing carts, pack bullocks or ponies. The country is studded with British cantonments 200 and 300 miles apart, where supplies can be got to replenish the commissariat department—the traders' shops containing all that may be desired, from Holloway's pills to moderator lamps, and from Hall's gunpowder to bitter beer and cod-liver oil. All articles are generally at fair prices, the distance from England and the irregular market considered.

The "promiscuous" traveller cannot, of course, expect, on first landing in the country, to get servants of the best class, the more so as they would be aware that their work would be hard, and their situations only temporary; but good rough-and-ready men will always be found on the look-out for service, and prepared to start on a day's notice.

The only parts of the country which are much shot over are those in the immediate proximity of cantonments, say within fifty or sixty miles. Beyond this radius game may be found in sufficient quantities to satisfy the most greedy sportsman; and in the pursuit of some species he will find no lack of the danger which gives zest to the chase.

In the event of sickness or accident, skilled surgeons are to be met with in every cantonment. Indian hospitality is proverbial, and the patient might reckon on being courteously received and well cared for. Formerly, such a thing was hardly necessary, but now-a-days one or two good letters of introduction at starting would be found useful. In India everybody knows everybody, and the stranger would be passed on from one cantonment to the next.

With the exception of his guns and rifles and their ammunition, an outfit for a six months' excursion might be got together in a day at any of the Presidency towns.

If the sportsman goes in for hog-hunting, a couple of good horses are desirable, and these would cost from £20 to £100 each, according to the weight or luck of the rider. The more expensive horses are, however, by no means always the best hog-hunters, and I have known more first spears taken off seasoned screws and strong galloways with a turn of speed than by high-priced horses; blood and pluck to stand a charge being, however, indispensable.

A second-hand hill-tent, twelve or fourteen feet square, a copper basin, a couple of fold-up tables, two cane chairs bound with leather, a light sleeping cot, and, above all, a comfortable arm-chair, are all the furniture required, together with a thin mattress and a few sheets, blankets, and towels. If the party consists of two or more, a double supply of everything is most convenient. On a change of ground being contemplated, all would dine comfortably together, and after dinner one set of servants would start off with one tent and one set of equipments. The sportsmen would rise at or before daybreak, and, after a cup of tea and a bite, might shoot their way to the next camp, where they would find the tent which had come on in the night ready pitched, and their tubs and breakfasts all comfortable.

Leaving England early in October, Bombay might be reached *vià* Marseilles in twenty-one days. Four hundred miles by rail would take the party to Ahmedabad, and the months of November, December, and January might be spent in the plains of Guzerat and Kattyawar. Here the Saiseen antelope or black buck abound, as do also the chinkara or gazelle and the nylghae. Hog are also to be found in parts, and panthers, wolves, and hyænas would occasionally vary the sport. In Kattyawar bustard are plentiful; quail and snipe are to be met with in large numbers, while every sheet of water in the country teems with ducks of every description. Waders of many kinds would afford interest to the naturalist, and the coolen or blue crane, which is found in large numbers, forms a valuable addition to the table of the sportsman. Hares are also plentiful in many places ; the grey and painted partridges are common, and rock or sand grouse are found on light and dry soils. If the hunter cares to vary his amusements, foxes and jackals will always give fair sport before a "running dog."

In the "Geer" of Kattyawar lions are to be found, though not in such numbers as formerly ; but I believe there are no tigers in this part. I have, however, never shot in that jungle. Wild boars and nylghae are plentiful ; but the country is rugged, and not suited for hog-hunting on horseback. Panthers are met with in considerable numbers.

I would not recommend this country for the hot weather, unless the pursuit of lions is an especial object; and even then not unless very good "shikarees," or native hunters, could be got. I think a better bag would be made in the valleys of the Nerbudda and Taptee.

From the plains of Guzerat and Kattyawar the sportsman might return to Ahmedabad, and thence to Bombay. Starting again about the end of February, some 200 miles by the Great Indian Peninsular Railway would bring him to the Asseerghur jungles, which are numerously stocked with tigers, bears, panthers, bison, pigs, the sambur or Indian red deer, chetul or axis, and several smaller kinds of deer.

By this time the country would be tolerably well dried up, and a large portion of the grass in the heavy jungles would have been burnt. Until the jungles are cleared there is little hope of sport, however numerous the game.

It would be well to secure and pay two good shikarees

from January 1. This might be done by a letter and a remittance of two or three months' pay to the Commissioner of Nimar, or some local official. Before the arrival of the sportsman at Asseerghur, from which place the party should start, the shikarees should go over the ground and determine the best line of country to be traversed. By this means much valuable time would be saved.

From the ravines on the Taptee River the party might cross to the Nerbudda; and in the Hoosungabad and Baitool countries, and thence down both banks of the river towards Burwye, a good bag might be made.

The best sport will always be got in the months of March, April, and May, as the trees are then free from leaves, and the scarcity of water drives all game to the immediate proximity of the rivers. As a rule, I have found that more tigers are shot in partially inhabited districts, and if a fair amount of game can be found in these, they are always to be preferred for many reasons. The cultivation attracts the deer and pigs, which are the favourite food of the tigers. Failing them, they have the cattle of the villagers to fall back upon. Bears prefer less disturbed countries ; but these are generally to be reached by a ride of a few miles, and the facilities in obtaining beaters, carriage, and supplies, more than compensate for the little extra trouble in reaching the ground.

The trip that I have thus briefly sketched might be thoroughly made out by the end of May. Soon after this the rains may be expected, and by this time the hunters will probably have had enough of it. Should they not care to remain in the country till next cold season, two or three days will bring them back to Bombay ; and at the end of the three weeks' journey home they will arrive in town for the best part of the season, and can have an opportunity of displaying their sunburnt faces to their friends in "The Row," as they gracefully loll against the railings at "Fool's-corner."

I calculate that the cost of such a trip as I have described would not be much more for the season than that of a moor in Scotland ; certainly less than a deer-forest. After providing for their passage-money to and from India, and the small outfit they would require, £50 per man *per mensem* would be ample for all charges. During the cold weather, when employed after antelope and small game, the expenses would not amount to that sum. Large game shooting is more expensive, as rewards have to be given to shikarees to keep them lively, beaters have to be paid for, young buffaloes for baits, and various incidental charges; but for antelope, gazelle, nylghae, and duck, snipe, and quail shooting, the expenses are but little, as beaters can be got from the villages at about 4d. a head, and, except for quail-shooting, very few are required.

If large game is shot in British territory, the Government rewards would considerably diminish the expenses. Fifty rupees are given for tigers, 15 for panthers, 12 for bears, and 5 for wolves and hyænas.

If the sportsman does not intend to hunt hogs, he can mount himself well on the ponies of the country at about £10 a head, and two such ponies ought to do all his work.

A riding camel is a most useful beast in camp, and a good one, with easy paces, should be got in Central India for about £15.

COLD WEATHER EXCURSION.

For antelope-shooting a light cart is very desirable, and a pair of good strong bullocks, fast walkers. The deer are generally in open places, where hardly any cover can be found to conceal the stalker. They are accustomed to see the carts of the villagers, and are not scared by them, but allow them to approach within 100 yards. The hunters can either shoot separately or in pairs. If they are content with alternate first shots (which is in my opinion the more pleasant and sociable arrangement), one cart and a pair of bullocks are sufficient for every two guns. The sportsmen should have their own bullocks for this purpose, and they should be good and highly fed. With the light shooting cart they will travel across country all day, and, being accustomed after a short time to the European faces and the crack of the rifles, they will not shy or give trouble when approaching deer. By hiring the village bullocks as required, a good shot is often lost, and the driver being ignorant of his work is a constant source of irritation to the sportsman. The cart such as I have described might be bought in Surat or Ahmedabad for £3 or £4, and a pair of really good bullocks would cost about £16 ; but they would be readily sold at the end of the season. Similarly, ponies might be got rid of without loss ; but a market cannot always be found for the more expensive Arab horses, and these are not absolutely necessary in a shooting excursion.

Leaving the tents, the hunters may ride, their rifles being carried by their attendants. On seeing deer, they should dismount at some distance, and, making over their ponies to the grooms, and leaving all superfluous men with them, the guns alone should advance with the cart. They should not go straight at the deer, but make as though they would drive past them, the hunters always keeping the cart between them and the deer. They must on no account drop behind or walk apart from the cart, or the deer will be uneasy and suspicious.

Should the deer commence to move, and cross the front of the cart, no attempt must be made to head them. If they have the slightest idea that they are being driven, they will move off, and that herd will not again be easily approached. But by edging off behind them no alarm will be caused. If there are two guns with the cart, the shooter should walk last, and both should be on the far side of the cart from the deer.

When an opportunity presents itself, the shooter should raise his rifle just behind the driver, and by the time the tail of the cart is clear of him he will have probably fired. The cart should not be stopped, nor should the shooter, if possible, drop behind to fire, as, except in districts where the deer are but little disturbed, such a proceeding would at once make them on the alert, and they would begin to move off.

After a herd of antelope has been fired at once, they should not be again followed at the time. They will not again stand for another shot, but will keep moving ahead; and by their scared appearance they will alarm and carry on with them all deer within sight in the line of country they may take. On the herd going off, therefore, whether any have been bagged or not, their direction should be observed, and an opposite line taken by the hunters. Picking out the best bucks from every herd, a dozen or more good shots may be got in a day; and one great advantage of the cart is that on a buck being killed he can at once be placed in it, and the party can proceed in quest of more game without delay.

On the shot being fired, the ponies should be brought up at once; but if during the stalk the herd should move towards the spot where they have been left, the grooms should go quietly to a distance, as I have always found deer much scared by the sight of horses standing about the plain.

Grooms should always carry a good hog-spear; there are many occasions when it is handy. Antelope with a hind leg broken will give a good horse a run for miles; with a foreleg broken they will go long distances, but should the ground be rough they are sooner distressed. It will seldom be found necessary to spear a wounded buck in a run, as he generally gives in when he finds the horse close with him. He will then throw himself down in some bush or patch of grass, and may be laid hold of. It is well, however, to carry the spear, for at times it may come in useful. Antelope shot through the body should not be ridden at once; if watched, they will probably lie down, and in half an hour may be picked up.

The foregoing remarks also apply to the pursuit of the chinkara or gazelle, and the nylghae. The does of all these antelope are generally easier to be got at than the bucks, but, except for food, the sportsman would not care to shoot them; and in Guzerat there are few places where a good buck cannot be found, and in many he may come home with four, six, or eight in his cart. When the herd is shy, the does generally lead off in the flight.

In the course of a day's shooting the hunter will frequently come across water, and, taking a smooth-bore either in the cart or carried by an attendant, he may vary his bag by a couple of hours of duck or snipe shooting. In Kattyawar he will often fall in with bustard and floriken, and altogether he will have no cause to complain of the scarcity of the game. Bustard, like antelope, may be approached with the cart. Large shot will bring them down.

In some of the fresh-water ponds fish are plentiful, and in the brackish pools in some of the rivers towards the Gulf of Cambay huge prawns are numerous. For the capture of these I always carried a casting net in the shooting cart, and was frequently enabled to improve my dinner by an extra course.

In some parts of Guzerat the natives of the Bunneah caste

are much averse to the destruction of animal life, and endeavour in every way in their power to thwart the sportsman ; and, as they are generally the grain-dealers and money-lenders of the place, they have sometimes considerable influence among the rest of the inhabitants, and can occasion small annoyances by withholding milk and other supplies from Europeans.

When an intelligent officer is in charge of a district, these little games are not often tried on, and these gentlemen are not allowed to annoy others who may not have the same religious views as themselves. But occasions have been known when, in a fit of fervour, they have not hesitated to incite the villagers to personal violence against Europeans who had offended them, either by the pursuit of game or the slaughter of some obnoxious Pariah dog who had intruded his impure presence in the neighbourhood of the camp.

Sportsmen would do well always to shun the close proximity of villages, even though good shade may not be obtained at a distance. During the presence of cholera and other epidemics, the cleanliness of an encampment is a great guarantee to health, and all ground near any native town or village is more or less filthy.

The water-supply should be carefully attended to, every care being taken to secure it as pure as possible, and the attendants should be discouraged from coming more in contact with the villagers than is necessary for procuring the requisite supplies of food, etc.

Hot Weather Excursion.

The success of the European hunter in quest of large game in India will depend greatly on the ability and diligence of his shikarees, and their subordinates. If the ability exists, rupees will generally draw out the other requisite.

It will be remembered that the best season for shooting is in the hottest months of the year, and during that time the work of following and hunting beasts, when their exact locality has been ascertained by the shikarees, will be found sufficient exertion. This does not refer to bison, sambur, and chetul shooting, as they are generally shot when stalking in the early mornings or evenings. But with tigers, bears, and panthers, the best plan is to have the game marked down by the shikarees; and if good men are employed, they will, except in very difficult countries, always succeed in following a beast to the spot where it lies up for the day.

Various methods are adopted, but I have found, for tigers and panthers, that baiting the country brings more game to the bag than any other plan. This is done by the shikarees, who, on arriving on fresh ground, proceed to hunt up the country far and wide for tracks, and by careful examination of the ground, and assiduously " pumping" the cowherds, tolerably accurate estimates of the prospect of sport can generally be formed.

The presence of a tiger in the country having been ascertained, young buffaloes must be procured, and these can be bought at from three to six rupees each, according to their size and the rapacity of their owners. They are tied up in the afternoons at the meetings of paths or ravines, and near pools which the tigers frequent, being attracted both by the water and the herds of deer and pigs which come down to slake their thirst. They should be tied by a stout cord to some stump or root, so that if possible they may not get the rope into a complication. They should, moreover, be tied in an open space, so that they may be seen from a distance. Sometimes, on the approach of a tiger, they will lie down, and by keeping still escape observation.

The tiger will, however, generally kill the buffalo and devour half of him, always beginning at the point of the buttock or inside the thigh. If the rope is not very strong, he will break it and drag off the carcass to some covert ; but in either case, if he is not disturbed, and eats well, he will lie up in the nearest spot where he can get good shade, or shade and water combined.

By the first streak of dawn the shikarees will be out examining the country, and looking after the baits. All the buffaloes found alive should be taken to a cool spot for the day, and they should be well fed and watered. If one has been killed, the shikarees will quietly approach the spot, and endeavour to find out where the footprints lead to. Especial care is requisite at this early hour, as in the cool of the morning the tiger, unless very lazy and much gorged, is apt to move if disturbed, and there may be great difficulty in again marking him down that day.

Towards seven or eight o'clock the sun will be powerful, and the shikarees may advance nearer. Should the tracks lead into a thick covert or mass of rocks, or other spot where the tiger may be supposed to have lain up, the shikarees will proceed to ring the game by carefully examining the ground for footprints, at some distance all round the covert. If no footprints are to be seen, and the place is in their opinion a good one, they will quietly mount trees commanding a good view of the ground.

The tiger will probably change his position, and, if there be a pool of water, will come out to drink and roll in it ; or some inquisitive crow will perch over him, and drawing attention by cawing, will indicate his position to the shikarees, who, on being certain of his presence, will send off one of their number to camp to bring up the hunters.

Some men in India insist on each shikaree always carrying with him a supply of water in a leathern bottle. With that and his pipe a native will sit in a tree, and keep watch over a beast for a whole day. Without the water they may be tempted to go in search of it, and the game may move unobserved, to the eventual disappointment of the hunters. If the party can command the services of more than one really good shikaree, it is well to assign to each a line of country, otherwise they are apt to be jealous, and sometimes spoil sport.

By this means I have been able to cover a considerable district, and by having a horseman at the head-quarters of each detachment ready to start off at once to the main camp with intelligence from the shikarees, the prospect of the day's sport may be known by 9 A.M., by which time the hunters will have breakfasted comfortably, and the sun will be sufficiently hot to prevent game from moving to any great distance if disturbed. By following the above plan I have received information from three places at once of tigers marked during the morning.

I had more men and horses at my disposal than a stranger could expect, but even on a small scale the plan will be found a good one ; and in many parts of the country a man on foot will not take much longer than a horseman to run into camp with intelligence.

There are of course occasions when game has to be beaten for "on spec," and I have frequently made a good bag though leaving the camp with but slender expectations.

On arriving on the ground selected for the day, the party should quietly dismount and hold a long palaver with the shikaree. This time is not thrown away. Then the ground should be carefully but quietly examined, and the run of the beasts ascertained. There is generally some covert not far off, which the tigers may be expected to make for when started, and all this information can usually be gathered from some of the natives of the spot, who will have been induced by the shikarees to assist them in marking the game.

Tigers are found in great variety of ground. At times I have found them lying almost in the open, or in ground quite clear of under-covert; on other occasions they lie in high grass or in dense bushes. Rocks, caves, and ravines with water, are favourite spots, and above all the tiger seems to delight in the thick shade of willows and cypress as found in large masses in the partly dried-up beds of rivers.

The mode of attack will depend on the ground and the means at the disposal of the hunters, but much of the success of an expedition will rest on having at least one good elephant ; and to insure this, I would recommend the hunters, before leaving England, to endeavour to get a good letter of introduction to the Governor of the Presidency where they may intend to shoot. There are some good elephants in the Commissariat department, and I believe one or more of these might be got for their keep—say 5s. each per day. Many of the native chiefs have good elephants, and if they know that they will be well used they will generally lend them in their own territory ; but, if possible, I think it would be preferable to obtain one from the Commissariat. This arrangement should be made at once on landing in India, and if necessary a howdah should be made during the cold weather, and all the gear got ready before the month of February.

None but really staunch elephants should be employed— a runaway is most dangerous—and a good and plucky mahout is essential. An elephant will no more go steadily up to a tiger when driven by a funky mahout than a horse will at his fences when ridden by a bad and nervous rider ; and the least hesitation or retrograde movement on the part of the elephant at a critical moment may spoil or lose a shot, and perhaps enable a vicious tiger to get in and make good his charge.

The elephant is generally required to drive a tiger out of cypress, long grass, or scrub jungle ; but the great advantage of having him with the party is that, on a tiger being wounded, he can be followed up at once. It is madness to follow on foot a wounded tiger into long grass or dense bush, and I have known many fatal accidents from such rashness. I well know that it is hard to leave a bloody track, but without an elephant, no tiger ought to be followed into such ground as I have described. They may sometimes be followed up successfully, if the mass of hunters and beaters will keep together, but no reliance can be placed on such a scratch pack ; and I have seen a crowd of beaters start and scatter in a moment at the mere growl of an angry tiger. With an elephant there is no danger to speak of. The wounded tiger can be almost always followed and brought to bag, unless he has managed to escape into some cave or mass of rocks.

In many places the elephant may not be required at first, or till the tiger is wounded. The covert may be surrounded by trees, and no better "coign of vantage" can be found. The experienced hunter will at once detect a good seat on some branch for himself and gunbearer.

If the party consists of two or three guns, straws may be drawn for places. This is a good plan ; it prevents all discussions as to who gets the best chance of the shot. When the elephant is required, the choice of tree or howdah can similarly be determined by straws.

Should guns not be available to command all the passes,

intelligent natives may be posted on trees in one or more with orders to cough or tap with a stick on a branch. This will generally be sufficient to turn the tiger on the shooters.

On the guns being placed, the beaters should commence at some distance from the spot where they know the tiger to be; the more noise they can make the better. If suddenly roused, the tiger may dash by the guns and give an uncertain shot; but by commencing to beat at a distance, he has time to rise, and move off quietly; and, as they seldom look up, he will at times come under the very tree from which the hunter quietly awaits his approach. By this means I have shot tigers within fifteen feet of the muzzle of my gun, before they were aware of my presence.

If the tiger is wounded and goes on, the elephant must be called into requisition, and all beaters left behind. Neglect of this precaution will often be followed by bad accidents.

Bears may often be shot on foot, and by two guns together, with comparative safety; but they are tenacious of life at times, and savage when wounded. They generally select a quiet spot to lie up, but care little for heat, notwithstanding their black colour and long hair. When convenient, they inhabit caves and rocks, but I have often shot them in grass, where they had been lying throughout the day exposed to all the power of the Indian summer sun.

Most of the remarks which I have written regarding tigers apply also to panthers. The latter are most savage and dangerous animals, and too much precaution cannot be taken in hunting them. They can conceal themselves anywhere, and when attacked will charge repeatedly and in the most determined manner.

On no occasion ought the beaters to be exposed to danger more than is necessary, and they ought never on any account

to be sent into a covert where a wounded beast is known to
be. In India news travels fast, and the report of a beater
killed or mauled will precede the hunter from camp to camp.
If the natives hear that their lives are likely to be recklessly
exposed, they will not assemble to beat, and the shikarees
will find great difficulty in obtaining men to assist them in
marking game.

If a tiger has only been slightly wounded, he will do mischief; if badly, he will probably be found dead next day; but
he should never be followed up into thick covert, unless with
an elephant; and all men on foot should be directed to mount
trees or keep well out of the way. I purpose illustrating the
truth of these remarks by anecdotes which have come within
my own experience; and as I bear the marks of both teeth
and claws, I hope my observations may have weight in
warning any gentlemen who may be desirous of entering on
a sporting campaign in the East of the danger of rashly
exposing themselves or their followers when in pursuit of
savage beasts.

A bad accident to one of the party entails the removal of
the sufferer, if not killed on the spot, to the nearest cantonment where medical aid can be obtained. His friends have to
accompany him, and the expedition is either at an end or
much valuable time is lost. With common and reasonable
care, and a little resolution and self-denial, all this may be
prevented.

PRESERVATION OF SKINS.

A few remarks on the preservation of skins and heads (not
human) may, I think, be useful here.

Deer's heads may be cleaned by boiling till all the flesh
leaves the skull; but the base of the horns should be en-

veloped in paste to prevent bleaching by the hot water. The nose bones should be carefully looked after, and, if loose, should be fastened in with glue. If wanting, the appearance of the head is much spoiled. Deer-skins should be pegged out in the shade, hair downwards, with wooden pegs, and rubbed over with finely-powdered alum.

Tiger, panther, and bear skins require more attention. The beasts may be killed at a distance from home, or in such a locality that they cannot be carried out without much difficulty and probable injury to the skin. In such a case they can be skinned on the spot, and the carcass left on the ground. When shot, a tiger should never be allowed to lie on hot ground or rocks in the sun. The heat is so great, that it will soon blister off the hair, and a good skin may be lost. It should be moved very carefully, and never dragged on the ground or over rocks. When tied on an elephant, care should be taken to prevent the ropes from chafing, or the hair will be rubbed off.

Tigers should be skinned on the same day that they are shot. The after appearance of the skin will greatly depend on the manner in which it is taken off. The hunter should himself superintend this part of the business, or only entrust it to one of his men whom he may have previously instructed. The cutting should be done by his own hand as follows :—

1st. Place the beast on his back, and cut the skin from the lower lip to the point of the tail. This cut should open the tail to its extreme point, beyond the last joint, else the tip is apt to go bad, and the hair will come out.

2d. Cut the skin down the middle of the ball of the fore paws, and so down the leg to the middle of the chest.

3d. Cut the skin from the inside of the ball of the hind feet, inside the hock and up the middle of the inside of the thigh, falling into the main cut about six inches from the root of the tail.

By carefully following these instructions, it will be seen that when the skin is spread out, the outline is not jagged or unseemly, and that the yellow is almost entirely surrounded by a band of white. This adds greatly to the beauty of the skin.

Panthers and chetahs may be done the same way. After the skin has been cut as described, the village skinners will do the rest.

Black bear skins are generally kept, though I don't know why, unless as trophies, for they are not useful nor ornamental, the hair being long and coarse.

When taken off, all skins should be made over to the village *chamars* or skinners, who will go over them with their own peculiar knives, and remove from them all flesh and fat which may be adhering. Each man should have an inch-thick board, free from nails, and a foot or eighteen inches square, to work upon. The ears should be skinned down as far as possible, as also the toes, each separately, and the bones removed to the last joint. The lips should be pared as thin as can be without damaging the roots of the moustache. All bullet-holes should be sewn up with a stout needle and thread.

On the skin being thoroughly cleaned, it should be pegged out, hair downwards, with wooden pegs five or six inches in length. A large number of these pegs should always be kept ready. The pegging out should be done with care, and the legs on both sides should be stretched in the same positions, else the shape of the skin will be spoilt. The proper proportions of length and breadth should also be preserved.

The skin should be pegged down in some spot which is completely shaded throughout the day; and the ears, head, and feet, should be well painted over with a strong solution of arsenical soap. The rest of the skin may be rubbed with finely-powdered alum ; but a brush over with arsenical soap is also good. The soap should be kept in a tin pail, and laid on with a strong brush.

If white ants are numerous about the spot, men or boys should be employed night and day to tap the skins all over with a light stick every half-hour. This will prevent the ravages of these insects, otherwise at the end of two days, on lifting the skin, the hair may be found eaten off in large patches.

After two days the skin may be taken up, but the head and neck will still be found to be wet, and these parts should be very carefully handled at this time, or the hair will rub off. The skin should now be placed, hair uppermost, where it may get just a little sunning, a free current of air passing under.

In about three days it should be quite dry, and then should be placed on a broad litter of long bamboos, and carried on men's shoulders from one camp to another. In this way a dozen or more skins can be carried by four men. Should a change of camp be necessary before the skin is thoroughly dried, it can be taken up, and by placing it on the top of the heap, and abstaining from handling it, it will travel in safety, and can be again pegged down at the end of the march. This will be found a superior method to any other. If placed on a cart, the skins will be much rubbed and damaged.

A trustworthy man should accompany the skins when moving from camp to camp ; the coolies are apt to singe the moustaches as a mark of contempt or defiance, and to steal them to wear as charms. When in camp, tent-pegs should be driven in to keep the litter clear of the ground, so that white ants cannot get at the skins.

Handsome skins should be brought home simply dried as above described. The Indians do not tan well, and I have seen many a good skin spoilt. Skins packed in a tin-lined box with camphor should arrive in good order. They should be folded, not rolled, or the hard points in the leather round the peg-holes may rub off the hair in other places. I recommend Mr. Stammwitz, of Argyle Street, as a good man to mount skins. He does them well, and at a very moderate charge.

The skulls of tigers, bears, and panthers may be cleaned by boiling after the fleshy parts have been removed with a knife. As soon as the skull is cleaned, the whole of the teeth should be covered with a coating of beeswax a quarter of an inch in thickness, so as completely to exclude the hot air, else the teeth will splinter like dry wood. This operation should be performed at once. Any claws that are loose should be removed and kept separately, or the natives will steal them for charms.

A peculiar bone, detached from all others, is found in the muscles of the shoulder, in tigers and panthers.

CHAPTER II.

ON landing in India on the 8th of January 1847, I was placed
on duty in the garrison of Bombay, where I remained for five
months. At the end of that time, having been posted to a
regiment in the Southern Mahratta country, I was directed to
join. Meeting with a brother officer similarly situated, we
hired a country boat, and sent our baggage, servants, and
horses on board.

The craft was a botella, or ordinary coasting boat, undecked,
with a small cabin in the stern, from the roof of which the
tiller was worked. The crew consisted of about ten men, and,
the wind being fair, we made our run down the coast in about
a couple of days to Vingorla, where we landed.

It was my first visit to the mainland of India, and having
read from my youth up of its varied game, I longed to see
and judge for myself. Hayward, my chum, was imbued with
a like spirit, and we subsequently made many excursions
together.

We were detained a day or two in procuring pack bullocks to carry our baggage to Belgaum, and in the meantime had leisure to examine the new country and its inhabitants. At the travellers' bungalow we met an officer of the Belgaum garrison—a very sharp fellow. I rode with him one evening, and having made a considerable detour, we found ourselves at dusk close to the house, but separated from it by a creek thirty yards wide, which we had crossed further up. I was not aware of the depth, but my companion told me to go on, and assured me that it was "all right." In another moment the water was over my saddle. Finding myself in for it, I held on, and, half swimming my horse, reached the opposite bank. Looking back, I saw my friend on the other side. "Ah!" cried he, "the water is deeper than I thought;" with which remark he rode off by the way we had come, while I returned alone to the bungalow, a wetter and a wiser man.

The march to Belgaum occupied five days. Not knowing the customs of the country, we generally rose at daylight, superintended the loading of the bullocks, and then marched with them till about 10 A.M., by which time we had got over some eight miles. If we came to a suitable stream, we unloaded, had a bathe in the river, and breakfasted, moving on again to the next staging bungalow in the afternoon. We were of course "griffins," and our mode of procedure was that of griffins; but what cared we? We enjoyed ourselves thoroughly, and pursued and shot doves for the pot with a zeal and energy worthy of a better cause.

On the second day we reached the foot of the Ram Ghaut, a steep pass in the mountains, leading up from the Concan to the table-land of the Deccan. I believe that, had we known how to set about it, we might have got bison and sambur here; but ignorance was bliss, and when I shot a large red squirrel at the foot of the Ghaut, I was happy for that day, and busied myself with taking off and preparing the skin.

The jungles below the hills swarmed with fireflies, lighting up the trees on dark nights.

We reached Belgaum on the fifth day, and, after a halt of two days, proceeded on our way to Dharwar, fifty miles, which we accomplished in three marches.

It was now the beginning of June, the rains were setting in, and not much shooting was to be got.

To the east of Dharwar is a vast level plain, extending sixty or eighty miles, and highly cultivated. In parts the antelope are numerous, but we did not then understand the use of the stalking-cart, and got but few. I well remember my satisfaction on bagging my first black buck. He was with a small herd, and I had succeeded in getting within 150 yards of him. Not having much confidence in the steadiness of my hand, I made my shikaree lie down flat on his face, and, lying down myself at a right angle, I rested the rifle on his back. On being struck, the buck kicked out with both hind legs like a jackass, and went off at speed. I watched him for some distance, and then, supposing I had missed him, signalled to my groom to bring up my horse. On mounting I observed an unusual object on the plain, and cantering up I found the buck stone dead.

In this plain the deer are much hunted by the Hirun shikarees, or antelope hunters, who snare them by an ingenious method. To a line about 200 yards in length, made of the sinews of deer, they attach snares, to each of which is fastened a wooden pin eight inches or ten inches long. The snares are also made of deer sinews, and the whole is very strong. They are placed at intervals of about eighteen inches.

When carrying the line, the hunter passes his left arm

through all the snares, so that it is covered from the shoulder to the wrist. A stalking bullock is employed, and is led by the shikaree, who also carries a number of sticks five feet in length, with bunches of feathers attached to one end, the other being pointed. Stooping on the far side of the bullock, he proceeds towards the herd, and, on approaching sufficiently near, he plants the sticks into the ground, 20 or 30 yards apart. Having so disposed of half the number of his sticks, he commences to lay his snares, which he does across the plain, dexterously setting each in the ground by the peg attached to it. From the end of the line he plants his remaining bunches of feathers, and moves off. His confederates then show themselves, and, by simulating the movements of cultivators, quietly drive the deer towards the snares. When they calculate that the proper time has arrived, they howl and run forward, and turning from the feathers the herd runs over the snares, one or two deer generally being caught by the leg. The snares being all attached to the main line, the deer are then easily caught.

Bustard are taken in the same way, but the driving has to be quietly conducted, else they would take flight. They are fine birds, weighing from 20 pounds to 24 pounds each. I have frequently, when stalking them in comparatively open ground, suddenly lost sight of them, and, after searching in vain for some time, have seen them rise from the ground I had just gone over. They will lie flat on the ground, and conceal themselves in a marvellous manner. One morning, when riding across the plain, I observed one walking about in the open ground. I moved slowly towards him, and he did not rise till I was within ten yards. I have often, in Central India, had good shots at them from the back of a horse or camel, but they are very shy of a man on foot.

It was in this plain of Dharwar that I made my first and last personal acquaintance with the sting of a scorpion. I was seated on a bank, waiting for my horse to be brought up, and had been pounding the black friable turf between my feet with the butt of my rifle. Scorpio had been disturbed, and quietly walked up the stock and stung me in the point of the finger. I instantly shook him off, and stamped upon him; but the pain was most acute, and shot up the arm at once. Binding a handkerchief tightly round the finger, I sucked the injured part, and the pain began to subside as the poison was drawn out. In half an hour I did not feel it; but some time after a callosity formed over the spot. Experiencing a peculiar sensation, I opened this one day with a penknife, and dug out the point of the sting, which had been broken off and remained in the wound.

To the westward of Dharwar, within a few miles, are some good lakes, or tanks as they are called, much frequented by wild-fowl in the cold weather. There are also many good snipe grounds, and quail and florican in the season are tolerably plentiful, though by no means in such numbers as in Guzerat. About ten miles to the westward are considerable jungles, stretching away towards the Western Ghauts. In these we found a fair amount of spotted deer and pigs, and also jungle sheep, a small antelope with flat goat-like horns, three inches or four inches in length.

We generally had these jungles beat by a number of men, taking up our places at the different passes. At one of these beats a large boar and a couple of jungle sheep had fallen to my rifle, and I was on my way to rejoin the other guns when I came on a herd of cheetul or spotted deer crossing my front about sixty yards off. They were just over the brow of a hill covered with grass and jungle, and sloping abruptly down for

150 yards. Running in a few paces, I fired at a doe ; but by the time the smoke had cleared, the herd was out of sight. I was confident that I had held straight ; but on going up to the spot I found nothing. I followed for some distance in the direction which the herd had taken, and, finding nothing, returned along the base of the hill. Nearly opposite the spot where I had fired, I caught sight of the white stern of a deer among some long grass, and, aiming rapidly, rolled it over. It turned out to be the same deer at which I had fired above, and my first shot had broken both fore legs close to the body ; notwithstanding this, she had managed almost instantaneously to disappear, and, but for my luck in coming across her, would have been lost.

In the next drive I heard a shot from one of my friends, and soon after a pariah dog which had accompanied the beaters came down in my direction, giving tongue loudly, and evidently after something. Guided by the sound, I rushed off, and crashing through a thicket came into an open spot, thirty yards across, in the middle of which stood a mighty grey boar. He was crippled in one of his fore legs, but was able to keep his head to the dog, on whom he fixed his small vicious eyes, his long white tusks gleaming in the sunlight. The instant I appeared, he wheeled round towards me, and I believe in another moment would have charged ; but a shot between the eyes bowled him over.

Formerly tigers must have been numerous close round Dharwar, and, though we never fell in with any, our old shikaree always endeavoured to soothe the pangs of disappointment by assuring us that he had seen many shot in those self-same coverts. He constantly quoted two gentlemen, named Walker and Campbell, as having been mighty hunters, and I fear we did not always receive the accounts of their exploits in a spirit of meekness.

I have since learned that Campbell was either "The Old Forest Ranger" himself, or his brother. Both were well known in that country.

One morning a man came running into the fort, and informed us that a panther had taken up her abode in a rocky hillock about ten miles from the cantonment. Hayward and I started off with a friend who was staying with us, and on arriving at the village we were conducted to the place by half a dozen semi-nude savages. The hillock was not more than fifty feet high, and was situated close to the edge of the heavy jungle. The summit was a mass of rocks and green bushes. As we were all on foot, and could not tell the exact spot in which the beast might be expected, we formed up three abreast, and advanced very cautiously in expectation of a charge. Ascending the hillock, we peered about among the rocks for some time without seeing anything. At length we found a small den formed by several masses of rock, and as our eyes became accustomed to the darkness we spied what we supposed to be the head of a panther. We were on the point of firing when the object moved, and we then discovered it to be two small cubs lying together, and apparently asleep. We captured these without much trouble, and then hunted about the jungle in the immediate neighbourhood, in hopes of getting the mother, but she never showed ; so, tying up her offspring in a blanket, we carried them off to the cantonment.

In these jungles were numerous pea and jungle fowl, and frequently, when we were waiting for larger game at passes, they would come by in long strings, passing close under the trees on which we were seated. Troops, too, of the "lungoor" or large grey monkey would come dancing along, with black careworn countenances. It was interesting to watch them unobserved—grey old patriarchs and youthful mothers, with their young clinging convulsively to their necks and waists as they bounded along. To see them spring from tree to rock, it seemed a marvel that the infants did not get their brains knocked out.

About three miles to the south of Dharwar are the Edeeguttee jungles, which we generally found good for spotted deer and pigs; but the coverts were very thick, and consisted almost entirely of corinda bushes. These grow to the height of about twenty feet, and are evergreen. The leaves are about two inches in length, and, while the outer part of the bush appears impenetrable, the interior is generally hollow, and affords cool shade to wild animals during the day. The branches are armed with strong thorns.

We were driving this jungle one morning, when five spotted deer came by me. I was standing at the top of a rising ground, but the bush on all sides was so dense that I could only get a view at one or two places, and then only for distances two or three yards in width.

I had my eye on one of these openings, and as the deer crossed had a snap-shot at a fine buck. I had hardly time to see whether he was hit, but on the beaters coming up, we examined the track for a short distance and found blood. As we followed the prints, the buck dashed out of a thick bush, and I again fired, taking him behind the shoulder, but without dropping him. He then got away into a very dense mass of bushes, but was discovered by some of the beaters, and, after assuring myself that the opposite side was clear, I again fired and finished him. On examination, we found the three balls had entered behind the shoulder, within three inches of each other. Considering that I was shooting with a 14-bore gun, his tenacity of life was wonderful.

Immediately to the south of Edeeguttee, about three miles,

runs a range of very stony hills, with deep ravines filled with rocks and bushes. In these we frequently shot pigs. On different occasions we started panthers, but never succeeded in bagging one. Hyænas were less fortunate, and we slew several. Langton, of my regiment, shot a very large one, whose striped sides he had at first mistaken for a tiger. As he wished to preserve the skin, we proceeded to remove it on the ground, and had taken it off all but the tail, round the root of which a rope was tied, and, while Langton and I held on to the rope, half-a-dozen natives hauled bravely at the head and legs. The skin was strong and tough; but at last it stripped off, and came away with a run, the beaters tumbling backwards down the hill in a heap, while we rolled over in the opposite direction.

A hare rose at my feet one morning near these hills, and as she went off at speed I bowled her over with a bullet.

But the happy hunting-grounds of Dharwar lay in the Dandelly jungles, thirty-five miles to the S.W. Hayward and I had long been anxious to visit them, but they were said to be malarious, and our commandant was shy of giving us leave. In those days we did not believe in fevers, or at any rate were quite willing to risk them in the hope of sport; so perhaps it was as well that we did not get our own way, for I believe that till the ground is thoroughly dry the jungles are not safe.

It was towards the end of April that, at the close of a long march, we reached Hullihal, about six miles from the bungalow, on the banks of the Kala Nuddee.

The latter is a noble river, flowing through the heart of the jungle where we were to shoot. As we intended to push on again in the afternoon, we made a halt under some trees, and sent one of our servants into the village for supplies.

After a long time our messenger returned, saying that the native government official declined to furnish any, adding that he had stated that his resolution was fixed, even if a subsequent request should be made by our parents. Being hot and hungry, I suppose we were displeased, for we at once set out to see the gentleman in person. We found him in his office—a wide, open, verandah—seated on cushions, and surrounded by minor officials. He was a large man, and his sole garment consisted of a sheet, apparently embedded in folds of fat at the spot where his waist should have been, and hanging down over his nether man.

He gazed on our dusty coats and sun-browned faces with a listless apathy, quietly chewing a large mouthful of betel nut; and it was not till sundry pokes had been administered with the points of our sticks to the softer portions of his capacious person, and our wants had been reiterated in forcible and emphatic language, that the requisite orders for supplies were given, and we returned to our people.

Towards the afternoon we again marched, and our fat friend sat down and wrote an account of our brutal treatment to the collector of the district. Had we been better acquainted with the manners and customs of the country, we should have been beforehand with him; as it was, we forgot all about the matter, and made up our minds for a pleasant camp in the Dandelly.

We subsequently received an official letter from the collector in charge of the district, and had some small trouble in settling the complaint of the obese gentleman, who, however, on our return march supplied everything at once on our arrival without delay.

At a village a few miles from Hullihal we were joined by the shikarees of the country, Messrs. Emaum and Moideen.

The latter was an intelligent little man, and well acquainted with the jungles, but was in a way, I believe, under subjection to Emaum, who was, to say the least of it, a very remarkable man. He was by birth almost a pure negro, with all the characteristics of the race both in face and person. He generally moved in light marching order, his dress consisting of an unclean turban, and a strip of cloth passed under a string, which he wore round his waist. Over his shoulder he carried a brown blanket. His accoutrements were a long flint gun, a belt with sundry bags attached, and a long knife. By creed a Mahomedan, he was, I regret to say, addicted to strong waters, and when he came to us he stipulated that his daily wage should be one shilling and two glasses of brandy. He was, however, so far mindful of his duty to his employers that he never, except on special occasions, took his drink till the day's work was over. He seemed much pleased at the prospect of sport, and informed us that he had a strong predilection for flesh—a craving which, he added, had not been lately gratified. Moideen was the son of old Kamah, mentioned by "The Old Forest Ranger," in whose words the following anecdote of his early life is well told :—

"While sitting at breakfast we were alarmed by hearing cries of distress proceeding from the Jagheerdar's hut, and on running out to ascertain the cause, we found old Kamah in a furious state of excitement, his left hand firmly fixed in the woolly pate of the hopeful scion of his house, and belabouring him soundly with a stout bamboo.

"We inquired what crime young Moideen had been guilty of, to bring upon him such a storm of parental indignation, and learned, to our astonishment, that it was all owing to his having killed a tiger !

"One of his father's tame buffaloes having been killed by

a tiger on the previous day, the young savage had watched for him during the night, and shot him from a tree when he returned to feed upon the carcass.

"This most people would have considered a very gallant and meritorious exploit on the part of a lad of fifteen, but the old forester was of a different opinion.

" ' It was all very well,' " he said, " ' for us who lived in the open country to wage war with tigers, but with him, who lived on sociable terms with them in the jungle, the case was different. I have no quarrel with tigers! I never injured one of them, they never injured me, and while there was peace between us, I went among them without fear of danger.

" ' But now that this young rascal has picked a quarrel and commenced hostilities there is no saying where the feud will end.'

"And for this breach of good fellowship between the family of Kamah and his feline neighbours, the unfortunate youngster was being beaten to a mummy!"

The shooting in the Dandelly was carried on entirely by stalking. We rose long before daybreak, and had a light refreshment ; then each taking one shikaree, we set off in different directions, returning home about 9 or 10 A.M.

The principal game was bison, sambur, cheetul or axis, and pigs. There were also bears, tigers, and panthers ; but in those extensive forests the chances of getting them were small.

We rested during the heat of the day, and about 3 P.M. again set out, returning to camp after dark. The shikarees were well acquainted with the jungles, and by their advice we always walked in their tracks, while they, carrying the spare gun, led the way and kept on the look-out for game.

Emaum was generally my companion, and he certainly was a very good marker. His senses of sight and hearing were

D

very acute, and he used to declare he could smell bison when the wind was favourable. We had in our camp about a dozen baggage ponies, each with his attendant, and after a successful stalk we generally took these and went out after breakfast to cut up and bring in the meat. We had a sort of pic-nic on these occasions, and it was fearful to see Emaum indulging in his African propensities, and bolting huge pieces of raw bison's flesh.

We were joined by Emaum and Moideen about four miles from the bungalow on the Kala Nuddee, which we intended to make our head-quarters for some weeks ; so, on the following morning, sending on our baggage by the road, we each took a shikaree, and started off through the jungle in different directions.

Our attendants requested that we should trust entirely to them to find the game, and that all our attentions should be engaged in avoiding making any noise by treading on dry leaves and sticks.

My first shot was at a doe cheetul, at which, however, I would not have fired, had not Emaum urged the want of meat in camp. She was about eighty yards off, feeding in an open glade in the bamboo jungle. My shot took her behind the shoulder, and Emaum's long knife did the rest. He was much pleased at this beginning, and expressed his intention of eating largely of flesh. The deer was soon skinned and cut up ; but Emaum said that nothing must be wasted, and, emptying out the entrails, he packed them in the skin, and so we set off to camp, where we were soon after joined by Hayward, who had shot a sambur.

One morning, when shooting in this jungle, I fired at a spotted deer, which at once made off, and, as it showed no signs of being hit, I concluded I had missed—especially as I had not heard the thud of the bullet on his side. On going up to the spot where the deer had been standing, Emaum bent down, and pointing out some hairs on the grass, pronounced it "no miss." The hairs had been cut by the ball on entering, and lay just below where the shoulder of the deer had been, the spot being plainly indicated by the deep marks of the hoofs in the ground as it started at my shot. Following up the track, we came on the deer lying dead. On other occasions, I have been similarly assured that deer had been wounded, and have brought to bag beasts that otherwise would have been lost.

The bungalow was situated in a lovely spot, about sixty yards from the river's bank. To the rear of the house was a huge banian tree, alive with minahs, parrots, and green pigeons; and on all sides were clumps of giant bamboos seventy feet high, standing out like feathers against the clear sky. The river here was about one hundred yards across, the somewhat broken bed of the stream changing just above into a fine deep pool. We made this place our head-quarters for about three weeks, stalking morning and evening in the jungles, and generally having some fresh additions to make to our game list every evening.

I did not get a shot at a bison till I had been out some days; but one morning when I was stalking with Moideen we came on fresh tracks. My companion plucked some blades of grass, which had been cropped, and pointed out how the broken edge had not dried, from which circumstance he knew that the game was not far off. It is remarkable how little impression these large hard-hoofed animals leave on the sunbaked earth, and, though sometimes the footprints are plain enough, at others, they can only be distinguished by a practised tracker.

We proceeded very cautiously in single file, Moideen leading, and after going about half a mile we heard the bison a short distance in front. The herd was about to lie up for the day, and had betaken themselves to a mass of thick young bamboos.

There were several of them; but near the edge of the thicket, with her face towards us, lay a cow, and, from her position, we saw we could not advance without alarming the herd. I was anxious to get a bull, but, fearing that in attempting to do so I should lose all, I made up my mind to take the cow. She lay in deep shade, and I fired at her shoulder, on which she sprang up, and, together with the rest, dashed off to the left.

My battery was but a poor one, consisting of a 12-bore single rifle, and a 14-bore double gun. I caught the latter from Moideen, and fired both shots at a bull as they rushed off. Reloading, we took up the track, and soon came on blood in large quantities, and a few hundred yards ahead we came on a bison, standing with his stern to us, at the side of a patch of jungle grass eight feet high.

We decided on moving round this grass, to get, if possible, opposite his shoulder, and on going to the right we suddenly came on the cow. She caught sight of us, and, wheeling round, stood head on. Expecting a charge, I got behind a tree, and as she stood looking at me, with her nose poked out, I fired at her head, and she fell dead in her tracks.

We had supposed that this was the beast whose blood we had seen; but, on examination, we found that as she lay in the bamboo thicket her hind foot had probably been drawn up behind the forearm, and in firing I had sent the first ball through the foot, breaking both toes. Being unable to run in this crippled state, she had wheeled round on finding herself pursued, and my second shot had taken her just above one nostril, and had passed up the head into the brain.

Seeing that she had bled but little, we knew that the bull must have been hard hit, and endeavoured to follow up the track ; but the blood soon ceased to flow, and the footprints getting mixed up with those of the rest of the herd, we were unable to make anything of them ; so, returning to the encamping ground, we had breakfast, and then, taking our ponies, we proceeded to skin and cut up the beast.

Our camp followers were in high glee at the prospect of meat, and on our return they cut up the flesh into long strips, and dried it on ropes and bamboos suspended from tree to tree. In a few days it became black and hard, and was then tied up in bundles like firewood till required for food.

We kept the tail, tongue, and marrow-bones, and some of the meat, for our own larder. The flesh was somewhat tough and stringy, but after a long diet on scraggy fowls and goat we were glad of any change. The tail made capital soup, and the tongue and marrow-bones were excellent.

Most of the jungle on the left bank of the river had been burnt ; that on the right only partially. As the fire sweeps along, it is not uncommon for dead trees to ignite near the root, and as the fire smoulders, the tree falls. It will continue to burn for days, and the fire travels out to the ends of the branches, leaving the impression of the tree on the ground in white ashes. At these times the sambur approach, and stand in the smoke to rid themselves of the flies. They also lick up the ashes for salt. We frequently came on them about these burning trees, but our shikarees assured us that on being disturbed they would not return till the second day.

One morning, Hayward and I, having set out with our shikarees in different directions, chanced to meet in the jungle, and, seeing one of these burning trees close by, went up to it and sat down to have a smoke. Presently a splendid buck cheetul came quietly across the open glade in front of us. We sat quite still, and he never observed us till within seventy yards, when he drew up and stared. He was a handsome beast as he stood in the bright morning sun, with his dark-brown sides flecked with white, and his fine antlers thrown back. Hayward, who sat somewhat in rear of the rest of the party, quietly raised his rifle and rolled him over, and we carried him off bodily to camp.

While encamped in the Dandelly I had a narrow escape of being charged by a bison, owing to want of proper attention to my rifle. I was out one morning with Emaum, and as we were emerging from a thicket of young bamboos we came on four bison feeding on an open space. The clearing was only about fifty yards wide, and in the bamboos on the opposite side we could see the rest of the herd moving about. The wind was favourable, and we were not observed, but any retrograde movement on our part might have alarmed the game ; so, quietly sinking into a sitting position, I raised the heavy single rifle to my shoulder and sat motionless, trusting to the dark brown colour of my clothes and Emaum's skin to escape observation.

I was anxious to secure a heavy bull, and, supposing that one would be in the herd, I reserved my shot for him, and allowed the four in the open to feed unmolested. One of these was a fine young bull, and presently he turned his head towards me and fed up to within fifteen yards. He was getting too close to be pleasant ; so, aiming at the point of his shoulder, I pressed the trigger. The cap snapped, and the bison started back a pace or two and looked hard at us. Had they charged, we should have been smashed, as we were sitting among young bamboos no thicker than a man's finger, and no friendly tree was near. Without lowering the rifle from my shoulder, I whispered to Emaum to fire, which he did with the double-barrel smoothbore, taking the bull diagonally from the point of the right shoulder to the rear of the left arm.

All four wheeled round and dashed away through the thicket. Emaum, however, assured me that he had fired with a good aim. I then set to work to fire off my rifle, and after some time succeeded in doing so. Shooting into an ant-heap, I picked up about half a yard of burning cloth, which my servant, to whom I had foolishly entrusted the cleaning of my rifle on the previous night, had left in the barrel. I made a note of the fact for future guidance. Reloading, we took up the track of the herd, and after going about 200 yards through the jungle came on the bull, lying quite dead.

As a rule we found that when a bison fell to the shot, it was wise to give him more lead at once, as they will frequently rise and get off. On the other hand, when a bison ran some distance, and then fell, he seldom rose again, and was nearly always bagged.

I was out with Emaum one morning before I had learned this fact, and as we advanced through some bamboos we heard bison moving a short distance ahead. Bending down to the ground, so as to get a view under the thick leaves of the bushes, we could see the heads and feet of the advancing herd as they grazed on the young grass. Some of them were within thirty yards, but their bodies were quite concealed. I had heard that a shot in the forehead would not penetrate, but having no other chance I determined to try, and, sitting down so as to get a good sight of the heads, I watched my opportunity. A large cow was head on, and aiming a little above her eyes I fired, and she fell. The remainder of the herd crashed away and disappeared as Emaum and I dashed forward.

He begged I would fire again, as the cow would probably rise and get away, so, standing over her, I fired both shots of the smoothbore behind her shoulder. Remarking that all was now right, Emaum drew his long knife from his girdle, bent back the head, and muttering some words of the Koran, proceeded to cut the throat. Unless this operation is performed in life, no good Mussulman will eat of the flesh. When meat was scarce, however, I have seen them satisfied with a very slight movement on the part of the dying animal.

I had just reloaded the smoothbore, and Emaum had already made a deep incision in the stout skin of the throat, when, with a desperate struggle, the cow shook him off and got to her knees. Emaum sprang to the nearest tree, and, catching up the loaded gun, I gave the poor cow two more shots behind the shoulder, and she sank down.

We were much troubled in our stalking on the right bank of the river, owing to the jungle being only partially burnt, and the ground was covered with huge dry teak leaves eighteen inches across, which rendered all stalking hopeless. We were informed that the burning had been prohibited by the officer in charge of the district, as being injurious to the young timber.   This we did not believe, the more so that the jungle had been burnt every year from time immemorial, and, notwithstanding, trees of every growth were flourishing. Several good stalks having been spoilt, we determined to fire the jungle, knowing that, in addition to getting rid of the objectionable leaves and dry grass, a fresh green herbage would spring up in a few days, and that game would be attracted.

Breaking out some stout **dead** bamboos, we jumped on them till they were in splinters from end to end, and suitable for torches, and then, **striking a** light, **we raked up some dead** leaves and made a fire. While engaged at this work, **I was** bending **over** the flame, when my powder-flask fell from **an** inner breast-pocket **and** dropped into the blaze. My first impulse was **to bolt,** but I was a long way from home and **had** no other flask, **so I** launched a desperate **kick into** the burning **mass.** I caught the flask on the toe **of my** boot, and sent it spinning right **into Emaum's face.** He was some yards off, and was not a little astonished, though not much hurt. We then lit our bamboo torches, and, walking across the wind, poked them into the leaves at intervals of **ten yards.** In half an hour the **whole jungle was a sheet of flame, and, satisfied** with our afternoon's work we started off home.

In the jungle, a few miles from the bungalow, was **a very** pretty lake, to which we occasionally went to spend the day, stalking morning and evening on the way. Going to one of these pic-nics, I came on a herd of bison, and **got a fair broad-**side shot at a fine young bull. **I heard the shot tell, but he** dashed off and disappeared. **Emaum was** sulky, and taxed me with having fired too soon, but **I made him** take up the track, and, finding blood, he recovered his temper.

. After going some **distance, as we crossed a** small dry **watercourse at the foot of a hill in the** jungle, **we saw the** bull **standing above us, eighty yards off.** He was evidently distressed, **but we could not tell** where he was hit. Presently he gave **a good broadside shot, and,** kneeling behind a fallen tree, I fired. He staggered, and then we saw one of **his fore-**legs was disabled.

Whether he tried to come at us, **or whether** he was unable **to run** in any other direction, I cannot say ; but he came down towards us on three legs at a terrific pace. He passed within a few feet of where we lay, and as he went by I gave him another shot behind the shoulder, and he fell all in a heap at the bottom of the watercourse, where another shot finished him.

The lake was a charming spot for resting during the heat of the day, though its proportions were of course reduced by the month of May. All round the edges might be seen the tracks of deer, bison, and pigs, which evidently came down in large numbers at night to the water. The reeds were filled with large blue waterfowl of the coot and waterhen kind, having long toes, which enabled them to run freely over the network of weeds which covered the surface of the water. Hayward killed one of these by a fine shot from the rifle at about 150 yards.

We had spent a pleasant day at this lake, and were prepared for a start home, when we observed a heavy storm gathering. The only shelter in the place was an old hut, about as large as a carriage umbrella, which had been erected by cowherds. It was constructed of slips of bamboos and teak leaves, and doubtless would have kept off a heavy shower twelve months before. At this time, however, it was rent and torn by the wind, and large patches of the thatch had been blown off. Into it, however, we crept, and covering up the locks of our guns, lit our pipes and waited for the storm to burst. We chaffed Emaum a good deal, as, in reply to a remark from me about mid-day, he assured me we should have no rain. We did not wait long for it, and for over an hour the rain came down in a perfect deluge. Our frail protection only seemed to concentrate the heavy drops, which poured through in every direction. The thunder was deafening, and the lightning appeared to strike into the ground all round us. We were somewhat uneasy lest the metal of our guns should attract it ; at length we carried them off, and laid them down in the open ground at some distance.

The storm went off as speedily as it came, and, wringing the wet out of our clothes, we dried our rifles and set off home.

The morning after rain generally brought game to the bag. All old footprints were of course obliterated, and, the ground being soft, any beasts that had recently passed were easily tracked, and the leaves and grass being wet enabled us to move noiselessly through the jungle. We were therefore out early on the next day, and, my beat on that morning lying on the other side of the river, I crossed with Emaum in the canoe before daybreak, and by the time that objects were distinguishable we were several miles from the bungalow.

As we skirted a fine open glade in the forest we observed a large herd of cheetul on the far side, and as we were advancing to stalk them we came on fresh marks of a bison—a solitary bull, which had evidently fed and lain down at the covert side during the night. He had not left the spot more than half an hour ; so, taking no more notice of the cheetul, we followed on his track. He had moved deep into the heavy forest, and as we followed we came across another herd of cheetul. Catching sight of us, they dashed off from right to left, making much noise. We stuck, however, to the track of the bull, and found he had been lying down close to the line on which the deer had crossed. They had disturbed him, and he had moved ; but we could see by the prints that he was not scared, and had moved slowly, feeding as he went.

Proceeding with much caution for a quarter of a mile further, Emaum suddenly halted, and pointed out the bull about sixty yards in advance. He stood in a small green space, twenty yards in diameter, on the side of a hill. Beyond was a dense thicket. On this side of him was a ravine, from the sides of which grew bamboos, and one straggling clump of these, about twenty yards from us, came in the line of sight for the bull's shoulder. It was a moment of much perplexity. The bull was by far the finest I had seen, and we knew that if he advanced five paces he would be out of sight. He stood broadside on, and, as the intervening bamboos were four and five inches apart, I determined to take aim between them, and, raising the single rifle, I fired. The bull made a start forward, and stood for a few seconds on the verge of the thicket. I told Emaum to fire with the smoothbore, which he did at once, and the bull disappeared. Emaum was much disgusted, as the bull had shown no signs of being hit. However, I carefully examined the bamboos through which I had fired, and, finding no mark, I assured him that the bull was not unscathed. We had just reloaded when we heard loud snorts from the thicket, and the African features of Emaum relaxed into a broad grin as he sprang behind the nearest tree in expectation of a charge. The ravine, however, was between us and the bull, and I knew that we were tolerably safe. Presently we heard more snorts, and a heavy fall, followed by a crashing of bamboos. Emaum shouted that the bull was down, and was lashing out; but we could see nothing owing to the density of the covert. Soon the kicks seemed weaker, and we advanced, running forward from tree to tree. There lay the mighty bull at his last gasp. He had not run thirty yards from where we had first seen him, but had stood, sending the blood from his nostrils over the bushes, many feet higher than his head. My shot had taken him about half-way up his body, behind the shoulder, and Emaum's farther back. As he lay on the ground we measured him, and made him out to be about seventeen hands high at the shoulder, with fine well-preserved horns.

These large solitary bulls are at times very savage. They separate themselves from the herds, and their lonely life seems to make them vindictive and morose. When wounded they will charge repeatedly with great ferocity, and on these occasions the nerve and activity of the hunter are put to the test, and woe betide him unless he succeeds in gaining the sheltering trunk of some tree. Emaum informed me that he had a narrow escape on one occasion when he had wounded one of these bulls. He was pursued, but succeeded in getting behind a tree. The bull drew up about twenty yards from him, watching his opportunity, for the forest was of large growth, and Emaum could see no tree up which he had any chance of climbing before the bull could overtake him. At length he bethought himself of his blanket, which he carried over his shoulder, and as the bull drew back for another charge he placed the blanket on the end of his long gun, and holding it out from behind the tree shook it defiantly. Accepting the challenge, the bull lowered his head, and came on with a rush. Catching the blanket on his horns, he dashed on through the jungle, while Emaum, bolting off in the opposite direction, made good his escape.

We found the best way to preserve the skulls of bison was to bury them up to the horns in the earth for three or four days, after removing the skin and as much flesh as could be got at with the knife. At the end of that time the horns might be pulled off after a few blows from a tent-peg. We then dug up the head, fastened a rope round the bone of the horns and flung it into the river, where the fish soon cleaned the skull.

On one occasion only did I see a tiger in the Dandelly. I

came suddenly on him one afternoon as he was rolling on some dry sand in the bed of a watercourse, but he saw us, and was off before I had time to shoot.

Hayward also fell in with one under peculiar circumstances. While walking quietly in quest of game, he heard a great swearing of monkeys, accompanied by the cries of deer. As the noise appeared to approach, he stood, and soon saw numbers of cheetul and sambur coming on, apparently in a state of great alarm, while troops of monkeys sprang from branch to branch, crying in the manner peculiar to them when alarmed by the sight of a tiger or panther. Hayward and his shikaree stood motionless, and presently the head and shoulders of a tiger appeared from behind a clump of bamboos. Catching sight of them, he dashed off; but Hayward had a right and left shot at the deer, and got two sambur.

Tracks of tigers having been seen near the river, Emaum proposed that we should sit up one night over a cow which was to be tied up for a bait, and a platform was made in a tree for this purpose. The place was not, however, well selected, and as the moon rose we found the cow lying in deep shade. Two tigers came by together about midnight, and passed within thirty yards of the cow; but the old beast laid her head to the ground, and they passed on without seeing her.

We frequently came across pigs, and sometimes saw some very fine boars. Returning home with Emaum one evening empty-handed, we saw a sounder* of pigs rush across our line 100 yards in front of us, and as we moved up to the spot we heard one of their number crying after them. This was an old sow, who, I suppose, had been busy with some choice root which she did not like to leave, and so had been left behind. She

* Term used in the language of Boardom for a "herd."

stood on a ridge about eighty yards to our right, with her head towards us. I told Emaum I should either miss her or shoot her between the eyes. I was lucky enough to do the latter, and ran up to the spot with visions of pork chops. Friend Emaum, however, notwithstanding his love for strong drink, was a staunch Mahomedan as far as pig was concerned, and steadily, but respectfully, declined to lay a finger on the noble beast. I was obliged, therefore, to cut off the head and carry it home myself, leaving the carcass to the jackals. My rifle I made over to my companion, but I do not think that even the prospect of soused countenance would again induce me to carry a pig's head four miles on my shoulder.

When meat was plentiful in the camp, Emaum was sometimes apt to be lazy in following up a wounded bison. I was out with him one evening, and, seeing a herd at some distance feeding towards us, we lay still and allowed them to come on. They advanced within thirty yards without observing us, and singling out a good bull, I aimed at the point of the shoulder and fired. He swung round, and went off with the herd. Emaum declared I had missed, but this I knew to be impossible, and insisted on his taking up the track. The ground was hard, and we were unable to distinguish from the others the prints of the beast which was supposed to be wounded. After going a quarter of a mile I saw a few small specks of blood on the leaves, but soon after even these ceased. Emaum then said that the wound was evidently but slight, and that, as we were far from home, night would come on, and we should lose our way in the jungle unless we returned at once to camp. I replied that, if necessary, we could sleep in the jungle, but that in the meantime we must follow the track. This we did, and soon came on the bull lying stone dead. Emaum was probably aware that we should find the bull dead, and that consequently the flesh would not be lawful food for him and his co-religionists ; hence his laziness.

We were sorry to leave the Dandelly jungles, but our leave was up, and we were obliged to return to cantonments. Hayward also had had good sport, and we had a fair show of sporting trophies packed on our baggage ponies on our return. In commemoration of the expedition, our washerman, who accompanied us, cut a bamboo about eighty feet in length, and, hiring coolies on the road, bore it to the fort at Dharwar, where we afterwards saw it supporting a flag at his favourite shrine. We fully intended to have made another exploration in the following year ; but getting our marching orders in autumn, we moved to Kolapoor, and since then the Dandelly jungles have been to me but a dream of the past.

CHAPTER III.

THE country around Kolapoor in the Deccan is not very good for sporting. There are no large jungles within two or three marches, and, owing to the rocky nature of the ground, even the uncultivated districts are but thinly wooded, giving no covert to large game of any sort, with perhaps the exception of a few panthers ; and these can hide so easily among rocks, or in the holes of porcupines, that they are seldom to be met with.

At the time I write of, the present cantonment was not established, and the military force—which, after the campaign in the southern Mahratta country of 1844-45, was considerable —had been located to the south of the town, on the ground sloping to a large lake. The houses of the officers were scattered on spurs of land jutting down among the rice-fields from the higher ground. Each regiment had of course its own lines assigned ; but, as the force was reduced on the pacification of the country, many of the bungalows, being left untenanted, fell into decay, and on our arrival only a few were occupied, and our officers were spread over a large area with most unmilitary irregularity. The garrison consisted of two native infantry regiments and a horse battery of European artillery.

No large game being found within a day's shoot, we were obliged to be contented with what we could get. Foxes and jackals were plentiful, and we set to work to collect greyhounds, or rather long-legged dogs of all sorts. We had some Persian greyhounds, but found they could not stand the hot weather, when they invariably pined off and died. With Polygars we were more successful; but the best dogs of our pack were from a large Arab mother and a thoroughbred English dog, which had been brought out by an officer of my regiment. They were large, handsome hounds, having the dash and speed of the English dog, while from their mother they inherited hard and durable feet, which enabled them to stand over the rocky hills and ravines in which we generally found our game. As greyhounds I fear they would not have passed muster in this country, but they were well adapted for the work they had to do. Every dog "ran cunning;" and, in fact, had they not done so we should have had few kills to chronicle, for the country was covered with rocks and stones and scrub jungle, and earths were plentiful.

Our season did not commence till about December, by which time the higher crops had been removed from the valleys running up among the hills, and the grass was cut in most places. After February the weather began to get very hot, and the dogs could not stand the sun after 7 A.M., so our hours of sport were limited to the early mornings.

Our usual plan was to send out the dogs a few miles from the cantonment before daybreak, and then follow on horseback, so as to be up with them as soon as there was light enough to see clearly. On our arrival the dogs were cast loose; we generally ran from two to four together, and sending the dog-boy home, wandered over the hills and ravines till we found.

Together with the greyhounds I always had a small terrier,

and we frequently found her most useful in bolting a fox from his earth. Poor old Smut! she lost her teeth early in life, but she would force herself into any place, and at times we had hard work to extricate her from some complicated hole among masses of rock and roots.

The foxes were of the usual Deccan breed, small but fast, and would double and turn before the dogs with wonderful agility. The jackals, too, were strong and active; but they give but a poor run before good dogs, unless the ground is rough and they have a good start, and then they will frequently escape.

The dogs knew their work, and kept near the horses till they saw their game, when they would dash off over the most rugged ground in a manner that would astonish a man only accustomed to legitimate coursing.

Riding quietly along, we would frequently start two and three foxes together, and I have seen as many as four jump up at once from some hollow, where they had been basking in the morning sun after their nocturnal wanderings. At such times we had to trust to our luck to get the dogs on any particular fox, and if our pack scattered the chances were against us; but we seldom came home without one or two brushes to show for our morning's work.

When a fox went to ground, the terrier came into play, though she had neither teeth nor strength to draw him; but we found that, as a rule, if the fox were followed into its earth by the terrier, and there bullied a little, all we had to do was to get her out, and withdraw with her and the other dogs to a distance of fifty yards. If we then kept quiet for a few minutes, the fox, apparently satisfied that its retreat had been discovered, would often bolt out and make off, giving a second, and for him often a fatal run.

I do not recollect ever bolting a jackal in this manner, nor have I ever heard of a fox having been so started from its earth in this country ; but the hint, if new, may be worthy of the attention of foxhunters, and may secure a kill when blood is wanted.

In addition to foxes and jackals, we also fell in with hares ; but we preferred going after these with beaters, in the cooler days of the rainy season. We moved in line on these occasions, carrying guns, with our horses led behind us, and the dogs at intervals held in slips. Partridges, quail, and florican, were tolerably numerous ; and if a hare got up in rough ground unsuited for the dogs, his career was stopped with a charge of No. 5, otherwise we jumped on our horses and gave chase. We were annoyed sometimes by herds of antelope ; they would lead the dogs a dance of miles, and by the time we got them back they were generally quite ex-hausted. They never seemed to grow wiser in this matter, but having on one or two occasions killed fawns, never hesitated in their hopeless attempts to run down full-grown antelope.

One course was checked in a singular manner. The dogs, four in number, were close round my horse, and sighting a black buck they dashed after him. After going about 100 yards, I saw an unlucky fox jump up just in front of the leading dog. He whisked his tail and attempted to get under weigh, but the dogs were on him like a railway engine, and I saw him flung up and come down among the pack, who made short work of him. The antelope was of course forgotten, and I congratulated myself on the turn of events. Running loose, the dogs became very intelligent. At first they would start off even after a hawk or other bird skimming along the ground, but in this they soon learned wisdom, and came to know what they ought to follow.

Riding over this rough ground, it was requisite to have a horse strongly bitted and thoroughly in hand, at the same time giving him his head sufficiently to enable him to pick his way over bad ground. I was one day riding a valuable horse, which, having been raced, had become almost a run-away. Finding that he pulled less with a plain snaffle than any other bit, I foolishly rode him in one on this afternoon. I was accompanied by two friends, and we were soon after a fine fox. Before we had gone 100 yards I felt that the horse was away with me, and, as we were on smooth ground, I determined to keep him on it till I could manage him. Bearing heavily on one rein, I kept him going in a large circle till I succeeded in stopping him. By this time my friends, with the dogs and fox, had crossed some low ground, over which I had to follow, and no sooner did I attempt to increase the pace than my horse again bolted.

The hollow was full of huge holes many yards in width, formed by the action of water in the rainy season, and one of these coming in our line, I only escaped a smash by a desperate wrench of the rein, whereby we were enabled to clear the corner of the pit. When I rejoined my friends I found they had lost the fox among some bushes, and shortly after we again moved on. Finding a hare, my horse bolted for the third time ; but, as the ground was clear, and he was going in the right direction, I did not much care.

I was far ahead of my companions, and going at racing speed, when my steed fell as if shot through the head. I suppose he must have crossed his legs, for I could see nothing to throw him. I was sent flying about ten yards over his head, and came down on the hard sun-baked ground with a force which would require to be felt to be fully appreciated. I was badly bruised, but managed to pick myself up and return to my horse, which lay where he fell. I had shaken him on his legs, and was about to remount, when my friends came up. One of them was our regimental doctor, and he naturally inquired after my health. I replied that I was all right, though a good deal knocked about. On attempting, however, to raise my left hand to gather up my reins, I found it was powerless, and the doctor then called out that I had broken my collar-bone, and was all down on one side. True enough, this was the case. He dismounted, and unrolling my muslin turban he trussed me up, and with his assistance I mounted his horse and returned to camp, where I was laid up for some weeks.

Our dogs frequently started off in pursuit of some unlucky mongoose, an animal like a large blue ferret. The poor beast was at once pulled to pieces, much to our regret, for they are inveterate enemies to snakes, with which the country is infested.

I was awoke when in bed one night by the growling of a small dog which lay at my feet. My bed was the only furniture in the room, the floor of which was covered with a bamboo matting. At first I suspected thieves, but at length observed the dog fix its eyes in the corner of the room, where stood a tumbler of oil with a wick burning. Near the lamp I saw a snake close to the wall, and, snatching up my sword from under the mattress, I jumped out of bed. The snake wriggled under the matting, and as I could see where he was, I gave a smart cut down on him. The sword went through the matting and into the plaster floor ; but on my attempting to withdraw it I gave the lamp a jerk and extinguished it. The situation was unpleasant. My feet were bare and un-protected, the room was dark, I could not tell how the snake had fared. I managed, however, to regain my bed, and shouted till a servant came with a light, when we found that I had cut fair, and the two ends of the snake lay wriggling under the mat.

The game round Kolapoor was much reduced by the hunting expeditions of the Rajah, which were frequent in the cold weather and during the breaks in the rainy season. His party consisted of several hundred men, mounted and on foot, and about thirty brace of greyhounds. They moved across the country in a long line. Everybody who had a gun fired, and all the dogs were slipped at any running beast that got up.

The lake below the cantonment was full of fish of large size; and in the cold weather a fair amount of ducks and snipe might be got.

About twelve miles off were the hill forts of Punalla and Powagurh, rising about 800 feet above the low ground. Here some of the political officers had bungalows, which gave a pleasant retreat from the heat of the cantonment. To the eastward of these forts was the hill of Jotebaz, crowned with picturesque temples, where large numbers of Hindoo devotees were wont to congregate. On the north side of this range was a good deal of scrub bush, well stocked with peafowl, hares, partridges, and a small species of jungle antelope. My chum Hayward and I frequently shot over these hills, and invariably made good bags.

Fourteen miles to the west of the cantonment lay some good coursing ground; and thither Langton, of my regiment, and I, set out for a three days' trip, taking with us an old native officer of the corps, who was fond of sport of all kinds, and generally kept two or three good dogs of his own. Bheema was a native of Malabar, an intelligent man, and a good and trustworthy officer. His sporting get-up was very fine—short drawers from the waist to the middle of the thigh, an old cloth jacket, and a black blanket ; about his person were hung numerous bags containing flint and steel, tobacco, food **of sorts** (including parched grain, sugar, **and** salted shrimps), **shot,** powder, and ball ; on **his shoulder he** carried an old flint musket.

We found foxes in great numbers, and one day coursed seven, killing six. The ground was very rough, and Bheema, who was on foot and declined a mount, predicted that we should break our necks, but our ponies kept their legs, and we had no spills.

On the last day of our leave we had just struck our tent, and were about to load the baggage ponies, when a severe thunderstorm came on, and in five minutes we were drenched to the skin. Within an hour every watercourse was a raging torrent, and we knew that for the present it was hopeless to attempt to return to camp.

Turning into the village, we found some horsemen of the Rajah's Irregular Cavalry picketed at a temple, and with these we fraternised, and gave them a goat, which they forthwith slew and cooked. Here we halted till the moon rose, and having got some dry clothes from among our baggage, we made ourselves comfortable. About 11 P.M. we started on our march home, and, the water having by this time subsided, we arrived without further adventure.

I was ordered off with a detachment to escort treasure which was coming from Belgaum, and was sent out five marches to meet it. At our second halting-place some villagers brought in an unhappy boy who had been horned in the leg by a buffalo. The calf of his leg was nearly torn off, and was hanging down over his ankle. It was in vain that I assured his friends that I was no surgeon. They said that they had great confidence in a white man, and begged me to do my best. I beat up among the detachment for needles and thread, and, having prepared a number of threads with two needles on each, had the boy laid on a table, and brought the calf into its proper place by sutures at intervals of about an inch ; then, directing cooling diet and water dressing, I made the lad over to his parents. We marched early next morning, and I never had an opportunity of learning the result of my attempt at surgery. The natives, however, at times get over wounds and lacerations in an extraordinary manner, and he possibly recovered, though it struck me at the time that there was much danger of tetanus.

On this march I passed through a country swarming with antelope and bustard, but I was suffering at the time from a sharp attack of rheumatism in the shoulders, and was unable to hold up a rifle.

I was out one morning with an old village shikaree, and, disgusted with several bad shots, returned to the tents. The man asked permission to try his luck by himself ; but, as his weapon was only a short and very rusty old matchlock, I never expected he would succeed. About two hours after my return he made his appearance, bearing on his shoulders a fine black buck which he had successfully stalked and brought down.

A friend of mine once made a rather remarkable shot when on the line of march, in command of a treasure-guard. His party consisted of about 100 infantry and some horsemen, the infantry with loaded muskets. As not unfrequently happens, a large herd of antelope were feeding near the road in the open plain, and, quietly getting his men on the proper flank of the treasure-carts, he halted, faced outwards, and fired a volley at the astonished deer. A charge was at once executed by the cavalry, and the result was, I think, seven deer brought to bag. The muskets were the old brown Bess ; with Sniders an even better account might have been given of the herd.

A brother officer had been out on leave at the Phoonda Ghaut, where the road from Kolapoor descends the Western Ghauts to the port of Wagotun. He reported well of the prospect of bears, having shot one or two, and badly wounded another, which had escaped. He proposed that I should return with him, so we got ten days' leave and set out.

It was the early part of the rains, and the weather was cool and pleasant; we did not, however, find much game. There had been a few bears, but they had been disturbed and had changed their ground, and we found no very fresh marks.

We shot a few of the small deer known there as " Peesaie." They are about the size of an English hare, very handsome, having sides spotted something like a cheetul. Our shikaree here was Shaik Adam, a very respectable old Mahomedan, and in his younger days he must have been a strong active man. When employed with us he, of course, carried a spare rifle, but his own shooting-iron was peculiar. The barrel, which was of great length, was that of a matchlock ; he had procured an old Government flint lock, and the stock had been fashioned and fitted by some primitive village carpenter. His charge was a handful of coarse native powder, measured with the ramrod in the barrel, and a long plug of lead hammered on a stone to fit the bore. The barrel was of soft metal, and if much knocked about was liable to become bent, a circumstance which naturally affected its shooting. A bad shot was, however, not unfrequently put down to the evil influence of some Hindoo demon, who was supposed to be employed by Brahmins and Bunneahs to counteract the flesh-eating and life-destroying tendencies of the worthy Shaik. On such occasions a kid was generally presented as a propitiation to the nearest Hindoo shrine, and the musket was handed over to the blacksmith to have the barrel straightened.

We were encamped among the hills far from any village, when my companion got a bad attack of fever and ague, and was unable to leave his tent.

As we intended to stalk sambur early next morning, I went out with Shaik Adam before daybreak, and we had a long walk over likely ground, but returned at nine to breakfast, having only had a distant view of one sambur.

Shaik Adam had arranged for a beat in the daytime, and had assembled some men ; so we again went out, returning at 4 P.M., without having seen a hoof.

My friend was better, and being hungry we sat down at once to dinner, and had just finished when a herdsman came running in and said his cow had been killed by a tiger about three miles from our tents. The Shaik and I at once set off with our guide, hoping that the tiger would return about sundown. As we approached the spot, which was in a rugged part of the jungle, the cowherd pointed to the bush where the cow lay, and we saw something moving close to the carcass. We naturally thought this must be the tiger, but it turned out to be only a fine old peacock who was quietly scratching the ground by the murdered cow. No part had been eaten by the tiger, but in her neck were the marks of the four fangs.

As there was not much daylight left, we at once climbed trees, and waited patiently for the arrival of the beast. The sun went down, and the darkness came on, but still we sat hoping for the tiger, till we could not distinguish the white carcass of the cow beneath us.

I then proposed that we should descend and return to camp ; but the cowherd declared we should be eaten by the tiger, and that we should never be able to retrace our steps at night through the jungle and ravines. In this he was backed up by Shaik Adam ; and, being somewhat inexperienced, I bowed to their mature judgment, and made up my mind to pass the night in the tree.

As we had made no platform or arrangement of any sort for squatting, the prospect of sitting for eight hours on a small branch was not invigorating, the more so that we had been on the move since daybreak in the morning. My first proceeding was to tie the guns to branches, and then to cut up my turban into lengths for stirrups, as the blood descending into the feet when kept long in a hanging position gives a very painful sensation.

The padded cover of my cap was employed as a cushion, and another portion of my turban to tie round the waist to the tree at my back, and so to keep me in position in the event of my falling asleep.

These little arrangements concluded, I smoked myself into a state of somnolency, and passed one of the most uncomfortable nights I can remember. So eager were we to bag the tiger, that even when the day broke we retained our positions for some time, in the hope that he would return to the cow ; but we never saw him.

Returning to the tent, I found my chum still in small health, so we determined to move to Phoonda, where an officer of the Quartermaster-General's department was employed in making a road through the pass, and from him we hoped to get some medicines. We accordingly rode in after breakfast, leaving the servants to follow with the baggage and tent. Captain Delhoste received us hospitably, and made us comfortable at the travellers' bungalow, which was situated on the crest of the mountain, commanding a magnificent view of the pass and low country. We made a halt here of a couple of days, during which my companion was fortunate in shaking off his feverish attack.

Soon after our arrival, and before that of our people, two villagers came in bearing on a pole a dead bear, which they said they had killed. Knowing the weight of a large bear, we were astonished to see them move so easily under their load, but, on closer inspection, we found that the bear had been skinned and rudely stuffed with hay. After some questioning, the men confessed that they had found the bear dying, and had knocked him on the head with their axes ; and from various bullet-holes in the skin, and their description of the place where they found it, we had no doubt that it was the same bear which my friend had wounded and lost in his former expedition. We gave them a small reward and dismissed them, and as Shaik Adam had not come in we arranged to have a little sport with the defunct bear.

I had it carried to some distance from the bungalow to a mass of rocks and bushes on the face of the mountain, where we drew out the pole and partially concealed the bear among some long grass. On the arrival of the Shaik, we told him that a bear had been severely stung in an attack on a bees' nest, and was so blinded as to be unable to make his way through the jungle.

We added that he was supposed to be lying up among some rocks not far off, and as my companion was not fit for work I proposed to the Shaik that he and I should go in search of it. He at once acceded, and soon appeared with his own gun. Placing a couple of caps on a rifle, I went out with him, and, directing him to keep close, moved down on the spot where we had placed the bear. When about ten yards off the Shaik caught sight of it, and halting, pointed it out to me. I at once raised my rifle, and exploded the cap. Up went the long gun, and taking a careful aim my friend pressed the trigger, but the only result was a flash in the pan.

Telling me to stand ready with my other barrel, he again cocked his piece and attempted to fire, with no better result.

Muttering something uncomplimentary to the musket, he passed his right hand behind him, and, drawing out a long knife, commenced to hammer the flint with the back of it, steadily keeping a look-out on the bear all the while. Satisfied with his operations, he again raised the gun, which this time exploded with a report like a young cannon. I retreated a few paces, warning the Shaik to beware of a charge ; but he replied that his aim had been sure, and that he had done for the bear. We then advanced, and a slight puff of wind from the direction of the bear saluted our nostrils with a not too savoury odour. With a disrespectful allusion to she bears in general, and particularly to those nearly connected with the deceased, the Shaik ejaculated " Bās marta," which is, being interpreted, " it smells."

I could contain my gravity no longer, but fled laughing to the bungalow, where I was soon followed by the indignant and much injured man. His feelings were much hurt, for he had the local reputation of a mighty hunter, and he knew that the story would spread, and that his village friends would make the most of it. He remarked in a dignified manner that he was an old woodsman, and that such a prank ought not to have been played on him by a youth of my tender years. I have since heard of a similar joke being played on a gallant officer, who was taken out and made to shoot at a railway wrapper, having on it the representation of a panther-skin, which had been cunningly hid away among some long grass.

We restored the Shaik to good humour with a glass of brandy, and in the afternoon went out with him, and bagged a number of spur-fowl.

In the river above the pass we saw two fair-sized fish of

the species known as murrel. They were lying close to each other near the surface of the water, and, aiming between their heads, I fired with a heavy rifle. The Shaik, who had in the meantime disrobed, sprang in and recovered both fish. Neither had been struck, but the concussion of the water had stunned them, and they were on the bank before they had time to recover.

My friend being restored to health, we arranged to move to the Mombait jungles, about four miles to the north of Phoonda. The road was only practicable for men on foot, and horses; so we had to collect coolies to carry our tent and baggage. These were sent on with Shaik Adam, who was directed to go out on reaching the ground, look about for marks of game, and ascertain the prospects of sport generally.

We started on horseback one afternoon, but, as we did not take the direct route, it was sundown before we reached the camp. We found the coolies and servants busy pitching the tent, and bringing in wood, grass, and water. The Shaik had gone out alone, and it was nearly dark before he came in. He said he had been along the crest of the Ghauts, and had visited several caves of bears, finding fresh marks. He was on his way back to the camp, and was entering on a piece of clear ground, about 200 yards in length, having a footpath down the middle of it. On coming out into the open, he saw a bear walking leisurely towards him along the path, and as he was not observed he quietly slipped aside and concealed himself behind some bushes. The bear, meanwhile, came slowly forward, and when within ten paces, the Shaik gave it the contents of the long gun through the heart. The bear fell in its tracks quite dead, but to make sure he rammed down another charge, and fired again behind its shoulder as it lay on the ground. He then cut boughs of trees, and, having covered up the beast, returned to the tent to procure men to carry it in.

A party of our coolies at once set off with him, but on arriving at the spot where the bear had been left, they found it had disappeared. The boughs lay scattered about, and marks of blood were on the ground, but the bear was gone ; and it being now quite dark, the men came back and reported matters to us. We of course conjectured that the bear had only been stunned and badly wounded by the Shaik, and had managed to recover sufficiently to get away among the dense bush, which on all sides surrounded the spot. The Shaik, however, who was a man of long experience, and skilled in all matters of woodcraft, assured us that he had left the bear dead, and he believed some beast must have carried it off. It was too late to do anything then, so we settled to go out at daybreak and clear up the mystery.

The jungle-cocks were crowing in the ravines when we turned out in the morning ; and after a light breakfast we set off for the spot whence the bear had disappeared.

As the men had reported, we found the boughs strewed about and much blood on the ground, but the daylight enabled us to see that the carcass had been dragged along the ground, so we prepared to follow up the track. For some distance it led through the open glade, through which the Shaik informed us the bear had advanced just before he shot it ; after this, it went through some thick scrub jungle, and then along the stony bed of a dry watercourse.

Here the jungle became very thick, and the thorns and branches were so interlaced across the bed of the stream that we were obliged to stoop, and at times to crawl along on all fours. We were about 500 yards from where the bear had been left, but the blood on the stones enabled us to follow the track with ease.

We kept a sharp look-out ahead, expecting to come on the wounded beast, and at length, in turning an angle of the nullah, we caught a glimpse of a bear moving up the bank in the thick bush. We were unable to get a shot at him, but kept our rifles ready, and on coming up to the spot we found the dead bear lying on the stones. It turned out to be a large female, and the one which we had seen moving off was evidently the he bear, who, finding the carcass of his spouse on the previous night, had managed to push or drag it all this distance. We were much struck by his conjugal affection, as his grief was no doubt genuine, and not, as is perhaps the case with some other animals, simulated out of deference to public opinion.

He must have moved the body with great care, and evidently hoped that if he could only get her home to their cave, he would be able by assiduous nursing to restore her to health. She was a large bear, and very heavy and fat, but he had moved her throughout the night with such gentleness that the skin was quite uninjured.

We carried her to the tent, and, after skinning, cut off all the fat, collecting a large quantity, which we boiled down and bottled off for our lady friends in the cantonment. I have been told that any efficacy which may exist in bear's grease " for promoting the growth of the hair" is only to be found in the fat cut off the loins and hams—in fact, the external grease, and that the internal fat of the animal is no better than that from a sheep or bullock. On this subject, however, I must consult my hairdresser.

We found the neighbourhood of our camp a good deal disturbed by herdsmen and woodcutters, and during the two following days I only came on one lot of bison. At one of these I had a fair shot at about sixty yards, but wishing to get nearer I was advancing through some thick bush, when I alarmed another which I had not previously seen. He dashed out of a mass of creepers, and I had a snap shot at him, but he held on, and we could hear the herd crashing along the side of the mountain, dislodging gravel and stones, which rolled down with much clatter. We looked in vain for traces of blood, and returned to camp empty-handed.

Our leave being now nearly up, we had to move back towards Kolapoor.

My friend had been out some time previously in the jungles along the Ghauts when on his way to the coast. At one village where he was encamped he heard great stories of numbers of sambur which frequented the spot, and how they came out at night to graze about the cultivated lands. He accordingly directed his servants to be on the look-out in the neighbourhood of the tent, and, as the moonlight was bright, he hoped to get a shot. Towards midnight a sambur was said to have been seen in a field not far off, and, taking a rifle, Pogson sallied forth. Seeing a dark object among some low bushes, he made a successful stalk, and when sufficiently near loosed his piece. The animal made off, but one of the servants, on hearing the shot, came up with a dog, which was at once put on the track. The dog went off, but, as he did not return for some time, Pogson went back to the tent. At length the dog appeared with much blood about his muzzle, and, making up his mind that he would find his game in the morning, my friend went to bed again.

At an early hour he was awoke by the sound of voices, and on coming out he found the whole village community assembled in front of his tent. The head men came forward and informed him that they were all much distressed and shocked at finding the Sahib had shot a very holy cow, which had been allowed to roam at will about the village. They then took him to the spot, where, sure enough, lay a red cow dead, with a bullet-hole through her shoulder, and the marks of the dog's teeth in her throat.

Pogson expressed much regret, and offered to pay for the cow, but was informed—no doubt much to his own satisfaction—that the cow was sacred, and could not be sold for money. The villagers behaved very well, and said it had been the fate of the cow to die by the Sahib's bullet, and there was an end of the matter.

About the close of the year we received our marching orders for Guzerat. This district we had always heard of as abounding in game of all sorts; and we were not sorry to leave the Deccan, where, to say the most of it, our bag had been but small.

We marched to the port of Wagotun, on a river about twelve miles from the sea. Here we found a number of coasting boats, twenty-two I think, waiting for us; and we were told off to these according to their capacity.

A few of the boats had cabins; these were assigned to married officers. I had a party of about seventy-five men and women, for many of our men moved with their families. Our boat had a split bamboo mat for a deck, and the men took up their quarters on it as best they might. The boat had no cabin, and the only spot which afforded any shade from the sun was under a platform, whereon sat the steersman. This was by courtesy supposed to be my cabin, but it was filled with bags of provisions for the men; and during the eleven days occupied in the passage I sat above in the sun, and tried to console myself with the idea that I was serving my country.

CHAPTER IV.

It was late one evening when our boat reached its haven in the creek known as Tunkaria Bunder, one of the chief ports in Guzerat for the export of cotton and opium. Notwithstanding the great trade of the place, there were no facilities whatever for the landing or shipping of goods, and the coasting vessels were simply moored to the bank of a muddy creek.

We were all glad to get ashore. The caste of many of the men had prevented them from cooking on board, and they had subsisted during the voyage on parched grain and sugar. These now set to work to collect material for a heavy feed ; but, as it was too late to pitch tents, we all returned to sleep on board the boat. I had my bed made in the stern of the vessel, and made up my mind for a comfortable night's rest.

About midnight I was awakened by finding my cot flying across the boat, and I was brought up against the side in an avalanche of boxes, etc. There was a great outcry among the men, and on extricating myself I ascertained that the boat, which had been moored on the mud, had been left by the receding tide, and had consequently heeled over, and lay completely on her side. We had some difficulty in settling down again, and on the day breaking we all landed and joined the camp. We were halted here two or three days, waiting for some of the boats that had not arrived. When the whole regiment was landed, the head-quarters moved on Baroda, and the major, another subaltern, and myself, with three companies, were told off for detachment duty at Broach.

I was much struck by the numbers of wildfowl and game of all sorts which surrounded us. Every field was swarming with quail, and in every patch of rushes we found snipe, while the pools furnished ducks of many kinds, and waders innumerable. Here, for the first time, I saw the coolen—a large blue crane, which comes in great numbers in the cold weather ; and I here fell in for the first time with the sarus, a huge bird, also of the crane family. They are very numerous in Guzerat and Central India, feeding in the corn-fields, and in the neighbourhood of tanks and rivers. They are generally found in even numbers. Every Jack is supposed to have his Jill, and, according to native report, the death of one is soon followed by that of the other. I have at times seen them in large numbers together, generally in the sandy bed of some river, where they assemble during the heat of the day, or at night. The bird is of a light blue colour, with some white about the tail ; the head, and about eight inches of the neck, are bright red, but nearly devoid of feathers. The natives regard them with some degree of veneration, and they are seldom molested by the European sportsman.

Soon after landing I was out after snipe, having with me several small dogs. I was beating a patch of rushes, when I saw two of the huge birds above mentioned flying towards me, uttering their peculiar cry. I had loaded with No. 8, but

I dropped a ball into one barrel, over the shot, and, crouching down, awaited their approach. They came on with the intention of alighting among the rushes, and had almost touched the ground, when they saw the dogs, and turned upwards. The male bird presented a large surface, and I fired, sending the ball through his breast, and at the same time peppering him with the small shot. He fell dead, and we secured and carried him to camp, where I gave him to some of my men, who declared that he would be as good as half a goat. He was about six feet in length, from the toe to the extremity of the beak. I have often thought that these birds would be good for food, but I never heard of any European trying them ; nor do I think that during all my residence in India I ever fired at another.

The road for the first few miles from Tunkaria is about the worst in Guzerat, and consists simply of a number of parallel ruts, so deep that the bottoms of the carts often scrape the earth between them. In these ruts the dust accumulates to the depth of many inches, and when raised by the march of a body of men it becomes very distressing.

We started one very cold morning at about 3 A.M., our detachment being in front of the regiment. I was mounted on a pugnacious pony, but I was too cold to attend to him, and, having got him into a rut behind the band, I lit my cigar and rolled myself up in my cloak. We had thus advanced for some miles, when the march was checked by some obstruction, and as we halted the dust rose thick and white. Suddenly my pony gave a scream, and rose on his hind legs, and I could just make out that he was in furious combat with the major's horse, when we all seemed to tumble over together. I thought I should be jammed against the bank, but managed to kick myself clear. Some of the men rushed forward and secured the horses, while a friendly drummer dragged out the nearly expended major, who had sustained a sharp contusion on the shoulder. On assembling at breakfast, I received the thanks of the regiment for my laudable endeavours to accelerate promotion.

After the first march we left the main body, and made our way to Broach, where I was stationed for some ten months.

On the south bank of the Nerbudda, which flows by the town in a stream half-a-mile in width, we got some first-rate quail-shooting. Below the town we found birds in immense numbers in the fields, and higher up we made large bags in the bastard cypress along the bank of the river. They were so numerous that a couple of guns could kill seventy and eighty brace with ease in a few hours, and frequently they rose so fast that we were obliged to cease firing to allow our guns to cool. The natives catch large numbers in traps made of the stalk of the millet, which they shape into a small box and bait with a head of grain, the trap being like a figure-of-4 trap. Numbers also are killed with arrows having a blunt head of hard wood as large as a florin. The natives stalk them as they dust themselves in the cart-ruts, and often kill several at one shot. I am not aware whence these quails come. They appear about the end of November, and are gone again by March. In this respect they are similar to the mass of the wildfowl and snipe, which I suppose are driven down by the cold from the north. Our bag was generally varied by a few brace of gray and painted patridge and hares, and not unfrequently by a civet or large wild cat.

Further up the Nerbudda, near Nandode, where the river enters the jungles, tigers are found ; but, though I went on two occasions for several days at a time, we were unable to make anything of them, owing to our not knowing the country, or having no authority among its inhabitants. On the first expedition, my friend and I had just passed through a village at some distance from any jungle, and had been assured by the villagers that tigers were unknown among them, when we were addressed by a man in charge of some cattle, who begged that we would shoot the tigers which had killed several of his beasts. On our doubting his statement, he drew our attention to numerous footprints, almost obliterated by those of the cattle which had passed over them. They were in all directions, close up to the houses, and the tigers seemed to have been walking about the village all night. We were much astonished at this, for I had never before known tigers wander so close to human habitations. The man informed us that they came from a belt of ravines and jungle about two miles farther on, and about a mile from the bank of the Nerbudda. He accompanied us for some distance, and showed us their tracks, both new and old, along some cart-ruts formed in bringing grain from the fields. As the moon was near the full, we determined to sit up in trees at night, and rode on to our camp to make the necessary preparations.

We at once sent off men, who erected two platforms in trees about half-a-mile apart. Round the edges of these seats we had screens formed of boughs, selecting those with soft leaves, to prevent any rustling or noise. Goats were tied with strong ropes on the south side of the trees, about fifteen yards from our hiding-places, in such positions that, as the moon came round, they would remain clear of the shade. My tree was on the path, that of my companion nearer the village, both in open cultivated ground, but clear of crops. About nine o'clock I saw a tiger come across the field and stand in the clear moonlight about 100 yards from my tree. I had made up my mind that he would come along the road and I should get a good shot, when suddenly another tiger came skylarking at him, and, with a playful growl, they both ran across and disappeared behind a rising ground.   I had waited for about half-an-hour, hoping to see them again, when I heard my friend fire, and soon after some men came to call me, and I left my tree and joined him.   The tigers had come close to where he was posted, and one of them came straight at his goat, sprang on it, and, having killed it, walked forward for a few paces with his tail straight up in the air.   At that moment my friend fired, but unfortunately missed, and the tiger went off at speed.   In his way lay a cactus hedge nine or ten feet in height, and this he appeared to have taken in his spring, for we found the footprints deep in the light soil on the far side. The tigers did not return.

On the following evening we sat up in trees on the other side of the ravines.   On this occasion my platform had been built in a prickly babool tree, and was only accessible with a ladder.   My friend, having seen me in my place, carried it off to enable him to mount his own tree, about a quarter of a mile off.   The moon did not rise till some little time after sunset, and having been out all day I was tired and fell asleep, with my rifle projecting from a small porthole in the screen of boughs.   I suppose I turned in my sleep, and thereby raised the stock of the gun, for I was awoke by hearing it rattling through the branches, and on looking down I beheld it on the ground with the stock broken.   Having no means of descent, I was unable to recover it, so composed myself to sleep till morning, when my companion returned and enabled me to come down.   No tigers had appeared during the night.

Next day we crossed the Nerbudda, and went to the village of a small chief, who assured us that his country swarmed with game, and that the village was nightly beset by all manner of savage beasts. I knew enough of these gentry to prevent me from placing much reliance on his statement ; however, we had no better amusement in view, so we rode off to his place, and had platforms again made in trees. I was posted in the bed of the river, and was close to the village ; but the chief assured me that that was the principal resort of all the tigers in the country. A goat was tied up below me, but he seemed to consider himself in no danger, and after watching for some hours I fell asleep. I was awoke by the goat moving about and bleating, and on peeping out I saw a large hyæna walking round him, and apparently in doubt as to whether he should make a meal of him. As there was no prospect of nobler game, I thought I might as well make game of him, and, as he seemed much inclined to rush at the goat, I fired and shot him through the loins, disabling his hind quarters. Hearing some of the chief's people above me in the village, I called out and told them to knock the hyæna on the head and take him away, in the hope that, as morning was still far off, some other beast might come. Three or four men at once came running down the hill, and I could see their swords gleaming in the moonlight ; when they found that there was nothing more formidable than an old hyæna, they went in at him with the most determined courage. Next morning, when we came down from our trees, I found the ground covered with blood, and all the marks of a great struggle.

My companion had seen nothing, so we went up to the village to get a drink of warm milk. The first thing we observed on coming up to the house was a cart, upon which was lashed the ignoble carcass of the hyæna, in order, as the villagers said, that we might take it to our own camp in case we wished to preserve the skin. We went up to the spot and examined the beast, which we found cut and slashed with swords in all directions, and altogether presenting a very gruesome spectacle.

On turning into the courtyard of the chief's house, we found him and his merry men just rousing themselves from the dose which overtakes habitual opium-eaters ; for they cannot be said to enjoy what other men call sleep. I never saw such a wretched-looking parcel of vagabonds. Generally I had seen them rather smart and dandified in their attire, but they now, one and all, looked more dissipated and untidy than I can describe. Their beards were tangled, and I could not help laughing as they tried to open their gooseberry eyes and wish us good morning. They had not had their morning dram of opium ; and till it was ready for them they squatted round the verandah of the courtyard, with looks of the most hopeless imbecility. Soon a woman of the establishment appeared, and, taking a piece of cotton wool, spread it out about the breadth of a saucer. She then took a lump of opium, which she scraped and rolled up in the cotton. The whole was then saturated with water, which she squeezed and sopped into the palm of her hand till she succeeded in producing a strong brown liquid. She then went to the chief, and, holding her hand to his lips, poured the opium into his mouth, after which the cotton was again saturated with water, and the operation repeated, till every gentleman had had his " morning." The effect was wonderful ; in ten minutes they all began to brighten up ; and when they had washed their faces and bound on their turbans, it would have been difficult to recognise the seedy-looking fellows of the previous half-hour. This custom of eating opium is almost universal among the Rajpoots of Guzerat and Central India. Every man carries it, and on two chiefs meeting they take opium together, as Scotsmen are popularly supposed to take snuff.

After a drink of warm milk we returned to our tents, shooting partridges on the way. Passing through a bit of jungle, I saw a large hawk fly up from the ground, and on going to the spot found a hare which he had just killed. It was only a little damaged about the head, so we carried it off and had it jugged for dinner.

Hearing of some bears at a place called Wuggeria, where there were some low hills, we moved our camp there. We found three small table hills lying close together, having their sides covered with stunted trees, while round the tops were precipitous rocks and caves, giving good shelter to bears. A tiger was also reported to frequent the neighbourhood. An old Mahomedan shikaree offered to show us the ground, and we went out under his guidance. He led us along the top of one of these hills to a spot overhanging a mass of rocks, into which we heaved some big stones. Two bears rushed out, and went down the hill at a headlong pace. We opened fire and knocked over the largest, but he picked himself up and went on. We could see he was severely gruelled, and, reloading, scrambled down after him. We found him lying in a small ravine, and he at once charged, with loud grunts, but we again bowled him over, and he made off ; being again shot in the rear, he turned and made a last attempt to charge, but was dropped dead. The smaller bear got off unscathed, and we could see him crossing the ravines in his flight for a considerable distance.

Our leave being up, we had to return to Broach.

During the next hot season, when we were quartered at Baroda, Hayward and I organised another expedition to the Toorun Mall hill, in the Akranee Pergunnah of Kandesh.

We made first for these hills at Wuggeria, but on inquiring for the old shikaree, we were informed that he had gone to the happy hunting-grounds, so we had to procure another guide. Early next morning we ascended one of the hills, with some men from the village, and carefully examined all the rocks along the crest. We had been looking down from one spot, where there were large masses of rocks, and seeing nothing, we had moved away some paces, when we were startled by the discharge of a matchlock just behind us. We hurried back, and found one of the villagers seated on the edge of the rock, whence he had fired at a hyæna. As we were scolding him for shooting without orders, six or seven hyænas ran out from the rocks below us, and made off down the hill. The noise we had made alarmed a large bear, which had been also lying among the rocks, and it made a rush for its cave, which was close by. We opened fire, and, confused by our shots, the bear went at a hole too small to admit it ; and as it struggled in the entrance, we emptied our remaining barrels. It managed, however, to withdraw its body, and disappeared under a huge mass of rock. Beneath this was a cave, having another small opening tending upwards to the edge of the rock, and having on its immediate left a perpendicular mass of stone, many feet in height. We could hear the bear in the cave below ; and on looking down through the opening above mentioned, I could see its eyes below me. From the position of the hole, however, I could not get my rifle to bear upon him, except by firing from the left shoulder. This I did ; and from the struggles below, we knew that the shot had taken effect. After some time, one of my horse-keepers who was with us got down to the spot where the bear had entered, and, taking a knife in his teeth, he crawled in. I followed him, and we found ourselves in a small cave, the end of which was blocked

by a mass of rock, having a hole under it, through which the
bear had passed. Into this hole the man crept, and disappeared, till I saw nothing but his feet. Presently he called
out that he had hold of the bear, and requested me to pull his
legs. Laying down my rifle, I hauled away, and succeeded in
drawing out man and bear into the outer cave, whence the
beast was dragged by the rest of the party. I was much
pleased by the pluck shown by my man, for his entry into the
cave was a purely voluntary act on his part, and contrary to
the advice of the villagers, who, one and all, declared that he
would be killed.

In the dry bed of a river, close to the village, was a water-
hole used by the cattle, and we were informed that a tiger
came there every night to drink. We had been out all day
without getting a shot; and on our return late in the evening,
we found that some men, who had promised to have a platform erected in a neighbouring tree, had decamped, leaving
their work undone.

The moon did not rise till after nine o'clock, so we remained till then in the village, and then went down to the
water-hole, where we had a small breastwork of boughs
placed round the foot of an old tamarind tree. In the open
space in the bed of the river we tied up a goat, and throwing
our blankets into our hiding-place, we arranged our guns, and
dismissed all our attendants. As we came down from the
village, we had heard the tiger growling on the hill-side; but
though we remained on the alert a long time, we saw nothing
of him. It had been arranged that if the tiger came, and
sprang on the goat, we should lie still till he commenced to
eat, when we were to rise on our knees and deliver our fire.
Altogether, it was rather an insane proceeding ; but we were
young in those days.

About midnight Hayward was lying fast asleep, when I heard the growl of the tiger at a short distance on the hill behind us. I at once aroused my companion, and we could see by the movements of the goat that it was in a great state of trepidation. Presently we heard the footsteps of the tiger advancing on the dry leaves, and then all was still, save the piteous bleat of the goat as it strained at the rope. The tiger, I believe, stalked him behind the very tree under which we lay, and in a few seconds he made his rush. We kept well down; there was a struggle among the shingle, and then all was still. Thinking that the time had arrived for us to shoot, we raised our heads and saw—no tiger—no goat—no anything!

The rope had given way, and the tiger had carried his prey under some thick bushes, on the far side of the river-bed. We could hear him crunching up the bones as he made his meal; but he was in deep shade, and we could see nothing. About two hours after he moved to a muddy puddle, and drank. We then got an imperfect view, and had a snap shot at him, but he got away untouched; and we returned to the village much disappointed.

Next night we had a platform put up in a tree at another spot, and again tied up our scape-goat. We took up our positions, and had both been asleep, when, on waking, I looked over at the goat, and saw that it was tumbling about in a peculiar manner. I roused my friend, and after looking long in the imperfect light, we made out a panther, lying by the dead goat, with his teeth in its throat. As the beast lay on the yellow grass, it was with great difficulty that we could distinguish it. We got our rifles on him, and fired together, on which the panther gave one grunt, and rushed off among the underwood. On descending next morning, we examined the ground, and found both the bullets in the earth, within a few inches of each other, and on the very spot where the panther had been. We searched about, but did not find him ; and next morning we moved our camp. Two days after, some villagers, observing vultures attracted to the spot, again went to the ground, and found the remains of the panther lying among some dead leaves. We must have passed close to him in our former search, but his yellow jacket being so similar to the dry grass and leaves, we had failed to see him, and thereby lost his skin.

We had several days' severe marching among the hills to Dhergaum, where we left our heavy baggage and pack-bullocks, and set off to the Toorun Mall hill, distant some thirty miles, by a footpath through the jungle. We camped at the foot of the hill, and ascended it next morning. It is, I believe, about 4000 feet above the sea, and the change of climate from the low country was delightful. There are no human habitations on the summit, but we found a fine artificial lake, on the borders of which we encamped.

On the way up we came upon a huge tiger hanging on a tree. He had killed a cow belonging to some Bheels ; they poisoned the carcass, and, on his return, he had eaten freely, and there and then died. The Bheels had pulled out his teeth, claws, and whiskers, and then hung him up by his hind legs. The skin not being broken, the action of the sun had swollen the body to a huge size, and he looked truly gigantic ; but having hung for several days in an April sun, we did not care to inspect him very closely.

We spent several days on the top of the mountain. There were bison here, but not being present in any official capacity, we were unable to get men to show us the jungles, and were not sufficiently acquainted with the country and its inhabitants to work them properly. We bathed frequently in the lake, and shot a number of small jungle antelope and peafowl on the summit of the hill. On our homeward march we again passed Wuggeria, and went out on the hills during the heat of the day, hoping to fall in with something. As we were ascending a spur, we espied some animal lying under a ledge of overhanging rock in a bay formed by the contour of the hill to our right. We had no regular shikarees—only a few Bheels picked up as we were leaving the village ; these pronounced the beast to be a hyæna, and we decided on having a shot at him.

Carefully marking a tree on the crest of the rock above him, we made a circuit, and, ascending to the table-land, came out above the spot were we had marked him. Standing ready to open fire, we directed the Bheels to heave down stones, which they did, but nothing appeared. We concluded that the game had moved, but some of the Bheels crawled along the face of the rock like monkeys, and, on looking over, ascertained that there was an inner cave within that in which we had seen the animal lying. It was evident that on hearing us he had quietly risen and moved in, so we agreed to smoke him out. We, therefore, found a place where we could descend, and so passed round the base of the rock to the cave.

The outer part was triangular in shape—about seven yards wide at the outside, and four or five deep, having at the farther end an inner cave of about four feet high by two and a half broad. The outer cave was quite open in front, and seven feet high at the outside. From the cave the hill sloped sharply down, covered with trees and bushes.

Some of the Bheels advanced to the mouth of the inner cave, and looking in, saw one eye of the creature, like a ball of fire, at the far end of the den. We endeavoured to get a shot, but owing, I suppose, to some projecting piece of rock, we never could see both eyes at once, and two shots which I fired in were without effect. Meanwhile, the Bheels had collected a large bundle of grass and sticks, which we rolled up to the entrance of the inner cave, and having set fire to it, we all withdrew to the mouth of the outer to watch the result. There was a most thorough draught into the cave, and the flame was swept into it, but the beast made no sign, and at length the fire died down. We then had another large bundle of dry grass made up, but this time we mixed it well with green leaves. On this being fired, a dense black smoke arose, and was carried into the cave. It was such that we thought no beast could live in it ; but again the fire died out, and though the inner cave was filled with smoke, its tenant had made no attempt to come out. We had just made up our minds that he had died in the hole, when, from the inner cave, came a sudden rush of smoke, as if driven out by something advancing rapidly. We stood ready, and the next instant, through the embers of the fire, came—not a hyæna— but a large tiger, charging blindly, with savage growls.

Hayward carried a short rifle, with a ball of some three ounces in weight, and I had a double rifle of fourteen bore. In the instant that elapsed between the tiger's emerging from the smoke and his reaching the entrance of the outer cave, he was struck by the three balls. Two had taken him through the shoulder, and one through the loins, disabling his hind quarter. As he fell we could have placed our guns on his head—too near, in fact, to be pleasant.

Our followers behaved with great steadiness, and at once handed us our second guns. By this time the tiger had managed to drag himself from the cave, and having got on the slope of the hill, he was evidently unable to move up towards us.

When he first appeared, the Bheels were up the trees in an instant, but came down when they saw him fall, and assisted us to ascend the rock. This we did one at a time, the other keeping guard in case of accidents. The tiger, though disabled, was very savage, and had plenty of life in him, and crunched the underwood savagely. After some time we gave him his *quietus*, and carried him home to the camp. He was no doubt the same beast that had dodged us so cleverly at the well, but we had checkmated him this time. From his boldness he had long being the terror of the village, though we did not hear that he had killed any one.

After this exploit we returned to Baroda, and soon after I joined some friends in a three days' pic-nic to Dubka, on the Mhye river, where the Guicowar, who rules the country, has a preserve well stocked with antelope and wild hogs. Besides myself, there was only one of our party endowed with sporting tendencies, and his forte was more in the saddle than with the rifle. The Guicowar had given us permission to hunt, but had requested that no firing might be allowed in the preserve. We, therefore, encamped at some distance, and made preparations for an early start.

My companion was well mounted on a valuable Arab. I had only a rough but strong Deccan pony, so did not expect to take a very active part in the morning's work. The beaters had been sent round to drive, and as we rode through some thin cypress jungle, on our way to the point where we were to take up our position, we saw a huge boar returning to his covert from the open country where he had been feeding during the night. As we wished to get him as far as possible into the open ground before riding at him, we cantered ahead, and getting between him and the jungle, shouted, and turned him back. We slowly followed, keeping about a hundred yards apart, and well away from the boar. He went quietly for about half-a-mile, and then seemed to think he had gone far enough, for he stopped and faced round. He was in front of me at the time, and was hid by some low bushes. My friend called to me to look out, and at that moment the boar came charging straight at me. I had no time to get under weigh, but my pony behaved admirably, and stood like a rock. As the boar came on, I planted my spear in the top of his neck, just behind the head. The blade and a foot of the shaft were completely buried, but he gave a wrench and snapped the bamboo short off. I turned to a horseman who was with us, and who should have been carrying spare spears, but he had none, and when I looked round, the pig had disappeared. Where he went I cannot say, but I never saw him again. I thought then, and I think now, that had my companion done his duty, he should have finished him. The jungle was thin, and there was nothing to hide the pig; my friend was, moreover, well mounted, and had seen me deliver my spear, so he had no excuse. I was much vexed, for the boar was a rattler, with long white tushes. We hunted about for some time, but could find no trace of him, and as by this time we calculated that the beaters would be in the covert, we moved on, to intercept any pigs which they might start.

We had not been long by the covert-side before a fine young boar broke across the open; and this time I had no chance of a spear, for my friend was better mounted, and a good rider to boot. The boar held on till he came to some thin cypress jungle, over which we raced him, but were thrown out by some nasty creeks. He dashed through these, sending the mud flying in all directions, and by the time we had managed to cross where the bottom was sounder, he was far ahead. He then slacked his pace, and was apparently undecided as to what course he should take. In the meantime, we made play, and gained on him fast, but on seeing us he again went off at score, but he was now in clear ground, and my companion closed in and gave him a good spear. In another moment mine was through his ribs, when he made a sharp and plucky charge at my friend, who met him well, and turned him over.

By this time the sun was high, and we returned to our camp, which was on a high bank overhanging the Mhye river. The opposite shore was muddy, and all along the edge lay huge alligators basking in the heat. Walking along the bank, near the tents, with one of our party, I observed a large one which had crawled out, and lay high and dry, in such a position that we could stalk close up to him. We made a circuit, and coming straight in on the bank, saw him lying about thirty feet below us. We gave him four barrels before he could reach the water, into which he threw himself, lashing about with his tail with great violence. From the mud which he raised we could see he had not gone far, and the water being much tinged with blood, we knew that he was hard hit. We returned to the tents to get some long poles wherewith to stir him up, and on our return we found he had come out, and was lying dead upon the bank. He was a strong heavy beast, over twelve feet in length, with most formidable jaws. I had him carried to the tents, where I removed his skin and preserved it. In his stomach we found a hatful of pebbles, some of which were as large as small billiard-balls ; these he had swallowed probably to assist digestion.

In shooting alligators, I have generally found that unless shot dead by a ball in the head, or the base of the neck, they will struggle into the water, but that, if left alone, they will return to the shore and die on the bank. In the same way the large turtles which frequent the Indian rivers will also come ashore when shot through the body. I suppose they are distressed by the water entering through the bullet-holes in the hard skin.

About twenty-five miles to the east of Baroda is the hill-fort of Powaghur, standing at a height of 2500 feet above the sea. It is much frequented during the hot weather by the officers of the cantonment, with their families. The base and sides of the hill are clothed with heavy jungle, well stocked with sambur, and having a fair sprinkling of tigers, bears, and panthers.

The sambur lie in the ravines, far up the hill-side, and require hard work to bag them. My friend Hayward did more execution among them than any one else, and his plan was to ascend the mountain before daybreak, and take up his position at the head of one of the spurs of the hill, at the highest point accessible to the deer. Beaters, who had been sent for the purpose, would then come up the ravine, driving the deer before them. The sambur would move up, till the rocks became too abrupt for them to ascend higher, when they would skirt the precipice to pass over the spur into the next ravine. The hinds always came first, then the smaller stags, and if there was a big one, he invariably came last. They were not therefore bagged without considerable exercise of self-denial on the part of the sportsman, for, as it could never be known that the old stag was with the herd till he made his appearance, it was not safe to fire at the small ones ; and if there was no big one, the chance of the lesser was often lost before the fact was ascertained.

Officers visiting the hill from Baroda generally made the journey during the night, as the toilsome ascent was best got over in the early morning. There was one man who, by his own account, had been a most intrepid sportsman, though we had never known him bag anything more formidable than a quail. One morning he started up the hill by the only footpath. The day had not yet broken, and on getting into the jungle he heard the steps of some beast following him. He halted, and the sounds ceased ; but on his advancing, they were again heard. Becoming somewhat nervous, he kept his rifle ready, and at length saw what his diseased imagination led him to believe was a huge tiger. He at once loosed his piece, and shouted loudly, but was only answered by the bleating of a goat, which had followed him from the village, and which he fortunately had missed in his excitement.

CHAPTER V.

THE district of Guzerat is the best in the Bombay Presidency
for game of all kinds ; and the town of Ahmedabad, directly
connected as it is by rail with the Presidency, is a most convenient starting-point.

In addition to the British Civil Station, there is a military
cantonment, and the latter has a good racecourse, where there
is an annual meeting, as well as sky races, generally got up
during the monsoon. Game of many kinds abounds within
easy distances; and in most parts of the country, antelope,
chinkara, and nylghae, are to be found.

The cold season, commencing in November, brings in duck,
quail, and snipe ; and, as soon as the rain crops are off the
ground, good hog-hunting can be got in many places. The
country is for the most part very fertile, so much so that Guzerat
is fairly styled the Garden of Western India. From a few
miles south of Baroda, and as far as Ahmedabad, the line of
railway passes through a succession of highly-cultivated fields
for upwards of eighty miles. These fields are generally fenced
with high cactus hedges, covered with flowering creepers, and
the whole is richly wooded with noble trees, the larger pro-

portion being mango.   To the west of the Samburmuttee river,
which flows under the walls of the town of Ahmedabad, the
country is more open and less cultivated, but in many parts
are immense tracts covered with wheat and cotton.   Conti-
guous to these are often found extensive salt plains, to which
the Saiseen antelope retire during the heat of the day, returning again in the evenings and at night to feed in the fields,
where they do great damage to the crops. The cultivators
seldom interfere with them, but endeavour sometimes to drive
them off by placing fuel in long stripes along the edges of the
fields.   In the evening they ignite these at the ends next the
wind, and the fire smoulders till morning.   The plan is not,
however, very efficacious.   The Jeytulpoor country, lying
south of Ahmedabad, is richly wooded, and in many parts
nylghae and chinkara are very numerous.   There are also many
good tanks, and in these, and in the rice-fields which they
irrigate, excellent snipe-shooting is to be had in the months
of December and January.   I seldom cared to shoot more
than twenty or thirty couple at one time ; but on one occasion
I remember two men going out twenty miles to their ground,
and shooting during that day and for three hours on the following morning, and returning to the cantonment with 120
couple of snipe.

I was at this time appointed to the Guzerat Revenue Survey,
a branch of an establishment which has done much to concili-
ate the natives, and to consolidate our empire in Western India.

Throughout India the population, with the exception of
Bheels and other jungle tribes, resides entirely in towns and
villages.   To each of these the land in the immediate vicinity
belongs, and it is either cultivated by individuals, or reserved
for grazing by the community in general.

Previous to our occupation of the country, the boundaries

of townships, except in cultivated districts, were vaguely defined. But now that life and property are secure, and the population has confidence, the cultivated area has greatly increased, and it has been found necessary to have all boundaries accurately laid down.

When the Survey was established, village maps did not exist, and the village accountants merely had rough books, containing vague and unsatisfactory entries regarding the tenure and rent of the lands.

A very large proportion of the best lands was alienated from the state, and held by individuals on old grants, subject generally to certain payments.

The rents paid to Government were excessive, and much land lay waste.

Moreover, on wells being dug, or other improvements effected by cultivators, they were at once subjected to an increased assessment on the improved value of their holdings.

For the correction of these matters the Revenue Survey was established.

The Guzerat Branch consisted of—

> 1 Superintendent ;
>
> 6 Measuring Assistants ;
>
> 2 Classing Assistants.

In the early days of the department these were all officers of the army, or gentlemen of the uncovenanted civil service.

The superintendent directed the whole, and assigned his work to each assistant.

The measuring assistants had each under him twenty native surveyors and eight learners.

The native surveyors were appointed to survey the various villages about the country ; and they conducted their work with chain and cross-staff.

They were at work at daybreak, accompanied by the village authorities, and in a rough field-book all entries regarding the tenure, holder, cultivator, and area, of a few fields, were daily made.

On going home these entries were written out in a fair book, and a plan, drawn on a scale, was made of each field which had been measured that day.

The fields were then daily added to the large map of the village under survey.

Roads, tanks, or ponds, wells, etc., were all shown on the plan.

Boundaries of fields were marked by stones or mounds of earth.

The classing assistants had each under him twelve native classers, and each had to go over as much ground as three measuring assistants.

Their duties were to examine and class the soil according to its capability.

This they did by ascertaining the depth and nature of the soil. All land was divided into first, second, and third classes ; and the standard was lowered as deteriorating qualities existed.

Mixture of lime, gravel, sand and clay, and salt, were held to be bad, as was also liability to flooding in the rainy season, or a surface whence the rainfall would at once run off.

All unculturable land was deducted from the gross area.

Finally, the area being fixed, the field was classed according to its merits, the great object being to secure, by constant supervision and co-operation, that lands of equal value should be entered by the various native classers according to the same standard, and consequently in the same class.

Ten per cent of all work done by native measurers or classers was tested by the European officers.

On the completion of the survey and classing, the books and maps were made over to the settlement officers, who were, usually, the superintendent of the survey and a revenue officer of experience.

These determined the rent to be paid on the lands, and they were assisted by the best local advice.

In this matter all minor details were duly considered—viz. the area; the soil; the distance of the land from the village and from water ; and the distance of the village itself from the nearest market.

The settlement was made for thirty years, and the rents fixed were so low, that not only were large tracts of waste at once brought under cultivation, but many lands which had been granted away on yearly payment were given up, the holders preferring to give the new and diminished rent.

The full value, up to the end of the settlement, was secured to the cultivator for any improvements he might effect.

The land was secured to the cultivator so long as he continued to pay his rent ; while, on the other hand, he was at full liberty to give it up at any time, on giving intimation previous to the 5th of June.

At the time I write of we had an institution called "The Hunt," got up for the furtherance of hog-hunting, and a small monthly sum was collected from subscribers. With this the Hunt paid for a shikaree, whose duty it was to go about the country and ascertain where pigs were to be found in rideable ground. The Hunt, moreover, paid for the cost and carriage of a large mess-tent and a mess-table, and provided candles and cards. On hunting days half the cost of the beaters was

THE START

also defrayed out of this fund, the other half being paid by
the sportsmen present.   The meets generally lasted from four
to six days—alternate days being devoted to hunting and
shooting.

The locality being fixed on, the mess-tent was sent out,
and every man intending to be present sent on his servants
with a small sleeping-tent and a goodly store of provender
of all kinds—both solid and fluid—and as many horses
and ponies as he could muster.   The shikaree and his assistants were out long before daybreak, and took up positions in
trees whence they could watch the pigs as they returned to
the coverts from their feeding grounds.   By eight o'clock he
generally reappeared, and gave in his report to the captain of
the Hunt, by whom the programme for the day was arranged.
About 9 A.M. there used to be a general shout for breakfast,
and each man's servant brought in a dish or two to the mess-
tent, and the table speedily groaned with viands of sorts.

The appearance of our camp was highly effective.   It was
generally situated in some grove of grand old mangoes.   In
the centre stood the mess-tent, amongst the trees were dotted
the small sleeping tents, and besides each of these were picketed
three or four steeds, whose numerous attendants lay about on
the ground wherever they could find shade.   By half-past ten
we were in the saddle, and seldom had far to go before reaching the covert-side.   The horsemen were sent to their places
by the captain, and though at times some were unruly, we
were, for the most part, orderly and well conducted.   Our
favourite meet was at Dongurwah, about thirty miles to the
north of Ahmedabad.   Pigs were always plentiful, and on the
alternate days there was abundance of game of all kinds, for
both gun and rifle.

The mess-table was always liberally supplied.   In addition

to beef, mutton, hams, and tongues, we had ducks of many kinds; teal, snipe, quail, Saiseen antelope, chinkara; and the marrow-bones and tongue of the nylghae, while his head was generally potted and served up cold; partridges—painted, gray, and rock—and hares in plenty; and, to crown all, pork chops and the soused head of the mighty boar himself.

The field was generally well attended, and sharp contests for the honour of the first spear were numerous. At times this emulation led to hot and strong discussions; for in the excitement of a chase, when several pigs were on foot at once, and when possibly the hunted boar might be changed during the run, it was not always an easy matter to say whose spear had drawn first blood.

I well remember an occasion when a warm dispute for the tushes had at last been decided between two rival horsemen by a toss-up. The beaters were proceeding to open the beast, and only then discovered, deeply buried in the boar's neck, the spear-head of a third horseman, whose claim to the tushes had been utterly ignored, but who had in reality drawn first blood. The boar, after being first speared by him, had in his course passed through a thicket of high grass and bushes, and on emerging on the far side was supposed to be a fresh one; hence the dispute which had so narrow an escape of an unjust decision. The head of the first spear had broken short off, and was completely buried in the muscles of the neck.

In some parts of the Dongurwah country there were dense thorny thickets which, though of no great extent, were quite impenetrable for horsemen, and on a wounded boar gaining the shelter of one of these, there was much difficulty in dislodging him. We had had a severe run after a very large old boar; he was badly speared, but managed to reach one of these, and all our attempts to induce him again to break cover were in

vain.   The beaters came up and advanced with fiendish yells,
blowing horns and beating drums.   Stones were showered into
the bush, and a sharp fire of blank cartridge was kept up by
a party of the Guzerat Kolee corps who had accompanied us.
The boar, however, knew the strength of his position, and
refused to show himself again in the open ground.   He
might, of course, have been shot, but such a proceeding
would have been regarded in the same light as the shooting
of a fox in Leicestershire ; so as we could not in honour ride
away and leave him, it was agreed that we should dismount
and go in at him on foot with our spears.

The project was a rash one, for though a spear is a handy
weapon when used from horseback in open ground, it is not
quite so suitable when going in at an infuriated boar in a
tangled thicket of thorns and long grass.   We did not, however,
give this part of the matter much consideration.   We were
about eight in number, and in the event of any one of us being
in difficulties we relied on our comrades.   The boar had taken
his stand in the centre of the thicket, which was some fifty
yards across, and we moved slowly in on him, with our spears
shortened and pointed in advance.   My greatest danger
seemed to be from my neighbour on the left, who, relinquish-
ing his spear, had armed himself with a sharp-pointed crooked
sword which he had taken from one of the beaters, and
which he held over his shoulder in painful proximity to my
countenance.

Towards the centre of the thicket the ground was somewhat clearer, and most fortunately the boar selected the
moment at which we gained this spot to make his charge.
With savage grunts he came crashing down on us, and evidently intended to make an ugly hole in some one, but we
stood steady, and the nearest spears were buried in his chest

and shoulders. His weight and impetus were great, and the tough bamboo spear-shafts bent under the strain, but we closed in on him, and he yielded up his gallant spirit.

The beaters crowded in and bore him from his lair, and on reaching the open ground, proceeded to "gralloch." On removing the intestines, a large quantity of blood was found in the carcass. Diving their hands into the body, they scooped out the warm blood and drank it greedily, wiping their en-sanguined fingers on their long beards and moustache. The effect was truly startling, but they seemed to enjoy it, and for all that I can say to the contrary, it may have been very good tipple.

Many of these men carried " boomerangs," a weapon I have never seen used in any other part of India. It was made of dark heavy wood, two inches broad, three quarters of an inch thick, and about two and a half feet long, sharpened . at the edges. These they threw with great force, and would not unfrequently knock over hares and partridges as they rose during the beat.

Although in hog-hunting it is advantageous to be well mounted, yet many spears are taken by men on steady old horses, held well in hand. Young high-couraged horses are often hard to hold, and, to enable the rider to work his spear properly the right hand should be free. I have seen the spear taken from a field mounted on high-priced horses, by an old stager riding a steady screw that would not fetch £10. One member of the Hunt often rode a small dark chestnut pony, about thirteen hands high. The man was over six feet in height, and it seemed incredible that the rat he bestrode could carry his weight. The pony was a most vicious little beast, and when at his picket would rush open-mouthed at any one who approached him ; but his blood and

RIDING FOR THE FIRST SPEAR.

pluck were undeniable, and it was a rare sight to see him and his rider hurl themselves into a ten-foot hedge and kick and struggle till they forced a passage. When let out at a boar, the pony thoroughly entered into the sport ; and, thanks to his speed and game running, his owner frequently carried off the spear.

Old boars are often very cunning, and will hang back in a thicket when the rest of the sounder breaks, stealing quietly off when the field is in hot pursuit of some of the smaller pigs. As a rule, they do not give so fast a run as a young boar or a long-legged sow ; but when brought to bay they are awkward customers, and frequently leave their mark on their pursuers. Our beaters were ripped on several occasions, but fortunately the wounds were not severe, and were confined to the legs. . The cut of a boar's tusk is peculiar, and is generally of the form of the letter **L**, like a tear in woollen cloth. Although, when charging, they come on with savage grunts, they seldom cry out when speared ; and a pig who dies with a squeal is generally regarded as an ignoble beast, having in his veins the blood of domestic ancestors.

I remember a joke played off on a man whose deeds in the saddle were not supposed to lose aught of their importance by his own description of them. Some youngsters of the cantonment, having purchased a village pig, had been in the habit of sending it out for a mile or two in a cart, and hunting it home with long bamboos. By this course of training, the piggy acquired wind and some degree of speed. At length, on a day appointed, he was taken out and secured by the leg in the covert. The usual party, with the addition of the mighty hunter, were assembled at the mess tiffin, when a native came up and reported a fine boar marked down. Horses and spears were called for, and, with the guide in advance, all proceeded to the jungle-side. Nimrod announced his intention of refraining from all active part in the proceedings, on the ground that it would be unfair for an old experienced hunter like himself to take the spear from a lot of young fellows to whom the sport was new. He was, however, assured that without his valuable aid the game would probably escape, and that it was therefore hoped he would not practise such extreme self-denial. On the riders taking up their positions, men were sent to free the obscene beast, which speedily appeared; and, in expectation of the customary chevy, made off at its best pace. By judicious management, all the field got thrown out with the exception of Nimrod, who was seen riding like a man, and coming up to the pig, hand over hand. Making a well-directed rush, with a triumphant shout, he speared the beast, and a few more thrusts rolled it over. The other riders now gathered round the redoubtable hunter, who was seen standing by the prostrate " gaumtee," waving his cap and brandishing his blood-stained spear. " Gentlemen !" he cried, " it was too bad of me ! but really when I saw the boar break cover, my blood got up, and I was quite unable to restrain myself !" At this moment, a villager, who had been previously well coached, came running up and demanded payment for his property. It was long before Nimrod again entertained the mess with his hunting exploits.

Although large boars often showed fight, and gave trouble, at times they were laid low by a single spear. One morning we were hunting in a difficult country, covered with scrub-bush, through which it was difficult to urge a horse at great speed, when a stout young boar was seen crossing the cover at some distance ahead. He was going at a sharp pace, and as he already had a good start, the word to ride was at once given. Away we went, threading through the bush at a smart gallop. Hearing us coming up, the boar halted for a moment, and again started off. We now settled down to the work, and were gaining on him, when one of our party, who had been at some distance from us when we started, came down on the pig at a right angle. The boar never swerved, but apparently charged straight ahead, and with the intention of cutting the fore legs of the horse from under him. How the horse escaped we could not imagine. The boar seemed to cross under his neck, and both were going at their best pace. In an instant the rider dropped the point of his spear between the shoulders of the boar, and with a convulsive struggle it rolled over, quite dead.

The thorns through which we hunted told heavily on the legs of the horses, and they were often much swollen after a hard day's work. A favourite remedy was the red earth from the nests of white ants, boiled up with the leaves of the neem-tree, till the whole formed into a thick paste. With this the legs were plastered, from above the knees downwards ; and the mud on drying formed a sort of bandage round the leg. In the early morning the horses were often taken down to the nearest tank, and kept standing for fifteen minutes in the cold water. These combined remedies seemed to draw out the thorns to the surface, whence many were extracted by careful horsekeepers ; and I have seen a man come up with the back of his currycomb covered with large thorns, which he had picked out from the legs of the horse under his charge.

During the meet,— on the days devoted to shooting, we generally started off in pairs, armed with gun and rifle, and taking a light shooting-cart to carry home the game. I was out one day with a civilian who was passionately fond of the chase in all its branches. We laid in a good lunch, and cooling beverages of sorts, and started off after breakfast. A mile or two from camp we came on a small herd of chinkara, and conspicuous among them was a fine buck. They were standing about, in a partially cultivated piece of ground, cropping the young shoots of bair-bushes. Dropping off our horses, we walked on the far side of the shooting-cart, which was slowly driven past the deer. Seeing us, they moved off for a short distance, and stood scattered over the side of a slight rise. The buck gave a fair chance, and the Collector dropped him neatly with a shot through the shoulders.

Placing him in the cart we again mounted and moved on, and soon came on a herd of nylghae. One of my attendants had asked me to procure for him the skin of an old bull, as he required it to make a shield. Observing a very fine blue fellow standing out by himself, at some distance from the rest, we decided that he was a proper beast for the purpose. On this occasion, it was my turn to shoot, and working up to within a hundred yards, I drew the bead on his shoulder. As I pressed the trigger the bull wheeled round, and the ball struck him too far back. He was, however, badly wounded, and went off slowly. Running back, the Collector mounted his horse, and gave chase. As he closed on the bull he delivered his spear behind the shoulder, and narrowly escaped a kick, which would probably have broken his leg had it taken effect. The spear-thrust proved deadly, and the beast fell over, after going a short distance. As we did not fancy taking him about with us all day, we dragged him to some thick bushes, where the vultures could not see him, and covering him up with boughs, we left him till we returned in the evening.

Farther on, we came on a herd of Saiseen antelope, but my companion missed a tolerably good buck, and knocked over a fat doe, which was grazing just beyond him. We now came on a country fairly stocked with hares and partridges, but as deer were likely to be scared by much firing, we did not interfere with them. In a patch of scrub jungle, we came on six or seven chinkara, and I shot the best buck. The rest ran a short distance and stood, when the Collector rolled over a doe in good style. Our bag was now, one nylghae, one antelope, and three chinkara, so we thought we had fairly earned our luncheon. Not far off was a well shaded by trees, where some cultivators were busy with their bullocks, irrigating a field. Here we halted. Our own bullocks were unharnessed and watered, and while we emptied the luncheon-basket, they and our horses took their mid-day feed of grain. Then a smoke and a confabulation, and we again turned homewards. On our way we shot two more chinkara, and picked up the blue bull which we had shot in the morning. Altogether, the load in the cart was about as much as it would hold. The blue bull was taken charge of by one of my gun-bearers, who removed the skin by cutting it down the back of the neck and spine, thereby preserving undamaged the stout skin of the chest and throat, which is prized as a defence against sword-cuts and arrows. After a long day in the sun, a tub and clean clothes were very refreshing, and the hour before dinner was pleasantly passed in arm-chairs, in an open spot, where we assembled to smoke our pipes, and go over the adventures of the day.

There was a sure find for pigs at Vinjool, about eight miles from Ahmedabad ; but the country was difficult, and hog were only got by hard riding and good luck.

Part of the ground was much cut up by rice-fields, formed into terraces, with mud-banks between them. These fields were baked in the sun till they became hard as bricks ; and woe to the unlucky man who got a cropper among them. We

were also frequently troubled by a nasty nullah, with steep
and treacherous banks, winding in a tortuous manner through
the line of country which the pig almost invariably took ;
and in many parts, the cactus and milk-bush hedges grew to
the height of eighteen and twenty feet—too thick for a horse
to crash through, but open enough below to allow of the passage of a boar.

We had a good meet here one fine morning, the attendance being larger than usual, owing to the proximity of the
cantonment. Several pigs had been marked into some low
hills covered with neem-trees, and having in parts a strong
undergrowth of bair-bushes. They were started, and made
off across the rice-fields at a great pace. We were soon after
them, and before long, a gallant officer was seen to get a
frightful header over a high double bank. The sounder
broke into twos and threes, and I found myself, and two other
men, after a stout young boar. He made for some enclosed
fields, and dashed through an eighteen feet hedge. Thinking
I saw an opening, I rode at it and crashed through, landing
in a narrow lane, minus my stirrups, which had been drawn
out of the catches by the resistance of the hedge, which was
strongly laced with creepers. Having readjusted the stirrups,
I again mounted and put my horse at the hedge on the other
side, and somehow we struggled through ; but by this time
my two companions and the boar had got a long start of
me. I had some difficulty in getting up to them, and only
did so in time to see the spear taken. The boar was only
slightly pricked, and getting close to the side of a high overhanging hedge of cactus, he held on at a good pace, and, by
crossing through where he found an opening underneath, left
us a long way behind. Finding a gap, we again closed with him.
He was now very savage, and as we came up he shortened

THE FIND.

his pace and prepared for a sidelong rush at the nearest horse, " verris obliquum meditantis ictum." Watching his opportunity, he suddenly swerved across, but was checked by a clever spear in the shoulder, and in another instant he was rolled over by a cross spear behind the elbow, which finished him. Meanwhile the rest of the field had divided into two parties; one of which had lost their pig in the nullah, and the other had slain a large sow. She had made a good charge at the finish, and before receiving the *coup de grace* had nearly bitten through the boot of one of her pursuers.

About mid-day we adjourned to the tent for refreshment, and by the time we had rested, the Hunt shikaree—who had gone off on the track of a small boar which he had seen stealing away in the morning—returned, having succeeded in marking him down. His hiding-place was watched on all sides by men perched on trees. We set out at once, and on arriving at the spot a few men were sent into the cover to dislodge him. Some of the field were rather noisy, having taken deep draughts of beer-mug, which had not only cheered but also slightly inebriated. Two of these gentlemen managed to head the pig, and turned him back into cover; thereby calling forth a well-merited rebuke from the captain of the Hunt. After some trouble, the boar was again driven out, and made for the much-dreaded nullah. The field, however, spread out and divided. One or two horsemen kept on the far side, and on the boar attempting to cross for a distant cover, they had a sharp skurry, and the spear was neatly taken by an officer of the Guzerat Horse. In the course of the afternoon another pig was started, but got away among difficult ground and escaped. While watching a corner of the cover, one sportsman saw two land tortoises crawl out of some thorn bushes, and dismounting, succeeded in capturing

both. We returned to the cantonment by moonlight, and as
we rode along, were favoured by some of the party with vocal
music of a high order.

In some parts of the country round Vinjool, chinkara are
plentiful, and it was here I had my first day's shooting among
them. It was during the height of the rainy season, and I had
come to Ahmedabad to attend the races which were held that
year. Bowles of the Revenue Survey had a good shooting-cart,
which we sent on with our rifles and lunch, and cantered out
after it on horseback. The millet and maize crops were high,
and we were not very sanguine, as, during the heat of the day,
the deer take much to the shelter of the tall crops. However,
after wandering about for some time, we spied a buck feeding
among some vetches, and succeeded in working the cart up to
within shooting distance. Bowles would not fire, as he wanted
me to have all the sport. I made a good shot, and dropped the
buck, but he rose at once and made off; we could see, however, that he was badly hit, and he soon slackened his pace
and lay down among some low bushes. Had we attempted
to go up to him at once, he would probably have risen and
gone off, so we quietly sat down and watched him for nearly
an hour. By this time his wound began to distress him, and
when we again advanced he allowed us to approach sufficiently near to give him a final shot. We then went on, but
saw nothing for some time, so sat down under a tree and
took our lunch. Again moving on, we started two bucks,
which were feeding in some high grain in our left, and they
ran out into the open ground. After going about seventy yards
they halted and stood head on ; I fired, and dropped one in
his tracks, shooting him through the chest ; and as the other
bolted off I gave him the second barrel, hitting him through
the body. He was completely doubled up, and soon after lay
down, when we captured him without another shot.

The heat of the sun during the monsoon is very great, and the glare from the large white clouds has a more scorching effect than at any other time. We felt it very much on this occasion, and having three deer in the cart, we thought we might move home. So, leaving our men to follow, we returned to our quarters.

By keeping quiet, and watching a wounded deer for some time, much trouble may be saved. Some men ride down wounded bucks on horseback ; but the plan is a bad one, and should be avoided if possible, as the other deer get scared, and subsequent shooting is spoiled. It is, however, requisite to keep the wounded animal in view, or a disappointment may result.

I remember one man who fired at a buck, and thought he hit it. He followed, and lost sight of the deer ; but soon after observed a brown object near a bush, which he supposed to be the wounded antelope. He was not much of a sportsman ; but, having heard us recommend the above course, he determined to adopt it. Sitting down, he lit a very long Trichinopoly cheroot, and smoked it out, and had, I believe, half finished a second, when the supposed buck turned out to be only a large hawk, which then rose, and flew lazily away.

When stalking antelope, it is well to pay some attention to the selection of any native attendant who may accompany you. It is an amusing and instructive sight to see a youthful sportsman crawling up to a herd on his hands and knees, while his servant, walking bolt upright, gravely follows at the distance of a few yards.

The result may be imagined.

CHAPTER VI.

MY chum, Harrington Bulkley, than whom a better fellow or more keen sportsman never breathed, had invited me and a friend who was staying in my camp to pay him a visit. So we made an early start one morning from the town of Dholka, and, riding eastward, crossed the Samburmuttee river, when a few more miles brought us to his tents.

He was most comfortably situated, in a good game country, and there was excellent snipe-shooting in the vicinity. On arriving at the tents we were informed that our host was absent in Ahmedabad, but was expected home that morning ; so, after a cup of tea, we ordered out the shooting-cart, and went in quest of a herd of antelopes which we heard were in the neighbourhood. We had not gone a mile before we came upon them, some fifteen in number, and among them four or five very good black bucks. My friend and I tossed for the shot, and the luck was in my favour. The deer had evidently not been disturbed much, for they allowed us to get within easy range. My first shot dropped a fine buck dead, and, as they went off, another fell to the second barrel. They were both large bucks, and, having had good feed among the irrigated fields, were in excellent condition. We then put them into the cart, and returned to the tents just in time to meet our host on his arrival. He gave us a good deal of light and pleasant chaff, and abused us for disturbing the game so near home.

It turned out afterwards that, though chinkara were plentiful, this was the only herd of antelope within some distance, and it had been carefully preserved in anticipation of our visit. During our stay we were joined by two gentlemen of the Civil Service, and had two days' good hog-hunting, killing several pigs on both occasions. We also made some good bags of snipe and ducks. Bulkley and I were employed together for some time at Meytal—a village about fifteen miles west of Dholka. This was an excellent camp for game, and on all sides the Saiseen antelope swarmed. I shot one very fine buck, with twenty-five inch horns. He was feeding on the side of a rising ground, about a mile from camp, and I was at once struck by the rich purple-black of his skin and the great length of his horns. I made a successful stalk, and put a ball in through the shoulders. He went only a short distance, and then ran into some thorn bushes, where he lay down and was easily captured.

Close round our tents were some low sandy hills, slightly rising above the plain, and covered with neem-trees and thorny bushes. Hares were plentiful, and we shot them from time to time, as required for the pot. The painted partridge was also common, and shared the fate of the hares. In Guzerat the shooting of peafowl was prohibited, in deference to the prejudices of the natives, who encourage them in the neighbourhood of the villages. They consume large quantities of grain—especially of wheat, which is seldom cut, however ripe, until a certain date ; and in many parts scores of peafowl may be seen feeding in the fields at all hours of the day. There were numbers of them round Meytal, and we frequently took a quiet shot at the younger birds among the thorn bushes. They were excellent when roasted, and made very good make-believe turkey. The Mekranees have a singular method of shooting them. When the peafowl are feeding in the early mornings and evenings, these men tie a mask, representing the head of a panther, over their faces, and crawling up to some bush or opening in the hedge, they thrust their heads forward and attract the notice of the fowl. The latter raise their heads and advance in an inquisitive manner, watching the supposed panther, which they frequently approach to within twenty paces, and are then easily shot.

About a couple of miles south-west of Meytal is an extensive plain. The ground is so impregnated with salt as to be uncultivable ; but during the monsoon a coarse grass springs up, and the place is resorted to by herdsmen with large numbers of tame buffaloes. The soft ground is cut up by these heavy beasts, and when again hardened by the subsequent action of the sun, is most disagreeable to ride over. I had a very severe run over this country one morning after a black buck whose hind leg I had disabled. I was unacquainted with the ground, and seeing the buck make off over the apparently level plains, I signalled to my groom to bring up my horse, and, mounting, gave chase. By this time the buck had got a long start, and having passed near some other deer which were out in the plain, they also took alarm and moved off with him. Had he been shot in the body I should have had difficulty in selecting him from the rest, but with his damaged leg there could be no mistake, though the pace at which he went kept him up with the others. I followed at a hand gallop, but found I had to put my galloway at his best speed. Sometimes we came on 'places where the hard mud stuck up in jagged lumps, and my horse made some desperate flounders. I sat well back in the saddle, keeping a steady pull at his head, and the pace alone kept him on his legs. After going about two miles the buck began to give in, and broke away from the rest of the herd; and as we were then on better ground I was enabled to press him. I at length succeeded in turning him, and I then knew that he could not hold on much longer. He now gave in fast, and, holding my horse well in hand, I took several more turns out of him, and he soon after dropped exhausted. The run was altogether a severe one, owing to the extreme roughness of the ground, and the mud, baked in the sun, was as hard as brick. On these occasions I generally carried a spear, though I seldom required to use it, for when a buck is so far blown as to allow a horse to come up with him, he will, in most cases, throw himself down, and may then be laid hold of.

A friend sent me a large red dog, which I found very useful, especially when following a wounded buck in long grass, rough ground, or high grain. The dog had, I think, belonged to some of the Brinjarra, or other wandering tribes, and was a strong powerful beast, though by no means fast. He was, however, wonderfully steady, and would never leave a wounded deer. Where antelope were numerous, I have frequently seen him pursue one right through a herd; and though the other deer, apparently with the intention of baffling the dog, would cross and recross within a few yards of his nose during the run, he would never leave the wounded beast, but would follow on till he succeeded in separating him from his fellows. The only difficulty was to get him fairly laid on at the outset, and for this purpose I had a cord passed through his collar to act as a slip. I kept one end of the cord tied round the wrist, the other loose in my hand, and in this manner I would mount my horse, and, keeping the dog on the right hand, would start after the wounded buck at a hand gallop. The old dog knew his work, and as soon as I was convinced that he saw which deer he was to follow, I slipped the cord and away he would go.

The Saiseen antelope, or black buck, is, to use an Irishism, occasionally found pure white.

I have seen five or six specimens, but they were all in the country to the south-west of Ahmedabad, and may consequently have been related to each other. These antelope are regular albinos, having white horns and hoofs, and red eyes. They can be distinguished at great distances, owing to the exceeding purity of their white coats, and, being seldom met with, they are much sought after by sportsmen. My friend Bowles shot one of these on the north-east frontier of Kattyawar. He was a very fine buck, having horns twenty-six inches in length. I had often seen one near Meytal, but he had been frequently fired at—often when he could only have been bagged by a fluke—and he had in consequence become very cunning, lying out during the day in some open salt plain, and only coming into the cultivated parts at nightfall. Many stratagems were employed, but to no purpose. Sometimes we stalked him with the shooting-cart, sometimes we tried to drive him, occasionally we tried to approach him with the coloured dress of one of the native women over our shooting clothes, but the buck was too much for us, and we never brought him to bag. I fell in with another of these albinos at Kote, a village some thirty miles south of Ahmedabad. It was a fawn, in company with one or two skittish does, and they were very shy. I worked after it one morning for many hours, but was unable to get within range.

The nylghae were met with to the north-west of Kote, and we often brought in a fat cow to the larder. The flesh, though somewhat coarse, is by no means to be despised ; and as beef proper was not obtainable, we were glad of the change from the everlasting mutton. We also shot some very large old bulls.

I was out one morning shooting for the pot, when I observed a herd of nylghae, and seeing some calves among them, I stalked to within a hundred yards, and, singling out a good one, fired. The bullet struck low, breaking the fore-leg near the body. I had no horse with me at the time, but my big dog was led by an attendant, to whom I signalled to bring him up. The herd had not gone very far ; and, taking up the dog towards them, I advanced till they began to move away, when I slipped him. The herd went off at a sharp trot, and the dog was gaining on them fast, and was close to the wounded calf, when the herd suddenly halted, and a number of cows faced about. They waited till the dog was within twenty yards, when they made a rush at him, striking violently with their fore-feet. The dog had no chance against them, and received some severe blows, but at last managed to get away, and returned to me much discomfited. The herd moved off, taking the wounded calf with them, and my visions of veal vanished into thin air.

The nature of the nylghae varies much, according to the locality in which he is found. In some of the more cultivated parts they are tame as cows, but in the big jungles they become very wary, and are nearly as difficult of approach as the sambur. An officer who was in camp with me, but who himself was no sportsman, expressed a wish to join me one afternoon ; so, ordering out the shooting-cart, we mounted our ponies and set off for some Babool jungle, which I knew was

frequented by nylghae. We had not gone far before a large
cow passed across the track. We moved quietly on, and I got
a fair shot. She went off, however, and on my slipping the dog
he disappeared in the jungle, and did not return for some time.
Blood was visible about his muzzle, but we never got the cow.
Some days after, we learned that the dog had run her down
and killed her close to a village, and that her carcass had been
eaten by the Dhers and other men of low caste. Soon after
we came on another herd, and this time I got a fair standing
shot, dropping a large blue bull. The rest of the herd went
off through some high grass, and with my second barrel I
bagged a fat cow. My companion was greatly excited. He
was of a practical turn of mind, and at once suggested that
meat so easily obtained might be turned to good account, and
that we ought without delay to enter into a contract to supply
her Majesty's navy with salt beef.

At a village a few miles to the south-west of Dholka we
fell in with two specimens of the boa or rock snake. They
were not very large, only about seven feet long, but stout.
They had taken up their quarters in an old tree, which overshadowed the tents. The main trunk and many of the
larger branches were hollow ; and a groom, as he lay on some
straw near his horses, observed one of the serpents project his
head from a hole about thirty feet from the ground. He
at once called out, and my friend Bulkley fetched his rifle
and put a ball through the head of the snake, which, after
a few convulsive struggles, threw itself from the hole and fell
at our feet. The other showed itself a day or two after, and
was also slain.

In the open plains about twelve miles to the south-west
of the town of Dholka were large tracts covered with high
grass, and these were frequently resorted to by panthers.

We were shooting antelope near the village of Surla, and were astonished to find the deer very shy and scared. In the course of the day we came on several remains of them, and the carcasses of two or three which had been but recently killed. On inquiring from some cowherds, we were informed that a panther had been seen, so we fixed an early day to hunt him up. Water was scarce and bad, so we had a few bottles placed in the luncheon basket, which amongst other things contained a bottle of whisky and several bottles of beer. On arriving at the village of Surla I had a nasty feverish attack, and was too seedy to go out. My two companions, however, went forth, with about forty beaters, and hunted up a strip of swampy ground covered with grass ten feet in height. The panther was soon started, and opened the ball by charging back through the line of men, who made way for him with great promptitude. The guns then moved back and the line faced about, and this time succeeded in driving the panther across an open space. Here he received a shot which disabled one of his forelegs, but he reached a patch of high grass, into which he disappeared. To follow him now became a service of some danger, as the whole party were on foot, and the panther, being wounded, was certain to fight. Two or three parties, of four men each, were placed in various directions, with orders to stand together and endeavour to mark the beast down if he left the grass. The remainder of the beaters were then formed into a wedge, and with the two guns leading, and all the rest howling and on their guard, with uplifted clubs, the word was given to advance. The panther lay till his pursuers were within a few yards, when he charged out, and was rolled over by a well-directed fire. He was a very strong beast and very fat, having evidently taken kindly to his venison. It was universally allowed that it was fortunate that he charged at the strongest point of attack, as, had he made his rush at one of the sides of the living wedge, he would probably have left his mark on somebody. The hunt had taken place in full view of the spot where I lay, and my friends now came up, calling loudly for cooling beverages. I at once proceeded to make a beer-mug, and having prepared the correct quantity of sugar and spices in a large jug, I poured in two bottles of beer and what I supposed to be a bottle of water. My servant poured out the compound into quart pewters, and the sportsmen tossed off the grateful fluid at a draught. As he put down the measure, one of them asked if I had "laced" the mug with whisky; and on my replying in the negative, he said he was sure the drink had some taste of spirit. The other man being of the same opinion, I examined the supposed water bottle, and found I had in mistake given them whisky with their beer, and between them they had swallowed the best part of a quart bottle.

Luncheon was at once prescribed as an antidote, and it succeeded so far that no evil effects were visible beyond excessive hilarity and a slight tendency on the part of my friends to roll in their saddles as we rode home. On the way we came across three bustard feeding in the open plain. They allowed us to approach within a few paces, and when they did take flight, they lit again within two hundred yards. We had, however, no guns, all our people being behind.

Thirty miles south-west of Ahmedabad is a large sheet of water called the Nul, covering many square miles. It is very shallow throughout, and in most places is only six or eight feet deep. During the cold season the entire surface of it is covered with waterfowl of every kind—geese, ducks of many sorts, teal in great variety, and coots in myriads. Snipe are found in scores all along the swampy borders.

Large numbers of coolen resort to the shores in the evenings, and their wild cry is heard in all directions. No regular boats were procurable; but the natives used rafts composed of reeds. These were made somewhat in the form of boats, the reeds being bound in bundles, in a mass, five feet wide, and about three in thickness, and fourteen feet in length. Towards the bow they were brought together, so as to form a point, and facilitate progress through the water. The rafts were propelled by a man at the stern, with a long bamboo. On our arrival at the Nul, we at once ordered several of these rafts to be got ready. We made comfortable seats of blankets in the forepart of our primitive vessels; and skirting along the edges of the high reeds, we enjoyed duck-shooting to our heart's content. Among the many handsome ducks brought to bag, we got some fine specimens of the pintail, which, when cooked, were excellent, though some of them were almost too fat.

The country round the Nul swarmed with antelope, and we slew many fine bucks. We also made some good bags of coolen, as they fed in the wheat-fields. They are found in great numbers throughout the whole of this district; and though very shy, and difficult to approach on foot, they will frequently allow a man on horseback, or with a cart, to come within shooting distance. At that time I had a steady shooting pony, from whose back I made many a raking shot, greatly to the satisfaction of our attendants, with whom they were very favourite food.

We were camped at one time—about the commencement of the hot weather—at a village a mile distant from the edge of the water. Our beds were always placed outside the tents, and we slept in the open air. The coolen were in the habit of rising from the shores of the Nul at the early dawn, and making their way in a long, wedge-shaped flight, towards the cultivated country. Our camp was in their line, and they passed over our heads, uttering their usual wild cry.

Thinking that something might be done with them, I loaded a gun with BB, and placed it at the head of my bed. Next morning I was awakened by the cries of the coolen approaching, and, taking my gun, I sat up in bed and waited for them. Presently they appeared—coming on in a long line over my head ; when I fired right and left, and brought down a brace of fine birds. I tried to do the same on subsequent mornings, but the birds had become shy, and avoided the line of our camp.

A remarkable shot which I made at an antelope from the saddle is perhaps worthy of record.

In company with a friend, I was riding across country to a new camping ground, when I saw a herd of fifteen or twenty does and one black buck. We had no shooting-cart with us, but our rifles were carried by attendants. I rode up to within fair shooting distance, and dismounting, fired at the buck, and missed him. The herd made off, but halted after going a few hundred yards. I had reloaded, and again mounting, I moved towards them. They were, however, scared, and bounded away. I put my horse into a canter, and followed for a short distance, when I halted, hoping that the deer, as they often do, would stand and give me another chance. But they kept on, and I again cantered after them ; but as they were evidently not inclined to stand, and were taking me away from the direction in which I wished to travel, I drew up my horse, and fired a random shot from the saddle at the retreating herd. They were all going at fair speed, and at the moment I fired they were 250 or 300 yards from me. Much to my astonishment the only buck which was in the herd fell dead in his tracks ; and on going up to him I found that the ball had struck him on the back of the head, just below his horns. My friend, who had been watching my proceedings from a distance, came up, exclaiming, " What a fluke !" and though I pointed out to him that no sportsman worthy of the name would fire at anything but a buck, and that the back of the head was the correct place to strike a retreating deer, I fear he was not convinced.

Another singular shot was made by one of our party. He fired at a buck antelope, and struck it on the side of the horn, about three inches above the head. The effect of the shot was to wrench off the horn from the spiral bone which it covered. In fact it was simply *unscrewed*, and by the force of the shot was sent spinning several feet into the air. The buck escaped, but my friend brought the horn into camp ; and its appearance fully explained this remarkable shot.

At the southern end of the Nul were immense plains, covered with high grass. These plains were many miles in extent ; and during the heat of the day, when the whole atmosphere was trembling with heat and mirage, we had often no little difficulty, after shooting, to find our way back to camp. Large herds of antelope lay, during the day, in the long grass, coming in at nightfall to the cultivated lands, and returning to the grass at sunrise. Between the grass and the cultivation was a dead level plain, almost bare of vegetation, over which the deer were wont to cross in the early morning. Having marked the most frequented lines, we had pits, four feet deep, dug in this plain. Care was taken to spread all the excavated earth at a distance, so that the surface of the ground should present no unusual appearance.

Moving out from our tents before daylight, we took up our

position in these pits, and waited for the deer. About sunrise they would come on, straggling across from the fields. They never seemed to suspect danger ; and as we sat in our hiding-pits, with our eyes on the level of the plain, it seemed impossible that we were not seen. So well, however, did our poaching stratagem answer, that I have frequently slain deer from these pits with a charge of shot. By this means we were able to select the best bucks ; and got many handsome heads. I had a long shot one morning at a gaunt hyæna, but I believe 1 missed him. I was, however, consoled soon after by bringing down a buck with twenty-six inch horns.

About this time a Eurasian gentleman, who was employed in the same department with me, asked for the loan of one of my guns, having none of his own, and being anxious to prac-tise shooting.

I sent him a double smooth-bore, which was soon after returned with the following note :—

"Sir—I have the honour to return you herewith your gun, sound and in good condition, with the exception of the stock, which is broken across.　　　　　———"

It is but fair to him to add, that he did not ask for another.

CHAPTER VII.

I WAS joined in camp by an officer of a regiment stationed at
the Cape, who had come to India on a visit to his brother.
He was a light-hearted pleasant man, ardently devoted to the
chase in all its branches; sang a good song, and smoked a goodly
allowance of strong tobacco. Thrown as I was, at that time,
greatly on my own society, my companion was doubly welcome,
and my shikarees and horses were at all times at his disposal.
On coming in from his first day's shooting he somewhat
startled us by the announcement that he had shot several
rams. We requested an explanation, and he then told us
that at the Cape the males of all antelope were styled "rams,"
and he had imported the term to India. Perhaps he was right;
antelopes are more goats than deer, and, I believe, horn-shed-
ding deer are unknown at the Cape. At the time my friend
joined me, the crops of millet were still standing, and the
Saiseen antelope and chinkara, or gazelles, lay up, during the
heat of the day, in the high grain. We used to beat these
fields with a party of men on horseback, all our grooms and
followers being mounted on every available horse or pony.
The grain stood eight and ten feet high, and men on foot could

hardly have preserved an efficient line. One day, having been detained at office work till 4 P.M., I went out with my friend to hunt up the fields near the camp. Placing our line of cavalry quietly along the side of a square field, we moved along the flanks to the far end. As I walked slowly ahead, I saw a buck chinkara turn the far-away corner of the field, and come running down straight at me. I was evidently unobserved, and I stood still till he came within thirty yards. We were armed with smooth bores, loaded with BB shot, and I rolled him over dead. At that moment a doe broke out from the field, and was going across the open ground, when I turned her over with the second barrel. We then beat two or three fields blank, and I mounted my shooting pony, and joined the line of beaters. As we moved through the high grain I saw a fine black buck lying down about twenty yards ahead. He apparently thought that we should pass without observing him, but, checking my pony, I fired, and he rose, and dashed back through the line. I was afraid to shoot again, as my men were irregular in their movements. One of them was some 200 yards in rear, and I heard him call out that he had seen a wounded buck. At that moment I heard a shot from my friend, who had gone ahead to the corner of the field, but being anxious to secure the buck, I gave the word to the line to retire, and went back after the wounded deer. We soon came on him. He lay in a natural position, but his eye was vacant, and he was evidently much exhausted. Quickly dismounting, I succeeded in laying hold of his horns, and he was soon gathered to his fathers. My friend's shot had killed a fine doe antelope, and we returned home at sunset with four deer ;—a fair afternoon's work.

The next hot season I was encamped, for some weeks, at Wasna Kelea, about five miles north of Dholka. The country was a good deal enclosed, but was well stocked with chinkara, and I generally brought in a buck shot in my evening walk.

My Cape friend was, I think, sorry to leave us. He was a most persistent sportsman, but somewhat jealous withal, and inclined to claim his full share of the bag. On one occasion we had discharged our rifles at a flock of coolen, from a distance of several hundred yards. Four barrels were fired, and the result was, " one killed." As we had fired into "the brown" of them, neither could claim the bird ; my companion, however, declared that it fell to his shot, and, not caring to alloy his happiness, I did not dispute his statement. We parted, and I have never seen him since ; but I have a vivid recollection of pleasant days spent with him in the Guzerat plains.

Shooting two antelope at one shot is by no means uncommon ; I have done so on several occasions. One morning, having worked up towards a herd with my shooting-cart, I got within range of the best buck. He was standing broadside on, and immediately beyond him were several does. I fired, and the buck started, but kept his legs and went off at speed. Instead of the usual sound of a ball striking a deer, I heard a sharp cracking noise, and as the does scattered I saw one of them kicking on the ground. Observing that the buck had gone off at his best speed, and had not bounded in the air as is their custom when unwounded, I kept my eye on him, and sent my attendant with the cart to pick up the doe, which had been shot through the head. The buck soon slacked his pace, and presently subsided into a walk. I felt convinced he was hit somewhere, but as he moved straight away I was unable to distinguish any wound with my spy-glass. I therefore quietly followed. After going about half-a-mile, the buck stood still, reeled, and fell. I at once ran up, but he was dead before I reached him. The ball had passed through the neck, cutting a large vein, and travelling on had killed the poor doe. The buck had bled to death.

To the west of Dholka is a long string of pools called the "Rore," which, during the rainy season, are united into a sort of river. In the hot weather they are merely a succession of sluggish ponds, and in some of these alligators congregate. They are, I believe, harmless, but probably only owing to want of opportunity. We fired at several, and some of these we found dead on the bank next morning.

They are very numerous in the Watruk river, near its junction with the Samburmuttee. Close to the confluence the former river makes a large bend, almost enclosing a considerable tract of cultivated land. I was shooting there on one occasion with a friend, when I wounded a black buck, breaking his hind leg. My companion signalled to his groom, who came running up with his horse and spear. Mounting, he at once gave chase. The buck made straight for the bend of the river, and, knowing that the stream was deep, and about fifty yards in width, I concluded that he would be overtaken and slain on the bank. I followed on foot, but on arriving at the river I saw my friend standing on the opposite side, drenched with water, and minus his spear and stirrups. The wounded buck had swum across, closely followed by the horseman. When half-way over, the latter saw the heads of alligators appear above water in most unpleasant proximity.

Numerous at all times at this spot, they were probably rendered more lively than usual by the blood of the wounded buck. The situation must have been disagreeable, and especially so when, on reaching the opposite side, my friend found his horse floundering in deep mud, and unable to mount the bank. Close to the edge the water was deep enough to cover the saddle, and, as the horse floundered, the stirrup-leathers came away from the hooks, and they fell to the bottom.

With great presence of mind the rider drove his spear into the mud to mark the spot, and, throwing himself from his horse, scrambled ashore. Retaining his hold of the reins, he managed to guide his horse along the bank, and at length got him to dry land. We vainly endeavoured to recover the stirrups. The water was too deep to allow a man to feel for them with his feet when wading, and too muddy for diving operations. The knowledge that the water was full of alligators did not encourage us in our search.

I have seen as many as thirty of these reptiles, some of them twelve and fourteen feet in length, basking on the mud in the noonday sun, within a few hundred yards of the spot where my companion crossed. The wounded buck escaped from us, but was no doubt soon killed by jackals and wolves.

Near the head of the Gulf of Cambay very good antelope-shooting can be obtained, but the country is bare and desolate to behold, and contains large areas of uncultivable waste. In few spots can a tree be found to shade the sportsman's tent, and this inhospitable region should only be visited during the cold months. I was encamped there with a friend in the latter part of the year 1855. We had lately arrived from Surat, and after a ride of about sixteen miles, from the town of Dhollera to our tents, we breakfasted, and ordering our horses and a shooting-cart to be got ready, went forth for the first day of the season. As we were neither of us new at the work, and preferred to combine sport with conversation, we shot together, taking alternate chances. At sunset we returned to camp, having four handsome black bucks in the cart. Antelope abounded in all directions, and before we left the neighbourhood we had a goodly show of heads and skins.

I was out one evening with only a native attendant, when I observed an unusual object on the black salt plain, about half-a-mile ahead. With the glass I could see something move, so, directing the cart to follow, I dismounted, and taking my rifle I advanced. When within 300 yards of the spot I saw a wolf rise from a slight hollow where it had been lying, then another, and a third. They stood looking at us for some time, and then went off slowly, watching us all the time.

I endeavoured to approach them by directing the cart to move in an oblique direction ; but they were very suspicious, and the distance between us seemed to increase. One of the three was much larger than his companions, and I turned my attention to him. He was an immense beast, with shaggy tufts of hair about his neck, and altogether seemed a very respectable patriarch. My rifle was sighted to 250 yards, and, despairing of getting a closer shot, I raised the highest sight and fired. I saw the dust fly as the ball struck the ground fifty yards short of the wolf ; but the line of fire was correct, and the ricochet took him almost through the heart. He dashed forward at a headlong pace, with his tail whirling in the air, and his head coming lower at every stride. After going a short distance he fell over—dead. I was much pleased with this shot, for the wolf must, at the time I fired, have been at least 300 yards from me, and I generally considered it good shooting if I could make sure of a buck at 100.

Shooting one morning near this place, I wounded a buck, which I followed on horseback for several miles before I secured him. I had left my cart far behind, so, sticking my spear into the ground, I attached to it a white handkerchief, to mark the spot in the grass. On rejoining the cart, I directed my men to bring in the buck, and rode off into

camp. When they arrived at the spot, they found a couple
of wolves feasting on the deer, and in nowise deterred by
the flag which I had set up. Wolves are very bold at times,
and will attack and carry off lambs and kids from the flocks
in broad daylight.

At a village named Gaumf, a few miles north-west
of Dhollera, we had good antelope-shooting. They seemed
to do considerable damage in the wheat-fields ; but owing
to apathy, or to the religious prejudices of devout Hindoos,
they were seldom molested by the natives. On the contrary,
the tendencies of some of the inhabitants were strongly
in favour of the most stringent game-laws. One of my
friends went out one morning after deer, and, after some
trouble, had succeeded in working his shooting-cart towards
a herd, when he saw a horseman wildly careering towards
the game, shouting frantically, and waving a white cloth.
The herd was thoroughly startled, and fled over the plain,
and the sportsman referred to, who was a man of a gentle
disposition and well-regulated mind, unwilling to suppose
that he would be wantonly annoyed, went in quest of more
game. A second time he was about to approach a herd of
deer which he had espied on the plain, when the horseman
again appeared, and, wheeling his horse in giddy circles,
again scattered the deer. A third time my friend went on
after a fresh herd, when it was suggested to him by some of
his attendants that the lively horseman had been told off for
the duty of scaring the deer by the Bunneah, or trading
community, by whom the taking of animal life is regarded as
a deadly sin. He therefore watched his movements, having
previously directed his own groom, with his trusty Arab, to
keep near the shooting-cart. A herd of deer now came in
sight, and seeing that the persecutor was again in attend-

ance and bent on mischief, the Highland blood of my friend was raised, and he resolved to stop the annoyance. Springing on his horse, he grasped his spear—nine feet of tough bamboo—and, turning the blade behind him, he cantered towards his tormentor. The latter now turned his horse, and, not caring for a closer acquaintance, urged his steed towards the village whence he had come. As far as *he* was concerned, the wrong man was in the right place ; and before he could reach a friendly shelter, the incensed hunter had overtaken him, and he received the chastisement he had so well earned.

Returning to our camp one evening, we were disturbed by an alarm among the servants, who said they had seen a large snake in a hollow fig-tree at the edge of the pond, and close to the spot which they had chosen for our kitchen. Presently one of them called out that he could see the tail of the snake, and, taking up hog-spears, we ran to the spot. The tail of the snake was plainly visible, and I succeeded in nailing him with my spear to the tree. My companion then made another dig, and pinned him, six inches nearer the head. The snake was large and strong, and was only drawn out with much difficulty ; but, by alternate spearing, we forced him out and slew him. He was of the daman or water species—about nine feet in length, and as thick as a man's arm. The natives say that these snakes are not venomous, but that they are capable of inflicting severe blows with their tails. I have never heard of an authenticated case.

Riding round a small lake one morning, I observed one of these snakes, seven or eight feet in length, lying motionless among the weeds near the water. Its head seemed swollen to a great size, and the mouth especially presented an unusual appearance. I carried a stout walking-stick, so, dismounting, I struck the snake a sharp blow. It gave a frantic wriggle, and disgorged from its throat a bull-frog of the largest size. The head of the frog was protruding from the mouth of the snake, which seemed to have already swallowed the rest of its victim. On being liberated, the frog disappeared among the weeds.

The country to the north-east of Kattyawar, on the border of the Dundooka Pergunnah, affords great attraction to the sportsman during the cold weather. In many parts good hog-hunting may be got ; and, owing to the country being seldom visited by European sportsmen, antelope-shooting can be enjoyed in perfection. I was encamped with a friend— now, I regret to say, no more—at the village of Raanpore. Several hogs were known to be in the sugar-fields near our tents, and we found and hunted them successfully. Of them more anon. A white antelope was said to be in the neighbour- hood, and we were anxious to bag him. It was one of those fine bracing mornings in the Christmas week, when one can almost forget what the heat of Guzerat really is, that we set forth. To increase our chance of falling in with the "albino," we agreed to hunt separately, each making a circuit towards a certain village about eight miles off. We left our camp about 9 A.M., and, mounting our horses, set out, accompanied by well-appointed shooting-carts, and attendants on foot bearing our rifles. I had not been long out before I observed a herd of antelope feeding in a cotton-field. Working the cart to- wards them, I dropped a good buck. Having cleaned and placed him on the cart, we moved on. Before long I had another shot, but the ball fell short, and the buck escaped. Unfortunately, I found that the deer, when scared, were in- clined to travel in the same direction as that in which I wished to hunt, and I had to make a wide circuit to avoid driving before me the herd containing the buck which I had missed.

I now came on a fresh herd, and acquitted myself better, another good buck being placed in the cart. However, I found I was getting far away from our point of rendezvous, and I was obliged again to alter my course. In a bit of un-cultivated waste, partially covered with thorny scrub, I saw a herd of chinkara feeding. Among them was a fine buck, who stood on a small rising ground, watching our advance. Leaving my horse, I went on with the cart, and the deer seemed to think we were not very dangerous, for they only moved across our front, and went on feeding among the "bair" bushes. Some of the does were very tame, but, as I wanted the buck, I reserved my fire; and my patience was rewarded, for he soon gave me a fair chance, and I dropped him in his tracks. There were two smaller bucks with the herd, but I did not fire again. Unlike the Saiseen antelope, the chinkara do not congregate in large numbers. More than eight or ten are seldom seen together. Four or five is a more usual number, and the bucks are often found singly. It was now past midday, and knowing that my friend would be waiting for me, I headed straight for our meeting-place. But my attention was soon called to large numbers of ante-lope moving in a northerly direction. The plain seemed alive with them, and I think several thousand must have been in sight. Far away, in a distant herd, I saw a white speck, and after examining it with the glass I became certain that this was the buck we were after.

The herds had evidently been alarmed, and I had no doubt that my friend had started them. Taking no notice of the others I moved across the line in which the herds were travelling. Some were shy, others gave fair chances, but I would not shoot. I hoped that by moving through the others, without alarming them, I might be able to pass in rear of the herd containing the white buck. As I afterwards learnt, my friend had fallen in with him early in the day, and had fired without success, and he was not again inclined to allow himself to be approached. The country was quite open and level; and even had the ground been favourable, the numberless deer scattered in all directions over the plain destroyed all hope of stalking him. I dodged after him for nearly a mile. I was far from home, and the sun was getting low. The deer seemed to suspect that all was not right, and I saw that my chance of a standing shot was small. At that moment some of the other deer took alarm at my horse, which was led at a considerable distance behind the cart. They trotted forward, and the white buck moved across my front to join them. He was about 150 yards from me. Aiming somewhat in front, I fired; the buck reeled, and then went off at a long trot. My second barrel missed, but as he did not increase his speed, I made sure I should get him unless daylight failed me. With the aid of the glass I could make out that he was shot through the body, but well forward. Presently, to my great satisfaction, he halted and lay down in a cotton-field. I waited for half-an-hour to allow the shot to take effect, and then mounting, I rode straight at him. He rose, and went off at a good pace. But I found I could keep up with him. At length I succeeded in turning him, and then I knew he was safe. He gave in soon after, and, well pleased with the day's work, we turned homewards. After going two or three miles, I directed my men to follow, and, mounting my horse, rode off towards our camp. I had not gone half-a-mile when I saw what seemed to me to be a very large jackal sitting in a cotton-field between the rows of plants. Checking my horse to a walk, I moved slowly along, to see how near he would allow me to approach. As I advanced the beast crouched down, keeping his eye fixed on me, and I then made him out to be a wolf. Without halting, I made a wide circuit, and moved back till I met my gun-bearer. Making the horse over to him, I took the rifle and advanced on foot towards the wolf. He had evidently been watching my movements, and had slunk away to some distance from the spot where I had seen him. At length he left the shelter, and soon after stood out in the open. Being under the impression that the wolf I had seen was crouching close by, I reserved my fire, and it was not till I had searched for some time that I saw I was mistaken. All this time the wolf stood looking at us from a distance of 200 yards. Raising my rifle, I fired. The light was very uncertain, and I had not much hope of bagging him; but I heard that the ball told, and, mounting my horse, I went after him. The shot had taken him through one of the hind legs, which swung helplessly as he ran. I was soon up with him, but gaining some low bushes, he dodged me for a few minutes.

At length I succeeded in spearing him, much to the delight of a shepherd who came by on his way home, and who held my horse while I finished off the wolf. Cutting off its head, I threw it into the cart, and reached home rather tired.

My bag was—two black bucks, a buck chinkara, the wolf, and the white buck. Bowles had bagged two black bucks, and missed the white one; after which he went off to the village at which we had agreed to meet; and, directing his men to feed his horse and bullocks, sat down under a tree. While peacefully smoking, he observed a number of villagers

assembling and coming towards him, headed by some of the
Bunneah caste. One of these came up and demanded by
what right the great sin of deer-slaying had been committed.
Seeing only one European, and knowing that he himself had
all the village at his back, this man was most impertinent ;
and, fearing violence, Bowles made a sudden move, and succeeded in reaching his rifle, which fortunately the crowd had
not observed. The gallant Bunneah was about to beat a
retreat, when my friend collared him, and, after giving him
and his followers an instructive lesson on religious toleration,
he was allowed to go ; but not before he had made an ample
apology, and many profound salaams.

CHAPTER VIII.

PANTHERS were often found in the neighbourhood of Raanpore, and several had been shot by Bowles before I joined him
there. Most of them had been killed during the hot season,
when all crops save small patches of sugar-cane, left for seed,
were off the ground. The canes being irrigated to keep them
green, the ground in these fields was always cool and damp.
The canes gave good shade, and the presence of a panther was
generally indicated by his footprints in the moist earth. Left
to themselves, the cultivators would have cut the canes on the
outside of their fields ; but, in the hope of getting rid of the
panthers, they were often willing to cut rides down the middle,
of a sufficient breadth to allow of a snap shot at a panther
crossing. My friend on these occasions shot with a double
smoothbore, with two balls in each barrel ; and, taking up his
position at the end of the ride, he would wait for the panthers
to be driven across by a line of beaters with drums and
tom-toms.

If the panther was missed, as not unfrequently happened,
the beaters retired, and, moving round outside the field, would
proceed to drive him back. Sometimes a panther would be
wounded and claw a beater ; but, on the whole, there were

not many accidents, and the cultivators turned out readily to join in the hunt.

One morning, when going out after deer, etc., we had occasion to skirt a small garden outside a village, and in some fine sand we saw the recent footprints of a large panther. The hut of the gardener was close by, and on asking him if he had seen the beast, he replied that he had heard him near the spot about an hour before the daylight that morning. The garden was bounded by a dry watercourse; and on the far side was a patch of rough ground, covered with high grass and mimosa trees. We had little doubt that we should find the panther here; and a few villagers having been collected, they formed a line with some of our own people, and beat out the cover towards the guns. The men had passed over the more likely spots, and were advancing over some open ground, when the panther—which had been lying in the grass under a small bush—rose and came bounding towards us. Bowles was stationed about fifty yards to my left, and the panther was passing within a few paces, when he rolled him over like a hare with a very clever shot. He was a very large male panther, unusually heavy and stout, with a beautifully marked skin. The villagers were much pleased and astonished, and brought out offerings of milk and sugar.

At our next camp chinkara were very numerous; but we were in a lazy mood, and sent our men out to look for tracks of panthers in the cypress jungle, lying by the bed of a river. Having heard of nothing by noon, we proposed to go out together to shoot chinkara. We were to fire alternate shots, and only at bucks, and were to return to the tents when we had shot ten. We had been out about two hours, and had five good bucks in the cart, when we were overtaken by one of our men, who said they had found a panther's track in the cypress. We therefore gave up the chinkara-shooting, and went off to the river-bed, which, at this time, was a broad expanse of white sand, without any water.

On either side were strips of cypress. We were posted on the river side of one of these, and our men went round to drive the panther across. They had beat close up to us; and I had seen nothing but a wild sow, surrounded by a litter of squeakers. I had ceased to expect the panther, and was picking off young shoots from the bush before me, when I saw the beast walking towards me, and within three paces. I was quite startled; my rifle lay in the hollow of my left arm, and as I jerked it into my hand, the panther sprang to one side. I fired hurriedly and missed. Some bushes intervened; and, when I next saw him, he was bounding across the open bed of the river. He passed through the cover, and up the opposite bank, and was lost in some ravines. Next morning we hunted in vain for his tracks; we never saw him again.

I made a note in my memory—"Never consider a beat to be over till the last man has cleared out of the covert."

It was about Christmas, in the year 1855, that we were last camped at Raanpore. We were greeted one morning on waking by the welcome intelligence of a sounder of hog having been seen in the early dawn entering a field of sugar-canes near our tents. We sent out our own people to verify the statement of the villagers; and, instead of guns and rifles, boots and spurs were the order of the day. About breakfast time our shikarees returned and reported that they had seen the tracks of several pigs, and that two were marked down in some sugar-canes. We were somewhat doubtful of our horses, for that of my friend, though a stout well-bred Arab, had only recently arrived from the dealer's stables at Bombay, and had

never been tried after hogs.   My own had been out before, and
I had killed pigs off him, but he was a hot fiery beast when
excited, though at other times gentle as a lamb, and would
follow me along the road like a dog.   We mounted at about
10 A.M., and moved off to the ground, where we found upwards
of thirty villagers assembled.   When we had quietly taken up
a position, the beaters entered the cane-field, and soon a large
sow broke and went off at speed.   We did not give her
much law, nor, indeed, did she require it, for the ground was
in her favour, being uneven, and intersected with watercourses.
Farther on, it was more favourable for horses, and we now
gained on the flying pig.   I could not pay much attention to
my friend, for my own horse pulled like a mad beast, and I
had some difficulty in keeping him steady.   At length we
closed on the sow, but her speed was wonderful, and she cleared
thorn-hedges like a greyhound.   Nevertheless the pace was
evidently telling on her, and I succeeded in delivering my
spear behind her shoulder.   The pig gave a sudden twist, and
nearly wrenched the spear from my hand, but I held on, and
got clear away.   In another moment my friend planted his
spear in a vital spot, and she rolled over, dead.   She was one
of those long-legged, lanky sows, which I have generally found
give good runs.   Their pace is much faster than that of an old
boar, whose sense of dignity usually prevents him from a too
hasty retreat from his foes.   After breathing our horses we
returned to the cane-field, as our men were certain that it held
another pig.   Their supposition was correct, and we soon knew
by the shouts of the beaters, who had now re-entered the covert,
that something was on foot.   Presently a fine stout boar jumped
out, and stood hesitating by the edge of the sugar-canes.   But
the line of beaters was advancing on him, and having apparently made up his mind about his line of country, he bounded

off. Fearful lest he should turn back to the covert we let him get well away before starting; but our horses had seen him break away, and mine was nearly wild with excitement, and danced as if on hot plates. At last we started, riding steadily together, with a strong pull on the bridles. The boar took over a fine open country, with light soil, and ground free from holes or cracks, and we saw that his fate was sealed. By the backward glance of his eye we knew he would do mischief if he could, and his long white tushes warned us to be careful. Letting out my horse a little, I suddenly closed on him, but he swerved, and was getting away, when at that instant Bowles planted his spear between his ribs. On receiving the thrust, he charged across the front of his pursuer, and the shaft of the spear, coming against the horse's chest, was knocked out of his hand, and remained sticking in the boar, who at once pulled up and stood at bay, determined to die game. Bowles' horse would not go near him, and it was in vain that he tried to recover his spear, for the boar always met him with a vicious charge. Watching my opportunity, I put my horse into a gallop, and delivered my spear as I passed. The thrust was a deadly one, and as the boar staggered, Bowles cantered past and succeeded in regaining his spear, and a few more thrusts laid low the boar. This run had taken us to some distance from our shikarees, who, with the beaters, now came up, and the boar having been hung on a pole was sent off to our tents. Meanwhile, our horses were attended by their respective grooms, the saddle-girths were slacked, and the gallant steeds had their mouths washed out with water while we smoked a quiet pipe under the shade of a mimosa tree. The beaters held an animated discussion over the events of the morning, and the merits of the horses and their riders. We should have returned to the camp after the last run, but we had been informed that a cotton-field in the vicinity was often frequented by pigs, and we settled that we should form a long line, and beat it up before going home.   Accordingly, after a halt of about an hour, we were again in the saddle, and on arriving at the ground we advanced at either end of the line of beaters.   After going about half-a-mile, we saw the men in the centre run back a few paces, and soon a young boar jumped up and went away. We followed him at once, and I now, for the first time, learned from experience, what I had often before heard, viz., that a pig going through cotton cannot get up any pace.   This is, no doubt, owing to the stalks and pods of the plants striking him on his nose and eyes.

We closed on him hand over hand, and I soon secured the tushes, which were of fair size, though small in comparison of those of the big boar we had slain in the morning.

He turned at once, and charged at Bowles, whose young horse behaved very well, and enabled his rider to stop him cleverly.   By this time I was on him again, and he was soon following his kinsfolk to our camp.   Altogether we were at Raanpore about ten days, and we made a fine mixed bag. Bowles intended to visit the Geer of Kattyawar, during the following hot season, for the purpose of lion-hunting, a pursuit which he had followed the previous year with some success. In addition to bagging several full-grown lions, he had succeeded in capturing a fine cub, which he brought to Surat, where it wandered at will about our house during the rainy season.   It was then about as large as a Clumber spaniel, and very good-natured, except at feeding time.   Having got out of a verandah on the first floor, it passed down the weatherboards, and, jumping to the ground from a height of about eight feet, strained its back and fore-legs, and soon after died. I have had bears, panthers, and tigers, at various times, as household pets, but none of them were so good-natured and docile as this young lion. We were sorry to break up our shooting-camp when we had to return to our respective districts ; and poor Bowles never lived to make his second excursion to the Geer, for within six months of our parting at Raanpore he was laid in the graveyard at Ahmedabad.

One of our favourite hunting grounds was at Santhul, about four miles east of Dholka. Here the Samburmuttee river flows over a wide sandy bed, having, in many parts, large patches of cypress, in the cool shade of which the wild pigs delight to lie during the heat of the day. My men were always on the look-out, and when I learned from them that there were fair hunting prospects, I sent intimation to my friends in the cantonment, and forthwith a meet of the Hunt was arranged, and was attended by all lovers of the noble sport who could get leave of absence.

At one of these meets I wandered out one morning near the tents, and came on the bed of an extensive pond, which, with the exception of three or four deep holes about eight yards in width, was dried up. As I stood near one of these holes I observed a large fish rise to the surface, and I at once concluded that all the fish of the pond were probably collected in these holes. I accordingly returned in the evening with one or two of the party, taking with me the casting-net which I always carried in my shooting-cart. This I threw into the largest hole, and drew it out filled with fish of several kinds, and of all sizes. Subsequent casts were equally successful, and we returned to the tents with a good supply.

I was hunting at Santhul with my friend Major Johnson, and in some sugar-canes near the river we started a stout boar. Johnson was well mounted on a hunter of good repute, while I had only my galloway, a strong beast about 13.3 in height.

He was, however, a very fast pony, and entered fully into the
spirit of the chase, and would double and turn after a boar
almost of his own accord. The pig made across an enclosed
country, and gave us some sharp scrambles over and through
the cactus hedges. At length he turned and made for the
river, the bank of which at this place was rather abrupt. We
were close on him when he dashed into the broad shallow
stream, but the uneven sand was scooped out in parts by the
action of the water, and we had two or three desperate flounders before reaching the other side. Here we came on a considerable breadth of cypress, which would be under water in
the rainy season, and beyond this, at a distance of some 300
yards, was the other bank of the river, a steep slope of 30 or
40 feet. The cypress covert was all ridge and furrow, caused
by floods, and was very awkward to cross at a rapid pace.
The boar held on as though he would go up the bank, and,
thinking to spear him on the ascent, Johnson urged his horse
to the front, but, with a sudden swerve, the pig turned up the
river, while the horse shot up the bank and was completely
thrown out. My galloway behaved admirably, turning sharp
with the boar, and, as we were now running up the sandy
furrows, we were enabled to put no more steam. The boar,
however, kept his lead, and Johnson, who was galloping along
the top of the bank, and unable to find a place to descend,
could not render any assistance. At length I began to close
on the pig, and had made up my mind that I was to get the
tushes, when, to my horror, my friend, with his horse quite
fresh, having found a path down the bank, came by me hand
over hand, and shooting past took the first spear. I gave the
second, and the boar fell dead. Johnson was greatly excited,
and his conscience smote him for depriving me of the spear
for which I had worked so hard. "By Jove," said he, "you

rode that pig well! I had no right to take that spear! It was an awful shame!" With that he commenced shaking me violently by the hand, and pouring forth expressions of admiration and respect. It would have been amusing for a looker-on to see two Britons standing by their reeking horses, in the bed of the Indian river, shaking hands over the gory carcass of the dead boar.

We were returning to our camp one evening after a day's hunting, and I was riding alone in advance of the rest of the party when I heard shouts behind me, and presently saw the caps of some of the riders bobbing along on the far side of a high hedge. I stood wondering what to expect, when a large porcupine came bolting through the hedge and ran across a field. I gathered up my reins and rode at him, but his quills were rattling, and my horse did not seem to know what to make of him. At last I managed to spear him ; but before I could turn my horse again, he disappeared into his burrow. The other sportsmen now came up, and with them a number of beaters.

About sixty yards off was a stream of water, running from a well to a neighbouring sugar-cane field. All hands were at once set to divert the runnel to the porcupine's hole, which we succeeded in flooding. The wounded beast, together with two or three others and a civet cat, bolted out and was slain. We had some of the porcupine's flesh cooked for dinner, much to the disgust of our servants, who looked on them as unclean beasts. The flesh seemed white and good, and I believe if it had had fair play in the kitchen, we should have liked it well enough ; as it was, I did not care much for it.

A favourite meet was at Suheej, a few miles farther down the river. I was camped at this place with my friend Bulkley in the month of May. The heat was intense ; but this was in

some respects in our favour, as the pigs were attracted to the
cypress in the bed of the river.   We left our tents about
9 A.M., our shikarees having been out before daybreak.   They
met us on the ground, and reported that several hogs had been
seen in the early morning entering the covert.   Soon after the
beaters began to move, a well-grown boar left the jungle, and
ascending the bank, went off slowly over the open country.
We gave him a good start, and then cantered after him.   By
the time we topped the bank he was well away, and we now
increased the pace and closed up to him.   On finding himself
pursued, he halted, looked round for a moment, and then went
off at score.   We now went at him in earnest, and both being
well and evenly mounted, we had a most exciting chase.   The
pace was good throughout, and the boar ran true for some distant sanctuary, which he was doomed never to reach.   I had
got the best place, being on his left quarter ; and as I made
a rush at him, I made sure of the spear, but with a sudden
swerve he shot across my front, nearly upsetting my horse,
and I missed him.   He was less fortunate with Bulkley, who
stopped him with a thrust behind the shoulder, and as the
blood streamed from his mouth we saw that his race was run.
He struggled gamely on for a short distance, but my second
attempt was more successful, and poor piggy was laid low.
We were now joined by our grooms and a few beaters, the
main body having been quietly drawn out of the covert by the
shikarees as soon as the pig broke away.   The boar was slung
on a pole and carried back to the river ; and having breathed
our horses we remounted and returned to our old places.   On
reaching the high bank which bounded the cypress covert, we
observed a monster boar crossing the broad shallow stream,
and making for a patch of cypress of some extent on the other
side.   In a position commanding a full view of this covert,

we had placed a native in a tree as a marker. As we could
see him plainly, and he made no indication of the boar having
gone on, we concluded he had lain up in the covert. We
therefore arranged to put the beaters again into the place
which we had first driven, and before long, another pig—a sow
this time—came out, and went off, taking much the same line
of country as the boar we had killed. She gave a very good
and fast run over some very rough ground, but our horses
carried us well and never made a false step. As we reached
some good riding ground we pressed in on her, and I took the
first spear ; on which she stood and seemed determined to act
on the offensive. Bulkley advanced at her at a walk—a
rather dangerous proceeding, as in the event of the spear
missing, both horse and rider are at the mercy of the pig,
which can make its rush and do damage before its foes can
get away.

Bulkley, however, stopped her, but so determined was
the charge that she managed to run in on the spear and bit
him sharply in the foot. Fortunately he was protected by a
stout deer-skin boot, and before farther mischief could be
done I had turned and given her the *coup de grace*. Again
returning to the river, we were met by grooms leading a
couple of galloways, which we mounted, sending off our
horses to the tents. We partook of a slight refreshment, and
as we smoked our pipes we formed the plan of attack on the
big boar which we had seen crossing the river.

The beaters being sent round, we took up our positions,
and stood anxiously waiting the appearance of the monster.
Tom-toms and drums were loudly beaten, horns were blown,
and guns fired, but still no signs of the game ; and it was only
when the last man left the covert that I began to suspect the
true state of affairs. Leaving the beaters, our shikarees pro-

THE "GRIM GRAY,"—Nº I BULKLEY TAKES A MUD BATH.

ceeded to examine the ground round the cypress, and on coming to within a few yards of the tree on which our lookout man had been posted, they came on the tracks of the boar, leading up the bank. The villain had either slept on his post, or had been amusing himself by watching our runs in the morning, and had allowed the boar to pass up the bank unobserved. The footprints were not to be mistaken, for the boar was of the largest size.

Leaving the river, he had made a detour of about two miles in the open country, which, though cultivated, was at this season quite bare of crops. Our men were equal to the occasion, and taking up the track they moved quickly along, scoring the ground at every few yards with a short stick across the prints of the boar's hoofs. We now found that he was crossing a wide bend in the river, and that the tracks would again fall into the bed of the stream. The trackers moved fast and sure, and we followed close in their wake with the crowd of beaters. At length we came to where a smaller stream joined the river, and on the ground between the two was a crop of irrigated maize, about ten feet in height, and looking very cool and green. The smaller stream was about fifteen yards in width, slow and sluggish, having about a foot of water, and an equal amount of black mud below it. We had crossed and sent the beaters to the end next the junction of the streams, when we heard much yelling and shouting, and next moment the boar came out at speed, and dashed down the slope into the stream we had just crossed. Bulkley was only a few yards from him, and driving in his spurs he rushed down the bank, regardless or forgetful of the muddy bottom. His horse seemed to turn heels over head, and as I checked mine and floundered slowly across, he was picking himself out of the black mud and shaking his steed to his legs again.

He had lost his hunting-cap, and his spear was buried in the grimy slush. I reached the bank in safety, and gathering up my galloway I went on after the boar. From his great size and weight I was sure he would make a good fight, and I saw I had work cut out for me, so I determined not to irritate him with a minor poke, but, if possible, to disable or check him till such time as my friend should emerge from the mud and come to my assistance. As the boar went along at an easy canter, I saw I should have no difficulty in overhauling him. We were going up the side of a field, having a high mud-bank on our right; and watching my opportunity I lowered my spear and pressed my horse with the spur. In an instant I was alongside of the boar, and had my spear within a few inches of his shoulder, when, with a savage grunt, he made a sidelong charge at my horse. The spear took him in the neck and checked him, but with a sudden wrench he broke the bamboo shaft, leaving the head imbedded in his muscles. Turning my horse sharp to the left, I got clear away, but having only the headless spear-shaft in my hand, my offensive powers were at an end, and I saw that my only hope of getting the boar lay in being able to keep him in view till my friend should rejoin me. In this way we held on over many fields. At times I pursued and tried to turn the boar, at others he pursued me, and then I was forced to "advance backwards." Still no signs of my friend, and I began to fear that either he or his horse had been seriously damaged. The boar had nearly reached the spot from whence we had first started him in the morning, and as he went down the steep bank into the cypress cover I pulled up in despair. At that moment I saw Bulkley coming along at a hand-gallop, and with a frantic yell I again set off after the boar. Aided by Bulkley, I succeeded in turning him towards

THE "GRIM GRAY,"—N°. 2. THE BOAR CHARGES.

the water, into which he hurled himself and lay still, apparently dead beat. Springing from his horse, Bulkley lowered his spear and ran in at him, but the boar rose and charged. He was stopped by a thrust in the neck, but his great weight broke the bamboo, and though Bulkley managed to get away unscathed, we had no spears, and were now powerless for all purposes of attack. Unwilling to leave the wounded beast, and hoping that some of our men with spare spears would soon come up, we followed him slowly down the river, and seeing some cultivators irrigating their fields near the banks, Bulkley rode off to them in the hope of obtaining some offensive weapon.

Presently he came after me armed with a short crooked sword, but by this time the boar was going down a part of the river where he had an abrupt bank six feet in height on his immediate left. Bulkley vainly tried to force him out, as he found it impossible to reach him with the short sword. At length he made a cut, but the boar charging at the same moment ripped his horse in the foreleg, and finding that he could not again get him to go near the pig, he handed me the sword and I took up the running.

We here came to a tributary stream, joining the river at right angles. Into this we plunged, and as the boar swam almost on a level with my saddle, I rose in the stirrups and made a cut at him with all the force I could muster. Had the weapon served me truly, I should have laid the boar in two halves, but the blade of the sword, being merely fastened into the hilt with lac, fell out, and the pig turned on me. I had just time to fend him off with my hand, receiving as I did so a slight cut over the thumb from his tusk.

Wheeling my horse round, I got away from him, when he crossed the stream, and, turning up the other bank, left the main river. By this time he was nearly exhausted, and our shikaree appeared on the scene, having followed the run on foot. Another sword was procured from some cultivators. The shikaree carried his own, and one of his men had an iron-bound club. Leaving our panting steeds, we made a simultaneous rush on the boar, as he stood at bay in the water. He made a last charge, but the swords cut fairly this time, and the huge beast succumbed.

I have been in at the death of many boars, but I never saw a run so full of excitement as that which I have now endeavoured to describe.

We returned to our tents well satisfied with the day's work, and the leading incidents of the last run were committed to paper in a series of four spirited sketches by the ever-ready pen of my light-hearted friend. I have them by me now, but the hand of the limner has been chilled in death, never again to grasp the spear or guide his gallant steed in the soul-stirring chase of the grim gray boar.

THE "GRIM GRAY,"—N°3. THE SWORD BREAKS

THE "GRIM GRAY."—No. 4. DEATH OF BOAR.

CHAPTER IX.

> " Ready he stood right valiantly,
>   But ere he had time to strike,
>   The tusk of the Boar, more prompt than he,
>   Deep through the flesh, above the knee,
>   Ripped with a stroke oblique."
>
> MAGINN'S ' HOMERIC BALLADS.'

IN hunting the wild hog, injuries from their tushes are sometimes received both by horses and beaters; but it is seldom
that the riders suffer. The wound made by the tusk of a pig
on the human leg is, as I have already said, generally of the
form of the letter **L**—like a tear in woollen cloth.

It is wonderful that injuries to beaters are not more frequent than they are; for a boar will constantly break back,
and when the line is advancing, through cypress or high sugar-
cane, he often cannot be seen till he is almost upon the men.
We seldom, however, had any difficulty in assembling beaters,
and though at times they naturally expressed an objection to
move in on a wounded pig, yet, on the whole, they showed
great pluck, and a proper enjoyment of the sport.

The injury done was not always in proportion to the size
of the pig, and I have seen a horse badly cut by a small sow
with teeth only half-an-inch in length. We had been hunting

her in the cypress covert, when she broke back, and, in the centre of a small clear space of ground, was met by one of our party who was cantering up to join us. He rode fair at the pig, which never swerved an inch, but charged straight at the horse. The steed was fresh, and tried to jump over her ; but the sow, without slacking her pace, seemed to throw up her head, and just touch the horse on the hind leg as she passed on. The jump given by the horse caused the rider to miss his spear, and, as he turned to follow the pig, we saw a clean cut, five inches in length, down the shank of the hind leg. The horse was of course laid up for some time.

On another occasion I pursued a boar which had been driven from a cane-field. He crossed the bed of the Samburmuttee river soon after I had slightly pricked him, and we were thoroughly splashed by the time we reached the other side. The boar was a heavy one, and lazy, and I was soon alongside of him. On being again speared, he stood at bay. Turning my horse, I walked towards him, and, as I advanced, he charged. He was, fortunately, very groggy, and, missing his stroke, he stood under my horse's neck. In vain I tried to shorten my spear, which was dripping with water, and slipped through my hand ; and, after several tosses of his head, the boar struck his tusk into my horse's chest. At that moment he was killed by a thrust from another of our party. Dismounting, I found my horse streaming with blood from a deep but narrow wound, which we only staunched by pinning the sides together, and binding them up with thread.

There was a good covert for hog at Rheenjah, about eight miles south of Dholka. I was encamped there in the hot season of 1855 with Bulkley, and walking out one morning near the tents, we came on the fresh tracks of a goodly boar leading into a sugar-cane field. A few beaters were collected, and we went out in the afternoon.　Bulkley was mounted on a large iron-gray Arab, which had been sent out to his camp by a young gentleman who, I believe, was anticipating a visit from bum-bailiffs.　I rode my galloway, having no fear that so heavy a boar would be likely to beat us by speed.　He was soon started, and at once made for some extensive cypress covert in the bed of the river.　We therefore gave him short law, but unfortunately turned him into another cane-field. Across his path lay a dry thorn hedge, over four feet in height, which he cleared at a bound, like a deer.　We had some difficulty in again dislodging him, but this time he took a more favourable line, and, after letting him get well away, we went after him.　The iron-gray got the better of his rider, and bolted between two thorn hedges.　A bushy tree overhung the path, and, as he dashed under it, Bulkley had a narrow escape, for his hunting-cap was knocked off, his spear sent spinning out of his hand, and he sustained a severe contusion on the shoulder.

My galloway behaved admirably, and, putting his ears back, followed the boar closely ; but on passing through some thin jungle he breasted a mimosa sapling, covered with long sharp thorns, and, as he brushed over it, he received a smart blow on the head from the stem.　The boar then crossed some open ground, and I was close on him, when he seemed to think he had taken the wrong line of country, and pulled up sharp—sliding along the ground on his hind-quarters—then, turning suddenly, he retraced his steps at full speed.

My horse checked himself in an instant ; but so sudden was the movement that I was thrown off my balance, and the sharp strain snapped my stirrup-leather, and nearly brought me to the ground.　However, I managed to keep my seat, and wheeling round I soon closed again with the boar. In front of us lay a cactus hedge, fifteen feet high, and seeing that he would escape unless I speared before he arrived at it, I crammed my horse at him. Before he could reach the hedge my spear was into him ; but, though badly wounded, he struggled on, and passing through a gap got away.

Fortunately, at this moment, I was joined by Bulkley, who came up on the other side, and, meeting the boar, turned him back. He was afraid again to face the open ; but, sticking to the hedge, whose overhanging branches prevented our getting at him, he kept dodging back towards the sugar-cane, which was not far distant. Judging that if he could only reach its friendly shelter he would be safe from his pursuers, he at length made a rush. Just then I found an opening in the cactus, and, joining Bulkley, we raced after him.

About fifty yards from the canes was a steep green slope, at the top of which we both speared him at the same instant. Bulkley drove his spear from his stern to his chest, while mine passed through across his body, and as we let them go the transfixed boar rolled down the slope and lay dead at the bottom.

Altogether it was a most exciting chase, and we had reason to congratulate ourselves on the finish, for had we not slain the boar when we did, he would have reached the canes, and we should not again have been able to make him break cover.

Suspecting that my horse had got badly pricked by the mimosa thorns, I dismounted and examined his head. I found one spike driven through the cartilage of his nose, and another broken short off, just above the eye. Both were so firmly imbedded that I had to draw them out with my teeth but no bad consequences ensued.   This was the last boar which I saw killed on the Samburmuttee.

In the hot summer evenings we found some amusement at Rheenjah in shooting ducks in the neighbourhood.   The sport was conducted in a lazy manner, for on these occasions we started off in a shooting-cart, and with pipes alight drove down to the bed of the stream, where we halted.   About sunset, the ducks would fly up and down the river, within easy distance, and we shot them from the cart.   They were large fine gray ducks, with bright orange feet.

The rains were now not far off, and we had planned an excursion in quest of large game in the country towards Lunawarra. Our party consisted of four; to wit, Ashburner, Arbuthnot, Bulkley, and myself; and we had secured the services of a good shikaree in the person of old Bheeka, a sergeant in the Guzerat Koli Corps, who, with several of his own men, had been sent on about three weeks before us to examine the ground, and ascertain where tigers were to be found, so that we should lose no time in moving camps in quest of game.

Ashburner and Arbuthnot had preceded us.   Bulkley and I started one afternoon from Ahmedabad, and rode out a stage on borrowed nags.   Here we found our shooting-carts in readiness with hired bullocks, our own having been sent on to Kuppurwunj, which we hoped to reach early next morning. But the hired bullocks gave us much trouble, and, at starting, bolted and upset Bulkley; then they shut up, and crawled along at a wretched pace.   Fortunately, as the day broke, we got fresh ones from a village, but it was late before we reached Kuppurwunj.   Here we breakfasted, and after a hot ride of many miles we arrived at Beerpoor, where we met our friends.   Our carts arrived late in the afternoon.

Bheeka was in attendance—he had been busy, and told us of about eighteen beasts, which he had either seen or tracked, within the range of our operations. In one place were five tigers ; in another two ; in another a panther, and so on. It was arranged that we should first move on the five tigers ; beating "on spec" some likely places on the road ; but we found nothing, and by the time we reached our camp at Muggoree it was about 3 P.M.

The tigers were said to live in the bed of the Watruck river, about a mile from the village. On reaching the tents Bheeka and his men were brought up for consultation, and it was settled that nothing should be done till next morning, as it would be well not to disturb the covert : Bheeka then retired. Before long a man came running in and said that there was a tiger close by, and that the monkeys in the trees were swearing in their peculiar manner. We jumped up at once, and sent for Bheeka, but that worthy, on receiving his orders at 3 P.M., had departed to his own quarters in the village, where he forthwith proceeded to get drunk. He came up, wild and incoherent, and we saw at once that no work was to be got from either him or his men. We went out, however, and I saw the tiger, a male of the largest size, moving along the face of the hill. Some of us ran on and tried to head him, but he slipped away, and not seeing him again we returned to camp.

At nine next morning we moved out and went towards the river. We had only one elephant, and as it had never been tried, it was not much sought after by any of the party.

After examining the ground, we found that the tigers had taken up their quarters in a piece of very rough scrub by the river-side, covered with large stones, long grass, and thick green willow bushes, many of which were bent over and weighed down by large masses of driftwood carried down by floods during the monsoons.

We were all new at the work, and trusted a good deal to Bheeka, who, when sober, was a good shikaree. By his direction we were posted in trees at various points on one side of the cover, while the beaters advanced into the jungle with loud yells and beating of drums. Very soon the father of the family appeared ; he was no doubt the big beast we had seen the day before. He came out either to Arbuthnot or Ashburner, who were posted near each other, and one of them wounded him severely, turning him back into the jungle. On hearing the shots the beaters promptly drew back, and could not again be induced to enter the covert, but the yelling was redoubled.

My post was in a tree at the upper end of a small watercourse, about a hundred yards from the edge of the thick willows. My rifle had recently been re-stocked by a native artificer, who had so arranged the triggers that if placed on full cock both barrels would go together, or nearly so. When deershooting, I got over this difficulty by cocking one barrel only.

Soon after the old tiger had been wounded I saw a tigress leave the covert and come up the watercourse towards my tree. Forgetting the peculiarity of my rifle, I cocked both barrels, and when she was within thirty paces I fired. My rifle went off with a great report and a sharp recoil, and I then found I had let off both barrels.

The tigress fell forward, and remained quite motionless, neither moving tail nor paws. My gun-bearer, who was seated beside me, passed the second gun, a smoothbore, and I sat ready to fire in case the beast should move. From her position she looked as if merely checked by the report of my rifle, and crouching for a charge. Meanwhile the beaters remained yelling on the far side of the river, where they had perched themselves on trees commanding views of the covert, which they prudently did not attempt to enter.

My three friends left their passes and came towards me, but halted when I told them of the tigress. As she remained motionless, I began to think she must have been killed instantaneously, so calling on them to cover my descent, I came down, and we went up to her. She had been struck by both balls. One had entered about the root of the neck on the right side, passing out behind the left forearm, the other had taken her through the loins, and the combined results were that she had sunk—stone dead—in her tracks.

I was not in very robust health about this time, and the effect of the sun, which was very powerful, brought on a feeling of deadly sickness ; and, soon after coming down from my tree, I became violently ill. My comrades gave me weak brandy and water, and poured water over my head, and in about half-an-hour the more acute symptoms subsided, but I was not fit to go on.

My friends were vexed at losing the big tiger, which they had wounded badly, and they determined to go into the covert together and hunt him out. I did my utmost to dissuade them, but they had been reading Rice's accounts of tiger-shooting, and assured me they would advance shoulder to shoulder, and proceed with the utmost caution.

Mounting a riding camel, I returned to the tents, and kept quiet for the rest of the afternoon. My friends returned about 5 P.M., not having seen the wounded beast ; they had gone into the covert as they had proposed, and had seen one small tiger, at which one of the party had attempted to fire, but his rifle snapped ; and, altogether, I thought they had reason to congratulate themselves on their want of success.

As our men assured us that there were still a tigress and two large cubs in the covert, we went to the same ground next morning, and took up the same positions. I saw the tigress,

which came out for a short distance, and then turned back
to the willows. Then one of the cubs came out: he was a
small beast, about six feet from tip to tip. He stood broadside on at seventy yards, and I dropped him dead with one
shot.

The beaters had again taken to the trees, and declined
to enter the covert, so after a consultation it was agreed
that Ashburner and Bulkley should take up fresh positions in trees, and that Arbuthnot and I should go in with
a few picked men and drive out the tigress.

The chief of the village had come out with us that
morning, with a considerable following. Ashburner had
lent him a carbine, and he and his men also posted
themselves in a tree near the edge of the willows. We
hunted about for some time, and, as I now believe, we were
fortunate in not finding the tigress, who would certainly have
left her mark on one of us. As we came up to a thick patch
of willows, near the edge of the covert, several shots were fired
in our front by the chief and his men, and we heard their
bullets *ping* in the air as they glanced off the stones. Our
position was not a good one. A tiger—probably wounded—
somewhere close to us, and an excited chieftain firing "promiscuous" into the covert.

We shouted to him to "cease firing," and made the best
of our way out of the jungle. Going up to him, we found the
chief had fired at and killed the other cub, which lay dead
near his tree.

A palaver was now held, and as we believed that only
the tigress remained, and that her temper would not be
improved by the slaughter of her offspring, we decided on
leaving her alone for that day. So, getting some men
together, we carried out the two cubs, and were starting off

to our camp when we heard shouts from the covert, followed by the cry that a man had been seized by the tigress.

It turned out that a party of men, unconnected with us, who were passing near the place, had heard the shots, and from motives of curiosity had joined our people at the spot where the chief had killed the second cub. When all had left the covert, one of these men missed the scabbard of his knife, and returned to the spot where the cub had fallen, supposing he had dropped it there. He was accompanied by one of his friends, and as they approached the spot they came on the tigress licking the blood from the dead leaves. She charged on them at once, and as the unfortunate men turned to run, one of them was dashed to the earth. The tigress seized him in her teeth by the waist, driving her fangs deep into his body, and shaking him as a dog would a rat. She then slunk back into the willows, and had disappeared by the time we reached the place.

We feared from the first that the man's case was hopeless, but we had him carefully carried to the tent, where we dressed his wounds, and did all in our power, but he sank fast, and died next morning.

Apart from the feeling of regret for the poor man, we feared the event would seriously affect our success during the rest of the expedition; for though we were in no way to blame, and the man had met his death solely by his own rash act in returning to the jungle, yet he had died in our camp, and we knew we should get all the credit of his death among the country folks. We gave his friends money for the funeral expenses, and they carried off the body to be burnt at his native village.

Soon after they had left we went forth to hunt in the bed of the Watruck river, a few miles above the scene of the previous day's disaster. Some of our men had been out in the early morning, and had followed up the fresh track of a tiger into the willows which fringed the banks of the stream. At this spot the river was about eighteen inches in depth from bank to bank, and the sides, which sloped down sharply to within a few yards of the water, were clothed with thick green bushes.

The main river was joined by several deep and tortuous nullahs, partially filled with dry grass eight feet high, which had escaped the conflagration in the annual burning of the surrounding jungle. Altogether the spot was very tigerish. Away from the bed of the river the jungle was bare and stony, and the black ashes of the burnt grass seemed to render the heat more intense. The trees were clear of leaves, and the only shade to be got was on the north side of their trunks.

On this day Bulkley and Arbuthnot wished to try the elephant, so they mounted him together, and proceeded to beat down the bed of the stream towards Ashburner and myself, who were posted in trees on the bank. My tree was in a good position on the edge of a deep nullah, and mounting, with my gun-bearer, we perched ourselves and sat quiet.

We soon heard the elephant trumpet, and a glimpse was obtained of the tiger by those in the howdah ; but the trees hung so much over the water, and were so large and dense, that the elephant could only be driven in the centre of the stream. Stones were flung in freely from above, but the tiger would not again show, though we worked after him for two hours.

All this time I was sitting in the tree exposed to the full force of the blazing May sun, and I had another attack, similar to that from which I suffered on the first day. My attendant would not let me descend, as he said he was sure the tiger was not far off. So, tying the guns to the tree, he passed his turban round my body, and kept me in my place. We called to Ashburner, who was not far off, and he left his tree, and came with several men to our assistance and helped me down. We then left the river-bank, and I was placed in the shade of the trunk of a tree.

I began to feel rather better, and Ashburner had shouted to the others to come and have luncheon. He was busy unpacking the basket, when we heard a great uproar from the river, followed by two shots, and snatching up our rifles, we ran forward in time to meet Bulkley staggering up the bank with his clothes all torn and bloody.

They had dismounted from the elephant in the bed of the river, where they were joined by some of the beaters, and were on their way up the bank to join us at luncheon. Arbuthnot was somewhat in advance, and Bulkley followed with a number of beaters, when the latter suddenly called out " The tiger! the tiger!" and fled incontinently.

Bulkley wheeled round, and at that instant the tiger charged out. It had been lying in the deep shade caused by a mass of willows, bent over by a heap of drift and débris from the river; and Arbuthnot, and the men with him, must have passed within a few yards of it on their way up the bank. As the tiger charged, Bulkley fired both barrels in his face, but, failing to stop him, turned and endeavoured to get away. His foot slipped, and he fell forward against the bank. At that instant the tiger seized him by the back, just over the shoulder-blade, and carried him off for about twenty yards. Bulkley had probably wounded him in his charge, for he now dropped him and retired into the bush, and did not again show. The wounded man picked himself up, and met us as we advanced, and we supported him to the spot where we had been sitting.

Cutting open his clothes, we found his back fearfully lacerated, but the discharge of blood was not great. The tiger had lifted him by the muscles of the back, and that with no tender grasp ; but we could form no idea of the actual mischief done.

A litter having been constructed, we raised him and set off for the camp. His pluck was wonderful, and he conversed freely with us on the road, and explained the whole matter. On our arrival at the tent we made all preparations for taking him to the Baroda cantonment, distant about eighty miles, where we could place him under proper medical treatment. Meanwhile we carefully washed his wounds, and over the whole laid a huge flour poultice.

We marched that evening, carrying our friend on a cot, borne on men's shoulders, and by daylight next morning we had got over twenty-five miles. A tent was then pitched in the shade, and we kept him quiet till evening, when we again marched, and so arrived, after three or four days, at Baroda. Quinine and castor oil were given, and the general health of the patient carefully attended to.

The British Resident at the Guicowar's court, having heard of our disaster, sent out a skilled medical man, who met us about ten miles from the cantonment, and 'under whose charge Bulkley remained for a mouth, by which time his wounds were sufficiently healed to allow me to take him to Surat, which we reached in five marches. I remained with him while at Baroda, where my regiment—from which I was detached on staff employ—was then stationed.

Another shooting party was out, and, as their leave was up, we daily expected them in cantonments. One morning

a man arrived with the news that one of the party had been
wounded by a tiger, and was on his way in. Soon after,
Langton, of my regiment, was carried in on a litter. Two
days before, having left his comrades, he was on his way back
to Baroda alone. Hearing of a tiger in the bed of the Mhye
river, he went after and wounded it. The beast got away
among some rocks, and as Langton was endeavouring to dislodge him, he charged, knocked him over, and bit him through
the elbow-joint and thumb. The tiger then left him, and his
people got him home to his tent. Men were procured, and
having placed him on a litter, they set off towards the cantonment.

In this way they moved all that afternoon, the whole of
the following day, and the third till 11 A.M., when they reached
Baroda. The wounded man was quite sensible, and free from
any great pain, and gave us a full account of his misadventure.
We got him put to bed, and he soon after fell off into a drowsy
state, from which he never recovered. A brother officer and
I watched him during the night, and at 2 A.M. I saw such a
decided change come over him that I at once sent for the
doctor, who was himself on the sick list. All that was possible
was done for Langton, but he never rallied, and died in the
afternoon. He was buried next evening with military
honours. He had been in a nervous and excitable state for
some time previous to the accident, but there was no doubt his
death was accelerated by undue exposure to the sun after the
shock which he had sustained.

Bulkley and I had a severe march to Surat, which was
distant ninety miles. The rain fell in torrents, and in those
days the railway was not commenced. All the nullahs were
unbridged, and some could only be crossed on cots, floated on
large earthen pots, procured from the nearest village.

Bulkley was carried in a palanquin by about twenty men, and I rode, having previously removed my horse's shoes, which otherwise would have been drawn off by the tenacious mud.

On several occasions the bearers had to carry the palanquin on their heads, while I dismounted, and wading and floundering waist-deep, crossed stretches of water a quarter of a mile in width. So bad was the road, that by starting at daylight and allowing a couple of hours' halt at mid-day, we did not reach the end of a march of fourteen miles till some time after dark. However, no damage was done to my patient, and in Surat he again came under the doctor's hands. The wounds refused to close, and for upwards of twelve months continued to discharge, giving at times excessive pain. By my advice Bulkley then went down to Bombay, where he consulted an eminent surgeon. This man placed him under chloroform, and laying open the wounds, extracted considerable portions of the shoulder-blade which had been splintered off by the teeth of the tiger, and were keeping up a constant irritation.

Soon after this operation the wounds completely closed up. The foregoing chapter is, I think, worthy the attention of young sportsmen, and may warn them from attempting to follow up wounded or otherwise infuriated wild beasts on foot.

CHAPTER X.

In the hot season of 1856 I marched from Ahmedabad to Indore in Malwa. I had always heard of this part of Central India as a good sporting country, but I arrived too late in the year to be able to organise an expedition, even had I been able to get the necessary leave of absence. The country was all new to me, and I knew that the information of the natives around the cantonment was hardly to be relied on. Game there was in plenty within sixty miles ; but without good shikarees little could be done by a stranger.

The Mhow cantonment was distant only fourteen miles, and some few of the officers employed shikarees ; but they were only to be got to work by high pay and large rewards, and, as a rule, confined their services to the garrison. The Vindyah range of mountains was close to Simrole, twelve miles from Indore, where the table-land of Malwa ceased, and the ground fell away to the valley of the Nerbudda river. The intervening country was very rugged ; covered with hills and deep ravines. Bradford, of the Madras Cavalry, started with me to explore this country, and riding to Baie, eighteen miles from Indore, on the Bombay road, we turned to the left, and after some miles along a jungle track we arrived at Kautcote, where our men had preceded us. The Maharajah Holkar had kindly lent us two elephants, but they were unsteady, and were driven by a couple of rascals who feared to take them near a tiger. Next morning we moved into the jungle, and encamped in a lovely spot by the banks of a river, a few miles from Kautcote. In the jungle were many iron-pits which had been worked in the olden day, but were now buried in grass and bushes, and given over to wild beasts.

We had not been long at our tents when one of our men came in and reported he had taken the fresh track of a tiger up to one of these pits, and was anxious that we should at once go and drive him out. On arriving at the ground we saw that the tiger had gone into some holes under a steep bank, so making a circuit, we posted ourselves above, and threw down stones. We had hoped that he would bolt out in front, but he showed no sign till we were about to give him up, when he suddenly appeared on our left, coming up the bank. I at once fired, but he dashed on, and in an instant was lost among the long grass. On examining the spot we found drops of blood ; but it was not safe to follow him on foot, for the grass was three and four feet high, and the trees and bushes would not have allowed the passage of an elephant. We were obliged to leave him and return to the tents.

Next day was blank, and we moved camp farther into the wilderness. On the way we came on some old marks of bison, and had a chance at a herd of nylghae, but would not fire, as we did not wish to disturb the country. As we approached a ravine running down from some springs, we observed a very large tiger standing in a streamlet about 200 yards from us. He had evidently seen us, and after a few seconds he moved up the hill-side, which was covered with bamboos and detached fragments of rock. On arriving at the spot where we had seen him, we came in full view of the huge beast, as he stood, a hundred paces above us, at the base of a large rock. He was watching us, with one paw raised like a pointer dog, and his head turned sideways towards us. Notwithstanding the distance, we were about to fire, when, with a series of savage growls, he charged down the hill, and rushing across the ravine, disappeared, and we saw him no more. The word "growl," which I have used above is, I think inaccurate, but I know not what term to use. A tiger when lying wounded in a thicket will sometimes "growl," but when he charges his cry is more of a deep cavernous grunt, very horrible to hear, and well calculated to try a man's nerves. On one or two *rare* occasions I have heard a tiger *roar*, and have oftentimes heard him growl, but the war-cry which he gives when charging is quite distinct from either of these.

After resting a while we moved towards the place where we had sent our servants and tents. The jungle had been only very partially burnt, and all the edges of the streams, together with large tracts of the more level jungle, were covered with grass two feet or more in height. We were skirting up the bank of a considerable stream, when we saw a tiger move up from the river on the opposite side, and disappear among the long grass. The jungle was fairly open, and we thought we might try our luck on the elephants ; so, calling them up, we mounted. We had to proceed up stream some distance, as the bank was too abrupt to allow the elephants to descend. Having at length effected a passage, we moved down to where we had seen the tiger, and there, among the grass, we found

half the carcass of a recently killed nylghae. Bringing the
elephants abreast we turned up the hill, and presently came
on three tigers sitting quietly in the grass, within thirty
paces of each other.   They seemed to regard us with great
unconcern. Whispering to the mahout to stop, I was in the
act of raising my rifle, when, with a shrill trumpet, my
elephant rushed to the front. I was of course jerked down
into the seat, and before I could recover myself the three
tigers had vanished.   Looking around for my friend, I found
his elephant had behaved even worse than mine, and had
nearly smashed him against the overhanging branch of a tree.
We deplored our hard fate, and abused the elephants ; but
had I known then all I know now, the blame, and probably
the punishment, would have fallen on the mahouts.

It was late in the afternoon when we reached our camp at
Ghora Puchar.   It was by no means a cheerful spot, and we
were informed that on a former occasion the groom of some
officer from Mhow had been killed here by a tiger. It was
suggested by some of our people that we might have a chance
of a shot by sitting up at night over a bait. Bradford had a
young buffalo tied up, while I sat over the remains of a nylghae
which had been killed two days before. Hyænas were
plentiful, and they fought over the carcass of the blue bull
all night, but no tiger came near me ; and Bradford was
equally unsuccessful.   On leaving my tree at daybreak I
made a short detour through the jungle, and on my way to
the tents I came on a large herd of cheetul. No good buck
presented himself, so, as we were in want of meat, I knocked
over a fat doe, which we carried to camp.

About this time we were told that the supply of flour was
running short, and that we must move in nearer civilisation.
In fact, we found ourselves in the hands of our attendants, who,

not being in our pay, and in no way imbued with the love of a woodland life, sighed for the bazaars and flesh-pots of Indore. These gentlemen no doubt gave the cue to the rest of the party, and we were constrained to retrace our steps. We had still two days more of leave, and these we determined to spend at our first camping-ground. The camp was therefore struck, and the tents and servants sent off by the most direct line. Taking our gun-bearers and a few of the aborigines who had joined us, we made a wide circuit through a very singular country. The whole of the grass had been burnt, and, in many parts, the surface of the ground was nothing but a sort of black freestone, which had, when in its liquid state, become mixed up with minute veins of quartz. The freestone had worn down under the combined effects of wind and weather, while the thin ridges of quartz stood out as sharp as knives, and were most destructive to our boots. Emerging from a small ravine, we came in full view of a large herd of sambur, headed by a noble stag. They stood watching us, but were too far to risk a shot ; and, after a short time, they went off, the hinds leading, then the smaller stags, and, in rear of all, the monarch of the herd.

None of the natives with us had any pretensions to being shikarees, and we wandered on in a purposeless manner, only endeavouring to eke out the day till our servants should have time to arrive and pitch the tent. As we ascended a rocky eminence we saw a large bear slink off, scared by the noise made by our followers. We found his seat, and to judge from the polished appearance of the rock it had been the resting-place of his ancestors for many generations, and possibly for centuries. It was on a slightly concave piece of rock, over which stood an enormous stone, resting on two or three points, and affording ways of escape on at least two sides.

Marks of bears were numerous, but we saw no others. It was late in the afternoon when we reached our tent, and, throwing off our garments, we plunged into the stream and enjoyed a good bath. We had a long talk that night after dinner, and laid plans for another visit to these jungles; for we could see by the marks in the forest that game was plentiful, and we were convinced that with good shikarees sport might be obtained. As it was, we had nobody with us who had any love of the chase, and the few people of Kautcote who attended our camp were only qualified to act as indifferent guides.

By 10 A.M. next day we had no word of game, so we set out on a further exploration. Passing a pool in the river, we saw a small shoal of the spawn of the murrel or sowlee fish. We knew that the parent fish were swimming below the shoal and would presently come to the surface, so, cocking my rifle, I waited their appearance. As one of them rose, I fired, and my men running in, brought it out. He was about seven pounds in weight. We then wandered up the river without seeing anything, and about 2 P.M. we had halted in the shade near some springs, not far from the stream. We lay about under the trees, and our people were scattered for some distance about the jungle. Presently one of them came running up, and assured us that they had seen a tiger lying close by. They suggested that Bradford should mount one of the elephants, and remain near where we then were ; and that I should accompany them and drive out the tiger. We accordingly crossed the river about a hundred yards below, and I was taken up among some rocks on the opposite side, from whence I had a good view of two fragments of rock on the other bank, meeting in a V shape, and overshadowed by a thick green willow. Behind these rocks

I was assured that the tiger was lying, and had been seen by some of the attendants as they were going down to bathe. The river was only some thirty yards in width, and our position was quite accessible had the tiger felt inclined to charge. After some minutes I saw him raise his eyes over the rocks, take a look at us, and sink down again. This he did several times, and at length, thinking I could take him in the head, I fired. He at once sprang up under the overhanging willow above him and disappeared, passing within a few yards of Bradford, whose elephant trumpeted loudly, and, bolting off, nearly killed him among the trees.

We never saw the tiger again. The finish had been quite in keeping with the other parts of our expedition, and we both vowed never again to go out with other men's servants, or to attempt to explore an unknown country without proper shikarees. Out of six tigers which we had seen we had bagged none, and one spotted deer was all we had to boast of. Wild dogs were numerous in these forests, and I saw three one morning close to our tents. The natives declared that, but for the presence of the dogs, we should have seen many more sambur and nylghae. In spite of our bad luck we enjoyed our ten days very much, and were sorry when we had to mount and return to cantonments.

When in the Kautcote jungle we had a good opportunity of noting the predilection of deer for salt. At some distance from our tent was a scarped bank in a dry water-course, and on its surface there was a strong saline deposit. The spot was much frequented by sambur, and the fact seemed known to the shikarees of the district, for, artfully concealed under the root of a tree at the top of the bank, we observed a seat whence, no doubt, many a deadly shot had been obtained. The tracks of the deer were numerous and fresh in the ground below, and, as far as they could reach, they had licked the salt from the face of the bank.

An old iron-pit in this jungle was shown to one of my friends, some years after my visit, by one of the natives of the place. He stated that he had on one occasion taken up a youthful British sportsman to this cave, in which a tiger had been marked down. A fragment of rock was hurled into the pit, and out bolted the affrighted tiger. "There," said the shikaree, pointing to the left, "there ran the tiger ; the sahib stood here ; and there" (pointing to a branch twenty-five feet straight over his head) "there is the mark of the sahib's bullet !" It is supposed that the tiger was not the only thing that was frightened on that day.

It was proposed by the Nawaub of Jowra, who had come into Indore for the Dussera festival, that some of us should go out some morning to see his cheetahs work. We accordingly made an early start, and set out for some ground which was preserved by Holkar, and on which was a good show of black buck. The Nawaub, who was a stout heavy man, rode a strong hill pony, which ambled along at a great pace, and the other officers of our party were mounted on Arabs in the hope of a run at something. In the open plain we came up with the Nawaub's men, about a hundred and fifty in all ; men mounted on screaming horses, and men on riding camels ; men on foot with guns and dogs, and men with camels laden with tents ; and last, but not least, men on elephants. There were other men in attendance on the two cheetahs, each of which rode on his own platform cart ; and, though hooded, were apparently aware that some amusement was in store for them. Several herds of deer were in sight, and they did not seem much disconcerted by the troop of men, horses, etc. etc. The place was not far from the town of Indore, and they were accustomed to such sights. After some talk, it was settled that one of the cheetahs should be taken up to the nearest herd; so the Nawaub, leaving the main body, requested us to join him. The deer seemed to mistake us for harmless wayfarers, for they fed quietly, while we passed at a distance of about eighty yards.

A cheetah was now unhooded, and on seeing the deer he at once glided from the cart, and taking advantage of every tuft of grass and inequality in the ground, he crept towards his prey. The deer were meanwhile lazily watching us as we went on without halting, and the poor beasts were only aware of their danger when the leopard made his rush. There was a wild scurry, but the cheetah was among them, and as the herd cleared off we saw him lying with his teeth in the throat of a goodly buck. His keeper now came up with a wooden ladle and a knife, and cutting the deer's throat he caught the blood in the spoon, into which in a few minutes the cheetah thrust his nose, and while he was lapping the blood the hood was slipped over his eyes, and he was secured and replaced in the cart.

As we moved on we saw several bucks feeding singly about the plain, and the Nawaub suggested that I should take my rifle and move on them with a shooting-cart. I advanced on a very black fellow with long horns. He was lying near a small bit of cultivated land, and as the ground was favourable I made sure of getting within easy shot; but when I was within about two hundred yards of him the buck rose, looked hard at us, shook his head, and trotted off to some distance, when he again lay down. We followed on slowly with the cart, and I was about to fire at him as he lay, but he again jumped up, and was shaking his head as before when I fired and dropped him. Some of the attendants ran in and cut his throat, and he was placed on the cart, with which I returned to the Nawaub and one or two gentlemen who had witnessed the death from a rising ground.

One of the party proceeded to overhaul the buck, and forthwith set up a shout of derision, for on examining the horns, holes were found which had been bored in them about two inches from the tips. The natives had no doubt caught him on some former occasion, and he had been let loose with catgut nooses attached to his horns—the object being to entangle any other buck with whom he might fall in and engage in combat. I got well roasted for shooting what my friends called a tame deer ; but, tame deer or wild, I had dropped him by a good shot, and so could afford to be chaffed.

Notwithstanding that we were in preserved ground, the crowd of followers by whom the Nawaub was accompanied had evidently scared the deer, and we were advised to go on for a mile or two, when we should be among fresh game. We accordingly mounted our horses and moved through a tract of grass land. Our company was numerous and noisy, and the chance of any addition to our bag seemed small at that moment. We were all laughing and talking as we rode along, when I observed, about sixty yards on our left, what seemed to me to be the points of a buck's horns, appearing just over the long grass. My henchman with my rifle was at my stirrup, and before any of the party were aware of what I was about, I had jumped off, and fired at the point where I imagined the horns should meet. The bullet told with a sharp crack, and the horns disappeared. On going up to the place we found a buck shot through the head. Had I not seen him, he would have lain still while the whole party of hunters — if we deserved the name—passed within a few yards of him.

At the foot of some low hills we saw a herd of deer feeding

in a cornfield, and the Nawaub called up the other cheetah with his attendants. The ground was very bare between us and the deer, and before the cheetah had got within distance, the herd saw him and bolted. The leopard, however, did his best, and nearly had one antelope, but, finding himself foiled, he gave in at once and was secured by his keeper. Meanwhile the deer went off to our left, where they were turned by some horsemen ; on which they passed in rear of us at a distance of several hundred yards. A rapid file fire was opened, but without effect, further than perhaps to cause the deer to bound higher than usual. The last shot was fired by one of the Nawaub's men, with one of his English rifles. The deer must have been nearly 500 yards off at the time, and to our astonishment one of them tumbled over. The shot was of course a fluke, but the shooter was not the less the hero of the hour.

The Nawaub now suggested refreshments, and soon a string of camels was seen coming up laden with tents, tables, chairs, and all manner of kitchen arrangements. Breakfast was at once ordered, and while the tents were being pitched we went out after some quail which had been seen close by. The Nawaub intimated his intention of shooting, and we had no wish to interfere with his sport, which we watched with great amusement. He was not a first-rate marksman, but one of his men could shoot very fairly, and when the Nawaub fired, he also loosed his piece, but of course took no credit for any result. On breakfast being announced we returned to the tents, where we found sundry and various cooling drinks, which were gratefully swallowed. In the afternoon we rode back to the cantonment, having spent a very pleasant day, although the sporting was not of a high order. The Jowra Nawaub was always most hospitable to all Europeans passing through his country. Our last meeting was in 1865, when I was his guest while on my way south from Rajpootana. Two months later he died of cholera, which was then raging at Jowra.

Towards the close of the year 1856 I accompanied the agent of the Governor-General through the Gwalior and Bundelcund states. We left Indore in October, and went north by rapid marches, so that, even had the country been favourable, we should have had little time for shooting. At this season, however, the jungles were filled with high green grass, and there was no prospect of shooting till the cold weather set in. We tried to beat a jungle near Ragoogurh, and indeed we started one large tiger, whose fresh footprints we found over our own on our way back to the tents, but we could make nothing of it, and did not again renew the attempt. At Seepree we encountered a violent thunderstorm. The ground was hard as iron, and in pitching the camp there had been a great destruction of tent-pegs. We were in the cantonment at the time, calling on some of the officers, and on returning to our camp we found it flat, with the exception of the big man's tent, which had only been kept standing by half-a-dozen men holding on to every rope.

The soil of the place was red, having a strong admixture of ironstone, and our tents bore the marks of that storm for many a day. To add to our discomfort, cholera had broken out among a large party which had joined us from Oujein, and had been communicated to our camp.

The disease was aggravated by the wet and discomfort, and for some days we had many deaths among our people.

From Seepree we moved on Jansi, having some very good snipe-shooting on the road. At one large tank they were especially numerous, and sometimes we had six and seven birds lying dead around us. We also made some good bags of ducks. I had an agreeable companion in Hunt, of the Bengal Lancers, who commanded the agent's escort.

At Jansi we called on the Ranee, who a few months later was destined to give so much trouble ; and we also went over the old Fort, where Burgess and his gallant companions fought so well, till they were led by treacherous promises to trust themselves to their merciless assailants.

After a detour to the south, we marched to Duttiah, where the chief, hearing that we were fond of shooting, offered to send out his men with us. We knew the sport would be but tame, but having nothing better on hand, we started off, taking only the chief's shikarees and our own gun-bearers. I always had a horror of native gentlemen when out shooting ; their utter ignorance of sport in any shape, and their inordinate love of noise and large followings, made them most undesirable companions. There are now and then exceptions, but they are like angels' visits.

On approaching the preserved ground we were met by the shikarees leading a tall and sagacious stalking bullock. A string was passed through his nostrils, and he was guided to the right or left by the rein being thrown on either side of his hump. We had not gone far when we came on a herd of nylghae, browsing among some thick bushes. One of them raised its head, and stood watching us at a distance of seventy yards. Hunt told me to shoot ; so, aiming at what I supposed was its shoulder, I fired. The ball struck timber, and when it cleared, I saw the white blaze of the shot on the trunk of the tree, which I had mistaken for the shoulder of the beast. Hunt had done better, for, as they went off, he dropped a good blue bull.

It was now settled that we should separate and meet again about 3 P.M., at a place about four miles off. We were each accompanied by a couple of the Rajah's men ; and those who came with me brought with them the stalking bullock. After moving quietly through the jungle for half-an-hour, we came on another herd of nylghae; one large cow was standing, broadside on, about eighty yards off. I dropped her with one shot, and one of the men behind me was in the act of rushing forward to finish her, when I checked him, and at that instant a blue bull bolted out into an open glade in the wood, and stood looking at us intently. Again my rifle cracked, and the bull staggered wildly forward for about fifty yards and fell. Fearing to lose the meat, owing to the throats not being cut in the orthodox manner, the men now ran up, and in a few seconds the poor beasts were lawful beef.

The style of shooting was by no means to my taste, but my attendants seemed highly satisfied, and looked forward to a great feast for themselves and their families, though they cared little for sport. Having covered up the dead beasts with boughs of trees, we went on a mile or two, when we saw a large cow nylghae feeding among some scrub jungle. The bullock was now brought into play, and stooping down behind him with one of the men, we allowed the beast to graze quietly, at the same time edging him up towards the game. The bullock seemed thoroughly to understand his work, and moved at the slighest hint from right to left. We got up within easy shot, and the cow was dropped with one bullet. Satiated with this slaughter, I intimated to my companions that we should now push forward to rejoin Hunt, who I knew would be ready for his luncheon. A man was therefore sent for a cart on which to carry home the game, and we moved on. Before long, a huge blue bull crossed our front, and stood within a hundred yards, with his shoulder well exposed. I raised my rifle and covered him, but thinking my companions and their friends would find they had sufficient occupation for their time and teeth, with the game already slain, I lowered my weapon, and soon after the bull went off.

Farther on, we heard some wild hogs moving in a thicket of bushes and high grass. Though I had spared the bull I thought a pork-chop might be desirable, so I crept forward. The sounder, however, had got our wind, and we heard them scurry off. One pig was left behind, and, on missing his companions, he set up a peculiar cry. Presently he moved out of the thicket, and stood in some long grass. I could just see his head, and I dropped him dead with a shot between the eyes. My attendant, by this time, regarded me with great respect. Four beasts had fallen to four successive shots, and he had not been accustomed, when sporting with his royal master, to see so large a result from so small an expenditure of ammunition. We now emerged into an open country, and were joined by Hunt, who had been most unsuccessful, not having killed anything since the bull in the morning. He had not had one other chance.

An abundant luncheon was now produced, and to it we did ample justice. Another party of the chief's men met us here. They had with them tame antelopes for stalking, and as neither of us had seen this style of shooting, we directed them to come with us in the afternoon. The tame antelopes were three in number—one buck, and two does—and their human confederate carried on his arm a screen of leafy twigs, having a small aperture in the middle, from which to shoot. The antelopes were held by their cords, five or six yards in length, and were so trained that a doe was always on each side, while the buck passed backwards and forwards between them.

A herd of wild antelopes was soon seen, and Hunt moved

forward with the trained deer and their keeper. As soon as they were observed by the herd, the reigning buck came forward, shaking his head, and evidently bent on having a fight with the new comer, whose does he no doubt intended, in true Oriental fashion, to sweep into his own harem. He was followed, at a few yards' distance, by the rest of the herd, and they all advanced steadily till within fifty yards of the stalking-party. Hunt would have dropped the buck had he had a fair chance of shooting, but he was so persuaded that he must be seen if he moved, that he kept his eye steadily fixed through the opening in the screen, which was placed too low to enable him to shoot conveniently. At this moment a horseman, who had been sent out by the chief to inquire after our welfare, came up on a screaming horse, and the herd went off at speed. Neither of us being inclined to go farther, we mounted our horses, and returned to the camp.

We marched next morning, and the chief sent with us his hunting cheetahs, with orders to their attendants to accompany us for several days on our journey. The country was not, however, favourable, and antelope were not seen. We went out one afternoon, on the report of a man who said he had seen deer. We found they were chinkara ; and the man in charge of the cheetahs informed us that these small deer were too active for this sort of work. We therefore left the leopard behind some bushes with our horses, and, taking his cart, I went forward with my rifle. The deer allowed us to approach within eighty yards, and I dropped the buck with the first barrel. The doe darted off, and then stood looking at us. She was at least 150 yards off, and looked very small, but I bagged her with the second shot, greatly to the astonishment of the cartman. We then returned to the cheetah. Farther on we came on some more chinkara, and, at my request, the cheetah was slipped. We moved on quietly with the cart, and had a splendid opportunity of observing the leopard approach his game. Crawling like a snake over bare ground, and taking advantage of the smallest shrubs and tufts of grass, he crept forward. But the deer were in the middle of a bare field, and when the cheetah did make his rush, they saw him at once, and fled with amazing swiftness. No capture was effected, and we returned to the tents.

Our journeyings took us through Hameerpoor to Cawnpore and Lucknow, and we rejoined our own camp in Bundelcund, passing through Oorae. Here we were entertained very hospitably by two officers, who were on detachment duty. Food was scarce, and they trusted a good deal to their guns for provisions. It was then the cold season, and a large pot was kept constantly on the fire in the sitting-room, and into this all manner of eatables were thrust promiscuously, —hens, hares, venison, ducks, quails, potatoes, turnips, sauces of sorts, etc. etc. The mess was, however, excellent, and there was always a pleasing uncertainty as to the nature of the food which the spoon would fish up. We were a merry party of four, but a few months later I was the only one left to tell the tale. Two fell in the massacre at Cawnpore, and Hunt, with another officer, was shot by the mutineer cavalry of the Mehidpore Contingent at Mulharghur.

Our return march was *viâ* Agra and Gwalior to Indore. We moved too fast to allow of any chance of large game. At Kolarus we were taken out by some of the people of the place, but the jungles were green and very extensive, and we saw that the whole thing was absurd. Late in the afternoon, as we were returning home on our elephants, we saw several nylghae on a hill above us. They were moving among thick bushes, and more from a wish to empty my rifle than from any hope of killing, I fired. The elephant had been by no means steady, and the bull at which I aimed was moving, but I heard the shot strike with a loud crack, and I observed a commotion among the bushes on the hill-side. Some of our people called out that the bull was shot, so, dismounting from the elephants, we went up the hill, which was very rough and stony, and covered with thick corinda jungle. Forcing our way through this, we found the bull, who had been shot through both hind legs, just below the hocks. The poor brute floundered violently, and I would have finished him with another shot, but for my gun-bearer, who was anxious to secure the skin for a shield, so the poor bull was knocked on the head with an axe.

As we approached the staging bungalow at Dewas, we observed from the carriage two fine bustard feeding near the road. During our march I had made several unsuccessful attempts to obtain a shot at bustard, but these seemed tamer; so, leaving one of the grooms behind to watch them, we drove on to the bungalow, where I got my gun, and loading with BB, I mounted on a small pony and cantered back.

The birds were feeding, and took but little notice of me so long as I remained on the road, but as soon as they saw me move towards them, they rose and took a short flight. I followed slowly, and this time I managed to approach somewhat nearer; but as I was about to check my pony, they again rose. Quitting the reins, I fired at the largest, and he dropped his legs, but recovering himself, he flew on. I saw he was hard hit, and I kept my eye on him, and after going about a mile, I saw him fall. Riding up, I found him dead. He was a very fine bird, and weighed twenty-two pounds. Some of the feathers of the bustard are invaluable to the salmon-fisher.

CHAPTER XI.

IN the spring of 1857 I entered on the duties of an appointment under the agent to the Viceroy in Central India. This
entailed the political supervision of the country bordering on
the Nerbudda river, lying between Western Malwa and the
district of Khandesh in the Bombay Presidency. My head-
quarters were at Maunpore, fourteen miles south of the Mhow
cantonment. The northern part of my charge lay in the
Vindyah mountains, the southern was covered with heavy
jungle, terminating in the Satpoora hills, and between the two
ranges, 1600 feet below the crest of the Vindyah, flowed the
broad stream of the Nerbudda.

The greater portion of the district was thinly peopled by
Bheels. Of these men, Sir John Malcolm, in his Memoir of
Central India, writes, " The Bheels are quite a distinct race
from any other Indian tribe, yet few among the latter have
higher pretensions to antiquity." According to popular tradition, the god " Mahadeo, when sick and unhappy, was one
day reclining in a shady forest, when a beautiful woman ap-

peared, the first sight of whom effected a complete cure of all his complaints."

"An intercourse between the god and the strange female was established, the result of which was many children ; one of whom, who was from infancy alike distinguished by his ugliness and vice, slew the favourite bull of Mahadeo, for which crime he was expelled to the woods and mountains; and his descendants have ever since been stigmatised with the names of Bheel and Nishada, terms that denote outcasts. . . . The cultivating Bheels are those who have continued in their peaceable occupations after their leaders were destroyed or driven by invaders to become desperate freebooters ; and the wild or mountain Bheel comprises all that part of the tribe, who, preferring savage freedom and indolence to submission and industry, have continued to subsist by plunder."

The above was written about thirty-five years previous to my acquaintance with the Bheel tribes. Since that period they are much settled down, but the presence of a British officer among them has always been found requisite for the general peace of the country. I was fortunate in being selected for this duty, as the wandering life among the hillmen, to which it led, gave me many opportunities for the pursuit of wild animals ; and while engaged in the chase, supported by the valuable assistance of the Bheels, I was enabled to become personally acquainted with many of them, and to acquire a knowledge of their habits which often proved of service in my official duties. By the more civilised portion of the inhabitants the Bheels are dreaded as robbers and freebooters, and to a certain extent some of them do prey on society ; but during my wanderings among them, which extended over nine years, I never lost the value of one rupee ; whereas, had I attempted to pass a night encamped in the neighbourhood of a town or village in the plains of Malwa, without a watchful guard, I should probably, on waking in the morning, have found my tent stripped.

In the month of April I had arranged to meet Hunt, who had obtained two months' leave of absence from his regiment, and we trysted at the point where the Bombay and Agra road crosses the Nerbudda at Khull. But I had previously to inspect the road for fifty miles to the southward, and on my way I diverged to the right and left, gathering information as to the sporting resources of the country. I left the main road at Goojree, two marches south of the Mhow cantonment, and, after moving about seven miles east, halted at the foot of the Vindyah range. My men had preceded me, and reported having seen both bears and sambur, but they had been unable to mark anything down.

Immediately in rear of our camp rose a steep hill of considerable height, and on its face, at various altitudes, were lines of bare rock and huge stones. The hill was covered with trees and scrub, and in parts the rank dry grass had escaped the annual jungle conflagration. About noon I was called out by one of my men, who, pointing to the black rocks on the hill-side, informed me that he had marked a bear among them, and had left his comrade on the watch, while he came into camp with the intelligence. The April sun was blazing down on the encampment, which was shut in by hills throwing off an intense heat ; and though I had small hopes of dislodging the bear from its cave, I thought that on the hill-side the air might be cooler, and accordingly started off at once with my men.

Toiling up the abrupt face of the hill, I found myself compelled to halt on more than one occasion, for the sun was powerful and oppressive. I suppose we had ascended 700 or 800 feet when our guide halted, and his friend, who had been perched on a tree, came down and informed us that the bear had not moved out from the masses of rocks into which they had marked him. I carried a 12-bore rifle, and another of the same calibre was carried by my henchman Bappoo, who had accompanied me from Dholka in Guzerat. We advanced cautiously, peering over the rocks ; but we found that they merely concealed the entrances to a complete gallery of bear-holes. Into some of these we hurled stones, and vainly endeavoured by shouts to induce the bear to show. Shots were even fired into the cave, but with no result, and at length, supposing that the bear must have moved unobserved by the watcher, or had made up his mind not to come out, I laid aside my rifle, and sitting down with my men in the entrance of a cave, we lit our pipes and enjoyed the view.

The prospect was grand and extensive, though the heated air rendered the distance rather hazy. We were seated on a spur of the Vindyah range of mountains, and the ground beneath us seemed to be nearly level, stretching away across the province of Nimar to the Nerbudda, which, from our exalted position, we could see winding through the valley like a silver serpent, as it crossed from left to right about twelve miles in our front. But we knew that our bird's-eye view deceived us, for the apparently level jungles below us were deeply cut up by rocky ravines, filled in parts with high grass and thorny bushes of the "bair," whose small round berries form a favourite food of their ursine namesakes. The trees were mostly salur, of moderate growth, devoid of leaves. The wood of this tree is soft and worthless, and a resinous gum of no known value exudes freely from its yellow bark.

Here and there small clearings might be detected, and an occasional Bheel hut ; and, in the more immediate vicinity of the river, were considerable patches of cultivation. On the north bank of the river could be seen the town of Mheysur, and four miles higher up, the small but pretty British station of Mundlaisir, the head-quarters of the political agent in Nimar. Beyond the Nerbudda, the country presented features similar to those on the north side ; jungle and cultivation intermixed, the more distant portions of the landscape increasing in elevation, till the horizon was bounded by the portion of the Sathpoora mountains lying between Sindwah and the hill-fortress of Asseerghur.

As we sat, Bappoo and another man had moved along the face of the hill some thirty yards, and were examining a cave when a bear rushed out on them. Bappoo fired, but missed, and the bear, greatly alarmed, went straight down the hill. Snatching up my rifle, I sprang forward and got a snapshot at the rapidly-descending brute. My bullet struck him somewhere behind the shoulder, killing him dead, and he fell over an almost perpendicular rock, twenty feet in height. Bappoo had a narrow escape, as, had the bear grappled with him, they must have gone down together, and he could hardly have escaped with his life. We had some difficulty in taking the beast up from the mass of rocks among which he had fallen, but the Bheels cut two stout poles, to which he was slung, and so carried to the tent, where we proceeded to skin him and boil down the fat.

I went out in the afternoon in quest of sambur, but saw none. The berry-like flower of the mowa trees was falling, and the wives and children of the Bheels were busy picking it up from the ground. Their presence in all directions through the forest was not conducive to sport.

The produce of the mowa forms an important item of Bheel domestic economy. The tree is one of the handsomest in this part of India.   It is of large size, with heavy rich foliage of a dark green.   During March and April few leaves remain, but at this season the flower, which is edible, ripens and falls.   These flowers are thick and fleshy in substance, pale yellow in colour, with a sweet sickly taste, and of the form of a large hollow grape.   They grow in bunches of from four to ten or more, at the extremities of the branches ; each flower being supported by a long spike running through it. As they mature, they fall to the ground ; and the entire Bheel population is employed in gathering them.   To facilitate this operation, all dead leaves round the bases of the trees are burnt, and the surface of the ground swept clean.

The flowers fall night and day, and are collected in baskets, and afterwards dried in the sun.   The mowa is a favourite food of both bears and sambur.   They travel long distances in quest of it, and when feeding under the trees are often shot from hiding places by the Bheels.   The privilege of gathering the mowa is jealously guarded by the people of each district ; but the boundaries of townships being only laid down by tradition, disputes frequently arise, and these occasionally end in bloodshed.   The flowers, when dried, are cooked in various ways and eaten.   A potent liquor is also distilled from them. Large quantities are collected by traders from the towns, and sold to distillers throughout the country.   The flower is succeeded by a fruit the size of a small apple, from which oil is extracted.

My time being limited, I gave the order to move camp to the Nerbudda, and thence to the fort of Sindwah, ten miles from the frontier of the Bombay Presidency, which I reached in four marches.   At Sindwah I fell in with a Mekranee, who was, or had been, in the employ of the guardian of the fort.   This man had, on a former occasion, joined one of my

friends who was marching up the country, and had assisted
at the death of a tiger in the bed of the Boorar river, six miles
south of Khull. The Mekranees are inhabitants of the country
to the west of Scinde, whence a number of the male population migrate into Central India and the northern part of the
Bombay Presidency in quest of employment in a semi-military
capacity. They are free lances, taking service with any one
who will pay them. Many of them are expert marksmen,
and skilled in the use of both sword and matchlock. Notwithstanding the services which he had rendered to my friend,
I did not think that the gentleman before me would prove
a very valuable addition to my sporting staff. He was evidently a great dandy, and appeared before me wearing a
pair of very high-heeled red slippers, which were no doubt
greatly admired by his lady friends, but did not strike me
as likely to be of service for quick work over a rough country.
However, he said he could show me a tiger, and he kept his
word.

I was on my return march to the Nerbudda, and arranged
for a halt at Tekree on the Boorar river, where the Mekranee
had preceded us. I had with me a very good little Bheel
named Himta, whom I had brought with me from Maunpore.
He also went forward to examine the bed of the river. On
my arrival they met me, saying, that assuredly there was a
tiger in the neighbourhood; they had seen his tracks in several
places, but had not succeeded in marking him down. About
10 A.M. I mounted an elephant, and we moved up the course
of the stream. After going two miles, we came on some close
patches of cypress and willow growing in the bed of the river,
which at this season was dry, except in the deeper pools. On
the banks were thick bushes, laced in many parts with masses
of creeping plants, through which an elephant could not have

forced his way. On either side the jungle extended over wooded hills. Altogether our chance of finding the tiger did not seem good, for the main river was joined on both sides by numerous deep and narrow ravines, in any one of which the beast might have lain up. In addition to the elephant which I rode, I was accompanied by another, of whose staunchness his driver was very doubtful.

Keeping all men on foot at a safe distance, I took Himta in the back seat of my howdah, and, directing the driver of the other elephant to keep abreast, we moved up the river, carefully beating out each patch of cypress. In this manner I worked for some time. Occasionally a hyæna would shuffle off with his back arched and ears erect ; and jackals would trot out into the bright sunlight, looking inquisitively at the advancing elephants ; but no sign of a tiger did we see. At length we came on a large herd of goats, some of which were feeding close to the river-bank, while others were lying down on the moist sand. We were about to leave a bed of cypress, which we had beaten out, and my elephant was standing on a slight hillock, when Himta caught hold of my arm, and pointed down into the covert, almost under the feet of the elephant. The cypress was thick, and about four feet in height ; but, looking down, I could see the striped back of the tiger, who lay perfectly motionless notwithstanding our proximity.

So dense was the covert that I was unable to distinguish head from tail ; but I knew that a two-ounce ball, either down between the shoulders, or through the loins, must prove an effectual stopper to any beast, so, quietly raising my rifle, I fired. With a savage growl a fine tigress scrambled out and vainly endeavoured to get away. Her hind-quarters were quite disabled, and I had no difficulty in overtaking and giving her the *coup de grace*. From this adventure I again learnt the great importance of thoroughly beating any covert in which a tiger or panther was supposed to be lying up, and of never relaxing my attention till the last corner had been carefully beaten out. We supposed that this tigress, when disturbed by us, was probably intent on watching the herd of goats ; but whatever her intentions towards *them*, we had, at least, earned the gratitude of the cowherds of the district.

I was glad to make for some shady trees overhanging the river, by the side of a long pool, where I dismounted, and sat down on the sand, while the mahouts removed to a short distance, and stood with their elephants in the deeper water. Meanwhile my men busied themselves scooping out wells in the sand, near the water's edge, for the natives of India are fully aware of the value of filtered water, and never drink direct from the pools in the jungle. Scraping out the sand and gravel with their hands till they got below the water-level, they dexterously splashed out the mud from the holes, and then, having allowed them to fill gradually with clear water, the men sat round and drank freely, using the broad leaves of the kakra tree as drinking-cups. The pipe was then passed from hand to hand, each man taking about three draws, and filling his whole body with smoke in the operation.

I was in the full enjoyment of my own pipe, when one of the elephants, uttering a fearful shriek, rushed from the pool, and narrowly avoided trampling on some of the men. A red bullock had been crossing the sandy bed of the river, some 300 yards above us, and, I suppose, was taken by the elephant (who had been rather excited by the morning's work) to be a tiger of gigantic proportions. In vain the driver shouted and held on to his ear with the boathook-like goad. The frantic brute rushed out of the river and up the bank. Fortunately he did not encounter any large trees, and after a run of half-a-mile he was stopped; but not before some guns which had been left in the howdah had been considerably knocked about. He continued so restless that we did not deem it advisable to use him again that day, so sent him off to the camp. In the afternoon we hunted farther up the river, but saw nothing.

Next morning the Mekranee returned to Sindwah, and I moved to Khull, where I met my friend Hunt. In the forenoon we moved six miles down the right bank of the Nerbudda to Dhurrempooree. Here our men examined the ravines descending to the river, but found only the tracks of a panther, and we soon knew that we should do well to move camp without delay, as there appeared little prospect of sport there. About mid-day, however, one of my men came in, having found the fresh track of a panther going into a porcupine's hole, in a small open ravine leading down to the river. Having no better work on hand, we went to the spot, and finding several openings to the burrow, we filled one with dry grass, mixed with green leaves, and setting fire thereto, we retired to the opposite side to watch the effect. Before many minutes a panther bolted, and was making off down the ravine, when we rolled him over.

Next morning we moved ten miles to the north, and encamped near the foot of the hills, at a spot indicated by Himta as being a favourite resort of bears. He had preceded us with several Bheels of the district, and was absent when we reached the ground. Late in the day he sent a man into camp with intelligence of two bears marked down at a spot about three miles from the tents.

We were soon on the road, and were led by our guide to a hill-face, sloping down towards a small river. Here we found Himta and his men seated in trees commanding a view of some long dry grass on the banks of a small watercourse running down the hill-side. Among the grass grew trees and bushes. The markers were unable to point out the precise spot where the bears had lain up, and it was therefore settled that Hunt should take up a position on the face of the hill above them, while I with three men advanced into the grass. We were to proceed quietly, and, if possible, get a shot at them before they moved. If we startled them by our approach, we calculated on my driving them up to Hunt, who went off to his post, accompanied by his two gun-bearers. Having allowed sufficient time to elapse, I advanced into the grass with great caution, closely followed by Bappoo, Buggoo Sing, jemadar of police, and Himta, the two former carrying my spare rifles.

As I was carefully endeavouring to avoid treading on the dry sticks, I came on a covey of the small bustard quail. These birds are generally found in the tree jungles, and sit in the grass closely packed together, rising simultaneously, with much noise, when disturbed. I had almost stepped on them before they rose; and as they flew up into my face I was a good deal startled. I had hardly settled my nerves when I saw the male bear about thirty paces in front of me, making off at speed towards the right. I fired at once, but the smoke came back on me; and, as it cleared away, I saw the other bear, not ten yards off, going away after the first. I let drive with the second barrel, on which she wheeled round and came straight at me, grunting viciously. I had no time to turn to get a second rifle before she was on me. Rising on her hind legs, she attempted to seize me by the throat in her teeth; and, as I fended her off with my left arm, she got it in her mouth, and crunched it up like a cucumber. Meanwhile, she was not idle with her formidable claws, with which she tore open my clothes, and gave me an ugly score across the ribs. At that moment Bappoo rushed in and shot her through the body. She dropped on all fours, but retained her hold on my hand with her teeth, tugging furiously to get me down. As we struggled, a young bear which she carried on her back, and which had been struck by my shot, fell dead at our feet ; and the old lady's temper was evidently not improved by the bereavement.

Bappoo behaved admirably. He again rushed to the front, and, raising his rifle, watched his opportunity for another shot. I called to him not to blow my hand off; and at that instant he fired, and the bear relaxed her grip and fell back with a ragged hole through her head. All this was the work of a few seconds.

I had now time to examine my hurts. My left wrist was nearly bitten through, both bones were smashed, and the hand twisted round. I was, moreover, cut across the ribs by the bear's claws. Holding up the wounded limb in a hanging position, I turned the hand round into its place, and supported it on the other arm, till Hunt, who had now come up, had cut some slips of bamboo, and bound the whole up with a turban. I was astonished at the utter absence of pain, for the wound was gruesome to behold.

The rage of the bear had evidently been kindled by her offspring being wounded. They generally bring out their young in some cave, or mass of rocks ; and, as soon as they can run about, the young bears travel over the country on the backs of their mothers, burying themselves in the long hair, to which they cling with great tenacity, holding their position at any speed, and over the roughest ground. While feeding or undisturbed they descend and run about, scrambling up again with great celerity on the least alarm. Had I pounded the bear on the head with my rifle as she came on, I might have turned her ; but the rifle was a new Sam. Smith, and I suppose I was afraid of smashing it. I had reason to be thankful to Bappoo for his cool and plucky conduct, as, with her murdered offspring lying between us, the bear would not have been easily driven off, and would probably have killed me. Mounting the elephant, which had been brought out with us, we went back to the tent, and I remarked to the jemadar that I feared I should not require his assistance in bear-shooting for some time to come.

I had in my camp a native dresser from the dispensary at Maunpore, and by him my wound was artistically bound up. Both bones of the arm were smashed ; the ulna was broken about one inch from the joint, and the ends protruded. The radius was also broken. I had on the third finger of my left hand a ring which had not been off for many years, and could not be removed. Knowing that my hand would pro-bably swell up, I lost no time in filing this off. Meanwhile, food had been got ready ; and, after partaking of refreshment, I mounted on a litter, borne on men's shoulders, and set off for Mundlaisir, distant thirty miles, hoping there to obtain good surgical treatment. A horseman was sent off before me, with a note to Colonel Keatinge, the political agent, ex-plaining matters.

The Bheels turned out at various places along the road, and carried me to Mheysur by daylight next morning. Thence, Colonel Keatinge's riding cart took me the remaining four miles into Mundlaisir. I had with me a leathern water-bag or "chagul" having a tin spout, and with it I kept the wound constantly wet. By this the inflammation was com-pletely kept under. Soon after my arrival my clothes were

cut off, and I was sent to bed by Colonel Keatinge, who
attended to my wants with much kindness.   Charley Hunt,
too, was in need of rest, having ridden beside me all night.
That evening Dr. Watson of the Bengal Army arrived after a
thirty miles' ride from Mhow, and considerably relieved my
mind by intimating his intention of endeavouring to save
the hand.   He pleasantly remarked that any man could cut
off a limb, but that it required a surgeon to save one.

I received much attention from all my friends at Mundlaisir,
and in about ten days was so far recovered as to be able to be
moved in a palanquin to Mhow, where I remained under the
surgical care and hospitable roof of Dr. Watson.   I have no
joint in that wrist, and can only partially close my hand, but
the limb is serviceable in most ways ; and as Watson used to
remark—" It is better than a hook."   My misadventure occurred about the 16th of April, and I was not able to take
the field again before the 20th of June.

CHAPTER XII.

THE year 1857 was a memorable one in India. The Bengal Army, pampered, petted, and badly disciplined, rose in mutiny. The officers of the army were not to blame. The system was wrong. Regimental officers had not sufficient power, and they lacked support from the Commander-in-Chief and the Government. Caste, in the army, was attended to ; and seniority promotion in the ranks was the rule of the service. Individual merit could not advance, nor individual incapacity retard, the promotion of the Bengal Sepoy. The irregular cavalry were insufficiently paid. Under these circumstances, it was not to be wondered at that designing and discontented men found in the army a willing tool in their schemes for the subversion of the British power in India.

The European force, throughout India, was also at this period reduced to a minimum, owing to the Persian war and other circumstances. The army rose in rebellion, but it lacked cohesion and organisation. Its action was not simultaneous, and the European officers, nobly backed by civilians of all grades, had time, in many instances, for preparations for the safety of themselves and their families. How they bore themselves, both before and after the storm burst on them, is now a matter of history. I do not think the British name in India lost aught of its prestige by the mutiny of 1857.

I was recovering from my encounter with the bear, and about the middle of June I was able to go about with my arm in a sling. Meanwhile we daily received the most alarming accounts of the progress of the mutiny. Station after station rose, and the advance of the rebellion was marked by terrible deeds of bloodshed.

Indore, the head-quarters of the agent to the Viceroy for Central India, is fourteen miles north of Mhow. It was garrisoned by detachments of infantry, cavalry, and artillery, of the Bhopal Contingent; of infantry of the Malwa Contingent; and of the Bheel corps—all natives : together with some guns and cavalry in the service of the Maharajah Holkar, whose capital lay about two miles from the British cantonment. The garrison at Mhow consisted of a horse battery manned by Europeans, the 23d Bengal Native Infantry, and a wing of the 1st Bengal Cavalry. Notwithstanding the assurances of some officers of their confidence in the fidelity of their men, I felt, with many others, that the native troops, at both stations, were only waiting their opportunity to break out. My trusty henchman, Bappoo, had mingled freely with the men in the lines at Mhow, and knew their feelings, and he warned me to be prepared for the worst.

About the 20th of June I was ordered to proceed down the road to the limit of my charge, and make preparations for the advance of a small column which was on its way up from Bombay. This column was, however, diverted, for the purpose of quelling a mutiny at Arungabad ; and, after making my arrangements at the Nerbudda, I returned to my own house at Maunpore. I was accompanied by an officer of the

Thuggee Department, with his wife and child, who had joined me at the Nerbudda. On the 1st of July they wished to go into Mhow, and having sent out a fresh horse for their buggy half-way on the road, I saw them depart, and went out for my usual morning drive.

I returned, and was sitting at breakfast, when I heard the sound of heavy guns in the direction of Mhow. The firing proceeded from Indore, fourteen miles beyond Mhow, where Holkar's guns had opened on the British Residency, raking with their fire the horses of the Bhopal Cavalry, as they stood at their pickets, within a square of four detached buildings, composing the Residency stables. The men of the Bhopal artillery and cavalry, and of the Bheel corps, were not in the conspiracy, and were scattered at the time throughout the cantonment. At the same moment a ruffianly rabble from the town of Indore, ripe for plunder and bloodshed, came rushing into the cantonment, eager for the sack of the treasury.

The European officers of the Malwa and Bhopal Contingent Infantry ran to their men, but were warned off, with threats and menaces. The guns of the Bhopal Contingent, two in number, which had been posted close to the Residency, replied to the fire of the attacking party, while a number of the Sikh cavalry troop of the same force, having succeeded in cutting away their horses from their pickets, rallied round Colonel Travers. The men of the Bheel corps who could be got together were drawn into the Residency; but these denizens of the wilderness seemed more taken up with the survey of the various objects of European art and luxury around them, and the contemplation of themselves in the large mirrors, than with any thoughts of the defence of the place. Colonel Travers, having got together some of his Sikhs, led a gallant charge on the Indore guns, sabring and driving on the gunners ; but the infantry who were in support opened fire, and compelled him to retreat ; and he and his men regained the shelter of the **Residency.**

At the commencement of the outbreak, the Resident, Colonel Durand, sent off an express to Mhow, calling **for the Euro**pean artillery. The battery was sent off **at once ; but it was** met half-way **by a** horseman, with the information that the Resident **had been compelled to vacate the cantonment, and** had gone, **together with such officers and other** Europeans, **with their families, as could be saved, in** the direction of **Sehore, escorted by the Bhopal guns, the** Sikh cavalry, and the **Bheel** corps. The station, **being** abandoned, was sacked and burnt by the insurgents, who murdered about **twenty**five European men, women, and children.

On receiving **this** intelligence, Colonel **Hungerford, who** commanded the European artillery, **at once returned to Mhow** with all speed, fearful least the **native troops should have taken** advantage of his **absence to rise in mutiny. The so-called** fort of Mhow was simply an enclosure about 150 yards square, and was used as a magazine. It was surrounded by a loopholed **wall, ten** feet high, **and two feet in thickness, with** small bastions at the four corners, and **was** originally, I believe, built to repel the Pindarries. Into **this Colonel Platt,** the officer **commanding, had, at the urgent request of his** officers, **allowed all the** European families to **be collected.** Later **on, the artillery were also moved into the** fort, but fearful of **hurting the feelings** of the native troops, the fort guard, which consisted of thirty men of the Native **Infantry,** was increased to fifty. Thus the day passed, **but as soon as** darkness had set in the whole of the **native troops** in the **lines rose in** open mutiny. The guns, loaded with **grape,** were at **once turned on the native** guard in the fort ; and they were ordered to throw down their arms. This they reluctantly did, and subsequently most of the muskets were found to be loaded. The gunners then kicked them out at the gate, and they went off.

Major Harris, who commanded the cavalry, had gone to dine at his own house : hearing the firing, he mounted his horse and rode towards the lines, but was met by a party of his own men, and he and his horse were there and then shot. Colonel Platt, who was very deaf, rode up to the fort, and called out Captain Fagan. This officer, till within a few days of the outbreak, had been adjutant of the infantry regiment. Apparently Platt could not hear the firing, but his trust in his men was great. He and Captain Fagan went off to the lines,—the Colonel confident that he could restore order. They never returned ; and their bodies were found next morning on the parade-ground, riddled with bullets.

The sky now began to redden with the blazing houses of the officers, when Hungerford, ordering out two of his guns under Lieutenant Mallock, supported by a few officers on horseback, made a dash down the central road of the cantonment. A few rounds were fired into the lines, which were instantly vacated by the dastardly mutineers, who fled to join those at Indore. Having plundered that station, they moved on Gwalior, and it was said they formed part of the force which was afterwards cut up near Agra by Colonel Greathed.

While these events were taking place I was in my house at Maunpore, where I had hastily got together all the men I could muster. What with my own guard of eighteen men of the Gwalior Contingent, road and hill police, and about twenty-five men of the Thuggee Department, left with me by my friend in the morning, I had about one hundred men. Holkar's agent, who was attached to my office, sent off several horsemen during the day towards Mhow, to ascertain what was going on, but none of them came back, probably finding more congenial employment at Indore. Towards evening the agent himself went off, and did not return. In the morning I had heard the guns at Indore, and after dark came the ominous boom of those at Mhow.

In anticipation of the outbreak, Bappoo and Jemadar Buggoo Sing had concerted with Himta a plan, by which I was, if necessary, to take shelter with the Bheels in the jungles of the Maunpore district. I was, however, unwilling to leave my house till I knew the true state of affairs. Thus the evening passed away. I sat reading in a room in the centre of my house, which was partially surrounded with a wide verandah, where my men were collected. About 11 P.M. my treasurer's agent came in perfectly livid with terror, and informed me that he had just come from Mhow; that Holkar had attacked the Residency at Indore, having been joined by all the troops at the station; that Colonel Durand and all other Europeans had been murdered; and that at that moment Holkar was encamped at Rao, six miles from Mhow, the garrison of which had gone over to him; and finally, that the officers and their families had retired with the European artillery to the fort at Mhow, and were to be attacked in the morning.

This cheerful intelligence created a great stir among my men, and Buggoo Sing implored me to leave the house, as he knew that many of the men, especially the Contigent Sepoys, were not to be trusted. He added that he had seen some of them stealthily loading their muskets, and that any one of them could easily take a pot-shot at me as I sat. Acting on his advice, I called in about ten men on whom I placed most confidence, and made over to them my own guns and those of my friend. At the same time I sent round to the stable for my best horse. I then went out among the men, and informed them that it was requisite that I should make arrangements for guarding the hill-passes, as, owing to the disturbances in the cantonment, disorderly persons would be abroad. The corporal on guard over the house was directed to keep order, and all were told to go to sleep quietly, and that they would receive further orders in the morning. Just then my horse was brought round, and I mounted and rode off with my small band. I have a vivid recollection now of an uneasy feeling of expectation of being shot in the back as we left the door; but no hand was raised, and I moved out into the darkness with a sense of great relief.

We left the main road, and, taking a jungle path, proceeded about a mile and a half, when we arrived at the Ajnaar river. Here the banks were precipitous, and it would have been dangerous to attempt to take a horse down the footpath in the dark. We therefore halted, tied up the horse, and having posted sentries, lay down till morning. When the dawn broke, we descended into the gorge, and took up our quarters for the day in a cave, whence I sent a man back to the house for one of my servants and a supply of food, brandy, etc. I was here joined and cordially welcomed by a number of the Bheels of the district, headed by Himta and a man named Oonkar, who assured me that they could give me safe protection for six or twelve months if necessary. In the evening we crossed the river, and went up into the mountain of Shez-gurh, where we encamped in the jungle; the Bheels leaving some of their men with us to mount guard during the night. These men quite seemed to consider themselves answerable for my safety; and that any disaster occurring to me while in their jungles would be discreditable to them.

I remained among them for a week, during which time I opened communications with the Mhow garrison, from whom I learnt that the report which I had received regarding the hostility of the Maharajah Holkar was incorrect, and that the mutineers, having plundered the Indore cantonment, had gone off *en route* for Delhi.   On learning this, I sent off a note by one of my own men to Holkar, from whom I received a very civil reply, in which he expressed his sorrow for what had occurred, adding that, like ourselves, he had been quite unable to restrain his men.   He concluded with expressions of attachment to the British Government, and assured me of his willingness to do all in his power to restore order.   On receipt of this note, I determined to return to my own house at Maunpore, and re-open the postal communications between Mhow and the Bombay Presidency.

During the whole time that I was out the Bheels were perpetually on the alert, and in the daytime they mounted sentry in pairs, perched on trees commanding the approaches to our camp. These double sentries were posted about a mile apart, and were armed with bows and arrows and swords.   On the approach of any one bringing letters or supplies they descended and asked his business, and on receiving his reply one man escorted him forward to the next post, while the other resumed his position in the tree.   To guard against any night attack they insisted on our moving our camp every evening after dark ; and inasmuch as any attacking party would probably make a rush at the camp-fire, my bed was always made in some quiet spot, about one hundred yards distant, and a couple of Bheels were told off to sit by me while I slept.   We were most fortunate in having cool and fair weather, only a few showers falling during the time I was out, so that the want of a tent was little felt either by night or day.   The side of the mountain of Shezghur, on which we had taken up our position, was admirably suited for concealment, being cut off from the open country by the deep rocky chasm of the Ajnaar river to the north, and closed in to the south by the mountainous range, which was thinly populated by Bheels only. The mountain was heavily wooded, and intersected by rocky streams.

Considering it advisable, for the sake of moral effect, to return to my house with some show of power, I gave the word for the Bheels to assemble, which they did to the number of about one hundred and fifty, armed with swords, spears, matchlocks, and bows and arrows. With these, and my own men, who had been with me throughout, I returned to Maunpore, where I found the garrison had weeded itself, the evil-disposed having gone off to join the mutineers.

Ten days after, I took a few men and rode into Mhow, where I met all my friends in the fort. They had not been idle, having collected supplies from the bazaar, and raised an outwork in front of the gateway, behind which were mounted some heavy siege-guns. Next morning I returned to Maunpore, accompanied by an Irishman named Moran, an old soldier of the 86th, who had been in the service of a civil engineer at Indore. His wife and master had both been murdered in the outbreak, and he owed his own life to having been employed at the time at some distance from the station.

A few days after I went down the road towards Dhoolia, in the Bombay Presidency, which I reached by double marches in four days, and where I met a detachment of 250 men of the 86th, with whom I returned to Mhow. There we met Colonel Stuart's brigade, which had arrived *viâ* Asseerghur. Soon after I was ordered to assume charge of the Nimar district from Colonel Keatinge, who was sent out as

Political Officer with the force under Colonel Stuart, for the siege of Dhar and the relief of the besieged garrison of Nee-much. He subsequently accompanied the force to Chundairee, in Bundelcund, where he guided the stormers up the breach. In this affair he was severely wounded, and for his gallantry he received the Victoria Cross : no man ever earned it better.

My official duties and the disturbed state of the country during the period I was in charge of the Province of Nimar, did not allow me much time for field sports. My head-quarters were at Mundlaisir, on the Nerbudda, but I also re-tained the Maunpore district. Before leaving my house there, I had built a trap for panthers, which I left with Buggoo Sing, who succeeded in catching several. The trap was composed of bars of stout wood, three inches apart, in the form of a box, seven feet in length, four in height, and four in width. At one end was a compartment to hold a live goat, the bars at this part being sufficiently close to exclude the paw of a panther. The partition bars were of iron, so as not to impede a full view of the goat from the door, which was at one end, and working perpendicularly in a slide. To the door was attached a trigger, communicating with the centre of the trap, so that any beast rushing in at the goat would free the door, which would drop down behind him. I should not have resorted to this contrivance had I been able to shoot these panthers, but they lay during the day-time concealed in rocks and caves, and could not be got otherwise.

Another trap was made of rough jungle-wood, tied with strips of bark, in the form of a triangle, eleven feet in length and six in breadth at the base. Across this triangle were tied other sticks, and on these were laid heavy stones. A forked stick, five feet in height, was then planted in the ground, on which worked a twelve-foot sapling, one end of which was attached to the apex of the triangle. By pressing this sapling over the fork, the point of the triangle was raised about four feet, and was kept in that position by a trigger fastened to the other end and passing down through the stones to a slight wooden partition of split bamboo, behind which, in a pit sunk in the ground, the goat was tied. The sides were closed by thorny bushes, and any panther attempting to take the goat from the front, freed the trigger and brought down the triangle with its weight of stones on his back.

Among the peons or attendants in the Nimar office was Shaik Munnoo, a young Mahomedan, fond of sport, and a good shot. He was a smart well-made man, dandified in his attire when in quarters, and generally might be seen with his turban stuck on one side of his head, one fold being allowed to hang over his neck in a jaunty style. His ears were adorned with large gold rings. Like most men of his creed and calling he was generally in debt, and when his creditors became too pressing, he used to apply for a few days' leave and betake himself to the jungle, where he would sit up at night, either over water or over the carcass of some murdered cow, and having slain a tiger or panther he would return to the station, claim the Government reward, pay his debts, and renew his credit.

My presence being required at a village about fourteen miles off, I sent Munnoo ahead to endeavour to mark down something, and followed next morning, taking with me the doctor of the station, who, though an indifferent shot, was fond of sport. On our arrival, Munnoo informed us that a cow had just been killed by a panther, and that he had erected a small platform in a tree close by, from which it might be shot at night. No part of the cow had been eaten, only the marks of the four fangs in the neck were to be seen. I took up my position about sunset, and soon after a fine panther came bounding out into the open. The light, however, was bad, and I could not be certain of my aim, for the moon was obscured by thin clouds. The panther commenced, as they always do, by tearing away the softer skin inside the thigh. At length I fired, but the beast bounded off unscathed. About two hours after it returned, and again I fired with the same result. I was much disgusted, and, rolling myself in my blanket, I went to sleep.

Just below where I sat was a jungle-path, and about day-break I spied a bear coming leisurely along it. I fired, and he rolled over, but picked himself up, and went off. Presently Munnoo appeared, and we took up the track, but soon lost it among some ravines, and I returned to the village. After breakfast we proceeded to a jungle some miles off, passing on our way round the edge of a fine artificial lake, along the shores of which we found tracks of tigers, panthers, bears, wild-pigs, and deer. Farther on, we beat out a very likely-looking covert, in which we found the fresh track of a tiger ; and in the moist sand of a small stream, well sheltered by overhanging bushes, I came on the spot where he had lain, as was evident by hairs from his coat lying on the ground.

We then beat a rocky ravine, taking up positions on trees. Soon a bear came out, and fell to my shot, but rose again and made off up the hill behind me. Bushes intervened, and I was unable to put in my second barrel. At that moment a police-horseman, who was on his way to join us, met him on the face of the hill. The bear charged, and, wild with fright, the horse reared up, and then suddenly swerving round, threw his rider. Ludicrous as the affair was, it might have proved serious for the man, but, most fortunately, the bear rushed at the horse, which broke away at full gallop. The bear then crossed the open ridge, and went down into the next ravine. We followed him at once, and running ahead, took up fresh positions. Soon after we heard the shouts of the beaters, and presently I saw the bear coming towards me. His general health was evidently impaired, and my next shot finished him. On removing his skin we found a small match-lock-bullet in the muscles of his shoulder. It had been there a long time, and was enveloped in a tough white sac.

That evening Munnoo took one of my guns, and sat up over the carcass of the cow, while I took up a position on another platform in a tree half-a-mile distant. During the night I heard Munnoo fire several shots, and nothing having come near me, I descended at daybreak and went up to him. Round the carcass of the cow lay the bodies of four dead hyænas; a fifth had been wounded, and we tracked him by the blood for some distance into the jungle.

I should have wished to explore these jungles farther, but my presence was required at head-quarters, and we returned to Mundlaisir. While descending to the ferry on the Ner-budda, we fell in with a large wolf, which allowed us to approach within a few paces before he moved lazily away. During our stay at the village we had resided in the dhurm-salla or shelter-house for native travellers. These dhurmsallas are open sheds, having a wall on three sides, the roof on the fourth being supported by posts. They are free to all comers. Immediately on reaching home I felt very unwell, and con-tinued so for some days, when my malady declared itself in the form of a mild attack of smallpox. I had no doubt contracted the disease in the dhurmsalla.

CHAPTER XIII.

HAVING work at Maunpore, I left Mundlaisir early one morning in the hot season of 1858, and rode into Malwa by a jungle-
path up the mountain-side. Anticipating that I should see
game of some sort on the road, I directed one of my men to
take a rifle and go in advance, awaiting my arrival a few miles
below the pass. Near the base of the hills I came on a herd
of nylghae. They crossed the path about 100 yards ahead,
and, passing over a wooded spur of the hills, disappeared on
the other side. Though they must have seen us they did not
appear to be alarmed; and, dismounting, I made my horse
over to my attendant.

I may here remark on the singular absence of fear of
human beings displayed at times even by the most timid
animals, if the former are passing along paths or highways. I
have frequently seen deer of all kinds, when grazing quietly
near a road, allow a party of men, mounted or on foot, to pass
near them without any signs of alarm. Any one, however
leaving the beaten track, or making any attempt to stalk
them, would at once create suspicion, and cause them to
move off.

Carefully ascertaining the direction of the wind, I made a

circuit, and picking my way up the dry bed of a torrent I got within seventy yards of a large blue bull. He stood broadside on, gazing back, apparently on the watch against pursuit. Catching sight of me he started off, and at that moment I fired. The bull dashed wildly forward for fifty yards, and fell dead. Startled by my shot, but uncertain whence it came, the cows ran up from a hollow which had concealed them from my view, and stood out on the hill-side; but I had already shot more than I could carry, and I allowed them to escape. On the way back to my horse I blazed the trees with my knife, and having collected a small pile of stones at the side of the path, I resumed my journey. On ascending the mountain I rode to some Bheel huts, and informed the inhabitants where they would find the beast. Men, women, and children at once turned out, furnished with knives, hatchets, and baskets; and I doubt not that before night the flesh of the poor bull was frizzling over many a fire.

From Maunpore I returned to the Nerbudda, having sent on my tents and people to Khull, where I found them encamped on the south bank. A small flock of sheep, which I kept for food, had been grazing that morning near the camp, and were attacked in broad daylight by several wolves. One sheep was killed before the shepherd could drive them off. Near the spot were some deserted huts, which had been occupied by a troop of irregular cavalry. I directed Munnoo to tie the carcass to a tent-peg, and conceal himself at nightfall in one of these huts. The wolves returned, as we had expected. Munnoo shot one dead, and wounded another, which got away.

Next morning I was riding about two miles down the Bombay road, when a troop of six or seven wolves crossed the path 100 yards ahead of me. As was my custom, I was accompanied by a man on foot with a rifle. Quietly dismounting, and making my horse over to my attendant, we moved on at the same pace, and on reaching the spot where the wolves had crossed, I saw several standing about in the jungle within easy shot. Selecting a large dog-wolf, I fired, shooting him through the body behind the shoulder. Although completely doubled up, he kept his legs, but as I could plainly see the bullet-hole in his side, I made sure he would fall, and ran on through the jungle, hoping to get a shot at another. This I failed to do, and on my return I found the wounded wolf had disappeared. I followed the track by the blood for some distance, but did not see him again, and had to content myself with the knowledge that he was past sheep-killing. Previous to this I had received intelligence of a tiger in the Boorar river, near Teekree, but having much work on hand I had been unable to go after him. But about this time a detachment of the 71st Highlanders was on its march up from Bombay, and as I intended to meet them at Sindwah, I hoped to find time to look up the tiger on the way. I therefore deputed Munnoo from Khull, ordering him to examine the bed of the river, and send me word at once if he saw a fair prospect of sport. He returned after two days, bringing the skin of the tiger, which was of the largest size. Hearing that a cow had been killed on the morning of his arrival at Teekree, he had sat up in a tree over the body, and on the tiger coming out, about sunset, he had shot him dead. I was rather angry at this termination to my hopes, and did not award to Munnoo the meed of praise which he evidently anticipated. When near Sindwah I came on the fresh footprints of four tigers which had passed along the road in the early morning. They were very distinct in the heavy dust— paterfamilias, the lady-mother, and two well-grown children.

I returned with the 71st detachment, and one of the officers being anxious to see some wild beast, I took him out in the jungles on the south side of the Nerbudda. I hardly expected anything, as we had but few people with us, and had not had time to send men out in the early morning. But, from the rocks on the edge of some table-land, thinly covered with thorny bushes, we started a panther, and, on examining the spot, found two cubs, which we carried off and made over to the soldiers on joining the camp.

As we approached Maunpore, I sent Himta ahead, telling him to bring all the local talent into action, and to endeavour to mark down something on the morning that we were to arrive. Accordingly, he presented himself as directed, and reported a panther in the bed of the Ajnaar river. This river, like many other streams rising on the southern boundary of Malwa, after winding for a short distance through the higher jungle, leaps down a precipice of about thirty feet into a chasm, walled on either side by perpendicular rocks of large-grained basalt, intersected in parts by veins of quartz. It was to a cave in the north bank of this river that I retired when the mutiny broke out at Mhow, and it was not far from this cave that the panther had this morning been seen to enter a mass of rocks in the centre of the river immediately below the waterfall. The cave was formed by an overhanging rock, from which water dripped incessantly. The water, being strongly charged with lime, caused the surface of the rock to be covered with incrustations in a stalactite form, wondrous to behold. Immediately in front of the cave rose a mass of heavy foliage twined with creepers, generally tenanted by green pigeons. The only drawback to the place was a very dirty recluse, who had taken up his quarters here, spending his time either in begging in the neighbourhood, or sleeping in a state closely bordering on nudity among the ashes of his fire. These pious occupations, I need hardly state, secured him the countenance and respect of all his native acquaintances.

Himta had left several of his men on the watch while he came to guide us, and having finished breakfast we set out. The party consisted of one officer of the detachment, the doctor from Mundlaisir, and myself. When started, the panther could only come down the bed of the river, which was only about thirty yards in breadth. Above him was the waterfall, and on either side walls of rock. We drew lots for places, the doctor getting the left bank, I the right, and the Highlander the centre of the stream. As soon as we had mounted into trees, the panther was started, and hugging the rock on the right bank, came towards me. I fired, but missed, and the beast passed close under me. Turning sharp on the branch, I again fired, and he fell dead. As we stood round the dead beast the Highlander commenced to congratulate himself on his good shooting, whereby he had slain the panther. Not having heard any report from his gun, I mildly suggested that I had been the fortunate marksman, but he declared so positively that the fatal shot was his, that I, looking on him as my guest, held my peace. Just then the doctor, who was standing by, passed his fingers into the barrels of his rifle. They were perfectly clean. It was a wonderful instance of the force of imagination.

Soon after this I marched to join a force employed in the Sathpoora Hills in the suppression of a Bheel insurrection. The Bheels to the north of Khandesh, headed by Khaja Sing, took advantage of the embarrassment of the British Government in the suppression of the mutiny, to return to their old habits of plunder ; and those of the Burwanee State, in the south-western corner of Nimar, having unsettled claims against their own chief, were not slow to follow their example. As in more civilised countries, there is always in India a number of men of irregular habits, ready to join in anything whereby they may obtain the means of subsistence without the necessity of labour ; and no sooner does any freebooter or disaffected chief evince a tendency to plunder, than many such at once offer their services. As vultures to a carcass, so are they attracted from far and near, and the disturber of the public peace is speedily surrounded by a band of Affghan or Mekranee mercenaries, swashbucklers, and vagabonds from the towns, ready for any mischief. The only qualification necessary for service is the possession of arms, and the promises of remuneration to be received generally depend on the nature of the work expected.

Soon after they had turned out in insurrection the Bheels of the Sathpoora received a most welcome subsidy. Owing to the disasters of the day, the value of the East India Company's rupee became much depreciated throughout India, and in consequence of this, silver, which, under ordinary circumstances, would have found its way into the Bombay mint, was forwarded into the interior, there to be coined in the Indore and other native states. At this time opium, for export from Malwa to China, was escorted to Bombay by armed men, hired for the trip by the native dealers ; and about 400 of these had been collected by some bankers at Bombay, and started from the railway terminus in charge of a string of carts laden with silver, *en route* for Indore. The news of their march, of course, preceded them, and doubtless an embassy from the insurgents was sent to treat.

When the convoy reached the British collectorate of Khandesh, they were informed by the officer in charge of the district that the Bheels of the Sathpoora were in rebellion, and would probably make a descent on the treasure, which was stated to be worth £75,000. He suggested that they should pass up into Malwa by the more easterly route *viâ* Asseerghur. This advice was not taken, and when the treasure-party had reached a spot six miles north of Sindwah Fort the Bheels came down on them in force. Little or no show of resistance was made by the guard, who, once they had satisfied their consciences by a mild remonstrance, joined heartily in the plunder. The treasure consisted of lumps of silver, many pounds in weight, coins of Chili, and five-franc pieces. Every man filled his waistband, and a large quantity was buried in the jungle by the Bheels. Many of the escort joined the insurgents, others continued their way to the Ner-budda, and were arrested by the police, who collected from their persons treasure valued at about £6000. No sooner had the news of the robbery got abroad than numbers of vagabonds of all castes from the large towns and villages, attracted by promises of high pay, joined the Bheels.

A strong native force was then sent out in April 1858 by the Bombay Government, and an organised advance was made into the heart of the jungles. The column was commanded by Colonel Evans of the 9th Bombay Native Infantry. They were encamped at Burwance, and having received reliable intelligence that the Bheels and their men were in a strong position in the jungle a few miles to the southward, an attack was planned. A small column was sent to make a feint at a pass to the eastward of the insurgents, who turned out in strength to oppose its progress. Meanwhile the main body made a détour, and advanced on the rebel camp from the west-ward. The Bheel force were exulting on their supposed victory over the smaller column, when the alarm was given that the Government troops were in their camp. They returned with

all speed, and a sharp fight took place, the Affghans and
Mekrances firing from behind the masses of rock and trees,
and making a determined resistance. In all about 300 were
slain, principally outsiders, for the Bheels themselves fled
early in the day, and by their knowledge of the ground made
good their escape. A prisoner having volunteered to show
some of the treasure which was buried in the jungle, a party
of men was sent with him. He guided them to a spot where
lay the decaying carcass of a bullock, and stated that the
treasure would be found buried beneath it. On digging, silver
of the value of about £12,000 was recovered.

I joined the force a few days after the fight had taken
place. Colonel Evans was then encamped on the Goee river,
in the jungle, twelve miles south-west of Burwanee. Soon
after I received a message from Bheema, the leader of the
Burwanee Bheels, stating that he wished to surrender, but
desiring that I should meet him in the jungle and let him
know the terms under which he would be allowed to come in.
The place of meeting was to be about two miles from the
camp, and I was not to be accompanied by any armed party.
As I knew that all but Bheels had fled from the jungles
after the engagement I acceded to his request, and replied
that I would meet him on the following day. I set out, accompanied by one native horseman of my own police, and
guided by a Bheel who had been sent by Bheema. Meeting
the officer commanding the Khandesh Bheel Corps, which
formed part of the force, he offered to join me, and as he was
personally known to Bheema, I assented.

On reaching a quiet spot in the jungle our guide requested
us to halt, and, running off, disappeared in the thickets.
After a short time he returned, followed by Bheema, who
was accompanied by fifteen or twenty Bheels armed with

matchlocks, swords, and bows.   I greeted him pleasantly, and after some conversation I told him the terms on which he might come in.   They were at once accepted, and he rode back with us to the camp, while his men returned to the forest. The news of his arrival created no small stir among the troops, and my tent was surrounded by the men, anxious to get a sight of the redoubtable freebooter, who was allowed to be at large on parole.   The result of these attentions was, that he took fright and fled in the night; and for long after he continued to be a thorn in the flesh both to his own chief and to the British officer in political charge of the district.   Soon after this the force broke up and proceeded to quarters, and my work in this country being only of a temporary nature I returned to Mundlaisir.

When encamped with the force we received intelligence of a tiger which had lain up in some long grass in the bottom of a small ravine.   I went out with two other officers, and having taken positions in trees, men were sent to hurl down stones from some overhanging rocks.   The tiger was at once started, and passed under the tree on which one of my friends was posted.   He fired, missing right and left, and the tiger went off into the jungle.   About this time I saw a specimen of the flying squirrel, which was brought in by one of the men.   It was brownish-gray in colour, and over two feet in length.   On either side a web of loose skin connected the fore and hind legs.   In springing from tree to tree these webs are spread out, and, acting like sails, enable the animal to make surprising leaps.   Another singular creature was captured one night near the tents.   It was nearly four feet in length and about one in height, tapering from the middle of its body to the nose and tail.   The legs were short, and the toes furnished with strong claws. The entire body from tip to tip was covered with strong, hard, yellow scales, the largest being about one and a half inch across. From its appearance we supposed it to be a species of ant-eater. When alarmed, it rolled itself into a circular form, the tail being lapped over the head, which it completely protected.

CHAPTER XIV.

By the autumn of 1858 the mutiny and rebellion in India had been effectually crushed. Scarce eighteen months had elapsed since the Bengal army had thrown off its allegiance to the British, and having possessed itself of magazines, treasuries, and fortresses, vainly supposed that it could establish a government of its own. It was narrated of a certain native chief who owed much gratitude to the British, that, at the commencement of the insurrection, he had consulted an astrologer as to the course which he ought to pursue. The reply was, "If you can utterly exterminate them, do so—but if one escapes, he will return with thousands." That chief stood firm. Had the Bengal army received as good advice it might have existed till this day. A few European troops were still to be found in the Indian garrisons. These held their ground till reinforced, and then, marching forth, they wreaked a terrible vengeance on their foes.

The Central India force under Sir Hugh Rose had ended

its victorious march from Indore by the capture of Gwalior ; and the rebel army, broken and utterly disorganised, had fled southwards under the leadership of Tantia Topee. This man was reported to have been the intimate friend of Nana Sahib, and to have been implicated with that miscreant in the massacre at Cawnpore. It was said that, despairing of success in the North-west Provinces, he hoped to gain the Bombay Presidency, and there endeavour to rekindle the flame of rebellion. Be that as it may, driven from Gwalior by Sir Hugh, he fled with a broken host of horse and foot, and arrived at Jalra Patun in Central India, where he took possession of thirty guns of various calibres from the Rajah. As ordnance these guns were contemptible, but the mere fact of an army having guns of any sort is sufficient in India to increase its importance.

To oppose the progress of Tantia, a small column under Colonel Lockhart (92d) was sent out from Mhow. It consisted of about 350 men of the 92d Highlanders, 400 of the 19th Bombay native infantry, two squadrons of the Bombay Native Cavalry, and two guns of the Bengal European Artillery. But on intelligence being received that the rebel force numbered about 20,000 men, and that Tantia had seized the guns at Jalra Patun, a second column under Colonel Hope, 71st Highland Light Infantry, was despatched. This column consisted of about 350 men 71st Highlanders, 400 men 4th Bombay Native Infantry, two guns Bengal European Artillery, and a squadron 17th Lancers. General Michel accompanied the latter, and eventually assumed command of the combined force. Captain Hutchinson accompanied Colonel Lockhart as political officer, and I was sent with Colonel Hope in a similar capacity. It was our duty to obtain information of the strength, position, and intended movements of the rebel force ; of the practicability or otherwise of various roads ; and to arrange for the advance of such money as might be required for the troops ; also to collect the requisite supply of food of all kinds. The latter was a work of considerable anxiety, and could not have been carried out without the hearty co-operation of the native chiefs in whose territories we were engaged ; for we were in pursuit of a flying enemy, the carrying powers of the commissariat department were very limited, and it was impossible to say on one day where we might be the next.

On receiving intelligence of the advance of our force from Mhow, Tantia moved eastward, and reached Rajghur, a fort about 120 miles north of Indore, and ten miles west of the Bombay and Agra trunk-road. General Michel advanced in a north-easterly direction, and on the 14th of September, about 3 P.M., came in sight of the rebel force. We had been marching since an early hour, and our men had suffered greatly from the intense heat, at no season more oppressive than during the months of September and October. On arriving at a spot whence the country fell away towards the river Neewuj, we saw the enemy about two miles off, encamped on the far side of the stream. A portion of their force had crossed to this side of the river, and had taken possession of the fort of Rajghur, which stands on the left bank. Conscious of the exhausted condition of his men, and aware that little could be done during the few hours of daylight which remained, General Michel halted his column for the night.

Before daybreak, on the 15th September, we were under arms, and moving down the narrow track descending to Rajghur. On either side the country was covered with thorny scrub, and intersected with ravines. As far as we could see from left to right, in the low ground, were the camp-fires of the enemy. A halt was ordered, and we lay down on the road till dawn. We then became aware that Tantia had moved, only a rear-guard of a few hundred horse remaining on the ground. He had marched in an easterly direction towards Beowra, on the trunk-road. We at once descended to the river; and, at the request of the General, I rode into the fort to bring out the chief, and learn what I could of the movements of the enemy. The gate of the fort was reached by a stone slope about eighty yards in length. I was accompanied by four troopers of the late Bhopal Contingent; and, on gaining admittance, I left two of them in the gateway to secure a retreat if necessary, and rode on to the chief's house. The fort presented a singular appearance, the streets being utterly deserted, save by a few old or decrepit individuals. The roadways and floors of the verandahs on either side were covered with horse-litter and smoking embers, and in all directions were strewed dinner-plates made of the leaf of the kākra tree—relics of the last night's feast. The chief met me at the door of his house, and at once proceeded to detail the indignities to which he had been subjected by his late unwelcome guests. His looks belied his statements, and I have no doubt they had spent a very jovial evening together. He accompanied me to the General, with whom I left him.

Our small body of horse, consisting of two squadrons of native cavalry and one of the 17th Lancers, was ordered to pursue, and my services as a political not being required while Captain Hutchinson was in camp, I accompanied them. The country over which the enemy had retreated was similar to that on the west side of the river—undulating and stony, cut up with many small ravines and watercourses, and covered with thorny scrub, through which the road wound over the natural surface of the ground. Skirmishers were

thrown forward to clear the jungle in our front, while the
rest of the cavalry kept the track. About a mile from Rajghur
we came on a dismounted gun lying on the path, and soon
after this, stragglers were overtaken and cut up by the skirmishers. On a steep incline, rising out of a watercourse, we
found two guns, which had evidently belonged to the Royal
Jalra Patun Horse Artillery. They had been abandoned,
and the harness, which had been cast off the horses, lay
beside them. At length we sighted the rear-guard of the
enemy, consisting of cavalry. They allowed us to approach
within range of their carbines, from which they fired a few
shots before going off.

We now came to a more level country, and on the left side
of the road, an open space, half-a-mile in length, and four
hundred yards in breadth, had been cleared of jungle, and
roughly cultivated. As our skirmishers advanced over this
ground, the rebel horse turned, and came on in considerable
strength, driving them in on our diminutive column. Sir
William Gordon of the 17th, who was in command, formed
his men up in line, and moved slowly on. Meanwhile the
open clearing above referred to was covered by the enemy's
sowars, who advanced shouting and brandishing their swords.
As we closed in on them they began to give way, and when
they saw us increase the pace to a trot, it was evident that
they did not mean to stand. On receiving the order to charge,
our men came on in admirable order, but the enemy turned
and went off. A few fell before our sabres and lances, but
the mass of men, which a few moments before had shouted so
defiantly, fled in the wildest disorder.

But it now appeared that they had been leading us into a
trap, and, had the execution been as good as the plan, they
would have thinned our ranks. Along the whole line of our

front they had posted their guns masked in the jungle, and no sooner had their own cavalry swept through them, than they opened in our faces, accompanied by a sharp fire of musketry. Sir William Gordon gave the word, "Threes left," and we passed within fifty yards of the muzzles of the guns. When clear of their front we retired to the other end of the open ground, where we halted. How we escaped being severely cut up was a miracle. Neither man nor horse was touched, and. we could only suppose that the guns had been laid for a longer range, and, owing to our sudden onset, the enemy had not had time to depress them. The infantry had probably contented themselves with blazing in the air. Long after we had halted, the round shot continued to fly over our heads, but no damage was done, and we quietly awaited the arrival of the General, with our own guns and infantry. These at length came up. The men had marched fast, and a brief space was allowed them to take breath. Meanwhile the enemy had again got their guns on the road, and were once more in retreat.

We followed, a portion of the infantry skirmishing in front to the right and left, and the remainder in column with the guns and cavalry. At length we reached the confines of the hard stony soil, over which we had marched since we left Rajghur, and before us lay a wide expanse of cultivated ground. But on this side of the cultivation was a stream, with soft boggy banks ; and as we came in sight of it we saw the guns of the enemy below us, struggling through the mud. Our own were then ordered to the front, and after a few rounds, the enemy fled, leaving their guns as they lay. The cavalry was again pushed forward ; and, having crossed the stream, swept through a small village and out into the open country. Half-a-mile ahead, we saw the rebels in flight,—a dense mass of horse and foot mixed up together.

It was now about 4 P.M. Our men had been in the saddle since 3 A.M., and had suffered a good deal from the heat. We had cut up a number of the enemy, and had taken all their guns ; and as any attack on the mass of the rebel force with our handful of cavalry must have been followed by some loss, and could have been accompanied by no adequate result, a halt was called, and the enemy went off, heading for Sironj. Men and horses were in want of water, and, guided by a fringe of date-trees at some distance to our left, we rode off to a small stream and dismounted. Here Lieutenant Shaw, of the 3d Cavalry, died of sunstroke. He was taken ill as we lay by the water, and was dead in twenty minutes. He was a man of a cheerful and kindly disposition, and was much regretted by all his comrades. He was buried at Beowra, where we rejoined the column, and from which place the captured ordnance was sent to Mhow. At Beowra we also buried several men of the 92d and 71st, who had died of sunstroke during the action. Our loss from the enemy was *nil*.

From Beowra, Captain Hutchinson returned to Indore, and after a halt of one day, the force marched on Nursinghur, and thence on Bhairseeah, the object of the General being to drive the enemy northward. From Sironj, Tantia, having obtained a considerable accession to his force from the Mahomedan population of the place, moved to Esaghur in the Gwalior territory, where he took possession of ten guns. He then divided his army ; one portion with four guns marching up the left bank of the Betwa, and the other with six guns crossing that river, and moving on Lullutpore. We were fortunate in falling in with both divisions. From Bhairseeah we also marched to Sironj, and thence to the village of Mongrowlee, thirty miles to the north-east, where we fell in with the right division of Tantia's force.

About this time we were joined by one of Scindiah's officers, the Sir Soubah or chief governor of the district, from whom I received much valuable assistance. From his scouts we obtained intelligence that a body of the enemy was coming southwards, and our march was so accurately regulated that we arrived on the ground at Mongrowlee on the 9th October, about one hour before they came in sight. We at once met them, and after some sharp firing they fled, leaving their four guns in our hands.

On the following morning General Michel, with all his cavalry, marched north to Serai, where we fell in with a column under Colonel Parke, 72d Highlanders. A considerable portion of his cavalry and horse artillery was transferred to our force. Our own infantry and guns had been directed to move due east to Malthone, on the north-west corner of the Saugor district. From Serai we also moved east, intending to cross the Betwa and advance through the jungle to Lullutpore. The river was deep and rapid, and the passage was attended with some difficulty, and on our attempting to push on a body of irregular cavalry by the direct route through the jungle to Lullutpore, they were fired on from the thickets, and driven back. The entire force was therefore moved round to Malthone, and thence we marched through a pass in the hills to Narhut.

At this time, the second division of the rebel army, augmented by the men who had fled from Mongrowlee, was encamped at Lullutpore, twenty-five miles to the north, and from that place to Narhut was the metalled road towards Saugor. As we had reason to believe that the enemy would attempt to turn our right flank, the General determined to intercept them, and had ordered the march on Sindwaho, ten miles to the north-east of Narhut, for the following morning. With this view I had sent men ahead to the surrounding vil-

lages, with orders to the head men to send in all requisite
supplies for our force on its arrival. About 11 P.M. I was
roused from a sound sleep by two of my messengers, who reported that the advance guard of the rebel force was marching into Sindwaho. I at once went off to the General, and
in half-an-hour orders had gone to commanding officers
directing them to turn out their men without bugle-sounds,
and be ready to march at once. We left the ground soon after
midnight (October 19th), and on arriving at Sindwaho came
face to face with the enemy, drawn up in line at the head
of a long rise of cultivation.

As we came within range they opened on us with their
artillery. We replied with shells, which burst over their
heads, causing great commotion. Meanwhile our infantry
were coming into line in echellon, but before they had time to
execute the manœuvre, the rebels turned and fled, their leaders
showing the way, as was their usual custom. Six guns fell
into our hands. The pursuit was taken up by the cavalry and
artillery, and a number of the rebels were cut up. Here and
there they made a stand, and fought to the last, causing us
some loss. Captain Harding of the 8th Hussars was among
the slain. They fled northwards, and we encamped on the
Jamnie river, about ten miles from Tearee, where we halted
for one day, and then marched west to Lullutpore.

This had been the station of a wing of the Gwalior Contingent Infantry, and the ruined cantonment bore sad traces
of the mutiny. Soon after our arrival I received a report
that the rebels were passing southwards by a jungle route a
few miles farther west. This was confirmed by a party sent
to reconnoitre. As it was important that Tantia should not
be allowed to reach the Bombay Presidency, we marched at
midnight, and next day arrived at Narhut, twenty-five miles

distant, the same place from which we had marched to meet the enemy at Sindwaho. At midnight we again marched, and halted a few miles north of Kurai in the Saugor district. The rebels were at that time encamped about six miles south-west of us, and were much distressed by the rapid moving to which they had been subjected.

On the following morning (October 25th) we again marched at about 2 A.M., and, taking a south-westerly course, passed through Kurai. At daybreak, as we cleared the town, we saw the rebels crossing our front. They straggled along the track, without any attempt at order, and among the various groups of horsemen could be seen the uniforms of many regiments mixed in confusion. Advancing on them, we cut their line in two. The leading portion went on its way southwards, but those who had been on our right, as we emerged from Kurai, turned back whence they came; and our cavalry, which was now broken into small detachments, closely pursued them, slaying many.

Marching in pursuit of the leaders we came to Bagrode, and here we found that they had again been attacked by a small cavalry force under Colonel Beecher. Several dead bodies lay about in the fields close to our line of march, and beasts and birds appeared to have profited by the occasion. Wolves, jackals, and vultures, were to be seen standing about in the fields, gorged and lazy. One wretch had fallen near a furrow, and lay in the way of a cultivator engaged in ploughing. Beyond guiding his bullocks round the corpse as he passed, he took no notice whatever, and the vultures, disturbed for the moment, hopped slowly back to their hideous banquet.

Tantia had now gained the shelter of the hills in the Vindyah range, north of Hoosungabad, and the tracks being impassable for guns and wheeled carriages, General Michel was obliged to move in a westerly direction to Bhilsa, a large town belonging to Scindiah, situated on the eastern side of the Betwa river, near its junction with the Bess, thirty-two miles north-east from Bhopal. Here we had an opportunity of visiting the Bhoodist remains known as the Sanchi Tope, an engraving of which appeared with a short notice in the *Illustrated London News*, March 5, 1870.—"These Topes were used for the deposit of relics, etc., and the Sanchi Tope is one of the most remarkable. The date of the Tope itself is 500 B.C., while the gateway is about 500 years later. Of the four gateways which originally surrounded it, the eastern is the most perfect. The others have suffered much damage from weather and other disastrous effects, and two of them are now nothing more than masses of richly carved blocks of stone, lying one on the top of the other. Of the eastern gateway a cast is at the present moment being made by a party of Royal Engineers, under a subaltern officer who has been appointed Superintendent of the Archæological Survey of India in the North-West Provinces, especially told off for this work by the Government of India. When finished the cast will be sent to England, and exhibited at the South Kensington Museum. In the meantime those of our readers for whom this magnificent memorial of Bhoodist art has any interest may find in Mr. Fergusson's exhaustive work, entitled *Tree and Serpent Worship*, very complete materials for acquainting themselves with its general features and details." Bhilsa tobacco is held in high repute throughout Central India. Here we parted with Scindiah's Sir Soubah, from whom we had at all times received the greatest assistance, both in obtaining intelligence of the movements of the enemy and in drawing supplies to the camp.

Tantia Topee had in the meantime reached the Nerbudda, which he crossed to the eastward of Hoosungabad. Descending the Vindyah by a rugged pass, we also crossed and advanced on Baitool. Tantia was on our left front heading for Ellichpoor, but hearing that a force would oppose his progress he turned west along the valley of the Taptee, crossing that river at Meil Ghat, and so passed through a large tract of heavy forest into Nimar, emerging at Khundwah. General Michel also moved west from Baitool through a wild and desolate country, in which supplies were not procurable. While in this jungle, the Banda Nawaub, who had hitherto been with Tantia, left the rebels, and, coming into our camp with his family and personal servants, surrendered himself a prisoner.

From Khundwah, Tantia passed through Nimar towards Burwanee, and the running was now taken up by Colonel Parke, with his column, then in the field south of the Nerbudda. The rebels crossed the Nerbudda near Burwanee, and headed for Baroda, in the Guicowar's dominions. Colonel Parke followed in close pursuit, overtaking them at Chota Odeypoor, where he attacked them and slew many. Tantia then fled north through the Banswarra jungle, emerging into the plains of Malwa near Pertabghur, where he was met and again smitten by a flying column under Colonel Benson, 17th Lancers. Colonel Somerset, with another column, then cut in, attacking and driving him north through the Kotah and Jeypoor territories, whence he was driven into Marwar by a force from Nusserabad.

Meanwhile General Michel, having arrived at Mhow *via* Mundlaisir, rested his men, and then marched north to Kotah, where we halted a few days. At this place Major Burton, the political agent, and his family, had been murdered early in the rebellion, and subsequently the Rajah himself was besieged in his palace by a strong insurgent force, which had taken possession of the town, which is strongly fortified, and stands on the right bank of the Chumbul river. But a column from Bombay, commanded by General Roberts, was sent against them. Having crossed the Chumbul in boats, that officer took possession of the inner fortress in which the palace stands. The town was then carried by assault. Our force was encamped near the ruins of Major Burton's bungalow. Its blackened walls bore many vengeful inscriptions, written by the British soldiers after the siege.

The Chumbul flowed in a deep smooth stream, 200 yards in width, at the foot of a high bank close to our tents. In the centre of the river were a few green islands of small extent, formed by alluvial deposit. These were favourite basking-places for numbers of alligators and large turtle, which afforded good targets for our rifles, and several were shot. There is usually a prejudice in India against using the fresh-water turtle as an article of food; but on this occasion we turned them into both soup and pies—very excellent.

The Rajah, having sent us invitations to join a great shooting party, we embarked one morning on the river in a number of large boats sent down for our accommodation. In all knowledge of woodcraft the Indian chiefs are, with few exceptions, lamentably deficient. Their great idea of "Shikar" is to go forth into the plain or woodland, accompanied by many men and horses. They are followed by servants of all descriptions, bearing emblems of office; and the noise of this small army, as may be supposed, is not conducive to sport. But the arrangements for this day were quite unique.

As we were rowed up the river we had an excellent view

of the town, with its walls overhanging the water. Farther
up, on the right bank, we observed a large and gaily-dressed
crowd ; and our boatmen and attendant ambassadors informed
us that the Rajah would embark at that point. Screeching
bands of music now struck up, and several boat-loads of
nautch-women were pushed out into the stream. Then came
the Rajah in a gorgeous boat, accompanied by courtiers, and
surrounded by other boats filled with armed men. The royal
barge was pushed up alongside of our own, and, after an inter-
change of compliments, we all rowed up the river in a grand
procession. On either side the rocks rose high and steep ;
and I noted many a spot, as we passed, where beasts might be
expected to be lying hid among the masses of stone and bush.
At length we came to a number of men, armed to the teeth,
standing on the left bank, at the water's edge. For some distance up the stream a fringe of broken rocks was backed by
a perpendicular cliff ; and we were now informed that "the
tiger" had been seen in the early morning to secrete himself among these fragments. In order that the king and his
guests might prosecute the chase without possible chance of
injury to themselves, it had been arranged that the boats
should move up the stream for some distance farther, and,
having taken up a position beyond the springing distance of
the most lively tiger, await the appearance of the game. The
tiger was to be driven from the rocks by the armed men before
mentioned.

The procession again moved on, and for the moment the
musicians ceased to blow, but the splash of the oars might
have been heard a mile away, and the noise of voices was
loud and incessant. Presently some one called out "The
tiger !" and we then saw a very small panther bolting along

the river-side 150 yards ahead of us. Shots were fired by king and courtiers, but the panther held on till he came to a fissure in the rocks, when he turned up into the forest, and we saw him no more. So ended the grand hunting-party, in which five or six hundred men had been engaged. The Rajah lamented our bad luck ; we replied that the tiger had still some days to live. Remarks complimentary to ourselves and derogatory to tigers were interchanged ; the bands again struck up ; the nautch-women commenced to yell ; and we rowed back to the town, where we parted from our host, and returned to camp. Poor man ! he had done the best he could for us according to his lights.

Some of the officers of the force went out hog-hunting ; but as I did not wish to risk laming horses on the line of march, I abstained from this sport. However, I went after deer in company with our Quartermaster-General ; and, at a short distance from camp, came on three chinkara grazing in some cultivated ground. Working our cart towards them I dropped one with each barrel. The third trotted off a short distance, and then, standing, looked about for his comrades. Quickly reloading, I again fired, and we picked up the three antelopes.

As the force was to cross the Chumbul on the following day, we proceeded to examine the ford, and as we descended to the river I saw a large alligator basking on a mud bank. He was broadside on, about sixty yards off, and lay motionless, with his jaws apart. I fired, and struck him in the neck. His head dropped, and he lay quite dead. We then descended and cut off his head, which we carried away as a trophy. On our way to camp my companion shot a buck chinkara.

Leaving Kotah, we proceeded to Nusserabad by easy

marches. General Michel was fond of shooting, and when within a few miles of the halting grounds he and I generally left the column and rode away across the country in search of some lake or swamp where we might find wild ducks. These were very plentiful. Our guns were carried by men in rear of the column, mounted on riding dromedaries, who could keep up with our horses at a canter. We usually joined the camp in the forenoon, and always had a good bag of ducks to share with our friends.

Throughout this march I lived in a small tent twelve feet square, known as a "pal." In shape it closely resembled the ordinary cottage of Scotland, having a ridge and two gable ends, in one of which was the door. The side walls were only four feet in height. It was supported by a long stick under the ridge, resting on two poles at the ends. This tent was simply a large bag, and could be struck or pitched in a few minutes. Its principal fault was want of rigidity in high wind, but this was counterbalanced by its portability. Here the various members of the staff camp assembled nightly after dining in their own tents, and honoured me with their company till bed-time. The General lay extended on my bed, his Aide-de-camp reposed in my arm-chair, while round the table in chairs, and ranged along the edge of the bed, sat the Assistant Adjutant-General, Assistant Quartermaster-General, Brigade-Major, Postmaster, Commandant of Artillery, Inspector-General of Hospitals, and any friends who had dined with them. The weather was sufficiently cold to enable us to appreciate a tumbler of hot whisky-toddy, and we spent our evenings very pleasantly, notwithstanding the certainty that sorrow would return long before the dawning of morn, and that at 2 A.M. "the general" would sound, to be too surely followed by the "assembly" at 3.

Throughout the native states in Malwa and Rajpootana we were much annoyed by thieves at night, and the dexterity of these villains was wonderful. With greased bodies they wriggled along the ground between the sentries, and stole articles from tents filled with soldiers. Night after night they entered the tents of the officers, taking away anything which they could move. I almost alone escaped, possibly because I was known to be the "Political Sahib," but more probably owing to the watchful guardianship of a black and tan terrier at the foot of my bed.

While we marched leisurely towards Nusserabad, the wretched Tantia was kept moving, and nowhere could he find rest for the sole of his foot. Column after column darted out from the British cantonments, all acting in unison, and all bent on avenging Cawnpore. For seven months we had been perpetually on his track, and it was now certain that his diminished band of men and horses could not hold out much longer. Driven through Marwar by the Nusserabad force, they crossed the hills into Meywar, where they found us in readiness to take up the pursuit. At this time it had become generally known throughout India that the royal amnesty which had been proclaimed was *bona fide*, and, acting on the faith of it, about 200 of Tantia's men came in and laid down their arms. The remainder fled again across Malwa, dispersing as they went, till Tantia, deserted by his followers, sought refuge with a chief of the Gwalior territory who was in rebellion against Scindiah. This man, anxious to secure the good offices of the British in effecting a reconciliation between himself and his own sovereign, betrayed Tantia to a party sent to arrest him. The latter was sent to Seepree, where he was tried and hanged.

General Michel marched his force from Neemuch to Shoja-wulpoor, where it was broken up, but detachments continued for some time to be employed in hunting down the predatory bands which had been brought into existence by the rebellion, and who now sought shelter in the jungle. My duties with General Michel being at an end, I was directed by Sir Robert Hamilton, then agent to the Viceroy for Central India, to assume the temporary charge of the Political Agency in Bhopal.

CHAPTER XV.

DURING the short period of my tenure of office at Sehore, my
official duties obliged me to remain at my post, and I had
but little leisure for the chase. The country was still in an
unsettled state, and as it had been decreed that a European
force should be located at Sironj, I was employed in forward-
ing men and material for the construction of temporary
barracks at that place. It was subsequently abandoned, as
the troops suffered much from fever, and a number of men
were laid up with guinea-worm in the legs and feet. How
these creatures find their way into the human frame is, I
believe, a mystery to medical men. They appear in all parts
of the lower limbs, causing intense pain, and much swelling of
the afflicted part. The worm, which is sometimes nearly two
feet in length and one-eighth of an inch in breadth, lodges
itself among the muscles and tendons. Shortly before it appears on the surface of the skin a small blister rises, and soon
after the head of the worm comes out. This must be secured
by rolling it round a small bit of cloth or other substance,
but no forcible extraction should be attempted. The part
must be kept moist and well protected, and such portion of

the worm as can be easily drawn out, is daily wound round the cloth till the whole comes away. Should the worm be broken by force or accident, it will recede into the wound, where it dies, causing suppuration and great pain before it is finally got rid of.

A few miles to the southward of Sehore lies a scrub jungle of some extent. In no part very dense, it contains many small ravines, filled with long grass and thorny bushes, affording good shelter to tigers, which occasionally wander up from the larger coverts, attracted by the cattle from the surrounding villages. Late one afternoon a shikaree whom we had stationed at this spot came in and reported that a villager had just been killed by a tiger. The man with two companions had been gathering gum from the trees, when the tiger rushed out on them from a patch of grass, seizing him in his teeth, and killing him on the spot. His comrades were unarmed, and fled to the village.

It was too late to do anything that afternoon, but all was prepared for an early start, and by sunrise next morning we had ridden out to the jungle, where we met our gun-bearers with three good elephants. I was accompanied by the civil surgeon and the adjutant of the local corps. As the country was very open, and the sun was still low in the heavens, I urged them not to fire long shots should the tiger rise on the approach of the elephants. I calculated that we should have no difficulty in again marking him down. All preliminaries being arranged, we went off to the spot where the tiger had been seen, and there, face downwards, lay the body of the unfortunate man. His clothes were torn, and a quantity of blood was on the ground ; but the tiger had apparently not been hungry, for no portion of the body was eaten, and as it had lain in the jungle all night, we were not sanguine.

Leaving a few villagers to carry home the dead man, we moved into some grass jungle, having previously posted men in different directions on high trees, with orders to keep a good look-out. The adjutant was on the left, the doctor in the centre, and I was on the right of the line. We had not gone far before the tiger, a very large male, rose from a small watercourse about sixty yards on my right front, and bounded up the opposite bank. He was too far off to allow of my shooting with certainty, therefore, trusting that he would lie up in the next thicket, I reserved my fire. The doctor, however, had caught sight of him, and, greatly excited, at once loosed his piece. I saw the shots strike the ground wide of the tiger, who increased his pace, and went off giving a few angry growls. We followed him up at once, and again I implored my companions not to fire unless they were certain that they could do so with good effect.

Half-a-mile farther on we again started the tiger—this time he was within a fair range of the doctor, who, however, missed him, and we feared that even my wonted good luck would not give us another chance. But the sun was now high and powerful, and as we knew that there was no strong covert within several miles, we followed on in the direction which the tiger had taken. About a mile ahead we came up to one of our scouts on a tree, who reported that the tiger had entered the bushes which fringed the edge of a small dry nullah running out into the plain. Quietly forming up the three elephants in line, we moved slowly on, and soon after saw the tiger going off about eighty yards before us. As he seemed thoroughly scared, I deemed it prudent this time to fire, on the chance of wounding him. The doctor also fired at the same moment, and the tiger lurched heavily to one side and disappeared among the bushes. I had just taken up another rifle, and we were cautiously advancing, when the enraged brute rushed to meet us. He was within twenty paces before we saw him, and was evidently inclined to do mischief, but again we opened fire and dropped him. He rose, however, in an instant, and again came on, roaring wickedly; but, apparently not caring to close with the elephants, he dashed through our line and went back up the nullah.

We quickly reloaded, and followed him up, carefully examining every bush and tuft of grass. In this manner we had advanced to the very head of the nullah, which terminated in a large green corinda bush. The tiger made no sign, and we began to fear that he might have slunk away to the right or left, but, determined to make sure, I directed my mahout to take me up to the corinda bush. The head of the elephant had almost touched the foliage, when the tiger, now mad with rage, sprang at him, seizing him by the root of the trunk in his teeth, while he buried his claws in the sides of his face. With a frantic shriek the elephant dropped his head, and endeavoured to pin the tiger to the ground with his tusks. It was a moment of intense excitement, and I was seriously alarmed for the mahout, who, seated on the neck of the elephant, was in great danger of being thrown down between the struggling brutes. My own situation too was by no means pleasant, for I was thrown forward in the howdah, and I dreaded lest the girths should give way. However, the "graith" was good, and I kept my position, and as the elephant with a desperate effort shook off the tiger, I found I had retained my three guns uninjured.

The tiger made off down the nullah before I could again fire, and it was some time before the elephant, who continued to dance and shriek with rage, could be sufficiently quieted to enable us to follow after him. Throughout the struggle, my companions, though only a few paces off, were unable to render any assistance, fearing to fire lest they might hit the elephant. About 100 yards down the nullah we came on the tiger, crouching under a bank. He at once charged, and this time left the marks of his teeth and claws in the head of the adjutant's elephant ; but he was now less lively, and one or two shots put in with effect rolled him over. He was a fine beast, a male of the largest size, with a rich dark skin. He was, moreover, very shaggy about the sides of the head, and was altogether a good specimen.

Soon after this I was transferred to the appointment of Bheel agent at Sirdarpore, in Western Malwa, to which was added the command of the local corps. The station had been burnt during the mutiny, and presented a most forlorn appearance. The houses of the commandant and adjutant were heaps of blackened ruins, and the hospital and guard-rooms were unroofed. The site of the regimental lines was marked by heaps of rubbish. It being desirable that we should be under shelter before the next rainy season, we set vigorously to work to collect material. Wood had to be cut, and carted from the jungles, lime to be dug and burnt, and bricks, both sun and kiln dried, to be made. However, we worked with a will, and in a few months were comfortably settled down. While the work was going on I made one or two hurried tours through the district under my charge, but had not much time to devote to large game shooting. I saw enough of the country to enable me to form a very favourable opinion of the prospect of sport. The extent of ground within my beat was in parts 80 miles in breadth by 150 in length, and comprised many fine tracts of forest and mountain.

Having occasion to visit Baug, a small town about three marches to the southward of Sirdarpore, I sent out my Sepoy escort with some of the Bheels of the place to endeavour to mark down a tiger, and about mid-day I got word that one had been tracked into an old iron-pit in the jungle. I at once went out, and on reaching the spot we had a consultation as to the position which I was to take up to give me the best chance of a shot. The Bheels were in favour of one tree, while I set my heart on another; and at length, yielding to their supposed superior knowledge of the locality, I gave in, and climbing up sent them round to start the beast. A tigress soon appeared, trotting lazily along, and I had the mortification of seeing her pass out of range and under the very tree in which I had wished to sit. Quietly descending, I stopped the beaters from coming on, and mounting my elephant I went off in the direction she had taken. I had not gone 200 yards before I came on her sitting at the foot of a small tree, and apparently careless of our approach. As I advanced she rose and disappeared over a small hill in the jungle. I followed, and on reaching the summit I saw her standing in the hollow below me. I fired, striking her near the spine, but though much disabled she succeeded in reaching an old iron-pit, in which she disappeared.

My men handed me a number of large stones, which I placed in the howdah, and, directing the mahout to move the elephant up to the edge of the pit, I hurled the boulders into the hole. The tigress would not show, and after some time my men came up with their bayonets at the charge, and from the spot where they stood could see the wounded tigress as she lay under a ledge of rock in a corner of the cave. I descended from the elephant, and while I stood ready to receive the tigress, if she should charge, the top of a tree, which had been left by woodcutters, was rolled by the men over the mouth of the pit, thereby effectually securing us against a sudden rush of the wounded beast. She was then killed by a shot between the eyes, and was with difficulty lifted out.

I heard of more tigers in this neighbourhood, but had no time to hunt them, as I was obliged to return to the neighbourhood of the cantonment at Sirdarpore. I therefore pushed on, and on ascending the Vindyah range, went out in quest of bears. I fell in with five of these one morning ; two in one ravine, two in another, and a huge old fellow by himself. I was very unlucky with them ; and though I wounded two I bagged none. However, I was consoled in some measure by securing a fine panther, which I shot from a tree on the rushy bank of a small watercourse, which ran through cultivated lands.

Several native chiefs having come to my camp on business, it was suggested that we should get up a shooting party, and I accordingly sent out some of my best shikarees in several directions. About noon next day, a horseman came in and announced that two bears had been marked down in a ravine about six miles off, near the village of Ringnode. I sent word to the chiefs, and they soon assembled with their usual motley array of followers, armed with guns, spears, and swords. They also brought two elephants, but were doubtful whether they would stand a charge. I ordered out my own, which, though by no means perfect, was tolerably steady.

These being sent forward, we followed an hour later on horseback, and on arriving near the jungle, I was met by a horseman whom I had sent out with the markers on the previous day. This man assured me he had marked a tiger in some thick corinda bushes, lying on the bank of the nullah in which I had shot the panther a few days before. I supposed that he must have seen another panther, which his excitement had magnified into the nobler animal, but he persisted that it was a tiger proper, which had retired into the thicket to feast on a wild pig which it had killed in the early morning.

Leaving the main body of my companions I went forward to examine the place and fix on the plan of action. Through a finely timbered and cultivated country ran a small watercourse, at this season quite dry, but fringed with high dead grass, and having at one spot, on both banks, masses of corinda bushes, twenty yards in depth by two hundred in length.   Outside were open fields, from which the opium crop had been recently gathered.

Having no confidence in the shooting of the chiefs, and being at the same time anxious to give them an opportunity of distinguishing themselves, I directed them to advance down the nullah on the elephants, while I went quietly forward on foot, and mounted a tree at the farther end of the thicket.

As the elephants came on, the tigress, for such it was, showed herself for an instant, and then retiring under a dense mass of green foliage, lay perfectly quiet. Shots were fired and stones were hurled, but she would not move, and even had the strong thorns not been too much for the elephants, I do not think the chiefs would have cared to go up to the spot where she lay concealed.

At length I determined to alter our tactics, and shouting to the others to clear out of the bushes, I left my tree and mounted another at the other end of the covert. A strong wind was blowing towards me, and I directed my men to fire the grass at the far end of the thicket. In a few minutes the high grass was burning fiercely, but the ground under the green bushes was bare, and the tigress, having chosen her position well, made no sign. The fire soon died away, and as it was now near sunset I feared that we should go home empty-handed. Just then, the horseman who had marked down the tigress came running up to my tree, and implored me to go in with him on my own elephant, leaving all the rest of the party outside. He was greatly excited, and having taken off his long riding-boots and drawn his sword, stood ready to guide me to the bush in which the tiger lay concealed.

I called up the elephant and went forward, my guide leading ; presently he lay down on the ground, and peering under the bushes assured me that he could see the tiger. I directed him to mount a tree, and as soon as I saw he was in safety, I ordered the mahout to drive the elephant forward. This he at once did, and at that instant the tigress charged. The elephant stepped back till it was clear of the bushes. The tigress burst out, I fired down, striking her through the loins, and as she fell over, the elephant turned and fled. It was soon, however, brought up by the mahout, and we again advanced at the thicket into which the tigress had disappeared.

But she was now very savage, and as we approached, she came charging out into the open ground. Again the elephant spun round and went off, and as I looked over her stern, I saw the tigress, in spite of her wound, fast gaining on us. Two more strides, and she would have seized the elephant by the hind leg, but at that moment I grasped the front rail of the howdah in my left hand, and firing my rifle pistol-fashion, I dropped her in the middle of an open field. The flight of the elephant was soon checked, and finding that the tigress did not come on, she permitted herself to be driven up close enough to allow me to put an end to the scrimmage by a final shot.

The whole affair had been witnessed by the chiefs, who, with their followers, were standing together about two hundred yards from the scene of the conflict. I did think once or twice that I heard the ping of a stray bullet, but if I did, they sped harmlessly. All hands soon assembled round the tiger, and loud and energetic were the exclamations of " Wah ! Wah !" as the opium-boxes were passed freely round.

Soon after we mounted our horses and were on our way back to the camp, when we came on the body of a dead pony over which an elderly cultivator stood, rending the air with his lamentations. He said his pony had been killed by a spear-thrust from one of the chiefs in my train, and as he named the man, I directed him to attend next morning, promising to inquire into his case. I requested two of the chiefs to settle it, and they adjudicated their neighbour to pay twenty-five rupees as compensation. In the defence it was stated that the pony, with the cheerful playfulness of his race, had come too near the plump and well-fed mare of the stalwart Rajpoot, who had received him on the point of his lance.

The land where this tiger was shot was for the most part cropped with poppies. The opium-cultivation is greatly attended to by the population of Malwa, and a large portion of the land-revenue is derived from this source. The poppies are generally grown on the best ground. The land is frequently ploughed and manured to the fullest extent practicable. A strong supply of water from wells or rivers is essential.

The ground is usually divided into small beds about eight feet square, separated from each other by ridges of earth, and all connected by runnels with a main channel leading from the water. On the seed being sown, the water is turned on, and while one man with a pair of bullocks keeps the stream running from the well, another is employed diverting it into the different divisions of the field till the whole is irrigated.

The water is raised either by a rude Persian wheel or by a leathern bag worked with a long rope over a wheel fixed above the well. The Persian wheel is simply a drum, over which passes a chain of earthen pots attached to a rope : these fill as they touch the water, and on ascending, empty themselves into a trough, whence the stream passes on to the land to be watered.

As the poppies come into flower the fields present a very gay appearance. Some cultivators prefer one colour—white, red, or purple—others go in for variety. The irrigations are repeated about eight times during the growth of the crop. When the flower falls the work of collecting the opium commences.

Armed with small instruments having three short steel points, the cultivator and all his household go over the whole field, carefully scoring each poppy-head. From the wound thus inflicted a milky juice exudes, and in a few hours assumes a dark colour, and becomes consistent. This is then scraped off with a small blunt knife, and the opium thus collected is carefully stored. Each poppy-head is scored and scraped three times. When dry, the heads are collected, and the seed shaken out. Much of the opium is consumed in the country, but the greater part is exported to China. Previous to its transport to the coast a high duty is paid to the British Government. This duty varies according to circumstances. It is now £60, and has stood as high as £70 per chest of 140 lbs.

In Bengal, licenses to cultivate opium are granted on the understanding that the juice is to be delivered at a fixed price to the Government factories at Patna and Benares. It is there manufactured, previous to being sent down to Calcutta, where it is disposed of, at monthly sales, by auction.

The net average amount of our opium revenue during the last five years, for which the accounts have been laid before Parliament, has been £5,781,890.

In the year 1867-68, the last for which the accounts have been laid before the House, it rose, after all expenses had been paid, to £7,049,447—between one-fifth and one-sixth of our whole net revenue.

CHAPTER XVI.

FIVE miles westward of the town of Dhar, near the village of Sooltanpoor, lies a fine ravine which has long been celebrated as a haunt of tigers. It is the birthplace of one of the countless streams which, rising in the Vindyah range, find their way down to the Nerbudda.

Near the head of the gorge is a dense mass of corinda thicket, under which runs a clear stream ; and hearing that a tiger had been seen in its neighbourhood I started from my camp at Dhar in search of him. I had no regular shikaree with me, and had to make the best arrangement in my power with the men at my disposal. On reaching the ground I selected a tree, close to the edge of the stream, at the lower end of the covert, and sending the men to beat down from the head of the ravine, I mounted on a branch and awaited their approach. Before long I saw a very large male tiger leave the bushes on my right front, and skirting the side of the ravine, it passed over a stony ridge into the next gorge. I quickly descended and followed on the track with some men, but the ground was very hard and stony, and we could make nothing of it.

Just then I was informed that one of the men whom I had sent to beat had been wounded by another tiger, and on returning to the covert I found a man slightly bitten in the shoulder. Neglecting my strict injunctions that all should keep together, this man had wandered away by himself, and was coming down the bank by a footpath, close to where I had been posted, when a second tiger, which had come forward to the end of the covert, rushed out on him, biting him as described. His wounds were not serious, and he had only himself to thank for his troubles.

Not wishing to disturb these tigers that evening, I returned to camp, and arranged for another attempt on them a few days later. This time I placed men on trees on both sides of the ravine, directing them to throw stones and drive the tiger back, should he attempt to break up the side.

I soon heard a troop of monkeys swearing in the thicket above me. Some of the men on the banks also telegraphed that a tiger was on foot. My position was unpleasantly near the ground, but it was the best that could be got, and I quietly waited for the beast to show. In a few minutes he walked out and stood on the path close to the spot on which the man had been wounded on the previous occasion. I fired, and he spun round and disappeared in the bushes. A few seconds later he broke cover near the top of the bank above me, and was going off at a good pace. I had a fine view of him as he passed along the sky-line, some seventy paces above me, and firing quickly, I saw him swerve over, and observed his hind leg dangling from the stifle. He then turned down the bank, and threw himself into a thick corinda bush, where he lay quiet. Calling out to the beaters to give me time to take up a fresh position, I descended, and making a circuit, climbed another tree lower down the ravine.

The men then came on in a close body along the top of
the bank, down which they hurled volleys of stones.   On their
arriving near the spot in which the tiger had lain up, he made
an attempt to move, but his hind-quarter was quite disabled,
and the men called out to me to come and finish him.   I proceeded cautiously, as, though unable to ascend the steep bank
to where the beaters stood, the tiger might have rushed down
on me.   His attention was however occupied ; and on reaching
the men I formed them into a compact phalanx.   We then
advanced on the bush, and as the tiger scrambled out towards
us, I laid him low with a shot through the neck.

I subsequently visited this ravine with Captain Ward,
who succeeded me as superintendent of the Dhar state.
I placed him in the same tree, and had the satisfaction of
seeing a fine tiger move down the covert towards him.   I was
mounted on a tree on the left bank, and might have fired
effectually, but I wished my friend to get the shot.   The
tiger went on, and was passing within a few yards of the
muzzle of his rifle, when he fired, wounding him through the
shoulder.   The beast dashed forward, and disappeared over a
mass of rocks, 150 yards farther down the ravine.   We followed after on an elephant, and finding him much disabled,
gave him the *coup de grace*.   After this, Ward and I shot
together whenever we could find time and opportunity.   I
have shot with many men, but I never met with one so sure
with rifle, gun, or pistol.   He always carried a Colt's revolver
in his belt, and as he was in constant practice, some of his
shots astonished me.

One evening when out riding, we observed several vultures seated on a hillock.   Ward dismounted, and supporting
his right with his left arm, he fired his revolver, remarking
that he would move them.   One of the vultures fell over

dead, the others flew away. Next morning I measured the distance with a cord, and to the best of my belief, the bird was shot at 375 yards from the muzzle of the pistol. The weapon was a medium-size Colt's revolver.

While I was at Dhar I occasionally shot florican in the grass plains to the east of the town. As the grass was two and three feet high, I ordered out all the horsemen in the place, and forming them into a long line, we beat the ground carefully. With seventy men I could cover a good bit of country, and when a bird rose, I dismounted and followed him on foot, generally bagging him on the second rise. On these plains we occasionally started antelopes. Hyænas and wolves too were met with. I had a rifle carried by one of my men, and one evening observing the head of a hyæna peering over the grass about 150 yards ahead of us, I fired and rolled him over dead.

One morning a man sent me word that there was a panther in his house in the town of Dhar. Knowing that there were generally panthers about the gardens and sugar-cane fields outside the town, I at once went to his house, which I found surrounded by a number of people. The panther was said to be concealed among a heap of lumber in a dark loft, so I mounted on the roof and proceeded to remove the tiles. The open bamboos on which they were supported guarded me from any sudden charge ; and it was well for me that they were there, for the panther made a rush at the opening, but was shot through the head, and fell back dead. I had previously taken the precaution to clear all the people out of the lower part of the house, and could therefore fire down with safety. The panther was about two-thirds grown. He had probably entered the town at night in quest of a pariah dog, and b' ing scared by some early riser, had taken refuge in the loft where we found him.

Acting on the advice of a brother in Ceylon, I caused an iron trap for panthers to be constructed. It was like a huge rat-trap, but was furnished with springs at both ends, and weighed about 60 lbs. I caught several hyænas, and two incautious natives, but though it was on one or two occasions sprung by panthers, none were caught. One evening, when camped with Ward near Kode in the Dhar district, we baited this trap with a dead dog, and set it near a road leading to the village. Next morning the trap had been dragged away to some distance, and between the jaws we found the forefoot of a hyæna.

Soon after this I visited Mandoo, a grand though now ruined and deserted city on the crest of the Vindyah mountains, overlooking the province of Nimar. According to Ferishta, Alif Khan (the son of Dilawur Khan), who became celebrated under the name of Hoshung Shah, removed the seat of the government of Malwa from Dhar to Mandoo, A.D. 1404. Mandoo lies fifteen miles south-east of Dhar, and had been irregularly fortified, according to Hindoo accounts, by a prince named Jey Sing Deo, who, according to Hindoo fable, was assisted in accomplishing his work by the possession of the Parus Puttur, or philosopher's stone, which was found during his reign by a grass-cutter. Its properties were discovered by a blacksmith, who carried it to Jey Sing Deo, who, after using it to make gold enough to defray the expense of building Mandoo, is said to have given it to the priest of his family, who, displeased at receiving a stone, threw it, before its value was explained to him, into the Nerbudda. When sensible of what he had done he sprang into the river, in the vain hope of recovering it, but his efforts to reach the bottom were in vain. Credulous Hindoos believe that at the place where this occurred the Nerbudda became and continues unfathomable.

The site of Mandoo was very inviting; the mountain chosen by Hoshung Shah for his future capital is said to be thirty-seven miles in circumference. It extends along the crest of the Vindyah range about eight miles, and is parted from the table-land of Malwa, with which it is upon a level, by abrupt and rugged valleys of great depth and width, which descend from either side of the main gateway, both to the east and west, to the low country. On the brink of these valleys, and on the summit of the ridge of the Vindyah mountains, which form the southern face of Mandoo, a wall of considerable height was built, which, added to the natural strength of the ground, made it unassailable by any but regular attack ; and this advantage, which gave security to property, combined with the salubrity of the air, abundance of water, and the rich nature of the ground that was encircled within the limits of the new capital, caused it early to attain a state of great prosperity.

Hoshung Ghoree was succeeded by his son, Ghiznee Khan, a weak and dissolute sovereign, who was dethroned by his minister, Mahomed Khiljee, to whom Mandoo owed its fame and splendour ; and the magnificent tomb over Hoshung Shah, and the college and palaces that he built, give testimony of his respect for the memory of his benefactor, and of a regard and consideration for his subjects, which entitle him to the high reputation he has attained among the Mahomedan princes of India.

For the above description of Mandoo I have drawn largely on Sir John Malcolm's Memoir on Central India. The glory of Mandoo has indeed departed, and save by a few Bheels and a stray Mahomedan or two the place is utterly deserted. On all sides are ruins of palaces, terraces, reservoirs, and gardens, all fast crumbling to decay, and inhabited only by owls, bats, and wild beasts. The work of destruction is greatly assisted by birds, which carry the seeds of the banian, pepul, and other trees. These, dropping into the crevices of the stone-work, germinate and throw out roots, speedily rending roofs and walls. I believe some little has been done by the Dhar Rajah to protect the ruins, but the extent of the buildings is great, and the tropical growth too powerful, to give any hope that an impression will be made on the slow and sure work of time.

I was camped with Captain Blowers in the old city, and had, as usual, sent my men out into the jungle. About 10 A.M. they sent us word that they had marked down a tiger close to the gateway of the fort. On proceeding to the spot they showed us a mass of high grass and bushes, in the bed of an old artificial reservoir, formed in the jungle by throwing a bank across a watercourse. The place was quite dry, the action of the water having cut a deep gap in the embank-ment. We approached the spot very quietly, and I took up a position in a tree on the bank of the nullah below. I then sent instructions to the men to advance slowly towards the tiger, tapping the trees with their sticks, but without making any very great uproar. The result was as I had anticipated. The tigress,—for it was a lady,—came stealthily down the watercourse towards me, and was laid low by a couple of shots. My friend was in another tree about fifty yards off. We had tossed for choice of positions, and he had lost, but as he did not pretend to be a hunter, it was a matter of no regret to either.

I had heard of game in the rugged country lying on the banks of the Mhye, to the north of Sirdarpore, and accord-ingly I trysted Ward to meet me at Burmundel, a village about sixteen miles from the cantonment. Near this place, in a comparatively open jungle, were some bears' caves, situated on the side of a ridge of elevated ground. We directed our men to proceed to this spot after dark, when the bears would be out feeding, and to block up the entrance to the caves with stones, etc. We started early in the morning on elephants, and on arriving at the place, found three bears dancing about the caves in a state of great consternation. On seeing us they went off, but after going a short distance, they were turned back by some villagers, and again made for the caves. I met them on a narrow ridge, and as they came tumbling along after each other in single file, my elephant became so unsteady that I could not shoot with accuracy. The bears, however, turned and fled, the largest being wounded in the foot. Ward at once went after him, and ended a long chase by slaying him. Meanwhile, the others, making a circuit, regained the caves, and before we could overtake them they managed to effect an entrance, and went to ground.

We then moved in a northerly direction to Buckutgurh, where we found a gigantic old male bear in a corinda thicket, on the side of a ravine. No trees were at hand, so we stood together, and as he came out, we made short work of him. We saw two others, but they got away in a bit of rough country, and we could not find them again.

We then moved north to Dhotreea, about eight miles. Here our men marked down a tigress, and we went after her about mid-day. She was lying on the side of a wide open ravine, filled with scrub about six feet in height, through which were scattered dwarf salar trees. It was a very awkward place to work in. The ground was unsuited for an elephant, and there was nothing to indicate the direction which the tigress, if started, might be expected to take. The scrub jungle was too thick to allow us to shoot down on her

from above, and the only spot from which a clear view could
be got, was the face of the ravine opposite to where she lay.
This position was attended by a slight objection, inasmuch as
the tigress, if wounded, could charge straight at us. We had
just reached this place, when she rose from the base of a large
stone under which she had been lying, and stood for a moment
undecided. I whispered to Ward that we should not get a
better chance, and at once fired. The ball struck her about
the middle of the ribs, and crossing diagonally, came out
before the shoulder. The wound was a mortal one ; but she
wheeled round and dashed down the ravine to our left. Ward
put in another shot, and she fell over, and was dead before we
could get up to her. The heat at this place was terrific ; the
sun of May beat down on the black and scorched rocks around
us, while the hills and scrub jungle by which we were surrounded shut out every breath of air. Ward never paused to
look at the tiger, but set off at once for the nearest water,
which was said to be in the bed of a small river, about two
miles off. Hastily directing the men to get the tigress on
the elephant, and follow, I went after him. I did not overtake him till he had reached the river, where I found him
drenching his head with water from a hole which the men
had scooped in the sand. He assured me, that had he paused
on the way, he felt that he must have been struck down by
the sun. On our way back to camp a fine young pig was
shot by Ward ; and we improved our banquet by pork-chops
and soused countenance.

The Mhye river lay a mile to the westward of our tents,
and next morning our men were on the banks before daybreak, on the look-out for game. They marked a bear into
some very rough ground, and, posting ourselves together, we
sent them round to drive. The spot where we stood was sur-

rounded by high grass; but we got a good view of the bear as it came out, and dropped it. Recovering itself, it got into a small narrow ravine leading down to the Mhye. We had crossed the river dryshod about an hour before; but rain had fallen near the source of the stream, and it was now coming down in a turbid flood, sixty yards in width. The bear at once swam across; and after some delay we followed on an elephant, and our men took up the track. They picked out the footprints with great sagacity, and after nearly two miles we came up with the bear and slew it. We had good prospects of game in this neighbourhood; but we both had work elsewhere, and next morning we parted company.

The last-detailed bear-hunt had been witnessed with much interest by Ramla, a Bheel freebooter, who had given a good deal of trouble in his time, and had lately broken out of the jail at Mundlaisir. The thakoor of Dhotreea, a chief who was well acquainted with his movements, had assured me that he had fled from the country, and pretended to be much hurt at my ill-disguised incredulity. Some time after I sent for Ramla, who came in on safe conduct. He conversed pleasantly on the subject of his numerous misdeeds, and informed me that, seated on the hill-side, he had watched our pursuit of the bear from find to finish.

On my way back to Sirdarpore a Bheel was brought into my camp minus a hand and a foot. He stated that he had been thus mutilated by order of a petty chief in the Dhar state, who, suspecting him of robbery, had directed his limbs to be hewn off. The operation had been performed with an adze, and the stumps had been dipped in hot oil, to check the bleeding. I reported the matter to the agent of the Viceroy, who ordered the chief to pay the man for life, through my office, a monthly pension of ten rupees. I sent for both parties, and explained the order ; and, with a view to his longevity, I suggested that the Bheel should reside in my cantonment at Sirdarpore.   He declined to leave his home.

Some time after the chief waited on me, and suggested a reduction of the pension, on the ground that the man had grown fat and lusty, and kept a good pony—a state of things unbecoming one in his station of life.   I replied that the matter had been settled, and could not be re-opened.   Eventually it was reported that the man had died from the effects of a drinking-bout ; but I fear that the quality and not the quantity of the liquor was to blame.

CHAPTER XVII.

My friend Major Bonnor commanded the Bheel regiment at
Dohud, 50 miles to the westward of Sirdarpore, and having
been invited to meet him on the frontier, I marched through
the Jhabbooa country, and was encamped six miles south of
the town of Ranapoor, when I heard of a tiger in a small covert
near my tents. Major Bonnor, with Colonels Buckle and
Baigrie, was then encamped about 16 miles farther west, and
I had arranged to be with them on the following morning.

The spot which the tiger had chosen was in a small ravine
about 200 yards in length by 50 in breadth, and in shape like
the letter Y. The lower part was filled with a dense mass of
creepers, having large leaves shaped liked a camel's foot, and
handsome pink blossoms. The stems twined like ropes from
tree to tree. At the spot where the ravine divided there was
a small tree, into which I stealthily climbed with one of my
gun-bearers. Outside the upper ends I had posted men on
trees, with directions to shout and hurl stones at the tiger
should he attempt to leave the covert. The beaters had been
sent to drive from the low end, and I sat facing a rocky ridge,
which rose between the two smaller nullahs. The position of
myself and gun-bearer was not a very good one, for we were

not nine feet from the ground, but we could get no higher, so I had to make up my mind to shoot straight and trust to luck. On hearing the beaters advancing the tiger passed under the mass of creepers on my left, and went up the right-hand nullah, at the head of which he was turned by the men on the trees. Retracing his steps, he came down to the spot where I was posted. I could hear his feet on the dry leaves, but he was completely hidden by the heavy foliage. It was a moment of intense excitement. The sound of the footsteps ceased, then there was a patter on the leaves, and the tiger glided out immediately below me. He was not eight feet from the muzzle of my rifle, and in another instant would have disappeared under the creepers on my right. At that moment I fired, and the heavy two-ounce ball struck him on the base of the neck, dividing the spine. Death was instantaneous, and the mighty brute sank down in his tracks. So suddenly had all muscular power ceased that he did not even roll over, but lay with his head doubled under his chest, and his hocks sticking out. Neither tail nor paws moved. Fearing that he might only be stunned, I at once fired my second shot, but I might as well have spared my lead.

When the men came up they looked first at the beast and then at me ; and then, as if in apology for the part they had taken in his death, they made a sort of shame-faced salaam to the tiger, and stood on one side. This reverence was, however, only shown by the local Bheels. The men of my own regiment, who always accompanied me, had long since stifled their veneration for wild beasts.

As we were lifting out the dead tiger a horseman came up with a note from Baigrie pressing me to come to them at once, as they were in a country swarming with game, and required my valuable assistance. He added, "Come on at once ;

Bonnor shikars *en prince*, drinking still hock while the beat is going on, and the more noisy moselle when it is over." I sent back a verbal message that I had just bagged a fine tiger, and would be with them in the morning. On meeting I learnt that they also had heard of this tiger, and, fearing lest I should slay it before joining them, they had sent off their urgent epistle.

We had just finished a hearty breakfast when one of Bonnor's men came in and reported two bears in a nullah, about two miles from our camp. Colonel Buckle was busy with state affairs, so we went off without him. The bears were lying asleep in some long grass in a bamboo jungle, and our guides, taking us up three abreast, heaved down stones. The unhappy beasts had no chance. They made a rush up the side of the nullah, but the fire was sharp and straight, and they were killed at once.

The day was hot. Bonnor suggested refreshments, and commanded Ganymede to appear. I then saw that we were followed by a man bearing on his head a huge basket. We sat down under a shady tree, and from out a mass of wet straw, the rich wines of the Rhineland and Bordeaux were produced ; as also the beer of Bass, and soda-water of a skilful manufacturer. Spices and limes were also there in profusion, and the requisite supply of tumblers. For the proper mixing of the various drinks a large earthenware jug had been also sent out. We lit our pipes, and spent an hour very pleasantly, and then returned to the tent.

In the afternoon we were again summoned to the jungle, where another bear had been marked by our indefatigable hunters. We set out at once, but the bear, having been roused by a hasty shot, got away unhurt. Our men however pursued and headed him, and he was driven back. He then came down a slope covered with clumps of bamboos, and had he held on his course he would have come straight at us. I was suggesting the propriety of not firing till he was within a few yards of us, when the bear turned towards our right and was going off. Resting my rifle against a tree I waited till he had cleared a thick mass of bamboo, and as his head and shoulders appeared, I fired and the bear dropped. The shot was a good one, for he was about 120 yards from where we stood ; but my companions abused me for firing when I had been urging them to refrain. However, I should not have done so had the bear not turned. My shot had only wounded him, and as he came blundering down the hill, we ran in and finished him.

We halted at this place another day, but heard of no game, and as our respective duties called us in various directions, we broke up the camp. I did my best to induce Baigrie to join me, but he thought the Baroda country offered fairer prospects of sport. I think he afterwards regretted his decision.

On my return march to Sirdarpore I sent my men ahead to mark game on the Vindyah hills, and on reaching my tents, four miles from Tirla, I found that a couple of bears had been marked. The grass had been burnt, and the ground was perfectly bare throughout the jungle.

On the side of a very steep slope, thinly studded with tall trees, was a bit of rock scarped to the height of seven feet, and extending some twenty yards along the face of the hill. Under this rock were some holes, into which the bears had gone in the early morning. We went very quietly down till we reached the edge of the scarp, when one of the men pointing over showed me the snout and two fore-paws of a sleeping bear protruding from a hole at the base of the rock. At the mouth of this hole grew a peepul-tree, and the noise made by the rustling of its green leaves in the wind prevented the bear from hearing our footsteps. The body of the beast was inside the hole, and the only effect of a low whistle was to make him move his head to the right and left. At length I cast down a small peeble, on which he made a grab at it with his fore-paws, and then threw himself back into the hole with his hind legs protruding. At length he disappeared altogether, and though we threw down sticks and stones he would not show.

The afore-mentioned peepul-tree grew up the face of the rock, and I now directed one of my men to climb out into the tree, and having tied a stone into the end of his turban, to shake it over the mouth of the hole. The ruse succeeded admirably. The bear rushed out, and as he rose on his hind legs and furiously attacked the dangling turban, I shot him through the head, and he fell. We then went down to the mouth of the hole, and lit a fire of dry grass, wood, and green leaves. A dense smoke was carried into the hole, and soon after the she-bear bolted with the cub clinging to her back. I shot the old one, and then running in, captured the cub, which we took home alive.

On moving camp to Tirla I was met by the Chief of Jucnaoda, a sirdar of the Jhabbooa Rajah, who had invited me to hunt a tiger which had taken up its abode in some grass lands near his village. The thakoor was a pleasant old gentleman, who spent much of his time in the saddle. He was very fond of dogs, horses, and all matters connected with the chase ; but from the constant habit of eating opium he had ruined his constitution, and reduced himself to a shadow. Still the old man was game, and always ready to join in any out-door amusement.

I sent on my men and guns to the place where the tiger

DRAWING A BEAR.

was said to be, and as the sun became powerful, I rode over with the thakoor. We found my own party of twenty men, and about fifty villagers assembled ; and, riding to a small rising ground, we proceeded to examine the ground and arrange the plan of operations.

Before us lay a wide expanse of rough grass and bushes, having here and there an irregular and steep-banked nullah running down on a main watercourse, which bounded the ground on the side next to us. At some distance to our left, down the bed of the stream, stood a large peepul-tree. Higher up, on our right, was a mowa-tree, and my choice of positions lay between them. I decided on mounting the peepul ; and having told off my own men into three parties, and given to each a proportion of villagers, I sent them off with directions to extend so as to form an unbroken line, and to drive the grass down towards the peepul-tree.

All being arranged, I went off to take up my position ; but I found the tree too large to climb, the trunk being clear of branches for a considerable height. The situation was unpleasant, as the tiger might be expected at any moment. No time was to be lost, and I ran back to the hillock from which I had surveyed the ground, and signalled to the beaters to halt. I then sent word to them to bring the right forward, and to drive up towards the mowa-tree, into which I climbed, and found myself in a very commanding position. High up above me I had placed a look-out, and before long this man whispered that the tiger was on foot, and coming towards us. Presently he came quietly out of the bed of the main watercourse, and stood in the long grass looking back towards the advancing line. In a few seconds he came on again, and when he was within fifty yards I gave a low whistle, and he at once halted. At that moment I fired, shooting him diagonally through the root of the neck, and he fell forward quite dead. I fired again, but he never moved.

Meanwhile the beaters came on, and I saw a leopard break away out of shot. As the men approached me, the chief, who had remained stationed on the hillock with all his followers, sent a horseman up to my tree to ascertain what had become of the tiger. I told him it was dead, and at that moment lying in the grass about ten paces in front of his horse. Craning out his neck, he caught sight of the tiger—a full-grown male; and without another word he wheeled round, and went off to his master at full speed.

The whole party now came up; but the old chief, who had at the least expected a smart scrimmage, seemed quite sorry to see the beast, which had been for months the terror of the place, so easily disposed of. He shook his head mournfully, and exclaimed, "Wah! Wah! ek golee—kya zoolum;" literally, "One bullet! what injustice!" But he was consoled with the knowledge that his cows would now graze in peace.

CHAPTER XVIII.

ON the evening of the 29th of March 1862, Captain Ward
met me at Dhurrempooree, a town in Nimar, situated on the
north bank of the Nerbudda river. The stream at this place
is about a quarter of a mile in breadth, swarming with mahseer and other fish, and moreover plentifully stocked with
alligators.

The country to the north for some six or seven miles is
partly cultivated ; but the Vindyah range of mountains then
rises with rugged slopes, covered with scrub jungle and trees
of moderate growth. To the south of the river, on the border
of the Burwanee territory, the country, though apparently
level when viewed from a distance, is cut up with innumerable ravines, all running down to the Nerbudda. These
ravines, and indeed also the more level parts, are filled with
long grass and dense thorny bushes ; and though the district
is fairly stocked with tigers, panthers, bears, and deer, I was
never able to do much execution among them.

Our intended beat on this occasion lay at Kotra, about
six or seven miles farther down the river, where it is joined
on the north side by the Maun and on the south by the
Deb rivers. Both of these streams almost cease to flow dur-

ing the hot weather, but large stagnant pools remain in parts ; and in many places along the beds of the rivers the bastard cypress grows freely, intermingled with willows and other green bushes, which refresh the eye amid the general parched-up vegetation. These bushes are covered by the floods during the monsoon, when the dried-up beds are swept by mighty torrents ; but, though the water disappears in summer, the undersoil is moistened by the percolation through the sand, and the bushes retain their verdure, forming comparatively cool retreats for tigers, who, in addition to their ordinary prey of pigs, nylghae, and porcupines, are attracted by the herds of cattle which are brought down by their owners from the more dried-up districts.

We had received reliable information of the presence of game, and had sent on tents, servants, and " shikarees," that all might be in readiness on our arrival. We had only one elephant, but he was a staunch one, though dangerous at times, and, when employed with the troops on service in 1858, had killed a soldier who had incautiously come within reach of his trunk. The elephant, together with our gun-bearers and a native horseman, preceded us from Dhurrem-pooree before daybreak on the morning of the 1st of April, and it was still dark when my friend and I mounted our horses and followed them.

We had proceeded two or three miles along the track formed by village carts, which is all the apology for a road which the country affords, when the day broke, and we then observed, in the very cart-rut in which one of us was riding, the fresh footprints of a tiger which had passed along in the early morning. They were not to be mistaken in the heavy dust, but were in parts obliterated by the tracks of the ele-phant and our gun-bearers, who had evidently passed the spot in the dark. The prints, however, led in the direction in which we were going, and we quickened our pace, keeping them in view.

After proceeding about a mile, we came up with our men, who, on the day breaking, had at once perceived the tracks, and had sent off the horseman to bring back the elephant, which had outpaced them. We then dismounted and proceeded to load, and on the elephant coming up we again followed the track of the tiger. It continued for some distance farther along the same road, and then turned north, by a cross-path, for about a quarter of a mile, after which it struck into the jungle ; and, the ground being hard, we were at fault. Leaving our men, we rode forward, and carefully reconnoitred the country in the direction which the beast had taken. It looked very hopeless, stretching for miles in flat thorny scrub, with small open spaces here and there, and occasional thickets 20 or 30 yards in breadth. Half-a-mile in advance was a solitary tree, and it was agreed that I should make a detour, and climb this tree, on the chance of seeing the tiger, should it be started by Ward, who was to mount the elephant, and beat up the ground in my direction. We accordingly returned to the men, and, taking my two gunbearers with me, I set off for the tree, which I climbed, and soon after saw Ward advancing on the elephant, and moving about among the thickets.

Presently I heard a couple of shots. The report was so small that I concluded Ward had only fired his revolver into some covert too dense for the elephant to penetrate ; but soon after our horseman came up at a gallop, legs and arms flying in all directions, and informed me that the tiger was slain. I was not a little astonished, having been deceived by the report of the rifle ; and, descending from my perch, I rejoined

Ward, whom I found standing over the body of a fine tigress. The beast had probably travelled a long way during the night in quest of food, and on the day breaking had lain up in the first quiet spot. Ward came suddenly upon her, and finished her before she had time to rise. We were much pleased with this bit of unexpected sport, and making over our guns to our attendants, we remounted our horses, and rode off merrily to breakfast, leaving the men to follow with the tigress, which we had bound on the elephant, after taking off the howdah, to prevent damage to the skin. The howdah was carried in by some villagers who had assembled at the spot.

On reaching the camp we were met by our shikarees, their countenances wearing a peculiar grin, which, from long experience, I knew meant business. They informed us that on their arrival they had found fresh tracks, and had tied up sundry buffaloes on the previous evening in the most frequented spots. One of these had been killed during the night in the Maun river, half-a-mile above the junction, and the carcass had been dragged into a large patch of cypress in the bed of the stream. Markers had been posted on the trees along the bank, and only our presence was necessary to open the ball. Refreshed by this intelligence, we proceeded to breakfast, and soon after the guns and elephant came in.

Our followers, who had preceded us, had suffered a good deal from bees, several large swarms having been roused by the smoke of the camp-fires from the few trees at the place which afforded shade to our tents. The village cattle had, moreover, been in the habit of seeking shelter from the mid-day sun under these trees, and the ground was alive with ticks, by which our men had been grievously bitten. The bite of these insects is severe, and is followed by great itching and swelling, which lasts for two days or more. In such places we generally wore long riding-boots all day, but the feet of the natives were unprotected and they suffered accordingly.

At 11 A.M. we again set off, and at the end of a mile we arrived at the river Maun. The opposite bank was steep, and at its foot ran a long strip of cypress some 10 yards in width, and 200 or 300 in length. On this side the bed of the river was covered with cypress to the extent of several acres, and in the centre was a large pool of still water, in which the tigers (there were two) had repeatedly been seen by our markers to bathe themselves during the morning. The country on both sides was cut in all directions with small but deep ravines, very narrow at the bottom, and filled with long grass and thorny bushes.

As we knew the tigers were gorged, we concluded they would not leave the cypress, and we therefore both mounted the elephant and proceeded to beat them out, previously taking care that all our men were clear of the covert, and safely perched on trees. The tigers were soon on the move, and, guided by the waving of the cypress, which was five and six feet high at this part, we pushed after them. Presently both beasts were wounded, but accurate shooting was impossible, owing to the motion of the elephant and the density of the covert. The tigress was the first to succumb, which she did after one or two plucky charges; and soon after, the tiger, a fine heavy beast, dashed through the pool, and disappeared in the strip of covert on the opposite side. We slowly followed, advancing cautiously, for the cypress was varied by rocks and bunches of long grass. Suddenly, with a terrific roar, the tiger rose and came on open-mouthed; but the shooting was good, and the elephant steady, and he was hurled back, and again crossed the pool to the place where we originally found him. We reloaded, and following, found him very groggy, and put an end to him without further trouble.

Thus ended our first day's work. Three tigers had been found and bagged. We bound the last two on the elephant, and returned in triumph to our camp, where we found that, with the assistance of the village "chamars" (skinners) my servant had removed and pegged out the skin of the beast we had slain in the morning, and was ready to turn his attention to the last comers. The skins of these were also pegged out before dinner ; and as we smoked our evening pipe, and lay back in our comfortable arm-chairs, we discoursed the labours of the day, and went to bed hopeful for the morrow, our men having told us that they believed other tigers were in the neighbourhood, and that another lot of unhappy buffaloes had been tied up in the rivers and other likely places.

I forget whether one of these was killed during the night, but we went forth next morning (Wednesday) after a tigress which was said to have her cubs in the ravines near the river. A number of beaters was assembled, and a line formed, while we took up positions ahead, on foot. The tigress was soon started, but got off without a shot ; so, making a note of the line she had taken, we mounted the elephant, and going round to the bed of the river, moved up along the bank, and halted at the mouth of one of the small ravines. Our star was in the ascendant, for, as the beaters again came on, the tigress appeared on the bank above us, within thirty yards, and, firing together, we rolled her over into the ravine, where another shot finished her. Our men were anxious that we should not disturb the country more that day, as they supposed that other tigers were not far off, so we went quietly home with the main body of our forces, leaving our shikarees to make all needful arrangements for the following day.

On Thursday morning we were informed that a buffalo had been killed during the night close to the spot where we had slain the two tigers on Tuesday, and that the tracks led into the cypress. Thinking the beast would be too lazy to break cover, we placed additional markers on the banks on trees and other elevated places, and, mounting the elephant, we entered the jungle. The tiger was a cunning one; and on hearing us he sneaked down the covert for 300 or 400 yards, and then, leaving the bed of the stream, went up among the ravines. Our men ran after, and did their best to keep him in sight, but to no purpose; and though we searched far and wide, we could not find him; so, leaving word for the buffaloes to be again tied up, we returned to camp.

The tiger came down to the river in the night, again killed a buffalo, and again lay up in the cypress. We went at him after breakfast on Friday. He had moved to the strip of cover on the far side. As we beat slowly down on the elephant, he again broke shyly and scrambled up a very steep part of the bank, where four or five small watercourses, meeting at one point, entered the river by an abrupt fall. We fired several long shots, but failed to stop him. The elephant was unable to follow at this place, and we had to return and make a considerable circuit to ascend the bank, and then we found we had to turn the head of several ravines before we could arrive at that by which the tiger had left the river. We passed round the heads of all its tributaries, carefully examining the ground, but found no tracks, from which we gathered that we had succeeded in heading our game. The heat at this time was great, and Ward, who was not very well, began to be knocked up, so, getting off the elephant, he took shelter under a tree while I went to closely hunt up each small watercourse by passing up one side and down the other.

I had carefully examined them all, and had turned away in despair from the last, when I happened to cast my eye back, and there, within twenty yards, lying in the bottom of a small channel some eight or ten feet deep, was my friend, looking pleasantly at me. I quietly called to the driver to stop, and kneeling on the seat of the howdah I gave him two through the shoulder. He spoke at once, and scrambled along the bottom of the watercourse towards the spot where I had left Ward sitting. He did not go far, however, and, following him up, I gave him a final shot. The feet and claws of this tiger were badly blistered and damaged. The blisters were probably occasioned by his walk in the hot ravines on the previous day, and his claws were no doubt broken as he scrambled up the steep bank this morning. But for this we might possibly not have got him, for on both days he seemed to think discretion to be the better part of valour.

A tiger of this description is apt to mislead an inexperienced sportsman, as to the dangerous character of these beasts. Having seen a huge brute flee ignominiously before the hunters, he rashly concludes that all tigers will do the same, and conducting his subsequent operations in accordance with this erroneous theory, sometimes pays the forfeit with his life. Such was the sad fate of Captain Gowan, 6th Inniskillings. Descending to the water's edge, we cracked a bottle of moselle, and, after the inevitable pipe, moved homewards. The following day being Saturday, we determined not to shift our camp, though, having already killed four beasts close to the same spot, we were not very sanguine about finding more. Buffaloes were, however, again tied up in the evening, and next morning one of our men came in greatly excited, and said that a calf had been killed in the night, and that

four fresh tigers were in a patch of cypress in the Nerbudda,
close to the junction, where our markers had seen them. We
were not long in turning out, and on reaching the place proceeded to examine the ground. The tigers were in a covert
some 200 yards in length and 150 broad, thick in parts, but
broken into ridges by the action of heavy floods, and between
these ridges were open spaces of sand and shingle.   On the
bank at the angle of the junction was a point from which
a good bird's-eye view could be obtained of the bed of the
river, and round the corner, in the Maun, was the cypress
covert, in and about which we had hunted on the four previous days.

We arranged that I should stand at the angle, while Ward
beat up the tigers with the elephant. As he approached
the covert the scene became very interesting, and the tigers
moved rapidly from one ridge to the other. I had a perfect
view of the whole proceeding, and as the beasts showed we
fired with various effects. Several, I knew, were hard hit,
but so many were running about the covert that it was impossible to say which were wounded.

Presently, with her tail standing out behind her like a
kitchen-poker, the old tigress charged past my post, growling
savagely. I had a good shot in the open, but missed her very
disgracefully, and she went at full speed round the corner
into the Maun river. Meanwhile, Ward was not idle, and as
I watched his movements I observed a tiger enter a ridge of
cypress on the far side of the covert, and close to the stream
of the Nerbudda.

Soon after Ward moved up towards me and said they were
all dead with the exception of the tigress which I had let go.
I asked " how many were dead ?" he replied, "Three." "Then,"
said I, " there is still a fourth in the covert." Ward was in-

credulous, so I came down, and mounting the elephant beside him directed the mahout to move towards the ridge near the water. We beat it down very carefully with no result, but I knew the beast was not far off.

The side of the bank next the river sloped sharply down some eight or ten feet to the water, and was heavily fringed with a thick green shrub. I directed the mahout to take the elephant round and enter the water. This he did, and as we moved along in front of the bank, in water about five feet deep, we spied the tiger lying almost hidden by the bushes. Being anxious to save the skin, only one shot was fired, with the best aim allowed by the imperfect view. On receiving the shot, the tiger roared and sprang clean out from the bank towards us, and was shot in the water swimming at the elephant's head. He was a young tiger, but a most determined beast. When we towed him ashore he was found to be riddled with bullets. We thus had four lying together on the sand. They were all young tigers and tigresses, but as large as the mother, and only to be distinguished at a distance by their imperfect stripes. After a slight refreshment we followed the old lady into the Maun river, and soon came on her in the cypress. She died game, but the shooting was too good for her this time, and she had no chance.

On the death of the four, we had sent off to the camp for two light carts. These had arrived by this time. Two tigers were placed in each, and with the fifth bound on the elephant, the procession moved on the tents. We had within the week killed ten large tigers, the result of five days' work. Of these nine were killed within a circle half-a-mile in diameter. The villagers turned out in considerable numbers, and rejoiced in their own apathetic way. Had we not come, many of their cows would no doubt have suffered. They seemed to think it strange that so many beasts should have been disposed of without loss of human life, or accident of any sort.

The five tigers made a goodly show as they lay in front of our tent. Loud and noisy was the discussion over the slain, and many and varied were the accounts given by our men of the week's work ; while the principal actors, again ensconced in their arm-chairs, quietly smoked the fragrant pipe, and quaffed the beatific beverage of Bass, weakened with water, sweetened with sugar, flashed with ginger, and vulgarly known as "mug."

CHAPTER XIX.

FROM Dhurrempooree I marched westward through Nimar
till I arrived at Baug, where my friend Captain Blowers met
me. Though no sportsman, he was anxious to shoot a tiger,
and as they were seldom absent from the neighbourhood, I
hoped he might succeed. My men had been out since daybreak, and about noon sent word that they had taken the
track of a tiger up to an old iron-pit. On repairing to the
spot we found that the entrances to the excavation opened in
several directions, and that all were more or less obscured by
bushes. On all sides lay an extensive tree-jungle of moderate
height.

Having fixed on our positions in trees lying in the course
we expected the tiger would take, we sent a number of men
round to drive him out. He showed at once, but broke wide
of our positions, and though I put a bullet into him, he went
off at a sharp pace. We took up the track, and followed it by
the blood for some distance, keeping well together, with the
guns in front. As we proceeded we halted frequently to allow
men to climb trees and examine the ground before us, in
hopes of getting a view of the beast, for we knew that at no
time is the hunter in greater danger than when following up,

on foot, a wounded tiger.   Irritated with wounds and the heat
of the sun, the hunted animal will stop in the first convenient
spot, and, wheeling round with his face towards his pursuers,
he will await their approach, crouching among the grass or
rocks, and utterly motionless, with the exception of the last
three inches of his tail, which he twitches nervously, like a
domestic cat when watching a mouse.

But the jungle now became thick and thorny, filled with
fragments of rock, and we reluctantly gave up the pursuit.
Had we succeeded in finding the tiger, I believe he would not
have gone under without serious injury to one or more of us.

On the following day we went out in another direction
after a tiger which had killed and eaten the greater part of a
buffalo which had been tied up for him the previous evening.
He was in an open ravine formed by a sandy river-bed,
having on the right bank a small hill faced with huge masses
of detached rock.   Along the base of this hill were some
trees of considerable growth, interspersed with creepers and
brushwood.   In the bed of the river lay a patch of willow
and cypress about thirty yards in length.   Beyond was some
rough and hilly ground covered with tree-jungle.

We had taken our places in trees above the afore-men
tioned hill, and had sent men round to drive towards us,
when we heard loud shouts, followed by roars from the tiger.
Soon a man came running over the hill, and called on us to
join him, as the tiger had broken back.   We quickly came
down, and I had just reached the summit of the hill when I
heard a further uproar, and a cry that the tiger was coming
forward on us.   I sprang on a fragment of rock overlooking
the river, and saw the tiger coming up the sandy bed at a
brisk trot, and roaring loudly.   From my position I could
only get an occasional view as he crossed the open spaces be-

tween the large trees which grew below me, but, marking an open bit of white sand over which I saw he would pass, I stood ready, and as he came in sight I fired down, shooting him through the back. He swerved heavily, and ceased to roar. Then, rushing forward, he disappeared in the patch of willows. Calling to Blowers to follow, I ran down the hill, and we climbed into our old positions in the trees. The beaters came on upon the opposite bank, from which they threw volleys of stones into the thicket, hoping to drive the tiger towards us, but he rose, and crossing over, ascended the face of the hill, and disappeared among the rocks, close to the spot from which I had fired. We went cautiously up to the place, guided by a man perched in a tree, and found ourselves on a huge fragment of rock which formed the roof of the tiger's retreat. The entrance, however, was on the face of the hill, and was not to be seen from where we stood.

The men shouted and yelled, and dangled cloths over the mouth of the cave, but the tiger showed no sign, and we failed to make any impression on him by smoke or fire. We worked at him for upwards of two hours, but he would not move. To descend to the mouth of the cave would have placed us at too great a disadvantage, for the foothold was insecure, and a mere fall among the rocks would probably have broken bones. At length we heard a faint cry, which some of the men supposed to come from young bears or hyænas. After that all was still. We now held a consultation, and agreed that the wisest course would be to return next morning and explore the cave. We concluded that the tiger would probably die, and we should get him without further trouble. If his wound were only slight, he would leave during the night.

On the following morning, about 9 A.M., one of our men, who had been near the cave, reported having observed an unpleasant odour arising from below, from which he inferred that the tiger was dead. We at once went to the place, and climbing down the rock came to the main entrance, where a close inspection of the cave at once explained to us how the tiger, which lay under a mass of huge fragments of rock, had been unaffected by the smoke and fire with which we had assailed him on the previous evening. In the middle of the cave, resting on his back, lay the dead body of the tiger, a very large male. He had probably died when we heard the cry among the rocks below us. The night had been very hot, and the carcass had become swollen with gas till it looked positively monstrous. Beside him was a ghastly mess of masticated buffalo, which he had disgorged in his dying agonies. I entered the cave with several of my men, who proceeded to turn over the huge beast. In so doing they pressed upon the carcass, and the gas escaping from the bullet-holes nearly choked us. I was nearly stifled, but, holding my breath, I made a rush at the main entrance and gained the open air. It required a long and a strong pull at the brandy-flask to restore my equanimity.

After allowing some time for the atmosphere to clear, we re-entered the cave, but found it impossible to lift out the tiger. We therefore resolved on skinning him as he lay. This operation I left to the men, and we remained outside till it was completed. On cleaning his skull, I found he had been fired at on some previous occasion. The ball had struck him across the face in front of the eyes, passing through the bones. The side on which the ball had entered was marked by a clean round hole. On that on which it had passed out a large fragment of bone had been carried away ; but nature was busy repairing the damage, and the bone was throwing out growth. I have this skull now in Scotland. It was possibly the recollection of his former injuries which made him so noisy when roused on the previous day.

Owing to the time that had elapsed before the skin was removed I feared that it would go wrong, and I steeped it in a strong solution of alum. Notwithstanding this I was obliged to throw it away. Had I stretched and dried it in the usual manner it might perhaps have been saved. On the following day we moved our camp towards Sirdarpore.

We halted at the foot of the hills, in a very dreary and horrible country, to which we had been led by the hope of finding game. Colonel Baigrie had visited this spot in the year 1860, and was here charged and severely bitten in the arm by a wounded tigress. He owed his life to the nerve and good shooting of his companion. On hearing of his mishap, Dr. Gane, the medical officer at Sirdarpore, at once went out and had him brought into the cantonment, where he was carefully and successfully nursed.

At this camp shade and water were alike scarce. In the jungle, close to our tents, was a hideous idol, daubed with vermilion and smeared with oil. It was apparently an object of great veneration, and had been so plentifully anointed with oil by worshippers that the ground around it was completely saturated. Beside it a well had been dug out and faced with stone, but the walls had fallen in, and the oil, oozing through the soil, lay in the bottom in a filthy pool. As we could hear of no game, and were not bent on "striking ile," we beat a hasty retreat from this inhospitable region. We ascended the Ghaut by a long and rugged track winding through the hills. The march was a severe one both for servants and cattle.

I may here remark on the excellence of good Indian servants. Faiz Mahomed came to me as head servant in the autumn of 1858, as I was about to start with the field force.

He remained with me till I finally left India in 1865. During that time he went through a great deal of rough work, both on service and while accompanying me about the hills and jungles within my own district. While I was with the force my tent was always among the first to be pitched and the last to be struck ; and though men would come in and sit talking till late at night, thereby greatly reducing his hours of rest, I never heard a word of complaint from him. When marching on duty, or on shooting expeditions, he would serve dinner at sunset, and then, packing up all his goods, would see the carts loaded and start off with them about 9 P.M. The roads were mere tracks over hills and along dry watercourses, often encumbered with large stones, but by sunrise my tent was always pitched on the new ground, and my bath and breakfast ready for me on my arrival. The length of the marches was generally from eight to twelve miles. In all matters connected with the preserving of tiger and other skins he was very intelligent. During the whole time he was with me I had neither purse nor keys ; all was under his charge.

No stores of any kind being procurable within fifty miles, I generally got out a supply sufficient to last for six months. Wine, beer, oilman's stores, groceries, shot, powder, horse-shoes, etc., all were under his keeping. His pay was £1 a month, with feed for a pony, and the usual small percentage allowed on all bazaar purchases.

Ward was to meet me for some days' shooting on the Mhye, and I accordingly sent off my camp and joined him a few miles north of Dhotreea, in the Dhar district. Captain Bradford, the political agent in Western Malwa, also came into camp. Ward had been out with his own men, and had shot a bear, but, wishing to save the country till our arrival, had done no further mischief. Next morning we went after a couple of bears, which had been seen to enter one of a number of steep and narrow ravines running down to the Mhye. They were soon roused, and one coming out on our side was shot by Bradford and me. The other was wounded by Ward, and went off pursued by my men of the Bheel corps. We ran up to an elevated spot, from which we got a good view of the ground, and could see the bear crossing the ravines with the men in full cry. Now and then a shot was fired, but the bear still kept ahead, and gained what seemed to be a patch of thicker jungle. Here, I suppose, he began to give in, for we saw the men dive into the bush, and soon after heard several shots. Presently they all came out into an open space, bearing the slain beast, after the manner of a number of ants removing the body of a defunct wasp.

Two other bears were marked next morning near the same place. They had lain up among masses of rock in some open ground between the ravines. They were dislodged by a volley of stones, and bowled over as they went off. One, a large male, attempted to charge back, but the shooting was too good for him, and he succumbed. Hitherto we had heard of no tigers, and none of our party having hunted this ground before, we feared that we should get none. But, as we sat at breakfast on the third day, two of our men came in ; the one reported two bears marked down in the ravines beyond the Mhye, the other the death of one of our buffaloes, which had been killed by a couple of tigers in a ravine about three miles to the northward.

Refreshed by this intelligence, we were soon ready, and having sent Ward's elephant and the guns ahead, we followed on horseback, commencing the day's proceedings with the nobler game. The tigers were said to be in or about a small dry river-bed, fifteen paces in width, with steep clay banks twenty-five feet high. Here and there were thick masses of high green grass, which flourished in the moist sand. Connected with the main stream were numerous small nullahs wriggling down through the scrub-jungle on either side. No suitable trees were near the spots where the tigers might be expected to break. Bradford and I, therefore, arranged to stand together, sending Ward to beat down the river towards us on the elephant. It was not long before we heard the crack of his rifle, and soon after a fine tigress came out two hundred yards from us. Hoping that she would soon lie up, we refrained from firing, but she held on at a sharp trot, and though some of our men went after her, they were unable to mark her down. Meanwhile, Ward had done his work well. He had slain a very large tiger which he found in the long grass in the river-bed. On being wounded he at first attempted to get away into the surrounding jungle, but failing in his attempt to spring up the steep clay bank, he turned and charged viciously. Ward, however, shot well, and dropped him as he came on. He was a very old tiger, light in colour, and on his grim and scarred visage he bore the traces of sundry conflicts with his fellows. We proceeded to remove the howdah from the elephant, and having sent it back to camp by some of the beaters, we bound the carcass of the tiger on the pad. Had we tied him on behind the howdah, the skin would probably have been injured by the friction. These arrangements completed, we partook of refreshments, and then went off to look after the bears, over which two of our men had been on sentry since morning. We found them at the head of a small ravine, which terminated in an open spot in the jungle. They were quite concealed among the long grass, and did not rise till we were close on them. The larger bear showed first, and came out into the clear ground, where he was at once slain. The other fled down the ravine, but was speedily stopped, and they were soon on their way to camp. We had got one large tiger and a brace of bears, and were well satisfied with the day's work. Next morning we broke up our camp, each man returning to his own district.

CHAPTER XX.

TOWARDS the commencement of the hot season of 1863 I
visited the chief of **Allee Rajpore**, at the south-west corner of
my political charge. The whole of this country is occupied
by Bheels and **Bhillalas, a race** said to have sprung from the
intermarriages of Bheels with Rajpoots. They are in a small
degree more settled in their habits than the Bheels, and are
more intelligent cultivators ; but they often suit their manners
to their company, those who live among the Bheels frequently
joining in predatory excursions. The mowa-tree flourishes
over the whole district, and supplies a large portion of the
food of the inhabitants. The soil is light and sandy, and the
irregular patches of cultivation are intermingled with rocky
ridges and ravines.

Being aware that the chief was in the habit of going out
occasionally after tigers, I supposed he had some pet preserve
not far off ; and on my suggesting that I should like to
accompany him, he forthwith gave orders for his shikarees
to exercise their intelligence in their own department. Accordingly, on the day on which I intended to march I sent
off my camp to the Hutnee river, twelve miles to the east-

ward, and taking with me a couple of horsemen and my gun-bearers, I met the Rajah at an early hour. He was escorted by a large following of Mekranees armed with swords and guns. After riding about five miles we were met by the shikarees, who had been out since the previous day. They assured us that tigers were in the neighbourhood; but they could give no positive information as to their actual position. We therefore dismounted. The Rajah, who looked as if he had spent a severe night, drank water. Such of the party as were addicted to tobacco lit their pipes, and some worked up a little Dutch courage by a dose of opium.

After consultation I was informed that a tract of jungle was to be driven by beaters, while the guns were sent ahead to intercept the game. I went off with the Rajah, but I soon saw that every man present who carried a firearm considered himself a "gun of position," and as such entitled, like Lords in an English shooting party, to go forward. This promised ill for sport; but, being a guest, I resigned myself to my fate, and, mounting a tree at the place assigned to me, I awaited the approach of the beaters. The Rajah, accompanied by eight or nine men, sat in other trees about 200 yards to my right, while many others, in groups of two and three, posted themselves according to their fancy. A strong odour of tobacco pervaded the air, and the noise of coughing and suppressed talking, accompanied by the bubbling of hookahs, was incessant. My anticipations were fully carried out; we saw nothing; and at the end of the beat I went up to the Rajah, and suggested that I should have the arrangement of the next drive. This being settled, I took the Rajah, with two of his attendants, forward, together with my own gun-bearers and the head shikaree. All other men were directed to go with the beaters.

We posted ourselves on the side of a rocky hill overlooking a small sandy nullah. We had not been long in our places when the beat commenced, and I heard a tiger roar loudly. Soon I saw a tigress coming down on the opposite side of the nullah, into which she dropped, and then, turning to the right, came along the bed of the watercourse till she was opposite my post. Raising my rifle, I gave a low whistle, and she at once halted, offering me a fair shot. The ball entered the point of her shoulder, and passing diagonally through, came out behind the elbow on the other side. She gave one convulsive rush to the front, and fell over. The Rajah had witnessed the shot from his tree, and seemed much astonished. As I have observed on similar occasions, when hunting with Indian chiefs, he was somewhat disappointed at the sudden close, and would perhaps have been more satisfied had one or two of his men been clawed a little ; and this not from any bloodthirsty feeling, but simply to give a little zest to the day's work. On arriving at my camp, which I reached about dusk, I found that my own men had followed the track of a large tiger into a covert near the tents, and had anxiously been awaiting my arrival. It was then too late to do anything, so we lost that chance.

I had brought with me two of the Rajah's Mekranee shikarees, who were well acquainted with the country ; and, as they suggested that a ravine, which lay about five miles south of our camp, might hold game, we arranged to examine it on the following day. This ravine, known as the Sankree Tokree, is a tributary of the Hutnee river. It contains water throughout the year ; and the huge masses of rock, mixed with grass and bushes, along its bed, were frequently occupied by tigers. Being single-handed, I examined the ground very carefully before commencing the beat ; and at length fixed on a tree overhanging the right bank, near the head of the ravine.

The beaters entered below, and came on shouting and beating tom-toms. As they advanced I heard a troop of monkeys swearing, as they always do when a tiger or panther is on foot. Still I saw nothing; and, as the beaters were now nearly within sight of my position, I began to fear that the game had gone up the side of the ravine unperceived. But about 150 yards below me was a mass of detached rocks, and on stones being hurled among them, a fine tigress sprang out, and after coming a short distance towards me turned up the opposite bank. She was at least 120 yards off and moving fast, but a lucky shot took her through the loins, and, unable to face the steep hill, she turned and came scrambling along the face in front of my position. Reserving my fire, I allowed her to come on, and put a shot in well behind the shoulder, but just at that moment she gained the shelter of an over-hanging ledge of rock and disappeared. I was much vexed, for I feared she had got into some cave. However, I reloaded, and calling up two or three of my best men to cover my movements, I descended the side of the ravine till I could see the tigress as she lay. Taking a steady aim, I again fired, and she rolled down into the bottom, where she expired.

Next day we moved our tents, and encamped in the jungle five miles to the eastward, and within range of the Mogra ravine. My men were soon scattered over the country, and on the following morning sent word of game. Sending off my guns, I followed on horseback, accompanied by a trooper of my escort. The Mogra ravine is one of the best spots for game in that country, and I have seldom, if ever, drawn it blank. On this occasion my men reported a tigress and cubs. I selected a tree close to the bed of the stream, and having arranged myself comfortably, sent orders for the beaters to come on. As a tigress with cubs is always inclined to be dangerous, they advanced very slowly, keeping up an incessant noise. Presently my gun-bearer whispered that the tiger was coming on, and in a few seconds he emerged slowly from a mass of green willows, and came quietly towards me. He was evidently annoyed at being disturbed, stopping now and then and giving a quiet grin, which disclosed his long white fangs. I allowed him to come within fifteen yards, and then sent a two-ounce ball crashing between his eyes. He fell heavily forward stone-dead.

Meanwhile, the beaters advanced, and I hoped that they would drive out the tigress, but we never saw her. Three cubs, however, came out—small beasts about three feet long. These were shot by the beaters. The tiger I had shot was a large handsome beast, with a rich dark-coloured skin, which my men there and then removed under the deep shade of some green bushes by the water-side. I was half inclined to go in search of the tigress, but sundry native officials were awaiting my return to camp ; so, leaving my men to follow, I mounted my horse and rode off with my orderly.

We were passing through a wild bit of country—the entire surface of the ground being covered with black sheet rock, thinly sprinkled with short dry grass. Stunted unjun-trees grew in all directions, and the green of their small dark foliage formed a pleasing contrast to the leafless trees around them. We were cantering along the track at a brisk pace when I observed a large cheetah or hunting leopard standing among the trees near the road. The air was trembling with mirage from the intense heat, and at first sight I thought it was a royal tiger, for he loomed large. I hoped that my gun-bearers might not be far off, and that by heading the beast we might induce him to lie up in some covert till my rifles arrived. After looking at us for some time he trotted off, but, on my cantering across, he halted. This sort of thing went on for some time, and had the ground been more favourable for riding, we should have gone in at him, for I carried a revolver, and my orderly a sword and lance. At last, however, he seemed to think he had seen enough of us, for he made off at a great pace and disappeared into a rocky ravine.

About this time I had arranged to meet Hayward, an old brother officer, who was coming out from Dohud to hunt tigers with me in the Jhabbooa district. I therefore moved camp, and joined him on the third day at the town of Jhabbooa, where we were received with much civility by the young Rajah. But there was no prospect of game in the immediate neighbourhood, so we moved north about ten miles, and encamped at Bugore, sending off a party of men to Kullianpore, five miles to the eastward. On the following day towards the afternoon we were informed that a tiger had been seen in a jungle about two miles from our tents. The ground in this covert was level, and covered with trees and long dry grass. A dry nullah ran throughout its entire length.

Being anxious that Hayward should get the shot, I posted him in a tree in the place which I considered best, while I mounted another about sixty yards to his right. The beat was arranged by Dhokul Sing, a jemadar of the Malwa Bheel corps, who always commanded my escort, and on whom I relied to mark down any beast within ten miles of my camp. He was by caste a Naik, and had been a hunter from his youth up, betaking himself on all occasions, when off duty, to the jungle, and seldom returning without some eatable bird, beast, or fish. But at the same time his military duties were not neglected, and it was amusing to see him half-an-hour after our return to camp after a long and severe day's work in the jungle. Having divested himself of his dust-coloured hunting dress, Dhokul would appear in full uniform, dark green, and red facings, and drawing himself up would make a salute, and report his party "All well." On this occasion he was very eager, and having seen us settled into our places, he went off, and we presently heard the beaters advancing towards us. A few minutes afterwards a shot from Hayward's tree was followed by a loud roar. Then two or three more shots, and savage growls of a tiger evidently wounded. Soon after Hayward called out that he had wounded a large tiger, which lay disabled in the bed of the nullah, but having dropped his loading-rod he was unable to re-charge his rifle. He therefore suggested that I should come and give him his quietus. As the ground between us was thickly covered with grass and bushes, and I knew not the precise position of the wounded beast, I did not care to come down ; but at length, on being assured that the tiger did not seem inclined or able to move, I descended.

I had reached the ground when I heard renewed shouting from the beaters, and rightly judging that another tiger was on foot, I scrambled up again, just in time to see it break away to my right. In the meantime one of my men who was with Hayward had quietly got down from the tree, and having recovered the loading-rod, enabled him to reload and give the wounded beast the *coup de grace.* He was a very large male tiger, and we bore him home to the camp, where we spent the evening in pegging out his skin. Next morning we were summoned to Kullianpore, where tigers had been marked in two places. In the first beat, which was over some rough open ground, a tigress came out and was shot by Hayward. We then moved over to the river, where a large tiger was said to have lain up. Below the cypress in which he had taken up his quarters the covert became a mere strip, some twenty yards in width, and here Hayward took up his position in a tree, while I was posted in another on the far side of the bed of the stream. Unfortunately, Hayward had neglected to secure a proper seat, and had contented himself with having his *face* to the quarter from which the tiger was expected. It is seldom that the shooter, when perched on a branch, can turn quickly so as to shoot to the right. He should therefore place himself *facing to the right with his left shoulder towards the beat*. By taking this precaution he will secure a wide sweep for his rifle, and a beast will seldom escape.

On this occasion the tiger passed on the right of Hayward, who was unable to turn to take aim. From my position on the opposite bank I saw his dilemma, but could not fire till the tiger was clear of his tree, and by that time my view was obstructed by intervening bushes. However, I managed to wound the tiger, but did not stop him, and he went off down the river. A palaver was held, and it was settled that the guns should again go ahead while the beaters came forward cautiously in a compact body. Hayward therefore climbed another tree, while I went forward and stationed myself on the elephant to his right. As the beaters came on he observed the wounded tiger emerge from the thicket about 120 yards on his left, and, raising the sight of his rifle, he was about to fire, when another tiger came out in front of him and was passing within a few yards. Forgetting that he had raised the high sight, he transferred his aim to the new comer, and of course fired over him, thereby losing both. Altogether it was most unfortunate. We tried to follow up the wounded tiger, but could make nothing of it. The ground was unsuited for the elephant, and we had seen enough of him to know that he would be unpleasant to meet on foot. We therefore returned to camp, hoping for better luck next time.

On the following day we remained at home, but early next morning Dhokul appeared and reported a buffalo slain near the spot where the large tiger had been shot two days before. He added that, as the entire carcass had disappeared, and the ground was much trampled, we might expect more tigers than one. This day I had choice of positions, and I selected a tree in an angle formed by a bend in the bed of the nullah, and about fifty yards from the bank, for, as a rule, beasts will seldom follow the course of a stream or ravine round a corner, but will leave the bed and cross over the angle. In addition to my gun-bearer, who sat beside me, I posted a man high up in a tree to my front, with orders to give intimation by signs of the approach of any beast. Hayward was in another tree on my right near the bed of the nullah. Soon after the beaters entered the covert a very handsome tigress came out about forty yards on my left front. She was a fine lissom beast, with a long well-shaped neck, clean head, and a rich bright skin. I had a fair shot at her, but though I fired twice she was untouched beyond a slight graze across the forearm. Bounding away, she went off into the covert behind us, leaving me very much ashamed of myself.

Quickly reloading, I sat quiet, and soon after my look-out man held up one finger and pointed into the grass below him. Presently he held up two fingers, and two young tigers, nearly full-grown, came stalking out. I dropped them both right and left, and then gave each another shot from my second rifle ; but they got away into the long grass, and I feared lest they should damage the beaters. Shouting to them to halt and crowd into one or two compact bodies, I called up the elephant, on which I mounted, and having hunted them out of the long grass, I slew these two tigers. I then, with shame and confusion of face, explained to Dhokul how I had missed the tigress, and, as he believed she would not go far, we left the beaters, and passing outside the covert, took up fresh positions across the jungle about half-a-mile higher up. Hayward was again on the right, I in the centre, and as the ground was more than we could cover, I directed Dhokul to take up a position on my left. My signal-man I posted as before, and as the beaters came on he intimated to me that a tiger was moving towards Dhokul. Soon after I heard the report of his gun, followed by roars from the tiger, and then all was still.

After a short time I called out, and received a reply that the tiger had been hard hit and had gone back. As it was important that the beaters should not be allowed to walk blindly into danger, I directed Dhokul to descend from his tree, and, having passed round behind Hayward and myself, to get back outside the covert and prevent them from coming on. He was further told to bring up the elephant. Alive to the importance of the order, he came down, and was passing between me and Hayward when my signal-man called out that the tiger was coming on. Sure enough, there she was, coming right up the bed of the nullah at a long trot, and I at once recognised the tigress I had missed in the first beat. I trembled for Dhokul, for he was fair in her path, and shouting to him to mount a tree, I fired. Beyond a flesh-wound in the forearm I did no mischief, and with a savage roar the tigress charged straight for Dhokul. She was within a few paces of the man; another bound, and she would have had him. Screwing myself round on the bough on which I sat, I fired my second shot. The heavy ball crashed through her skull, and the tigress fell heels over head, and lay dead below us.

A wah! wah! of approbation came from my men, who had witnessed the shot, and peace flowed into my soul as I proceeded to reload. Dhokul took matters very coolly, and remarked that his " kismet " was in the ascendant, but he also added that the tiger just slain was not that at which he had fired, and which he was certain was too badly wounded to have charged in that style. He therefore went off, and this time succeeded in stopping the beaters and bringing up the elephant. We at once mounted, and, on pushing into the covert, came on the wounded beast. It also was a tigress, but very old and light in colour. She immediately charged, but was stopped before she could do mischief. Thus ended the day's sport, and we had good reason to congratulate ourselves on its result, for we had bagged four fine tigers.

We had enough to do on the morning cleaning and pegging out the skins. Though we halted at this place on the two following days we heard of no more tigers, and accordingly moved north-west to the Anas river, where we encamped on the right bank of the stream. A rough tree-jungle, cut up with ravines, stretched away on all sides, and about a mile below our tents rose an abrupt hill, having its summit scarped with white quartz rocks, while the base was fringed with bamboos and other jungle. At the southern end of this hill was a small ravine, and at its entrance a buffalo, which had been tied up, was killed and partially eaten two days after our arrival. We posted ourselves in trees on the slope of the south end of the hill, and sent our men round to drive the ravine down towards us.

We had not been long at our stations before I saw a very large male tiger coming stealthily up towards me through a thicket of bamboos. I hoped he would have come straight on, but he suddenly turned sharp up the hill. Seeing that I should not get another chance, I fired, but my view was intercepted by boughs of trees, and though the ball struck the tiger behind the shoulder, the wound was too far back to take immediate effect. He growled and rushed to the front, where he disappeared behind a spur of the hill, after which he turned and went back through the beaters, one of whom shot an arrow into him as he went by.

We determined to follow him up on the elephant, but the hill was so steep that we feared we should never get him up the face. But the mahout said he thought it could be managed, and at length, after great difficulty, the huge brute reached the summit. It was wonderful to see the sagacity with which he moved, supporting himself at some of the steeper parts on his tusks and knees, but steadily working upwards. On gaining the summit, we found ourselves in a tolerably level tree-jungle which had been recently burnt, and the footprints of the tiger were plainly visible on the white ashes of the grass. Blood too was plentiful, and in several places we could see where the wounded tiger had lain down. Dhokul with several of his men had hitherto moved in front of the elephant, following up the track, while we kept a sharp look-out in the open ground ahead. But as, from certain well-known signs, we now knew that the tiger could not be far off, we directed them to fall back, while we went slowly forward on the elephant. Presently we heard a low rumbling sound, which at first we thought was made by the elephant, but the mahout, halting, declared it was the tiger. On all sides the ground was clear of grass, but we could see nothing.

About twenty-five paces to our front was a small teak-tree which had been bent over along the ground, and which still retained some of its broad leaves. Immediately below this tree was a small furrow in the ground, in which, guided by his growls, we at length caught sight of the tiger crouching for his charge. But before he could rise, our two rifles cracked, and though he still came on open-mouthed and roaring savagely, he was quite disabled, and another shot finished him.

From the above may be seen the very great danger of following wounded tigers on foot. In the present instance the ground was open below and clear of grass, but so great was the hiding power of the animal, and so wonderfully did the black and yellow of his skin blend with the parched ground, that, but for our elevated position on the howdah, we might have walked unconsciously into his jaws. Close to where he fell we found the skull of a gigantic wild boar, which had possibly formed a meal 'to the beast we had just slain. While following up the tiger we captured a good specimen of the land tortoise.

Two miles farther up, the river becomes deeper and more confined, containing deep pools hemmed in by rocks. Here we occasionally saw troops of otters, old and young, disporting themselves in the clear water, and no doubt feasting plentifully on the fish, which were numerous. Near this spot several of our buffaloes were killed by a very large tiger. His footprints were enormous, but we were never able to trace him to his lair, and though on several occasions we hunted out every covert and ravine in the neighbourhood, we never saw him. Probably he had some safe retreat in a deep fissure among the rocks, from which he only emerged at nightfall. Two of my men sat up one night on a small platform in a tree over the remains of the last buffalo which he killed. Soon after dark the tiger appeared, but I imagine there was some jealousy between the men as to who should have the honour of the first shot, for they fired hurriedly and without effect, and the tiger went off.

Next day we broke up our camp, my friend returning to Dohud, while I set my face towards Sirdarpore. On entering my tent at the end of the second march, I was overpowered by a horrible odour, and taxed the servants with having encamped over the remains of some decayed carcass. The carpets were lifted and the ground examined, and a fire was lit in the tent to purify the atmosphere, but with no effect. At length I ordered the partition curtain to be shaken out, and in its folds I found a squashed rat, which had no doubt perished when the tent was struck three days before, and in the interval had attained a height which was truly epicurean.

CHAPTER XXI.

ABOUT the early part of the month of February 1864, I visited
Baug, in company with Captain P. Bannerman and his family.
This place, though now only a village, was formerly of considerable importance, and its antiquity is evidently very
great. The larger portion of the modern houses is built with
large flat bricks of very superior quality, which have been dug
out from the numerous buildings occupied by the earlier inhabitants, but now fallen to decay and covered over with earth
and rubbish. The town is overlooked on the north side by an
oblong fort standing on a spur of elevated ground. It consists of a thick wall of red sandstone, which, together with a
strong gateway, is in tolerably good repair. The Waugnee
river lies on the south side. Its bed is broad and sandy, and
during the hot months the stream ceases to flow. The
surrounding territory is a wild, hilly tract, covered with
thick thorny jungle. The soil is rich in iron ore, and in
many places the old iron-pits may be seen, long since deserted
by the miners, and now the favourite resort of wild beasts.

But Baug is chiefly interesting for the rock-cut Bhoodist
temples in its vicinity. On the left bank of the Waugnee

river, about two miles below the town, stands a hill of coarse freestone rock, the whole face of which, for several hundred yards,
has been deeply excavated. But time and the action of the
weather has brought down a large portion of the face of the cliff,
and the entrances to most of the caves are choked up with debris
and jungle, openings here and there being kept clear by the bears,
panthers, and hyænas, who are now the principal occupants.
The northernmost cave is still in good order. The entrance
is approached from the bed of the river by rude steps, and
passing in by a small gateway, a spacious hall is discovered,
excavated entirely from the solid rock, and having its roof
supported by huge pillars hewn out in the natural stone. At
the innermost end of the cave are gigantic stone figures, three
in number, carved on the face of the rock. The effect, when
viewed by torchlight, is very grand. With the exception of
numerous bats which cling to the roof, the sole occupant of
this cave was a weird-looking Hindoo recluse, who, when not
begging about the surrounding country, spent his time sitting or
sleeping among the ashes of his fire. This was his home day and
night ; and as he sat with his body covered only with white
wood ashes, and his long hair matted and browned by sun and
rain, he seemed a fit companion for his neighbours in the
adjoining caves. Truly the religious feelings must be strong
which induce a man to adopt such a life.

I had sent out my men at an early hour to mark game,
and had gone out for a ride with Captain Bannerman. When
crossing the river a short distance above the town, I came on
the fresh footprints of four tigers which had passed in the
early morning. The troop consisted of a large tiger, tigress,
and two three-parts-grown cubs. My men came in about
9 A.M., having found nothing, and looked rather ashamed of
themselves when I told them what I had seen. They at once

set off, and later in the day returned, having taken the tracks up to an iron-pit. We at once sallied forth, and, standing near the brink, hurled in stones, but the tigers had passed on. We hunted about for some time in the neighbouring jungle, and got a glimpse of one tiger, but returned home empty-handed.

Next morning, however, we got word of the tigress having been seen in a strip of out-lying jungle, and having posted ourselves in trees we sent men round to drive. Captain Bannerman was not skilled in woodcraft, and seldom handled a gun, but on this occasion he armed himself with one of my rifles, and sat in a tree about forty yards to my right. As the beaters advanced I heard the footsteps of a tiger among the dry leaves, and soon after I caught sight of one of the cubs making off along the face of a bank beyond Captain Bannerman. My view was greatly obstructed by trees, but I made a lucky shot and dropped the tiger dead. The tigress got away, and we did not see her.

An adjoining bit of jungle was beaten without success, but here we came on fresh marks of bears. High up in the branches of some lofty trees hung the combs of bees, and though the bark was white and smooth, and the trees clear of branches to a height of forty feet, they were deeply scored by the claw-marks, old and recent, of many bears.

Three miles to the south-west of Baug lay a ravine in which my men reported another troop of tigers, and four miles farther on was the Mogra ravine, described in the last chapter. The first ravine I hunted from Baug, I saw the big tiger, but he went up the side of a hill, out of shot, and got away. Dhokul, however, fired at and killed one of the cubs, a small beast, about six feet in length. On two subsequent occasions I hunted here, but though the tigress was often seen by the beaters she always kept clear of my post.

However, I shot a fine panther, which gave us some good sport, in a bit of open jungle, where he charged my elephant with great ferocity.

One morning the tigress was seen to enter a small ravine about one hundred yards in length, which we had hitherto deemed unworthy of notice. Creeping quietly forward, I climbed a tree in a good position, and as she came out I rolled her over. She was up again in an instant, and slunk back into the cover, into which I followed her on the elephant. Presently I spied her remaining cub lying at full length, broadside on, on a ledge of rock on the side of the ravine. I fired, and as the ball struck the tiger it bounded straight out into the air, and, falling on the slope, danced down to the bottom on its hind legs, like a cat in a child's picture-book. The wound was mortal, and it fell dead. Soon after I got a sight of the tigress, which lay hidden by some thick creeping plants. Not wishing to spoil the skin, I hesitated to fire till I could be sure of killing her. She suddenly rose, and, rushing off through the bushes, got away, and leaving the ravine, made off down the river. We followed for some distance, and it was only after I had almost given her up for lost that some of my men caught sight of her in a thick bush into which she had crept. This time I give her no law, and a shot through the head closed the affair.

On my way back to camp I was mounted on my riding camel, having Dhokul, who was as usual armed with his regimental carbine of the old Brown Bess pattern, on the seat behind me. On the side of a hill, near the tents, I saw several peacocks sitting among the rocks, and, halting the camel, I fired from his back, sending the musket-ball through a fine cock at a distance of about eighty yards.

About this time Captain Bannerman left me, and I moved

my camp to the Mogra.   I found fresh tracks of several tigers, but I was too early in the season, and the long grass in and about the ravine was unburnt.   I therefore determined to return to Baug, as it was my intention to hunt the whole country, in April and May, with some friends from the Mhow garrison.   I went out with some of my men in the afternoon, and having fired the jungle in many places, I went home.   I had just dined, and was sitting in my arm-chair outside the tent, when I heard a cry of " Fire !" and, jumping up, I saw the hill-side in a mass of flame, which was rapidly advancing towards our camp.   Fortunately a small clear space lay between us and the long dry grass, and we managed to beat out the fire without any damage being done.

On my way to Baug I again hunted in the ravine where I had shot the tigress and cub.   We had turned out a bear, which I shot as it passed under me, but had not fallen in with the tiger ; and I was preparing to start for the tents when one of my men drew my attention to a yellow object among a mass of rock and bamboo high up on the hill-side, about two hundred yards from where we stood.   He remarked that it resembled a tiger's head, and, sure enough, as we watched it, we saw the huge jaws gape as the mighty beast indulged in a good yawn.   As I feared that he would make off I quickly mounted the elephant and went towards him, but found, as I reached the base of the hill, that the view was impeded by trees and bushes.   Just then the elephant gave a loud shriek. The tiger rose.   I had an unsteady shot, and missed, and he went off over the hill and was no more seen.   I was greatly vexed, for I believe I lost this fine tiger through my own fault. Had I quietly posted myself in a tree, and sent men to drive, I should probably have bagged him.   But tiger-shooting, like other things, can only be learnt by experience.

That night I was sleeping in my tent at Baug, when my dreams were rudely disturbed. My three dogs—Bugler, Boomerang, and Batchelor,—rough-and-ready beasts, half-bull-dog and half-greyhound, were chained, one at the head, another at the side, and the third at the foot of my bed. Close to my head, in the corner of the tent, stood my guns and rifles, four in number. Below the pillow were two five-chambered revolvers, and on my right side, under the thin quilt on which I slept, lay my drawn sword. The night was very dark, and some watchmen, who had been sent as a guard by the village authorities, were sleeping soundly round their smouldering fire, when I was awoke by a fearsome yelling of dogs. A dreadful struggle was going on beside me ; the dogs were plunging about and tugging at their chains, but I could see nothing. I, however, at once guessed that one of them had been seized by a panther. Though armed with gun, sword, and pistol, I feared to use them in the dark, so, springing up, I shouted loudly, and flacked about with my blanket. The scuffling ceased, I heard a sudden rush and then all was quiet save the whining of the dogs. By this time my servants, who slept in a separate tent at some distance, were aroused, and came over bearing a lantern. Poor Boomerang was found with his throat fearfully lacerated, and in the dust outside the door of the tent were the footprints of a large panther. Had the dog not been chained, he would no doubt have been carried off and eaten. His head and neck were greatly swollen for some days, but he soon recovered, and was none the worse. For several nights I set my iron trap baited with a dead pariah dog, but the panther did not return.

Towards the afternoon a villager came in, and reported having marked a panther down in a jungle about two miles from our camp. I went out, and go ta distant view of the beast, but did not fire, and was on my way home when one of my men, who had followed us by a short cut, came up and informed us that he had seen a tiger close by. The jungle was a difficult one to beat, consisting of thorny bushes ten feet in height, and it seemed impossible to form any opinion as to the direction in which the tiger might break. I trusted entirely to the Bheels, and mounted into one of the few trees near the spot. Before me was a tolerably open space, which I hoped the tiger might cross. By the shouts of the beaters I soon knew the beast was started, and presently a fine tigress came out, and stood facing me at the edge of the thicket, sixty yards to my front. The chance was too good to lose. I fired at once, striking her fair in the chest, and, with a savage growl, she charged straight at me. She was very noisy, and, no doubt meant mischief ; but, apparently disappointed at not finding me on the ground, she dashed on, and, as she passed below, I gave her the second shot through the back. At the same time I shouted to attract her attention, hoping that she might halt and allow my second rifle to come into play ; but she passed over the ridge and disappeared. I followed on the elephant, and soon came on her, lying down and very sick. Another shot finished her.

Next morning I was informed that a large Brahminee bull had been killed during the night by a tiger, close to the village, and within a quarter of a mile of my camp. These bulls are usually turned out in the name of the Deity by some devout Hindoo. From that moment they are regarded as sacred, and roam at will through the crowded bazaars and cultivated lands, living, like some other church dignitaries, on the fat of the land. I went out to examine the scene of slaughter, and, under some trees, by a well used for irrigation, lay the dead bull, with the marks of the huge fangs of the tiger on his neck, and sundry claw-marks on his sides. Immediately beside the well the ground had been irrigated on the previous day for a young crop. About one hundred yards off was some green wheat, in which the bull had been feeding when first attacked, while farther off was a watercourse, used during the dry season as a road, along which the tiger had advanced. Following the footprints in the dust and moist ground, the whole scene was brought vividly before us.

Passing along the watercourse in his nocturnal ramble, the tiger had seen the bull grazing in the green wheat, and, standing with his two fore-paws on the side of the bank, had formed his plan of operations. Keeping under the shelter of the bank up to the nearest point, he had slipped quietly up on the cultivated ground, and had then crept along unpercieved till he reached the wheat. Crouching along the edge of the high crop, he had approached his prey unperceived, till within reach for his final rush. Then came the tug of war. From this point to the edge of the field the wheat was beaten down, and here, and in the moist ground beyond, the footprints of bull and tiger were deeply marked. No part of the bull had been eaten, and we hoped that the tiger, which was evidently a very large one, would return at night. My men made a platform for me in one of the trees by the well; but, as the moon did not rise till about 9 P.M., we were obliged to take other precautions. To prevent the tiger from dragging the carcass, we secured it with strong ropes, and near the hind quarter, at which part a tiger always commences to feed, I set my large iron panther-trap, carefully covered with earth and grass. I did not expect that it could long detain the tiger; but I hoped it would do so sufficiently to allow me to put in a couple of shots by the light of a large grass torch, which, with some lucifers, was kept in readiness by one of my men who watched with me.

This night-work always had a kind of charm for me, though I seldom brought anything to bag.

I liked to hear the cries of the night-birds, varied now and then by the peculiar chattering of hyænas, or the distant growl of a tiger, while the panther would indicate his vicinity by a series of short grunts, whence, from the similarity of the sound to the rending of wood, he was known among us as "the sawyer."

I was in my place at sunset, but, owing to some wedding festival in the village close by, an incessant tom-toming and drumming was kept up till midnight, when I fell asleep, having seen nothing. Towards morning I heard some beast tearing at the carcass, and looking over, I saw what I supposed to be a panther; but the moon was obscured by clouds, and objects were indistinct. At length I fired, the beast rushed off, and we heard him struggling among some high poppies. At daybreak we descended, and, as I had feared, found the track of a hyæna, which we followed to the spot where he lay dead. As a rule, I think animals of the dog tribe tear their food, while cats cut it more noiselessly with their side teeth. This hyæna evidently had resided in some iron-pit, and the ore had changed the usual dirty-white of his coat to a deep yellow.

That afternoon a three-parts-grown tiger was marked by my men near the spot where I had shot the tigress two days before. Only one small tree stood in the sea of thorny scrub, and in it I found an insecure footing at a few feet from the ground. As usual, my men arranged the beat admirably, and this tiger's jacket was pegged out that night by the side of those of his relatives. We had good reason to congratulate ourselves on the death of these two last tigers, for the country was close and extensive, and the amount of ground which my rifle could cover was very limited. But the arrangements of Dhokul and his men were, as usual, excellent. From Baug I moved north towards Sirdarpore, and encamped below the hills, near the village of Tanda. Here my usual good fortune took a turn, and I lost one of my gun-bearers by a sad accident.

About 10 A.M. Dhokul came in, having left some of his men on sentry over a very large tiger, which he had come upon suddenly that morning. I was not long in turning out, and, on arriving near the spot, we arranged the plan of attack. I was accompanied by Lieutenant MacTier, who had joined me that morning from Sirdarpore.

The only tree which we could find in any way suited as a position, was one standing near the head of a slope some fifty yards in length. This tree had, at about eight feet from the ground, strong shoots growing from the stem. On these I took my stand, accompanied by my gun-bearer, named Foorsut. At the foot of the slope a dry nullah crossed from left to right, and beyond it was a level jungle thinly covered with trees and bushes. The tiger was to be driven from our left down the nullah. Having seen me to my place, Dhokul went off to bring on the beat, and soon after the tiger came trotting down on the far side of the nullah. Unfortunately, my shot struck him too far back, and, turning sharp to the left, he went off at a great pace, while I fired my remaining three shots at random in the hope of doing further damage. Seeing the tiger go off, I did not at once reload, intending to do so when I descended to follow him up on the elephant. Suddenly, a man on a tree cried out that the tiger was coming back, and, on looking up, I saw him coming towards us at a sharp trot. On reaching the nullah, he crossed it, and slowly ascending the hill, stood immediately below our tree. With a breech-loading rifle I might have shot him ten times over, and possibly, as he was coming on, I might have reloaded that which I had, but I knew that any movement on our part would probably make him charge, and we were too near the ground to make such a contingency desirable.

All might have yet gone well had the man kept quiet. In an evil moment he spoke, saying that the tiger was below us, The beast looked up, caught sight of us, and at once sprang up the tree. Getting a momentary hold for his claws on the trunk, he seized Foorsut by the waistband with his teeth and dragged him down, and as he fell, bit him three times through the back of the thigh, inflicting twelve deep wounds. I shouted loudly, and hurled my hunting-cap at the tiger, on which he slunk off and went down the hill. Presently the men came up, and we made a litter of boughs and sent the wounded man off to the camp, where he was attended to by the native apothecary who always accompanied my office. I mounted the elephant along with Mr. MacTier, and we presently came on the tiger, at which I fired, and on going up found him dead. I believe he had died from the first shot. He was a full-grown male, very large and heavy.

The wounded man progressed favourably, and the bone of the leg seemed uninjured. He was doing well on the following day ; but on the morning of the second we observed a slight twitching of the points of the fingers. Towards 3 P.M. he fell off suddenly, and by 4 he was dead. This was a sad termination to what had been a brief but successful "chasse"— my bag, during the trip, consisting of seven tigers, a panther, and a bear.

CHAPTER XXII.

ABOUT the 31st of March 1864, our party met at Mundlaisir
for a long-projected shooting excursion. We were four guns,
viz. Captain John Evans, *alias* "The Bashi," 6th Inniskilling
Dragoons ; Captain Murray, 72d Highlanders ; Captain T.
Cadell, V.C. ; and myself. Previous to this the country south
of the Nerbudda had been explored by Cadell's men, while
mine had devoted their attention to the district north of the
river. By this means we had learnt the position of a number
of beasts, and were thus enabled to march from point to point
without loss of time. At Mundlaisir we met Mr. Nils
Mitander, a Swedish gentleman, who had come out to India to
superintend the erection of an iron-smelting establishment in
Nimar. The afternoon was spent in some final preparations,
and in the evening we took a boat and pushed out into the
middle of the clear stream, where we had a delightful swim.

Early next morning we were on the march towards a river which flows into the **Nerbudda** from the south, about ten miles above Mundlaisir. **Here, at a** village named Burnea, three tigers had been marked down in a large patch of cypress **in** the bed of the river, which lay in a country much cut up by ravines, and covered by thorny bushes of the mimosa. **They** were very shy, and **at once** broke away into the ravines. We followed, and after a long hunt, succeeded **in finding one, a small beast, 7 feet 8 inches** in length, which was shot by Murray. We hunted the ground very carefully on the following day, **but** saw nothing, and in the afternoon moved east to Kamkhera.

On the way we beat a dry nullah filled with long grass, and were fortunate in starting a fine panther which had killed a pony two days before. I had a snap-shot at him, but missed, and he broke away through a thick thorny jungle to the **left.** Here the Bashi **caught sight** of him, **and** put **a ball through** his body, but he made off, **and it was only after a long search** on the elephants, **that** I observed the white tuft **at the end of** his tail protruding from a mass of high grass. Calculating where his shoulder should be, I fired, killing him dead. He **was a handsome beast, 7** feet 8 inches in length, with a finely-marked skin.

We moved still farther to the east, and encamped at Zerbar, where, some of **our people having lit a fire** below trees **containing bees, we were** greatly annoyed. The bees came down in great numbers, and dispersed the whole cámp, stinging many **men and animals.** Our grooms fled with **their** horses to the jungle, while we sheltered ourselves **behind the** bamboo screens of the tents. The bees appeared **to entertain** special antipathy to certain goats and bullocks, and these **they** persecuted without mercy, following them most pertinaciously as they rushed for protection among their fellow beasts, who escaped comparatively scatheless. In the evening I went out with Bashi for a walk, and in a ravine about two miles from the camp we came on a sounder of wild pigs. Bashi dropped one with a fine shot, and we carried him towards the camp slung on a pole. Darkness came on, and we found ourselves struggling through rocks and thorns with our burden. At length we saw the camp-fires in the valley below us, and having shouted and fired a shot, we were soon joined by our men, who relieved us of our porcine load.

Next morning we went after a tiger which had slain one of our buffaloes. He broke back through the beaters, and was shot by a half-caste of inebriated habits who had come from Mhow, having attached himself to Captain Evans's stables. The tiger was a stout male, 9 feet 10 inches in length. The two following days were blank, and we moved our camp west to Bulukwarra.

Evans and Cadell had been obliged to return to their cantonments on some duty, but they rejoined us at this place in time to see a tigress brought in by Murray and me. We heard of her from one of the local police, who volunteered, for a consideration, to be our guide. Under his leadership we went out on elephants, and beat an open tree-jungle, having an undergowth of bushes and dry grass. The tigress was started by Murray out of a small dry nullah. His elephant was unsteady, and he missed. The tigress then crossed my front, and I was fortunate in dropping her. She was up again in an instant, and came on, but was turned, and took shelter in some broken ground, from which, with Murray's assistance, she was dislodged and slain. On going back to the spot from which she had started we found her two cubs lying asleep on the gravel, in the bottom of the nullah. These we brought home alive. From this camp we hunted the

Boorar river, down as far as Teekree, on the Mhow and Bombay road ; but though we passed some splendid coverts, and saw footprints in one or two places, we found nothing. Cholera was very prevalent at that time on the high road ; we therefore crossed without halting, and encamped in the jungle a few miles farther on towards the Nerbudda.

Still we could find no game, so we moved westward into the Burwanee country. On the way one of our men observed three bears as they entered some long grass on the side of a small ridge, in a bit of open jungle. Having seen them settled for the day, he sent us word, and on examination of the ground we found that the whole family might be easily disposed of. We advanced on them along the ridge, moving very quietly in single file, each man having his gun-bearer, with a second rifle, on his left. On coming abreast of the bears all turned to the right, and as we reached the edge the three unfortunate beasts jumped out of the grass about ten yards below us. We made very short work of them, and, as our rifles cracked, they all fell in a heap together. We then marched to Nulwye, a small village situated at the junction of the Deb river with the Nerbudda, and nearly opposite the Maun river, where I had made so good a bag with Ward the year before. On the way Bashi and I rode down a young gazelle, and captured it alive.

On arriving at Nulwye, we found that our men had two tigers marked on an island in the bed of the Deb, which at this season was nearly dry. It was settled that Bashi and I should beat down the island on the elephants, while Cadell and Murray took posts in trees. We had hardly entered the covert when the tigress appeared before Evans. As he raised his rifle, the elephant, checked by a nervous mahout, backed suddenly. Evans was thrown off his aim and missed, but the tigress, crossing over to me, was dropped with one shot. We left her lying, and proceeded to beat out the covert. Presently the tiger jumped up, also before the Bashi. Again the elephant backed, and again he missed. The tiger plunged into a mass of creeping plants, and then, turning to the right, entered a small ravine, and left the river. Cadell and Murray now joined us, and after searching for some time we again saw the tiger making off. Murray fired with an explosive shell, which burst close behind him, and he got away, and was lost among the ravines. This tiger escaped entirely through the misconduct of the mahout, and on our return to camp he was sent for and admonished. He was informed that any future exhibition of cowardice would be met by instant chastisement. The elephant, which had been lent by the Rajah of Jhabbooa, I knew to be good and staunch. The tigress which we had bagged was 9 feet 1 inch in length.

On the following morning a buffalo was found killed in the cypress near the mouth of the Maun river. We forded the Nerbudda on the elephants, and, after posting men to look out from trees, we entered the covert. After hunting for some time we came on the tigress, which we shot without much trouble. She was 9 feet in length, and on opening her we found four cubs, which would have been born within a day or two. We removed their skins, which were very prettily marked. We halted another day at Nulwye, but finding no more game, we sent off our camp to Oochawud, some miles higher up the Deb river.

We hunted in the bed of a smaller river on the way, and started a panther near a village named Kirnowe. The Jhabbooa mahout again misbehaved, causing Cadell, who was on the elephant, to miss his shot. He was at once visited with the promised chastisement, and his mind and body were so

much hurt that he bolted on our arrival in camp. We were
well rid of him, and the grasscutter, being there and then pro-
moted to the rank of mahout, proved a most efficient substi-
tute. The panther attempted to break up the bank of the
river, but was turned by my men, and retreated into some
close jungle of mimosa. On our advancing on him he charged
viciously, and gave some trouble before he was killed. He
was 7 feet 10 inches in length. Crossing over some hills on
our way to the tents, we saw a gigantic bear, but he was far
beyond rifle-range.

While seated at breakfast on the following morning,
intelligence came in from two of our parties of markers.
One man reported a bear, the other a large tiger, which
was supposed to be the same which had escaped at Nulwye.
The latter, of course, commanded our immediate attention. He was lying in a fringe of thick bushes on the left
bank of the river, but as his exact position was unknown, we
had some difficulty in fixing on the plan of attack. We expected him to break away to the left, where the country was
covered with grass and bushes. Here and there were a few
trees, and it was decided that Cadell and Murray should mount
two of these, while Evans and I advanced on elephants from
either flank along the bed of the river. As I proceeded to my
position a panther rose at the elephant's feet, but I did not
fire. As soon as the men in the trees were in position, we
advanced, and the tiger, which probably had a lively recollection of his previous persecution, left the bed of the river unperceived by either Evans or myself. He took the line which
we expected, but, being turned by a shot from the trees, came
back towards me, and, roaring savagely, threw himself into a
dense thicket. As I advanced on him he went off, and lay
up in a thin fringe of willows in the bed of the river.

Evans then took Cadell on his elephant, while Murray joined me.

Between our elephant and the tiger was a space of about 100 yards, covered with long green grass and large boulders. No sooner did the tiger see us advance towards him, than he charged from a distance of at least eighty yards, roaring as he came on. Our mahout behaved very well, but the elephant, which was greatly excited, shook his head and swayed his body so much that accurate shooting was impossible. We each fired both barrels, but the tiger came on, and I fully expected to see him on the elephant's head. The latter, however, wheeled round suddenly, knocking Murray and me together in the howdah in a most undignified manner. Fortunately the tiger contented himself with a demonstration, and, catching up my second rifle, I shot him behind the shoulder as he went by. He dashed on for thirty yards, when, reaching the edge of the covert, he turned sharp and crouched for another charge. The end of his tail was twitching ominously, when, the mahout having somewhat steadied the elephant, Murray rolled him over with a shell, and another shot finished him. The Bashi and Cadell, who had witnessed the charge, now came up, and indulged in many pleasant jokes at our expense, imitating what they called our double-wobble style of taking aim. The tiger was a fine heavy beast 9 feet 10 inches in length. On removing his skin we came on a small wound evidently two days old, and from it we extracted a fragment of the shell which Murray had fired at Nulwye, and were thereby assured of the identity of the tiger.

Returning to the tents, we had some luncheon, and then went off after the bear which had been marked in the early morning. She was lying in an intricate network of small tortuous nullahs, having steep clay banks, and we had some trouble in finding her. At length we caught sight of her, and she was instantly slain. She was accompanied by a cub, and, springing down, we hemmed it into a corner and captured it alive. We took it home to the camp, where it was fastened by a dog-chain to a peg before the tent. About midnight I was awoke by Murray calling out that the bear was loose, and on jumping up I saw it making off to the jungle. Shouting to the servants to loose the dogs, we gave chase. A soft haze hung over the forest, but the moon being bright, we were able to keep the bear in view. My trusty Batchelor shot by me, and in another moment was hanging on the ear of the bear, which shrieked in a fiendish manner. · We carried him back to the tents, where he was properly secured. Our night-dresses, consisting of flannel shirts and wide cotton drawers, were much damaged by the thorny bushes.

Next morning two bears were marked down on the side of a hill about two miles from our camp. They lay among a mass of broken rocks near the summit, which was flat and thinly wooded. We had ascended the hill, and were within fifty yards of the spot from which we intended to fire, when a gun was accidentally discharged. Knowing that the bears would be alarmed, we rushed forward, and saw them going down the hill at a headlong pace. Many shots were fired, and all, I believe, missed. Fortunately some of our men were below, and, seeing them, the bears turned along the face to the right. We reloaded, and, running till we nearly dropped, crossed over the table-land and posted ourselves along the crest. Eventually we bagged not only these two bears, but also a third, which was driven up by the men. I believe each of my companions got one : none came to me.

We then moved farther west into the Burwanee jungles, bordering on the Sathpoora hills, and encamped under a huge

banian-tree far from human habitations.   Here we were
joined by Messrs. B—— and W——, two gentlemen employed
on the Geological Survey, who were exploring these hills.
Next morning we hunted in the bed of a dry nullah a few
miles south of our camp.   A tigress with cubs was said to be
in the neighbourhood, and as we beat up some long green
grass one of the elephants halted and commenced to strike
the ground with his trunk, while he kicked about the gravel
with his fore-feet.   Presently two cubs ran snarling out of
the grass, but as we hoped to find the tigress we did not fire.
She was cautious, however, and had gone off into the extensive jungle by which we were surrounded on all sides.   We
searched for her on this and the following day, but without
success, so we shot the cubs, and marched north to Dhunora,
where there were some large patches of cypress in the broad
bed of a river.   On arriving at the ground about sunset, we
found a buffalo had been killed by a panther.   So, deeming it
a good opportunity for setting the iron trap, we laid it in the
sand by the carcass.   After dinner we went out with a lantern,
and on going to the spot found the trap sprung and a few hairs
from the belly of the panther between the teeth.   We set the
trap again, and found a hyæna in it in the morning.

We then beat out the cypress, and started the panther,
which I wounded slightly, but he went off down the bed of
the river.   Our men tracked him for about two miles, and we
at length came up with him.   He had taken shelter under
the prickly leaves of some young date-trees, and made some
very pertinacious charges before he was finally disposed of.
Farther down we came on the prints of a very large tiger,
which we followed in vain for several miles.   Next day we
marched, and encamped at Burwanee.

In the afternoon the Bashi and I went down to the

Nerbudda to shoot alligators.   We obtained a boat, and while punting across the stream, a large crocodile came to the surface about twenty yards from us.   I fired with a two-ounce rifle, striking him fair on the head, but he sank, and we could not recover him.   We then hunted about the still water among the rocks, and presently saw several alligators swimming about in a quiet pool.   A dark object appeared on the surface, and was immediately fired into by Bashi.   On going forward we found it was the dead body of a woman, which had probably been cast into the sacred stream by her sorrowing relatives ; for, like the Ganges, though in a lesser degree, the Nerbudda is an object of great veneration among Hindoos.   We were much shocked, and left the alligators to finish their meal undisturbed.

One of our horsemen was sent in next morning from Bhowtee, near the mouth of the Goee river, five miles to the westward.   He reported a tigress to be lying in the bed of the river, where she had retired after feasting on one of our buffaloes.   She got away without a shot, but was fortunately headed by some of our men, and returned to the covert.   As we moved towards her she charged viciously from a distance of more than seventy yards, but the ground was tolerably clear, and our elephants being steady, she did not get home. Though very plucky, she was a small beast, only 8 feet 4 inches in length.   Suspecting that we should find more tigers in this country, we moved our camp westward to the junction of the Goee with the Nerbudda, and sent parties of men to scour the country in several directions.   In the evening I went out with Evans, and we got a nice buck chinkara.   On a sandbank by the Nerbudda we saw a large flock of pelicans.

Intelligence came next morning from three different parties.

Two miles up the Goee two small tigers had been seen ; the track
of a large tiger had been followed up to a mass of cypress in
the Nerbudda ; while a buffalo had been killed at Morkutta,
four miles down the river. We started soon after breakfast,
having given orders for the camp to be moved to Morkutta.
We commenced with the large tiger in the cypress, and having
forded the river on the elephants, we drew lots for places.
Murray and I were stationed in trees on a high bank overlooking the covert, while Cadell, the Bashi, and the geologists,
went in on elephants. The covert was very dense, filled with
water-holes, rocks, and deep gullies cut by the action of heavy
floods. The men on the elephants had all the fun to themselves, and we had to content ourselves with listening to the
reports of their rifles, varied now and then by the roars of the
charging tiger, who gave some trouble before he died. He
was a short beast, being only 9 feet 2 inches in length, but
very stout and heavy.

Having still much work before us, we lost no time, and at
once recrossing the Nerbudda we proceeded to beat up the
tigers in the Goee. They were lying in some ravines near an
old ruined fort in the jungle, and on being started, passed
near Mr. B——, who dropped them both. Though only
young beasts, 6 feet 3 inches in length, they were very
savage, and one of them clawed an elephant severely on the
trunk. The day was far advanced, so we at once pushed on
for Morkutta, where we knew the markers were anxiously
awaiting our arrival. But when we arrived on the ground,
the sun was low in the heavens, and we feared that night
would overtake us before we had accomplished our work. A
consultation was therefore held, and we agreed to rest content
with our day's sport. We accordingly adjourned to the tent,
sending men to tie up another buffalo for the tigers, and on

their return they reported that they had hardly left the spot before the unhappy beast was slain. This was very satisfactory, as we knew the tigers would gorge themselves and lie up in the cypress.

Our men were out early next morning, and having carefully examined the bank, assured us, on their return, that the tigers had not left the river. About 10 A.M. we went out to the covert, which was within half-a-mile of our camp. An open bed of gravel extended for forty yards from the foot of the high sloping bank, and between this and the water was a strip of cypress, ten yards in width. At the lower end, towards our camp, the covert became wider and contained some high willow-trees. Murray and Evans were posted in these trees; I was on another on the side of the high bank overlooking the cypress; while Cadell and the geologists entered the upper end of the strip on elephants, and immediately started the tigers. They were three in number, one gentleman and two ladies. Several shots were fired by the party on the elephants, and one tigress was there and then killed. The other two came rushing down the strip, giving me a fine view of them as they went by. But, though wounded, they did not fall to my shots. Passing down the covert, they were fired on and turned back by Evans and Murray. The elephants were now closing in on them; again I fired from my tree, and they were met by a sharp fire from Cadell and his party. Presently all three lay dead, and were soon on their way to the tents, where we spent the afternoon in preparing the skins. Here we parted with Messrs. B——and W——, who went off to explore the hills.

At a short distance below our camp was the " Hurn Pahl," or "Deer's Leap," at which point the province of Nimar terminates, and the ranges of the Vindyah and Sathpoora mountains are merely divided by the river. The name of the "Hurn Pahl" is derived from the circumstance of the river being here obstructed by large masses of basalt, rising about ten feet above the ordinary level of the stream, and giving passage to the river through three very narrow channels, across each of which, it is supposed, an antelope could bound. Below this point for several miles the river is fringed with dense masses of cypress, in which we had hoped to find tigers, but our men, after a careful search, could find no fresh tracks. We therefore forded the river, and encamped on the opposite bank at Dhurrumrai. At this period the south-west monsoon was blowing up through the gorge with great force, and we were much annoyed by the fine alluvial dust in which we were enveloped night and day.

To the westward of our camp lay a very rugged ravine, the sides of which had been rent asunder by some grand natural convulsion. The rocks were divided by fearsome chasms such as would delight the heart of Gustave Doré. Into this ravine a patriarchal bear was marked by our men, and, after some trouble, he was dislodged from his cavern and shot by Cadell. Finding no more game here, we moved west and pitched our tents at Dhie.

Owing to the intense heat we always dined in the open air, and as bed-time approached our beds were carried out by the servants, and we slept with our four cots ranged round the dinner-table. Among the Bheels in the hills I had no fear of nocturnal thieves, but Murray, who had derived his ideas of native honesty from the civilised inhabitants of the plains, always took especial care to secure his guns at night. For this purpose an iron chain was passed through the trigger-guards, and the guns were thus attached to a large arm-chair beside him. One morning about daybreak I saw the Bashi steal from his bed, and quietly unscrewing one of the trigger-guards, release a rifle, which he hid under his mattress. Murray, on waking, looked as usual at his guns, and, finding one missing, raised a great outcry. We kept up the joke till breakfast-time, when his weapon was restored to him.

A Bheel now came in, having left some of his friends on sentry over two bears in the hills about five miles to the southward. The heat was very great, but on being told that by making a circuit we could reach the place by a footpath, we mounted our horses and went off, having ordered the camp to be moved westward to the Hutnee river. Our guide led us a dance of at least ten miles through a very strong country, and our men suffered greatly from the want of water. The bears lay on a hill-side covered with long dry grass and huge stones, and we had some difficulty in fixing on positions for the guns. The beat, however, was successful, and both bears were slain. They were fine large beasts, and as we had no means of transport, we prepared to skin them on the spot. In the bottom of the ravine was a single green tree, and, anxious to avail ourselves of its shade, we carried the bears to the edge of the hill, and sent them rolling down into the nullah. For our own consumption we carried water in leathern bottles, but our men were obliged to go off to a water-hole two miles distant, where they slaked their thirst, while we busied ourselves in skinning the bears. It was late before we reached our camp, where we were comforted by a bath and change of raiment.

Two miles higher up the Hutnee is joined by the Sankree Tokree ravine, and here one of our buffaloes was killed in the night by a tiger. The tracks led to a mass of rough grass and bushes in the bed of the Hutnee, and we beat this place out very closely with the elephants, but found nothing. We then took positions in trees, and sent men to drive down the ravine. They started a big tiger, which went up the side, steering clear of our posts. Expecting that he would have crossed over the intervening jungle, and gone down into the cover which we had first beaten, we went back, and having placed Evans and Cadell on trees, I was proceeding with Murray to beat up the covert towards them, when my elephant became greatly excited, and commenced kicking violently at the grass with her fore-foot. At that instant a tigress rushed out, but the elephant was so unsteady that I missed her with both barrels. Catching up my second rifle, I was more successful, and dropped her with a shell behind the shoulder. Another shot finished her.

While this little bit of by-play was going on, the big tiger which we had previously started, and which had apparently been travelling leisurely, was seen by Evans's gun-bearer to steal down into the bed of the river, where he entered a long strip of cypress on the far side. Wishing to cross this strip so as to get quietly down between him and the jungle, Murray, Cadell, and I, moved over on the elephants. But the tiger, which had been creeping towards us under cover of the cypress, rose suddenly with loud roars, and as he sprang on some masses of rock, I at one time feared he would leap into the howdah. We instantly poured in a volley with good effect, and, falling back, he went off down the covert. We had just reloaded, when he emerged eighty yards lower down, and was passing over some bare ground on his way to the jungle above, when we again fired, and he fell over in the open, where he lay roaring. As we made up to him, he rose and scrambled back to the cypress, whence he made one gallant charge before he died. We returned home well pleased with our day's work. The tiger measured 9 feet 4 inches, and the tigress 8 feet 7 inches.

In this chapter I have given the measurements of beasts from a memo, lately received from Cadell, who took them down at the time. Many men have talked to me of tigers twelve and eleven feet long, and in some countries they may attain that size, but, speaking from my own experience, I can only say I have not fallen in with them in Malwa or Nimar. I have seen tigers nearly ten feet long, whose skins could easily have been stretched, when fresh, to eleven or more feet, but the breadth would have been greatly diminished and the beauty of the skin impaired.

On taking up the bear-skins which we had got on our way from Dhie, we found that they had been completely destroyed by white ants. These horrible little animals had been busy, and the hair was eaten off in large patches. We found that the only safeguard to protect skins when pegged out was to cause a man to beat them night and day every half-hour with a cane. White ants, when at work, cover the object to be eaten with an incrustation of mud, underneath which they carry on their operations. They will not work when disturbed, and the concussion of the blows from the cane is enough to keep them away.

Here, much to our regret, we parted from Cadell, who was obliged to proceed into the Sathpoora hills on duty. Before he left we divided the spoils by lot. Having picked out the four best skins, we tossed for choice, and so on till all were divided. After which exchanges were effected, by private bargain, for such as were supposed to have any particular interest attached to them. Passing down to the Nerbudda by the bed of the Hutnee river, Cadell's elephant got into a quicksand, and was extricated with some difficulty. On such occasions, trees, boughs, and bundles of grass and brushwood are thrown to the sagacious animals, which they force down with their tusks and trample them into the sand.

The Bashi, Murray, and I, moved north, *via* Dhie, towards the Mogra ravine, which we reached in two marches. On riding into the camp we were met by Dhokul, who came forward with a look of deep dejection stamped on his expressive countenance. He informed us that a cow having been killed by a tiger a few days previously, the exasperated owner had poisoned the carcass. A tigress and two half-grown cubs returned to feast, and there and then died. The Bheels had hung the three bodies on a tree close by, where we found them emitting a noisome effluvium. These were the tigers whose tracks I had seen on my last visit to the ravine, when, in firing the jungle, I had nearly burnt down my tent. We were vexed on finding them poisoned, but could not blame the poor Bheels, who were only protecting their cattle. The father of the family was still to be accounted for, and he, having yielded to the temptation of one of our buffaloes during the night, was marked down in the morning by our men, aided by a Mekranee named Morad.

We posted ourselves in trees across the ravine, and our men, accompanied by a number of the local Bheels, went off to drive down towards us. The Mekranee was on the left, and from my tree I could see the tiger passing up towards him. He fired, as did also Evans, and the tiger, badly wounded, rushed growling into the bottom of the ravine immediately below my post. I sat very quiet, and presently saw his huge head and neck protrude from some green willows. I had a pot-shot at him, and dropped him dead. This tiger, when first started, had charged back among the beaters. One man was cut by his claw on the shoulder, but his evil passions not being then roused, he came forward without doing further mischief.

We then moved our camp to Baug, where we pitched the tents under a large banian-tree opposite the fort. In the evening, while sitting outside in the full enjoyment of a pipe, we saw two panthers on the wall of the old fort, on which they had mounted by a breach leading into the jungle. Taking rifles, we went forward, but by the time we had arrived within range the panthers had disappeared. From this camp we visited the cave where, with Blowers, I had shot the tiger two years before. Much of the surrounding jungle had been cleared away, but the bones of the tiger still lay in the cave, and one or two were taken away as souvenirs. A bear and cubs were marked down below the Bhoodist caves, and were all slain without much trouble; but during my visit in February I had apparently exterminated the race of tigers, for my men could neither see nor hear of any. At Tanda, near the foot of the Ghauts, a large bear was seen to enter a rocky ravine, but as we attempted to approach the spot it became alarmed and went off. Shots were fired, but without effect. Up to this date we had bagged every bear, tiger, and panther, at which we had fired since leaving Mundlaisir. Much of the credit was no doubt due to our shikarees, but our good fortune had been very great. Personally, I had received great assistance from my gun-bearers, of whom Futtah, a serjeant in the Bheel Corps, was invaluable. Futtah was a Bheel of the Vindyah range, quiet and unobtrusive, but possessed of great intelligence both on parade and in the jungle. He was, moreover, an excellent shot, and very steady and plucky on an emergency.

Another march carried us into my house at Sirdarpore, where we rested for a couple of days, during which time men were sent out to examine the grass-jungle near Jucnaoda. They reported a tigress and two half-grown cubs, and having posted ourselves in trees, they were sent forward by the beaters, and the two cubs shot. The tigress crossed a bit of open ground clear of the guns, and got away among some small ravines. We mounted the elephants and gave chase, having been joined by Jowan Sing, the son of the Thakoor or Chief of Jucnaoda. Failing to find the tigress, Murray and Evans went forward and mounted in trees, while the Thakoor and I beat up the jungle towards them. As I pressed my elephant into some long reeds the tigress bolted out to the left. I had a snap-shot at her as she went over a ridge, and disabled her hind leg, but she went on and disappeared into the next nullah. Halting in the bed of the main stream, I sent the Thakoor to beat down on his elephant. As he came forward, the ground became so rough that the elephant could not advance, and to my horror I saw him directing the beaters to go on and hurl stones into the nullah. In vain I shouted ; my voice was drowned in the din of tom-toms, and in another moment I saw the tigress charge up the bank towards the men, who turned and fled. Deprived of the use of one hind-leg, her ascent was greatly retarded, but she struck down the last man and bit him behind the thigh. At that moment the Thakoor fired, wounding her mortally, and she scrambled back into the nullah, where she died. Fortunately the man was not very badly injured, though he had some severe flesh-wounds. We sent him off at once into the regimental hospital, where he was skilfully attended by our doctor, who set him on his legs again. By this time the rainy season had nearly set in, and my friends returned to Mhow, having greatly enjoyed their excursion, which had extended over nearly two months.

CHAPTER XXIII.

THE country to the north-west of my charge was occupied by
a wild and turbulent race of Bheels, who resided in the strong
jungles in the northern parts of Jhabbooa and the adjoining
British district of the Punch Mahal, lately ceded by Scindiah.
To the north of these lay the petty chiefship of Banswarra,
and the Bheels of the three countries had long been engaged
in raids either on their neighbours or on the more peaceable
inhabitants under their own chiefs. Rightly or wrongly, it is
the custom of the country to ascribe all such acts of violence
to external foes, and on the occurrence of any foray or case
of cattle-lifting in Jhabbooa, the chief invariably reported the
matter to me, praying for redress. His communication passed
from my office to that of the British officer in charge of the
Punch Mahal, or the officer in political charge of Banswarra,
by whom it was generally returned with an intimation that
the persons charged were not only brave, but also virtuous,
and at the precise period of the alleged inroad were actively
engaged in the peaceful operations of husbandry. This reply
was forwarded to the complainant, and the matter rested there

till some of his people having effected a raid over the border on their own account, similar communications would pass with the same unsatisfactory result.

In many of their manners and customs the Bheels greatly resemble the old Scottish Highlanders. They are very clannish, and have great respect for the chiefs of their tribes, while the patience and pertinacity with which they avenge plunder or bloodshed, and the zest with which they enter on any predatory expedition, would have done credit to the most accomplished reivers and caterans of our own land. But it was necessary that the benign influence of the Paramount Power should be felt in these wild countries, and, to this end, international courts were held on the frontier, when all disputes were examined into and settled by the British politicals. The peculiarity of the procedure consisted in the Bheels themselves being constituted judges and arbiters in the various cases. Some time previous to the assembling of the court, lists of claims on both sides were exchanged through the British officers, and on the date of meeting being fixed all parties were duly warned to attend. All were directed to come unarmed, and all came under safe conduct, being assured that they would be safe from arrest for any imputed crimes. On the assembling of the court, previous to calling on the first case, a scale of compensation was mutually agreed upon. Buffaloes about fifteen rupees, oxen twelve, cows eight, and sheep and goats one or two rupees. The life of a man was fixed at one hundred and twenty rupees, while—tell it not in Gath—that of a woman was only valued at sixty. Wounds were assessed according to their gravity.

I met Colonel Buckle on one of these courts at Dohud, fifty miles west of Sirdarpore. Our object was the settlement of the claims against our respective districts. The agents of the various native states attended, and the Bheels assembled to the number of about seven hundred. The first case being called on, the plaintiff and defendant came forward. They were told to name two men each, as arbiters, from the Bheels assembled. These four were then directed to hear what both parties had to say, and, in the event of their finding for the plaintiff, to ascertain the amount of his loss. To ensure freedom from interference by other parties, a constable was told off to remain by them, and they then moved off. The arbiters were authorised to call up from the Bheels who were present any witnesses they might require. The next and subsequent cases were disposed of in the same manner. From time to time the arbiters came up and made known their decisions, which were then and there entered on the general sheet. The great advantage of this course of procedure was, that in nearly every case the arbiters were fully acquainted with all the particulars of the matter under investigation. The feeling of honour among thieves was strong, and it was heightened by the certainty that an unjust award would inevitably be followed by active reprisals on the property of the judges themselves by the injured plaintiff or defendant.

These courts were always attended by the most beneficial results, and for some time after they were held, life and property, on both sides of the frontier, were comparatively secure. By no other course could restitution be fairly accomplished, as plundered cattle and other property were, on being swept over the frontier, at once divided among the plunderers, by whom they were speedily sent off to a distance to their friends. Before the court broke up, a debit and credit account was made out for each chief whose Bheels were concerned. Those who had to pay to other states were called on to pay the money into court at once.

Lists of the decisions were given to all, and the settlement of the awards and penalties within their own districts was left to the chiefs themselves.

The heavy jungles in the country lying between Allee Rajpore and Guzerat were occupied by an aboriginal race called Naikras. Partaking of many of the Bheel characteristics, they are more wild and uncivilised. The unhealthy nature of these malarious forests is evident from the wretched appearance of the Naikras, whose sole clothing, among the male population, often consists in a cord round the waist, under which a narrow strip of cloth is passed. The hair is worn long and uncontrolled, and lies on the head in a thick and filthy mat, tanned by the sun to a russet brown. They are armed with the universal bow and arrows, swords, and a few matchlocks.

Some disturbance being anticipated among these wild men, Colonel Buckle moved his camp to the jungles near the mountain of Powaghur, and as a party of the Guzerat Bheel Corps, under Major Bonnor, was to join him from Dohud, the latter officer invited me to co-operate by joining their camp. I accordingly moved across the frontier, taking with me my usual escort of a serjeant and twelve troopers of the Central India Horse, and twenty-five men of the Malwa Bheel Corps. We spent some days encamped in these jungles, and, during our stay, the Naikras who had threatened to give trouble came in and were promised a settlement of their grievances, on which they swore upon drawn swords, and imitation footprints of tigers, that they would abstain from disturbing the peace of the country. The above form of oath was meant to imply that they hoped they might fall by the sword, or be eaten by tigers, if they broke their promises there and then solemnly made.

We had gone out one morning to shoot partridges and jungle-fowl near the camp, and were accompanied by a number of dogs of various kinds. Passing through some bushes, I heard a terrier barking angrily, and, rushing in, I found her facing a large cobra da capello, which was coiled with head erect and hood extended, by the side of a rat which it had just killed. Hearing the terrier bark, the other dogs ran in from all sides, and in another moment the whole were worrying the deadly reptile. Catching up a stick, I beat off the dogs, and then shot the snake. The dogs seemed none the worse, but I was certain that some of them must have been bitten. About twenty minutes afterwards we returned to the tent, where a dog was presently seized with convulsions, and fell apparently in great agony. His mouth and tongue became perfectly black from the virulence of the poison, and he was put out of his misery by a pistol-shot. Another dog was similarly struck down. By this time we had got out some spirits of ammonia, which we administered, but without effect, and this dog also died. A third was then attacked, but it had probably been bitten last, and the poison of the snake being partially exhausted, we managed to keep the dog alive till sunset, when it died. We were much grieved by the death of our faithful companions.

Leaving Colonel Buckle at this camp, Major Bonnor returned with me towards the Ruttun Mall Hill, a fine wooded mountain in the south-west corner of my district. On the way we passed through a very wild and heavily-timbered country. The valley along which we marched was flat and sandy, but in many parts our line of route was flanked by hills formed of huge detached boulders of gray granite, piled over each other to the height of 200 feet; they had apparently been left by glaciers. On either side of the narrow path was jungle-grass ten feet in height. The Naikras in this country were very troublesome in 1857-58 ; and the closeness of the jungle having greatly impeded the operations of the troops sent against them, several clearings of 100 yards in breadth and many miles in length have been made along the principal tracks. As the district is now entirely under British rule, it is to be hoped that these and other beneficial measures may tend to civilise these wild men.

On this march we shot many green wood-pigeons and jungle-fowl. Both, when cooked, were excellent, and the feathers of the latter have since been in great request by ladies for their hats, and by salmon-fishers for their flies. We halted two days at the Ruttun Mall Hill, spending our time in its wooded glades in quest of sambur. I had wounded and lost a fat hind, and was posted in a bit of very close covert by the Bheels of the hill, who had assembled under their chief to do us honour by driving the jungle. A stag passed at full speed about fifty yards to my right, crashing, as he went, through the thick underwood. I fired, but without much hope ; and, at the end of the beat, was preparing to go on, when it struck me that I might as well examine the ground over which the stag had passed. On a close inspection of the dead leaves, I found a few hairs which had been cut by my bullet, farther on a speck of blood, then larger quantities, and a hundred yards farther the stag himself, lying shot nearly through the heart. He was skinned and cut up on the spot, after which a bottle of Moselle was produced from the depths of the capacious basket in which Bonnor invariably carried his refreshments when shooting. On descending the hill that officer detailed the events of the day in some spirited verses of heroic metre, but I regret, for the sake of my readers, that I cannot here furnish them with a copy. On the following day we saw several sambur, including one very fine stag, but the only shot which we got was at a hind, which I missed in a disreputable manner.

We then moved north towards Dohud, where we spent a day or two in quest of bears. Two were found in a ravine a few miles from the cantonment, and were both slain. We were taken up to another brace, which we ought also to have bagged, but one of these, though wounded, escaped. The other fell dead, and my companion loudly vaunted the marvellous effects of his rifle-shell. I said little, but as we were a long way from camp we directed the men to skin the bear as he lay. One bullet-hole only was found, and under the skin on the far side lay my two-ounce conical.

Major Bonnor had at Dohud a tame tiger, which was allowed to wander about the house till his size rendered him formidable. He was very playful and good-natured, except at feeding-time. His favourite pastime was to go down with us to the lake, where he would swim out with the dogs, enjoying his bath intensely. The lake was full of large fish of the murrel species, many of which were shot by the men of the corps, who sat in trees overlooking the water, and killed them as they rose to bask on the surface in the mid-day sun.

Some time after my return to Sirdarpore, a man of the Bheel Corps, who was out with Futtah in search of antelopes, came and informed me that they had seen two tigers in some grass lands a few miles east of the cantonment. I was very incredulous, as the place was not one in which tigers were likely to be, though I knew that the spot was occasionally frequented by panthers. I went out, however, with Blowers, and having taken up positions in trees, sent beaters round to drive towards us. Presently two hunting cheetahs came over the hill, and crossed the river at some distance from Blowers, who fired without effect. They then went off over an open country, cultivated here and there with crops of millet. My men pursued them on foot for several miles, keeping them in view, and eventually turning them back towards the river, where they lay up in some high grain. As the men advanced, several jackals broke away, but just as they reached the end of the field, the cheetahs bounded out. I fired, and wounded one ; however, they went on, and passing through some tall hemp, swam over a deep pool in the river, and went across the grass lands. Here they were headed by a party of my men. The wounded beast, being unable to keep up with his companion, halted, and, creeping up to a small tuft of grass, lay down. We went up to him, and as he lay ready for a charge, I fired and turned him over. The cheetah, from his great length of limb, stands very high, and an imperfect view of him in the jungle will often lead to his being mistaken for a tiger.

Chinkara or gazelles were found on the hilly ground north of the cantonment, and I frequently went after them with Futtah. On these occasions we started off on my riding camel, which I drove, while Futtah, who sat behind me, carried my rifle. On sighting the deer, I would either dismount and stalk them, or send Futtah, who was a good marksman, and, like all his race, an excellent stalker, to take the shot, while I, moving off on the camel, assisted him by attracting the attention of the deer. We seldom went home empty-handed, and often had a couple of bucks slung to the saddle on our return.

After the rainy season the plains were covered with grass three feet in height, and here we found florican in considerable numbers. But the extent of grass was very great, and

the birds could only be started by having a number of beaters.
I therefore exercised my men occasionally at light infantry
drill over this ground. I could generally muster about two
hundred, and these I formed in a single rank, and extended
them by bugle-sound in one long line across the country. I
accompanied them on horseback, my gun being carried by
one of my men. Buglers marched along the line, and on a
florican rising from the grass they would sound the " Halt,"
and mark the spot where he alighted. I then rode up, and on
dismounting to shoot sounded the " Advance" or " Retire" as
might be necessary to raise the birds. When required, the
line changed front to the right or left by bugle-sound. In
this manner I combined business with pleasure, halting now
and then by the bank of some stream to allow the men to
smoke and otherwise refresh themselves.

In the jungle north of Sirdarpore I observed a singular
instance of amiability in a tigress. We had been after her for
some days, but she had always managed to keep out of our
way. Buffaloes were tied up for her in several directions ; and
one morning, on going to look after them, we found that the
tigress had passed within a yard of a calf without injuring it.
The track was plain, leading down a narrow path to the spot
where the bait was tied in the bed of a stream, and the foot-
print of the tigress was distinctly seen over that of the buffalo,
which had apparently moved on one side to allow her to
pass.

CHAPTER XXIV.

FINDING that a claim to three months' leave had accumulated, I applied for permission to join my friend Major Hayward, who was then employed in settling boundary questions in Rajpootana. Early on the first of January 1865, I left my own camp, which was pitched at Budnawur, in the northern part of the Dhar territory, and riding into Rutlam I was met by Captain Bradford, the political officer in Western Malwa, with whom I spent the forenoon. Since our last meeting he had been nearly killed by a tiger, and had undergone amputation of an arm. While out shooting with a party from Goona, he was seated on a low stump when he was charged by a wounded tiger. He sprang down and made a rush backward, hoping to be able to throw himself into a pool of water close by. But ne tripped and fell, and the tiger, seizing him by the arm, crushed the bones between his teeth. With wonderful presence of mind and fortitude Bradford lay still, and the tiger was driven off and shot by his companions. The nearest medical aid was at Auggur, sixty miles distant, and thither a horseman was at once despatched. Meanwhile, a litter having been made, the wounded man was borne in the same direction. Dr. Beaumont, the medical officer at Auggur, was fortunately a man of intelligence and decision. Taking his instruments with him, he mounted his horse and rode off to meet his friends, with whom he fell in twenty-five miles from the cantonment. The heat at this time was intense, and observing symptoms of mortification setting in, Beaumont there and then took out the arm from the shoulder-joint, and saved the life of his patient, who now shoots, rides, and plays cricket, with as much energy as ever.

Soon after breakfast we heard an outcry, and running out, saw a wolf with a kid in his mouth crossing the plain near the tents. On being pursued, he dropped the kid, and retiring a couple of hundred yards, sat down. I got an old rifle from one of the servants and went after him, but it had apparently been loaded with native powder, for the ball dropped at fifty yards from the muzzle. In the afternoon I rode on twenty-four miles to Jowra, where I was hospitably entertained by the Nawaub. He showed me a breech-loading gun, every part of which had been made from an English pattern by one of his own native artificers. The finish throughout was uncommonly good.

Next day I rode to Neemuch, sixty miles, and on the following morning joined Hayward at his camp, about ten miles from the fortress of Chittore. We frequently went out on fishing excursions, our party consisting of five, including two ladies. We caught a number of bright, silvery little fish, somewhat resembling trout, which took fly and minnow very readily. We also got some mahseer. These rose fairly in the streams to a small salmon-fly, but they were more frequently taken by a lump of flour paste, to which cotton wool was added to give consistency. I have since heard that these fish will frequently take a hook baited with the "goolur" or wild fig.

Observing a large alligator basking on a sandbank on the far side of the river, I made a successful stalk and shot him dead. He was nearly twelve feet in length, and desiring to hold a *post-mortem* examination on him, we proceeded to bind him on an elephant. The sagacious animal had not, however, been broken in to alligators, and the tail of the huge reptile having been allowed to dangle against his side, he swung round suddenly, and having shaken off his load, fled with the mahout in the wildest terror. Fortunately, the country was open, and the man kept his seat. He returned late in the afternoon, affirming that the elephant had only been brought into subjection after a dance of twelve kos— *Anglicé*, twenty-four miles!! The elephant was styled from that day forward the "Bara kos ke bhagne wallah," or runner of twelve kos.

One morning we came on a large party of native fishermen encamped on the bank of the Bunass river. Their operations were principally conducted at night with large casting-nets. On arriving at the fishing ground they busied themselves in preparing rafts composed of masses of long green reeds. These rafts were about ten feet in length, and three in breadth and depth. Each was calculated to support one man. While fishing, they moved in two files about twenty yards apart, while two rafts closed up the rear. Each man had a large casting-net lying ready coiled at his feet. He propelled his raft very noiselessly with a long bamboo. On a given signal all put down their sticks, and with much dexterity cast their nets simultaneously into the space between the rafts. By this means large numbers of fish were nightly captured. The smaller ones were kept alive during the next day in netted enclosures sunk under water, while large fish were attached to the bank by a long cord fastened round the tail. At sunset all were drawn out and killed. They were then packed on ponies, and sent off thirty or forty miles during the night to the cantonment at Neemuch.

A number of murrel were shot by our own men, who fired on them from trees and overhanging banks as they basked on the surface. While fishing for mahseer with paste we were much annoyed by river turtle of great size, which came readily to the baits, and generally broke our tackle. I succeeded in bringing one of these to the top, and as he rose, Futtah, who was seated on a rock above me, put a bullet through him from my rifle. The pool was deeply tinged with blood, but the beast sank, and, as usual, my tackle suffered.

We frequently found bustard in the plains, and I shot several fine specimens. On one occasion I counted nineteen together, but they were very wary, and we got none of them. I generally found that they could be approached most easily under cover of a horse or camel, and sometimes, when riding, they would allow us to come within a few yards before taking flight. As we moved north we came on a fine antelope country, and many good bucks were brought in. Large bags of geese, ducks, and snipe, were also made. One morning, when encamped near the Bunass river, our men marked down a tiger, and we went out after him. We had no shooting howdah, and after the little affair with the alligator, we had no confidence in our elephant, so trusted to finding trees from which to shoot. The jungle, which consisted of thick "kakra" and thorny "bair" bushes, was bounded on the left by the deep still reach of a river running down at a right angle to the Bunass, which was not far distant. The natives of the place assured us that the tiger, when started, would come down the bank of this river, and insisted on our mounting on certain trees which they pointed out. But, on inquiry, I found that the covert for which he would probably make lay considerably to the right, and from my knowledge of the habits of the animal I was certain he would take the direct route, and so pass far out of shot. I therefore insisted on posting two intelligent men on trees in this direction, with instructions to keep a sharp look-out, and, should the tiger come towards them, to cough and tap with their sticks so as to turn him on the guns. As I expected, the tiger was no sooner started than I saw him making off to the right, but the men worked him very well, and he returned to the bank of the river, where Hayward slew him from his tree. Being shot in the cold season, his skin was in very fine order, so having bound him on the elephant, we sent him off to camp, while we went down to the Bunass, where we spent the afternoon in trout-fishing. Some good mahseer were brought into camp by natives who had shot them with barbed arrows, to which fine lines were attached.

After this we marched in a north-westerly direction, and encamped at Mandul. Here there is a fine artificial lake, covering many hundred acres, formed by an embankment sixty yards in width faced with cut stone, and covered with trees of large growth, under which we pitched our tents. The lake was alive with ducks, geese, and water-fowl of all kinds, and we saw many large murrel basking in the sun. Some of these we shot, but they sank in deep water, and could not be recovered. From the village we procured a number of lines thirty yards in length. To each of these we attached a large hook baited with a frog, and tied them to pegs along the edge of the embankment. During our stay at this place we thus captured about a hundred good fish. The northern and western sides of the lake were fringed with tracts of high reeds, which we beat for wild pigs. We saw several, but they all escaped. In a green bank I came upon a number of holes tenanted by a large colony of otters, who, judging from the number of fish bones, fins, and tails lying about, had prosecuted a very successful fishing.

Marching north, we encamped at Shoogramghur, where the chief has a preserve swarming with wild pigs, which he was in the habit of shooting from an ambuscade, his men having baited the place with grain for some days previous to this very royal sport! Being anxious to procure a few pairs of large tusks, we obtained leave to hunt in this jungle. The covert consisted almost entirely of cactus bushes, in which we found pigs in great numbers, but the heavy boars kept out of our way, and we only shot a couple of small pigs for the pot. By this time my leave was drawing to a close, and from this camp we retraced our steps to Neemuch, where I parted with much regret from my friends. Hayward, I am sorry to add, has since died of fever. We joined the regiment at the same time, and have spent many pleasant days together. Two days' hard riding brought me back to my own house at Sirdarpore. On my way I slept at Jowra, where I was again the guest of the Nawaub, who shortly after died of cholera. He was one of the most intelligent rulers in Malwa, and was much regretted by all who knew him.

On my return I at once made preparations for an expedition in Nimar, and proceeded to Allee Rajpore, where I was joined by Evans and Froom of the 6th Dragoons. We moved down towards the Hutnee river, and found a large tiger in the Sankree Tokree ravine. Profiting by our former experience, I placed Froom on the high ground between the ravine and the Hutnee. On being started, the tiger at once went up the side, and he shot him dead. I was posted on the far side of the ravine, and on descending into the bottom was nearly overpowered by the heat of the sun, whose perpendicular rays, untempered by the faintest breeze, beat down upon my head. The tiger, which was a full-grown male, had fallen in a spot whence he could not easily be lifted, so we were compelled to skin him as he lay.

We then moved down the Hutnee towards the Nerbudda, and on the way started a panther out of a patch of green reeds. On being wounded he returned to the covert, and was only discovered after a long search, when he was found dying under an overhanging bank, completely hidden by the long grass.

We hunted a large extent of very fine covert in the Nerbudda without finding the print of a foot, and resolved on moving up to the Hurn Pahl, but the intervening country being quite impassable, we were compelled to go round by Dhie. On the south bank of the river, at a short distance below the Hurn Pahl, one of our buffaloes was killed, and on going out we found the tiger among some small patches of cypress interspersed with pools of water. We moved in to the attack on our elephants, and this tiger was also shot by Froom, without any assistance on our part. This was his first expedition after tigers, and we were obliged to speak seriously to him regarding the prompt manner in which he disposed of our hardly-found game! This tiger was then bound on an elephant, and I prepared to mount my own, on which Evans was already seated in the howdah. Elephants are usually mounted by small ladders hung on the side of the pad, but as these are apt to get torn off by bushes, we generally mounted by the crupper, assisted by the elephant, who, on a hint from the mahout, lowered his quarters, while he stretched out his hind-leg for us to step upon. Unfortunately, on this occasion, the forefeet of the elephant were on high ground, and as he lowered his hind-quarter to allow me to mount, the howdah was tilted back at such an angle as to pitch over the rifles which lay on the seat. The Bashi managed to retain two, but the third, an extra heavy double rifle, went over, and falling from a height of about six feet, struck me on the cheek and mouth, nearly driving my teeth down my throat. I suffered greatly at the time, and feel the effects of the blow to this day.

We then moved north to the Mogra ravine, where the tigers had been poisoned last year, and we found to our regret that no others had taken their place. But we beat the lower part of the ravine, and turned out a panther, which was shot by Evans. Higher up we started a large bear. It came out to Froom, who, possibly remembering our admonition regarding the tigers, missed it very creditably, and it went its way. Crossing over the hills towards the Jeeree ravine, we hunted some fine ground, but found nothing, and we then began to fear, what was indeed the case—viz., that we had nearly cleared every tiger out of the country.

In the Jeeree ravine, however, we found a panther, which passed below me at a great pace, and went on to Evans, who bowled it over with a fine shot. Lower down, in the same nullah, we started another very large panther, which was also shot by Evans. Being wounded, we went towards him, and he made a somewhat vicious charge, when a final shot put an end to him. This was a very old beast, light in colour, and much scarred about the face. Many of his teeth were broken and decayed. We passed on to Baug, and found a panther in some cactus bushes a short distance below the caves. He lay near the top of a very high bank, and as one gun was to be posted above, we drew lots. The position fell to Froom, who was rewarded for the toilsome ascent by getting the panther, which he shot in good style as it went up the bank. We hunted all the old iron-pits round Baug, but found no marks of tigers ; and the only addition to our bag was a large blue bull, which started up suddenly from a nullah, and was dropped as he went off.

From Baug we made a long march to the eastward, and camped in the Maun river, in a country which I had not hitherto visited. There was only one tree which offered good shade, and the ground below it was so infested with cattle-ticks, that we were continually obliged to wear our long riding-boots. But our hearts were gladdened on the following morning by the arrival of Dhokul, who with his men had marked a tiger and a panther into the bed of the river, a short distance above our camp. The tigress, for such it was, had taken up her quarters for the day among a mass of shingle and willows, on a bit of ground which had been swept by the stream in high floods. Men having been posted in trees to look out, we went at her on the elephants, and I presently caught sight of her crouching among the willows, and evidently supposing she would escape our observation. This idea, if entertained, I speedily dispelled by a shot behind the shoulder. Bashi also fired, and wounded her, but she doubled back and got away down the river. Our men on the trees now came into play, and she was observed by them to make for some small patches of cypress. We followed her up at once, but so well had she concealed herself that the elephants had passed within a few feet of her before she was observed. A shot brought her charging into the open ground, where she was slain.

We then went after the panther, who was lying among the rocks in a small but rocky ravine running down to the Maun. On being started, he made a rush up the bank, and disappeared under a huge fragment of rock. Bashi and Froom having posted themselves, I went above on an elephant, and commenced to heave down big stones. My left wrist having been partially disabled in my encounter with the bear in 1857, I am unable to grasp my rifle with that hand, and in shooting, the gun merely rests in its position by its own weight. A stone having fallen near the panther, he gave a sharp growl, and the elephant suddenly stepping back, I was thrown forward against the rail of the howdah. One of the knobs which divide the spare guns struck the trigger, and the rifle, which was heavily loaded, went off. The force of the explosion pitched it clean over, and being only loosely held in my right hand, it fell on the rocks below, breaking the stock. Just before this mishap, fearing lest they should be in the way, I had insisted on a number of our men leaving a tree which stood a few paces off, and into which they had climbed to see the fun. But for this percaution, one of them would in all probability have been killed, for the ball, on leaving the rifle, passed through the branches.

A few more stones served to dislodge the panther, but he bolted out with such a sudden rush that he got away up the ravine unhurt. Two of my men had been posted higher up, and as the panther came opposite to them, he halted on a ledge of rock. The men, who were armed, one with a single-barrel smooth-bore gun, the other with a Brown Bess carbine, fired together, and the panther fell dead. The two balls, at a distance of about sixty yards, had struck him behind the shoulder, within a couple of inches of each other, and on examining the slain beast, we thought the shooting was a credit to the men of the Malwa Bheel Corps.

Finding no more signs of game at this place, we determined on hunting the Maun river very carefully as far as Munawur, as we thought we should probably find something in the large patches of cypress which covered its bed. We therefore sent off the camp to Munawur, and next morning, mounting our elephants, we moved down the broad bed of the stream ; while our men, keeping along the banks on both sides, carefully examined the ground for footprints. We started one panther, which, on being wounded by me, crossed over to Evans, who shot him dead. After this we saw nothing save jackals and the footprints of hyænas, till we had nearly arrived at the end of our beat, and were within half-a-mile of the village. A few detached bushes stood out in the waste of shingle, and as they passed these, some of the men heaved in stones, and a fine panther bounded out. As he was too far for accurate shooting, we reserved our fire, and the panther, leaving the river, went slowly up the sloping bank. When he reached the sky-line we saw him halt for a moment, and then, with his long tail whirling in the air, he charged to the front and disappeared. The growls of the panther were followed by loud human shrieks, and on going forward, we found a man of the Bunjara tribe who had been sharply clawed. He was on his way to the village bearing his child on his hip, and followed by his wife, when the panther met him suddenly on the footpath, and charged as above described. Having directed him to get his wound attended to by my native doctor, we went after the panther, and after going some distance took his track back to the river, where he had lain up in a close thicket of young mimosa, whence, after some trouble, he was dislodged and slain.

We found cholera was rife in the village, so we moved at once and encamped at Kotra, near the mouth of the river. At this place we drew the cover blank, and could hear of no tigers. We halted two days, on each of which Futtah shot a nylghae. One of these he had wounded at some distance from the camp, and finding he had no more ammunition with him, he succeeded in driving the bull towards the tents. We were quietly seated, when he rushed in, and, catching up a rifle, went off at his best pace, calling on us to follow. Away we went, and, after a long chase, we overtook the bull and brought him to bag. The marrow-bones of these antelope are very excellent, and we saved them for ourselves, giving the flesh to the men. But though the bull was shot late in the afternoon, the heat was so great that they went bad before dinner-time next evening. From this camp we moved north, and pitched in the jungle at the foot of the hills. We only found one bear, which I wounded but did not get, and we then ascended the mountains and halted at Cheerakan. In the ravines at this place we collected a number of fossils. In the marl and earthy limestones we found many univalve and bivalve shells, bucci-num, ammonites, etc., and in many places the ground was strewed with specimens of the sea-urchin.

But we found no game, and ascending into Malwa, we en-camped at Sooltanpoor. In the ravine in which I had formerly shot tigers alone and with Ward, a bear was found, but he escaped into the mountains. Several parties of our men had been sent out to villages a few miles off, and on the following morning, at daybreak, as we lay on our cots in the open air, I saw one of them carried in on a litter. This was Tarrachund, a corporal of the Bheel Corps, who had been seized with cholera the night before. He was attended to at once by our doctor, but he was beyond human aid, and died about mid-day after great suffering. His body was at once carried out and burnt, and, aware of the importance of getting away from all traces of the disease, we shifted our tents that evening and encamped on fresh ground. Next day we returned to Sirdarpore, and then moved out six miles to Dutteegaum, where we watched some bear-caves in the evening. A small bear was fired at and wounded, but he escaped among the rocks, and we lost him. This was the last beast which we saw. Our expedition, though a pleasant one in many respects, had not been very successful, but this was fairly accounted for by the number of wild beasts which we had killed in the same district during the two preceding years. My men, too, were so thoroughly up to their work, and so persistent in their efforts to show sport, that hardly an animal escaped them.

In the preceding pages I have endeavoured to show, from my own personal experience, the various circumstances under which, in a somewhat difficult country, the chase was successfully prosecuted, and many wild and savage animals were slain, with but a small percentage of damage to human life or limb. To "old shikarees" I have little to teach, but those who are learning their work, or may be induced hereafter to vary the tamer sport of Europe by a campaign in the East, will, I think, find in my narrative some hints worthy of their notice.

The record of my doings might no doubt have been more acceptable to the general reader had it been more varied with matter other than mere slaughter, and had the tale of bloodshed been more frequently relieved by accounts of the geography, scenery, and natural history, human and bestial, of the country ; but all these have been well described elsewhere, and by abler pens.

THE END.

Printed by R. CLARK, *Edinburgh.*